W9-ADU-155

SALT

Books by Herbert Gold

NOVELS

THE BIRTH OF A HERO

THE PROSPECT BEFORE US

THE MAN WHO WAS NOT WITH IT

THE OPTIMIST

THEREFORE BE BOLD

SALT

SHORT STORIES

LOVE AND LIKE

FICTION OF THE FIFTIES (Editor)

ESSAYS

THE AGE OF HAPPY PROBLEMS

FIRST PERSON SINGULAR: Essays for the Sixties (Editor)

SALT

a novel by **Herbert Gold**

THE DIAL PRESS NEW YORK 1963

LIBRARY OF CONGRESS CATALOG CARD NUMBER: 63-10553

Designed by Alan M. Heicklen
Manufactured in the United States of America
By The Haddon Craftsmen, Scranton, Pa.

for tough customers, good friends

George P. Elliott and Leo E. Litwak

PART 1: PETER

"Lady," said the unhappy lord, "I have become a werewolf. I go into this great forest, into the thickest part of the wood, and I live by prey and rapine."

When he had told her everything, she asked him whether he went undressed or clothed.

"Lady," he said, "I go entirely naked."

She asked him, by God, where he left his clothes.

"Lady," he said, "that I will not say, I do not wish their hiding-place known, for if I lost them I would remain a werewolf forever."

He saw in her eyes a bitter resolve to discover the hiding-place. But he believed that he might yet keep this secret.

HERE IS PETER'S STORY FIRST, *in his station on that manhattan where he began to take Dan and Barbara on their ride. . . .*

I'm moving on. No more games! I'm different now.

With these three ideas (really one), Peter Hatten floated out of the tunnel of love. For nearly four years he had been desperately attached, like a child, to a woman who remained faithful to her husband, except on Saturday afternoons, on occasional and hastily arranged evenings, or during special festive business trips when she came to his door with overflowing joy and bags of groceries in order to cook him a meal. The deprived and anxious lovemaking of adultery had been their habit, rending each other's flesh ("It's been so long, so long!"), followed by discussions of her children and the impossibility—the impossibility—followed by stiff recriminations, a blue space of solemnity, an obsessive studying of the clock, and long farewell waking dreams as they lay curled together on his bed. The SPRY sign across the river flashed through the dusk of Riverside Drive into his studio. "It's time, dear."

Green-eyed, lazily lounging, lean, growing rich, finicky, and sometimes indignant: but still like a child Peter brooded in the dark upon his only true love. On five hundred evenings in the past, on five thousand in the future if he let her, Sarah would stir and say: "It's time, dear. I mustn't be late again."

She would not change. Nothing would change. And so finally, a few weeks after his thirty-third birthday, Pete decided to grow up. Goodbye to all that fanatic secret devotion. He taped a note to his door and just went out walking.

> Sarah. I can't stand disorder. There is too much disorder in my life. Please understand.
>
> Goodbye.

It was melodramatic, he knew; but how to live in melodrama without an occasional melodramatic letter? And he should have said "our lives," not just "my life." And that "Please understand"—the rule of economy would have cut it. Of course she would understand, of course she would not understand; he saw her wet face on the pillow, with her fearful husband unable to ask why she was crying—"a mood, dear, women have them"—her hair damp on the pillow while a moony husband watched her. Poor Sarah. Poor husband. But poor Peter, too. Goodbye.

He walked up Riverside Drive to the dry fountain near the foot of West 116th Street. A Columbia boy in a white cable-knit sweater was necking a Barnard girl. The kid was pushing too hard, making it a contest, poor kid. The girl was being scraped and crumpled against a lip of cement. She might have assented, but she was being forced to resist. Peter fastidiously looked away. He hated to see a girl being spoiled like that, twisted the wrong way, with the back of her knees bruised. Mis-educated. So much wrong education in love. So many prideful boys and girls led to tease. He strolled back home, trying to think of everything but what he was thinking about.

When he returned, the note was gone. She had slipped his key under the door, wrapped in fresh Kleenex, but without any mawkish comment—no word at all. A damn sensible lady she was. A damn fine sensible girl. Now she could stop making excuses to her husband. If she really had. If she hadn't really gone straight from Peter's bed into her husband's arms—she must have sometimes! Peter's jealousy was fired up suddenly, blinding him. He wanted to destroy that husband. He wanted to blast into submission the girls who took those husbands. The only tools he had, clever head, cool heart, easy dollars, useful health, were sufficient to do the service he required. Enough! He could fix his way through the girls of Manhattan, he made the rules and came out easy, he needed no Sarah to spoil the game. Enough of her! But then, like a bulb charged too high, jealousy flashed off, dead and destroyed, with a charred worm of filament inside. Peter saw the waste in burning to no purpose. He would return with intensified devotion to juggling and money, putting oranges into the air of his high studio and keeping up his record of short-term speculation. And setting the strong ones aside for the six-months' capital gain. And he would also be a friend in need to his frantic friend, Dan Shaper. A man can't make Manhattan real all by himself. A fellow needs a friend.

Now he tried her name once more: *Sarah*. Sarah. Sarah. Yes, over. He opened the refrigerator and gazed inside. It began its hot pumping labor at keeping cool. The last evident sign of Sarah's taking nourishment with him was the two pears she had brought as her Saturday morning gift—luxury fruits from a luxury fruiterer, deep yellow and green, carried in tissue across town from Madison Avenue. Well, those pears should be served at room temperature, but they were pretty good chilled, too. Gluttonous, destroying, he ate them both, hunched over the sink, his hands drenched in ripe pear juice. He washed. He opened the window. Bruised pear fragrance gone. Goodbye, Sarah; go home to your cuckold; farewell.

Peter too sat at home the rest of that evening, considering the inventory of his duplex one-room studio, now reduced by Sarah's absence to less than one room, and decided to get a new lamp for reading and to paint the walls white. He sank into a chair, long-legged, sharp-kneed in light flannels, the green eyes hooded by lash. No juggling tonight. No *Barron's Weekly*.

A new life was beginning. His eye followed the open redwood stairway climbing the wall to the deck on which he had a bed, a table, and a few books. This bedroom floated above his head like a cloud. There were still violets in the Japanese bowl which Sarah had given him to celebrate Pearl Harbor Day. *Because you drove the Good Humor truck onto the runway*, she had said. *Because I can't get off the ground with you there. . . .* The bowl was low, flat, and perfectly proportioned for violets. Sarah knew how to make him smile; she could be delicate and raucous. He would keep the bowl, but replace the flowers with fresh ones. A sprig of ivy. Mistletoe for love. Now he would become a suitor, a swain, and then in due course, a husband and father, each step succeeding the other in proper order, with a sense of time and growth. Goodbye to adultery, he thought, goodbye to timelessness. He opened his arms to a future of tender boredom, with a girl by his side always—this is the dream of the secret lover of a married woman—and since his arms had been opened, he went to take a banana off the refrigerator in the alcove. He huddled on a stool, peeled the banana, and filled his mouth with sweet paste.

All at once, he regretted his courage. Suddenly, as he tried to eat, the ceiling was cranked down upon him; he felt as if the redwood stairway were a slipping screw under the weight of Manhattan, his bed, Sarah's bowl; he hunched his back against a crushing blow. Love had almost taken away his freedom—the world of desire wanted to rob him of his life. Only the taste of fruit could save him now, and the banana was followed by a cold ripe peach. Again thick juice squirted on his hands. He ate like an animal and wiped his paws. By gluttony he distracted himself from the crisis of loneliness, and then climbed up the stairway to bed at a strange early hour on that Saturday evening, just as if he had made love to Sarah again all afternoon, diverted and distracted. A dinner of two pears, a banana, and a peach; he floated on his deck in swollen sleep before the smoky dusk of Riverside Drive had deepened into night outside his window; evasions, fears, indigestion, a sweating forehead, dreams of isolation.

But when he awoke, just after sunrise on a fine springtime Sunday in New York, he found himself with good appetite for the day. This tall pale young man, very graceful, with the easy stride of a tennis player and the soft middle of a man who had suddenly given up sport—he would go back to tennis, he would join a health club—strolled among early churchgoers, discovering the morning, and had the Sunday *Times* with his breakfast in a Rudley's. French toast because that was his mother's habit on Sunday. Eggs were for weekdays. The Sunday *Times* was for Sunday. He loafed the whole day through, with no afternoon longing for Sarah, no evening miseries, and with a thrill of anticipation came out of the subway to work on the street Monday morning in his familiar crowd of stenographers and secretaries and female junior executives. He sniffed the perfumes of Broad Street. He was jostled by a purse leading a lady. That girl did not have rhythm. A girl should have rhythm; she should consider being syncopated. He bugged out his green eyes at her, but she hurtled by. He paused, letting the crowd eddy about him, and concentrated on a brief game: Which unmarried one would now come forward to greet him? Which hopeful bright one? Who would climb the redwood stairway to his high deck, kicking off her shoes as she went? What fresh girl, full of juice, amid this crowd of carefully groomed or cleverly mussed ladies?

Then he sighed, rubbed his hands, and took the elevator up the shaft in a slab where it was his pleasure to talk to the dollars and cause them to flock together.

First there was a bit of personal business. He dictated a letter to his friend Dan Shaper in Cleveland. Dan had heavier problems than Peter's. He was strapped. That man had good rhythm, but he had strapped himself down. Today Peter gave him some imperative mail-order advice: *Come to Manhattan, come on aboard.* Poor fellow, he needed the distractions of this town, he needed to be a still ravished bride of noisiness. Peter knew that he could be a friend to this friend. Friendship made him eloquent: *Let me tell you something. New York is the town for you, Pal.* Well, not very eloquent. Peter sighed over his letter and wished that he were as good with words as he sometimes could be with the sharp decision. Dan deserved strong support now in his time of trouble. He had gone into a stuporous shock under steady blasting by his wife. It wasn't fair. Dan was not supposed to be a loser. Peter would never have guessed that his friend was so susceptible, and yet they had known each other through some hard times. They had made the war together, they had been tempered, they had smelled the burning wool from their G.I. overcoats as they backed against a stove, trying to get warm on winter maneuvers, and then they had been shoved like kindling into the chimney of Italy; they had something to be friends about other than gossip and drink and idle talk. Once they had complained about the chow and jumped in combat parachutes, low against the ground. Now they were ready to chase girls in the middle of their time on earth, and take vitamin pills, take regular exercise, avoid saturated fats. That was a possible program for himself and for Dan. Dan too could learn to jab and dodge and get in his punches. They could carry unlighted torches through Manhattan, rubbing the salt into their wounds, complaining, bragging, surviving in a too-easy, very hard time.

Peter affected cynicism, but he was not cynical. He was discouraged in advance. "I'm against divorce because it leads to marriage," he explained to a broody young lady named Irma. "Marriage is better never than late. I think about myself a lot."

"Oh you don't, you don't, you're really quite sensitive!" came one of the standard replies. Irma was a girl to be counted on. She would see him sensitive. He was calculating, too. Irma did not notice that. It was not part of her plan. He was really quite calculating, unlike his friend Dan, who affected buffoonery because he was really often a buffoon, making the best of his weaknesses. Peter had narrowed the world of his care to a very small focus: himself, Sarah, high white studio and oranges, the play of money, himself. But intense focus. He looked out of his greenish eyes with a hard bright stare; he met the world with these vigilant eyes, a double row of excellent teeth (for biting, of course), a high-bridged elegant nose with delicate bone separating green eye from green eye. Because of exercise and a habitual diet of salads with lemon, steaks with an occasional bottle of Heineken's, and fruit, he would keep his boyish litheness late in the day. He might frazzle and fray a little, but thanks to clean living, the cleanest, he would be the last of the boys of World War II. He later came to know the awed ballet girl who pronounced it that way: "Hey Pete, were you really in Worldwartwo?"

"Sure 'nuff, Irma. Carried a spear at Agincourt, with special choreography by Mark Clark."

"Gee, you look young," she said.

"Sometimes I am, pal." And the hard green fawn eyes crinkled in a smile. When he smiled, there was something sloe and feminine, like a male dancer, in his lounging ease with himself.

Except for Dan Shaper, who was like him, though less controlled, more given to mistakes, Peter seldom kept his friends for long. Other boys aged. They grew too old for badminton, late strolling, patient expectation; they married, had children, went to the suburbs, and showed the effects of heavy eating; he took younger buddies, with whom he might eat pizza at the V. T. Pizzeria near Columbia on Amsterdam Avenue, or a meat loaf sandwich at the West End Bar on Broadway, and talk about how things were changing—people were thinking of politics as an art form, like Westerns and musicals, and the dominant political style breaking on the horizon was daring to indulge in grammar. When he brought a girl like Irma to these places, she said, "You know a lot about New York."

"I'm alone a lot," he said.

Her reply was to look serious.

Many women, thinking him sad, wanted to bring him out. He was attentive but did not listen. If they liked to work, let them work. He had a short hard laugh. But he was thinking seriously, too. He made his reservation for the trip to Cleveland. Irma-girl or Elsie-girl or some other girl might make a good beginning for Dan's convalescence in New York. He had them all down in his address book which was a gift from—he forgot her name. There was a record of it someplace.

In the cab out to LaGuardia he shut his eyes, folded his hands, and worked his way into his very simple plan for the weekend with Dan Shaper. Having assigned himself the duty of rousing Dan out of the miseries, he considered it good tactics to impose cheerfulness over whatever else he tried to suggest. He would not let Dan get away with despair. Everyone goes through that. Black hours, sure; but who needs it? Remember how bushy-tailed we were that time in Paris—how awol and bushy were our tails?

Times had changed a little. He rested on the plane and was refreshed to do battle again. He understood himself pretty well—"operationally, that is," he explained to Dan Shaper on this rescuing mission. He checked in for a weekend at the Colonial Motel on Euclid Avenue. He didn't even want to see Laura, Dan's wife. It was over. Not seeing her was an operational way to say it was over. He never wanted to see her again. Dan was still trying to keep his marriage limping along and Peter tried to hint that he could make out better in New York. Hint? No, *inculcate*. He smoked a cigar and discussed the firm flesh of some girls he knew. When you pressed them with your finger, the flesh pressed right back. "That is youth and good condition for you, buddy," he explained.

They sat in a motel room in Cleveland, staring at the gray dead stare of the teevee, and talked things over. Dan said: "Lay off the girls for a minute, will you? Who're you kidding?"

Peter listened to Dan's troubles and gave back some of

his own. Yes, he knew what girls meant about his "sadness," though he personally thought himself more at ease than most people. Control. Control. "But of course I can't give or take very much. I'm a loner, that's true."

Dan make a deprecatory, disagreeing shrug.

"Oh with you, that's different. We're friends." In 1945 Dan had shamed and shoved him about a girl, then shoved and shamed him into transferring from the infantry into the paratroops, and stood hooked on line behind him in a flying tub as he went out over Italy with a B.A.R. strapped to his chest. Now, fifteen years later, Peter wanted to do the same for Dan. It was now Peter who was in control and cool—he believed that Dan must stop living in misery, by bravado. Times had changed. A wife was not a beachhead to die in. He had the right to cop out. Peter said: "Come on over, boy. I'll help. I'm pretty generous for an exploiter, too."

"Bet you'd be a good husband to Sarah," Dan said from deep within his own conjugal agony.

"Maybe. The opening wedge. But I chose wisely: She's against divorcing her husband because it might lead to. . . ." He dodged away from finishing. It was Dan's way to skip on, playing with words, risking himself into sentences and just sawing them off when he got lost. Peter was crisp, controlled, 'operational.' This time he pulled away. But finally demanded of himself that he face the truth. ". . . marriage to me."

Peter wished, because Dan was his friend, to let him know how he lived in New York. Someone had to know in order to make it real. There was no one better than Dan, and so he explained. Sweet-talking the telephone at his office downtown, Peter sometimes affected the faggy drawl loved by moneyed old ladies who liked to take their investments out on the wire for a morning ramble; at night, in another manner, it was with a crisp, sharp note that he psyched all girls but Sarah; and better than talk, he stared hard-eyed and outraged when they spoke nonsense, waiting for them to give him what he wanted because he knew he could outwait any girl but Sarah. When they bugged him, he lit a cigar, narrowed his eyes, and just waited. And consequently, because he did not care, they hurried, they offered, they came trotting down the hall with their heels like picks into their own hearts, knowing how much they cared because Peter Hatten had managed to tease them into an angry definition of themselves: *I'm chasing him.* 'Come in, come in, what a surprise,' he would say jovially at the door. 'I was just peeling an apple. Come in,' he said, being kind for a moment because she looked so scared, 'people don't just come calling any more. You're an old-fashioned girl, would you like half an apple?' He handed her the half with the stem, because that was the rule of etiquette about apples. The peeling fell in a neat spiral to the floor. When she couldn't bear this any more, the girl would bend to retrieve it and put it into an ashtray, and when she straightened up, she would find Peter's hard eyes calculating about her from a great distance. . . .

Dan listened to all this in the motel room in Cleveland as if Peter were giving the first inside report of life on Mars. Outside, it was rush hour on Euclid Avenue. The husbands of Cleveland were hurrying up toward the Heights or out west to Lakewood. Peter swiveled the eye of the teevee with his stockinged feet and named the luxuries of Manhattan—anonymous ambitions and the chirp of hope—"Oh yes, and they perfume the breasts sometimes. It's nice, it's like a sweet fog in your nose and ears. Umm. And they get firm thighs from being so young. They can't help it, pal."

"You're a Martian," Dan said.

"Actually," Peter explained, "I find it just as easy to put the peelings directly into the sink. But I'd like you to figure it out for yourself about girls. That's the big part of the game."

"I've been married too long to play. I can't get up the steam for it, Pete. It scares me."

"Hm. You'll learn. Call me maestro. It's Taste City. You just need a natural sense of rhythm, strong legs, and a cool heart. Scared is the least of the problems. *Bored*. But you don't necessarily have to freak out like me. I'm a little used up."

"I'm not sure I want to make it, Pete."

"Listen, once you're free again, you'll be surprised. You've got stuff in you." And he gave Dan the cool hard-eyed green stare. With cigar. With the bugged scowl. "I see talent there, kid—*talent*."

They both laughed and Dan tapped a shoulder with his fist like the old buddy he was. One more little lesson for Dan. Money. It was nice to get philosophical with someone he could really trust, a true friend. This uncle talk was putting Dan down a little, Peter understood that; but he needed to be put down so that he might spring back up; the bedraggled nephew needed advice. It was a pleasure to speak out, away from Manhattan, in Cleveland, after Easter, with the frayed city ready to begin the cycle once more and this old friend looking skinny, yellow, and lined in the cheek, like a miserable Spaniard: "You need to get money and use it."

"Easy go, easy come, eh?"

"All right. Let me put it to you at some length, pal. It ain't simple, which is why I insist."

"Insist. Please."

"Hm. Let's take the nice and possible girl. Not the scheming virgin, not the round-heeled maniac. I don't like those chicks who give you a roll on the foam for their thank-you, I had a nice evening. Naw, the nice girl. What does she want? She's looking for something—what is it? If you show her, say, a hundred thousand dollars neatly done up in a bundle with a rubber band around the whole thing and you say, Here, lady, it's yours, hit the sack with me: She'll put out a big fat no. Okay, maybe a tense one. But *no*. She's got to. Well, she might, but you see the point—*nize* girl. Okay. Why? Because she is interested in security and your bundle outrages her pride, it's an offense, it puts her down and makes her feel insecure. Unprotected. That's why because. But let me tell you something. You take those same hundred thousand dollars and separate them nicely and make her feel each and every one of them behind your each and every move, your car, your cuffs, your drinks, your fly, and man, she will just slide in beside you, pal, all gassed up and lubed, too, because there you are, there they all are, things are in order and she is *safe* and *sound* and *protected* in port. Now it is *diff*erent. Those are transformed dollars. Those dollars really like her a lot. She don't want them to fondle—this is that nice girl, remember—she just wants to be cared for by them personally. Now they spell Secure, boy. They sing Secure. Secure is the name of that story. Yeah. You see how I think? I got respect for woman's feelings."

Dan looked at him as if he were busy translating this into a language he could understand. Peter waited. Dan said, "You're blowing smoke in my eyes. You had simpler ideas at the U.S.O. Club at Benning. Also I ain't got the dollars."

Peter drew his smile tight around his cigar. "Boy, you are sure hard to explain."

"I love your stories, Pete. But try to see my life, will you? I'm poor, I'm married, I'm strapped in with my kids, and I think maybe I'll kill myself first thing tomorrow morning."

Pete frowned at his friend.

"But I appreciate your talking to me."

Peter bugged out his eyes at Dan. "I don't appreciate your jokes. You got your whole blessed life ahead of you. Kids survive—they won't survive your killing yourself."

"Okay, Pete. It's just an expression."

"So listen about the dollars some more. Let's be practical. You got to package them for the ladies and build a little green boudoir, family-proof, boredom, bomb, and history-proof. They're no good out in the open air with a rubber band—"

"Besides everything else—"

"Hear me first. One gracious-living dollar is worth ten boorish greenbacks, pal. Come on in, like I say. I'll teach."

"Besides everything else, I don't think I can make it in your zoo, Pete."

Peter considered that and tasted the smoke. "It's a *zoo?* Hm. Not bad. With trapezes. And you're an ape, too, pal."

They had the laugh of old friends together. It was the smiling ease of men who had been through troubles and trusted each other and didn't need to come on strong. They just took each other nicely. Having jumped through exploding steel together, they could fall free and limber in the clouds of a different time and place.

Early the next morning, Peter checked out of the Colonial Motel with a sense of having done his good deed. He could still feel Dan's fist on his shoulder. There was barely a twinge about Laura, with whom he had been in love fifteen years ago. Ah that tough Laura-girl. She was Mrs. Fill-Me-Up-I'm-Empty. Uh-uh. Not for Peter. Thank luck for that stroke of loss. But not for Dan anymore, either. Dan would have to wear himself down a little more about his sons, about his wife, but then he would be ready for Manhattan. Right now he was probably having one of those cold breakfast wakes with Laura—polite passing of things, the children being shushed, death in the heart. Well, death is required for resurrection.

Peter went straight from Dan's agony in Cleveland to the airport, straight by a Monday morning breakfast flight to New York—good eggs and toast—well, eggs slightly steamed, but marmalade in a plastic cup—and then by cab to his office downtown on the Street. When he opened his briefcase over the second coffee which his secretary brought him in one of the senior partners' Dresden cups, he shut away Dan's troubles. He shut Sarah away. Work to do. He sipped his coffee and squinted over a balance sheet and a prospectus on a company called Navigation Electro-Computer Corp.—aircraft stabilizers. Civilian. Defense hopes. The issue had come out at 12, had doubled in a few weeks, had retreated to 10, but showed signs on the charts of getting ready for a high ride. Well, now for the questions Peter needed to decide: Did they have a real product or just an over-the-counter yoyo? If a yoyo,was it worth going for the free ride up the string before it spun back down again?

If a real product, how long would he have to wait for results in prices on the pink sheets of the over-the-counter quotation bureau? Peter was operational. He preferred his coffee in a thick mug, but Mr. Winters liked to see him sipping from the firm's traditional transparent china. Operational. He put his head back and gazed coolly out his window into the irregular air of lower Manhattan, trying to find in the clouds and the granite towers a future for Navigation Electro-Computer Corp.

2

The phrase which defined Peter's employment—"I work on the Street"—always gave him a twinge of embarrassment. It meant that he worked on Wall Street: Saratoga Springs, Princeton, liberal arts, he followed this familiar path of the bright enough, lazy enough, not much skilled young man of good family. But during his wanderyear in Europe (parents dead, small legacy), the phrase "on the street" had meant prostitution, that only, and now he wondered how he had ever come to be pleased with his job. He sold stock to friends he had grown up with in Saratoga, the last vestiges of the old racing aristocracy (talk of famous horses); he picked up new customers in Southampton and in his clubs in town (talk of old Princeton days and the sick comics, talk of the "jet set"); he managed the portfolios of a few griping, talkative, bluehaired widows, who fancied him their clever son. And how endlessly they gossiped on the telephone! And the teas he had to share with them on their birthdays! They seemed to have several birthdays a year, though they never grew any older.

Peter had no real money of his own ("real money" is

capital, not earnings), but he had a courteous manner, a retentive mind, a head of pale, barely thinning hair which he kept meticulously brushed, and an attractive air of melancholy which nevertheless did not depress anyone; his mouth was small, firm, full, and intelligent; his eyes were green and light under eyebrows darker than his hair, habitually drawn together with an expression both complex and unthreatening; his words were direct, discreet, and courteous all at once, and also sheathed an edge of judgment in the silences between them. Such a young man repays study by the discerning executive, and so it came to pass with Peter Hatten. He was no longer a mere customer's man in the small house where he worked. When one of the senior men came down with a popular disease (male climacteric: tantrums and inefficiency), and had to be eased into an improvised chairmanship, the surviving members of the firm looked at Pete Hatten and found him good. He was given their most junior junior partnership and assigned to study electronics and chemicals.

Speculation—a new game in this. It was his secret office infidelity to the firm. Peter believed himself in touch with reality when he speculated. He lacked the greed and steady interest of the committed speculator, he would rather juggle his oranges perfectly than make money in three commitments out of five; but he had found a method for tapping the stock market of a profit. With but a mediocre grounding in economics, enough to check the basic strength of a company, he invented his own sly techniques in research. He had once met a goofy old fellow who claimed to make a living playing the market according to Marx—after leaving the Party with Trotsky, of course. Peter was interested. "Personally," Peter confided with the rare pleasure of telling a secret to a stranger, "I play the market according to Freud." Peter had a touch. He interpreted the newspapers and the fads; he sniffed out what the sheepish public would trample down next. "Snow plows in summer, air conditioning in winter, that's my principle," Peter explained to the geezer. "Of course that's only a way of saying it. You have to catch the wind in your nose as it comes up—hula hoops, missiles, books, *you* know."

The geezer made a terrible face, one left over from his arsenal as a professional proletarian. "You have contempt for people. You express a perfect lumpen bourgeoisie antisocial prejudice, classic of its type. Also," he remarked professionally, "you can get in touch soon enough? You pick say the hula hoop company before it tops out?"

"Yes. Yep to both your questions, one implied. But hula hoops is only an example, too. Think of international travel. Think of credit cards. Oh lots of things, pal."

The old goof, slumping into his usual chair in the board room before the nattering ticker, lifted his newspaper to indicate that the audience was over. He was reading a back issue of *People's World*. He hid his face behind it, but as Peter moved off, he felt an eye boring at him through the socialism of Daniel De Leon. Peter agreed that this was no way for a man to live. But, he asked himself, what percentage of Americans do any useful work? Eight? Eleven per cent? It would make an interesting bet for the office pool. Of course, they would have to set up criteria for defining the useful. From Peter's point of view, salesmen, rocket builders, elected officials, and investment counselors did not qualify. The man who had given him juggling lessons, a Sicilian smelling of cologne, with a studio above a private detective on 42nd Street, was perhaps the most useful person in his recent experience. Professor Corrasini was an honest man who smelled of cologne that did not pretend to be after-shave lotion. It was cologne all right. Also he had saved his life. He rescued him from the disaster of love; he turned him away from speculation—gambling—destruction.

Peter stretched his legs by strolling through the board room on a quiet morning of backing and filling. The ticker was slow. The shuffle of yellow paper out of the Dow-Jones machine stirred faintly on the floor as a few paltry reports were tapped on the moving roll. A girl ran up with a scissors to cut it and post it when she saw Peter's disapproving glance. He strolled on, glancing at the new Over-the-Counter pink sheets and a report on IBM from *Value Line*. He asked a question of the girl with the scissors and she said breathlessly, "Noon averages up zero point eight, Dow-Jones, Mr. Hatten."

"Bull market just horsing around," he said to her.

She smiled gratefully.

"Mind getting me a few reports? Step into my office in a minute, will you, please?"

She smiled with ravishment, twisting her engagement ring. She followed him back. He gave her the list on a memo sheet. His office was empty again.

Without wanting big money, without the itch for possessions, heavy cars, houses, women in furs and diamonds, Peter had begun to dream of big rises in puts and calls, selling short, extended margin accounts and supplementary bank loans. This way lay ruin. He bugged out his lazy, sharp, slightly askew green eyes at himself in the glass top of his desk. He did not have the nerve for the power which a fortune gives. Big money was a delusion and a distraction. No desire for it. He wanted focus, not distraction. Therefore, instead of following his fantasy into money madness, he juggled. Strolling on 42nd Street, Peter had read the sign:

> JUGGLING FOR THE BEGINNER AND ADVANCED PRIVATE INVESTIGATIONS LOVE MARRIAGE BUSINESS. STRICTLY CONFIDENTIAL. ROOM 441.

It enabled him to put off the suicide of gambling.

Peter sat for ten minutes in silence and then turned to his telephone to check a rumor that the foremost toy company in America was about to announce a mechanical space monkey that beeped like a man. Okay, good evidence for it in the irate denial of a broker close to the company; not certain: make a note: watch the charts. Speculating in reality helped to keep him in touch. Under control it was okay. There were few other things to count on. The oranges go up and come down; outer space dolls, enjoying weightlessness, might replace card tricks. His hobbies were becoming his way of life. Peter judged himself most severely (this can be a form of complacency). He secreted intelligence as an eye secretes tears; but, in fact, eyes serve properly to see the world with, and the wily substance squeezed out of Peter's mind was not always the clarity, force, and decision of intelligence, was often its refrigerated substitutes. In Cleveland, he had said to his friend Dan about a girl: "I can deny her anything." He practiced his skills; he kept in condition. He could take almost any strong experience and make little of it; he knew (knowledge can be complacent and false) that this is the direct opposite of the intelligent man's examination of a speck in order to discover the universe. Sometimes praying to God in a peculiar habit left over from his Episcopalian childhood, he now prayed only for concentration, more and more of it. The act of prayer was mostly a joke, of course. He found the posture graceful. It helped to prepare him for sleep. Even without it, he could fight off the itch to gamble. He could juggle. He could think—same thing to Peter. He sought a small profit.

The cold war ran along nicely, with absorbing perturbations. Electronics and chemicals did well, and somehow this was put down to the credit of Peter, although he assured both the senior men in the firm and his clients that scientists, generals, and politicians went their own odd ways without considering his hopes of fortune. He read the proper newsletters and studied the pertinent budgets. He had a feel for the winds as they rose. It was not all that complicated. Nevertheless, he was a messenger of good tidings, and the messenger chose sagely among companies and projects. The grandson of the founder, feeling better after a prostate operation, came in two days a week, called Peter "son," patted him on the back with his bald, spotted hand, and insisted on putting him up for his club. The Grandson was nearly eighty years old. Well he remembered the fine times before the Securities Exchange Commission had taken away a fellow's liberty and Frank Roosevelt was the result. "But we can still pick our friends and associates, they left us that, son."

Pete turned into the middle of his life and decided it was time to move on. Not really a grasping young man, he kept his faintly bohemian, one-room, double-deck apartment, defying convention by remaining on the unfashionable West Side just because he liked his view of the Spry sign across the river on the Palisades; he made a bow to his success by buying a Jaguar, which spent most of its time in a garage; he was ready to take a winter two weeks in Mexico and a summer two weeks in Paris. But the main resolution was about Sarah. And after less than a year of deliberation, he had lived up to it. He believed that he had finally left that note of goodbye under the knocker on his door only because she would not leave her husband for him. He wanted to pick his friends and associates, as the Grandson said, not be picked by them on their terms. She had cast him adrift.

Therefore the freedom of erotic adventuring after so much stern fidelity. Forward! Another Monday had rolled out of the machine. Pete sat in the driver's seat at his desk at 110 Wall Street, swung resolutely from the Manhattan skyline to the telephone, and took his first client call of the week from a widow who wondered if they shouldn't maybe switch from U.S. Borax to IBM. Luxuriously he closed his eyes upon his desk with its glass top, its one leather folder with his initials in gold—P.H., as in Pent House—and the serving of black coffee in a Dresden cup. On the one hand, IBM can buy up almost any new device of consequence, or improve on it, true. But on the other hand, U.S. Borax has all that borax in the ground and an active research department discovering new uses for it besides soap and high energy fuel. He drawled with relish through a recitative of advice. He loved these free improvisations upon a secure base of inside dope and hearsay; he had a sense of power because, in fact, he really knew his stuff. But then he was done. "And cetera," Pete commented to his first widow of the day. He had a little repertory of these banal, mysterious phrases with which he sawed off the old ladies before lunch.

But this time she replied crankily, "*And* cetera yourself, Peter, that reminds me. I just can't be alone on my wedding anniversary this year. Poor Mr. Warden passed away he died God bless almost seventeen years ago, so stop by, fiveish, will you?" By the shrill leer of intention in her voice, he felt it coming a split second ahead: "My niece—"

Okay, okay. He knew these herds of nieces—long-toothed spinsters with festoons of lace hanging from the collarbones to give grace to their no-bosom bosoms. Christ! No, he would not do that job. He would rather go sit at the Yale Club with the Grandson and smell leather for an evening. He would rather turn cold through a long night of poker, through the breakfast of cigarettes and gin and tomato juice and final obsessed dreaming of Jacks and deuces. He believed in love before inherited capital; he believed in freedom and control. This was not the way for Mrs. Warden to develop new uses for borax, either. But of course he would have to take the tea with her anyway, with pink cookies and napkins of a linen thick as white fur. And perhaps his friend Dan, arriving soon in New York after settling his marital disaster, might need to know an Elsie. He would have child support and a new job to worry about, and maybe an Elsie would do some good if he wanted to try making it that way.

The niece. Ah, Elsie, the niece. That profligate fate which has blessed New York, St. Louis, San Francisco, and a few other American places, seems to distribute pretty girls where they are needed, and often just when. Elsie was no long-toothed spinster with a coated tongue; she was no glamorous beauty, either; she was an electric and pert little breathless thing, freshly styled by Sarah Lawrence, who wanted to be an avant-garde actress (no other guard would do). "You mean you want to play lesbians?" Peter asked, in order to see her blush and make her understand that he was an exceptional stockbroker. He had decided not to save her for Dan Shaper. He had decided to be rude to her right now, himself.

The solenoid that controlled her blushing let the pinkness through. She fluttered her eyelashes. She was an old-fashioned girl with new-fashioned false eyelashes made of genuine lash. "What kind of stockbroker are you?"

"Let me tell you something. I'm a customer's man."

"Shush anyway, Auntie will hear you," she answered, and true enough, Auntie did hear them.

"You young folks must have lots to discuss, so you will excuse me? I am proud to say I don't understand the theater any more." And with a satisfied glower on her hairy, high-pressured face, the old lady turned off her hearing aid and went upstairs to dress for dinner.

They were alone and silent amid the diminishing afternoon and the reflection of light on silver. All her long life Mrs. Warden had believed that the light had a special quality on East 82nd Street. There were trees outside—East Eighty-Second Street trees—and a yellow-gray sky—the sky over East Eighty-Second near Park. The sky had been trained to support a mild sun and rich shadows and to reflect them through Mrs. Warden's velvet curtains. The late Mr. Warden had been no help at all. Consequently Mrs. Warden understood that it was necessary to leave nothing to chance or men. A high-pitched electronic whine sounded down the stairway. Mrs. Warden was eavesdropping. Elsie's small eyes, carefully extended by make-up, were thickly veiled by her industrious lashes; her small pert face would get prettier and prettier until it abruptly crossed the frontier into martyred matrondom. Together they listened to the mating call of Mrs. Warden's hearing aid. With a point of conscience, Peter realized that his silence was a paltry revenge on Sarah—he intended to take control this time. And with a still sharper point of exacerbated pride, he wondered if his silence did not in effect give the control to Elsie.

"There were," she said timidly.

He coughed and waited.

"Do you have a cold?"

He shook his head and waited.

"There *was*," she said. No interruptions. And then all in a rush: "A-girl-like-that-in-school." And her face went crimson in the last glow of sunlight under the blinds and through the curtains.

A trumpet sounded in Peter's ear; he had won! His delay did not give over control after all! She was waiting for his lead! (The trumpet was also Mrs. Warden asking if he wanted an umbrella some damn fool had left in her umbrella stand six months ago.)

"No," he said, taking the hint, taking Elsie with him. They enjoyed dinner together at the Boulevard de Paris on East 60th Street (an enlarged mural of the Metro map, a décor of French street signs, *enseignes,* and metal café chairs); they embarked upon an illuminating discussion of the troubles "a girl like that" can get into, and then, of all things, they went to a neighborhood movie. A neighborhood movie seemed somehow the subtle and complicated gesture: to remove her from her class, habits, and expectations. He continued this original program of variation against the pattern by taking her to bed on the following evening, without the movie. Afterwards he showed her how he juggled three oranges without dropping one, "except," he explained with regret, "maybe sometimes by mistake."

"You're simply beautiful, Petey. Ooh, naked."

"I practice a lot."

She tried to look serious and scholarly, like a connoisseur

of juggling, curled against the headboard of the bed—Peter believed in headboards for propping the feet against—and she used the sheet to reveal and conceal, respectively. She hugged it against herself. She moved very slightly, as if thinking a subliminal rhumba. She said: "Isn't your form dreamy—I mean awfully good? Juggling."

"I've gained a little weight lately." Carefully he replaced the oranges in their Japanese bowl. "I'll get better. It's a funny thing how the entire body is implicated—arches, thighs, chest, neck muscles, everything—though all you see is the hand-flips."

"You're perfect already."

"I do the best I can, bein' white and all," he murmured so she would not hear.

"Perfect," she squeaked, and now he had to take serious notice.

"Don't say that," he warned her very solemnly. "Perfect is perfect, and I know I'm not, Elsie, not yet. I have to resist gambling and over-eating sweets and premature—"

"Shush!"

"Premature sometimes, anyway."

Thereafter, for several weeks, they followed a rhythmically varied schedule, movie or bed, bed or movie, on alternate nights. Once they even had dinner at the Child's near Pennsylvania Station—but that was carrying the joke too far. As an apology he offered to introduce her to Professor Corrasini or take her to see the belly dancer at the Greek Brittania Café. She could have a dollar bill to shower madly on the dancer's navel. The primitive Middle-Eastern folk artist at the Greek Brittania had been Miss McKeesport, Pa., 1957, and had gone to a school for advanced belly-dancing on Tenth Avenue. While dancing for these cruddy Greeks at union scale she was waiting to be discovered by the Blue Angel or her one true love or a really good agent. Elsie asked how he knew so much about her. He said that he didn't.

By this time he discovered that he had almost exhausted the available stock of entertainments and he began to notice about Elsie those little defects which men gratefully seize upon in order to make excuses for their own diminishing ardor: Her handwriting slanted backwards. She could not walk barefoot gracefully, since the tendons of her feet had been stretched by high heels, and she was a ludicrous spectacle on her way to the bathroom in the mornings. She preferred the Germans to the French, and this seemed inexcusable (the usual grounds: plumbing and politeness). She was not perfect.

Worse, she wore her tiny eyelids covered with silver makeup and had the habit of modestly closing her eyes and fluttering the lids whenever she said something which implied faint flattery of herself. But as her entire repertory of philosophy, judgment, observation, and comment all softly praised her own perspicuity, generosity, and elevation of spirit, her face seemed to have no eyes for looking outward—only those two agitated, quicksilver, triangular spaces. "I never judge people. . . . I can always tell from the way a man says hello if he's nice or just out for what he can get—you know—by that I mean a good time." And when she spoke about the "girl like that" at school, she meant to add, and did: "I may be a rebel and all that, but at least I'm *normal.*"

What, thought Peter, must I do to get rid of Elsie? Before I am required to strangle her, that is. And do I run a chance of losing Mrs. Warden's account on grounds of having broken the windpipe of her niece?

He worried about this for several weeks, until Elsie announced that she had been offered the role of a corpse in a play by Ionesco, in return for which all she had to supply was part of the financing for the operation ("Off Broadway it's not very expensive") and a few harmonious moments with the producer (male—Elsie was *normal*). Peter and Elsie had a theatrical hamburger together, an offbroadwayburger, easy on the onions; they discussed the symbols of death and decay in Ionesco, the revival of theater in cafés, the juiciness of beef on Sheridan Square; he thought of playing poker, he thought of selling short; and thus, on excellent terms, with Elsie very proud of her silvery-lidded business and artistic heads, they parted. She gave the valedictory address: "I shouldn't have gone to bed with you—you know, made love—because I did so want to, Peter, and now I know what that leads to. I'm hot, I really am, that's the only word for it, excuse me. Gee, it sounds terrible when I put it that way, *hot,* but honest, I really am. I hope you shall pardon the word, Peter. Where was I? Oh. We were spending more and more of our time in bed, don't you think? and pretty soon we wouldn't go out at all, we'd just roll around having a perfectly lovely time, like pigs. Peter. And then my career would grind to a terrible stop. I mean it, honest. I'd never arrive at what I truly want in life, you know, really express myself. That's my problem, Peter."

"Dire."

She put both fists to her mouth, arms inward, elbows covering her bosom, head slightly bowed, thus constructing a poignant tableau dedicated to Sensitivity. "You're not kidding," she said.

Peter promised to come to opening night, but forgot about it. Elsie sent him a large glossy publicity photograph with the following message inked across her shoulder: "Lots of Luck to a Real Swell Fellow. Elsie." It surprised him. He realized that, given the proper luck, Elsie would have a shrewd and humorous understanding of the world by the age of sixty. She was a survivor. He had let himself off too easily with her.

Mrs. Warden restlessly shuffled her holdings about a bit (General Dynamics and Getty Oil), and then was quiet. Elsie's play lasted four nights. The Dow-Jones averages continued to show an irregular advance. Electronics and specialties did much better than the averages.

Peter took a space of vagueness in the exasperated concentration of Manhattan. He decided not to mind letting himself off easy. That might be the best way.

3

But the life of this mild Wizard of Wall Street was suddenly much too quiet. He found himself shocked awake in the night, trapping his dream before it fled; Sarah's drowsy caresses were a sensation, not an idea. In his sleep he could not force Sarah to be an idea; he felt her head on his shoulder, her hair on his cheek. He shivered himself awake; he shuddered, sat up, and blinked at the lifeless walls. It was not afternoon, it was night. It was not Sarah, it was a memory of Sarah. Elsie had blown through his life like a trial subscription to an unwanted magazine; his loneliness returned. It gnawed at him as it had in the Army before he met Dan Shaper, as in his first year at Princeton, as it did when he wandered Europe after his parents died, checking on the Pitti Palace and the Place des Vosges. They were still there. They had not moved. His mother and father had left him alone and he had studied how to move within silence and longing. This loneliness was his oldest adversary, vanquished by learning to live alone. It was the only way he knew to purge the worm. Of course, control required the actions of controlling. He lay staring at the ceiling until the dawn came; he poured his breakfast of cold Super K from the box; or he dressed and went out again at midnight. The newsstand at West 96th and Broadway sold *Encounter* and the *Partisan Review* twenty-four hours a day; a bar on West 4th Street featured a Wednesday Amateur Strip Tease Night; there was chamber music at the YMHA on East 92nd Street. There were Broadway, off-Broadway, and off-off-Broadway theaters; and all over town, culture and distraction asked the privilege of filling the idle hours. Peter drank coffee at 2:00 A.M. in an Israeli coffee house with Mexican primitive paintings on the wall. He was served by a girl who admired his elegance and his green eyes and asked her friend in a stage whisper if he were an actor "or something."

That's right, an Or-Something, Peter thought.

He left the coffee house because the sentimental noodling of a guitar did not make him want to sing along. He strolled down Broadway and gazed at the stylish loiterers, the beatnik girls all in black, the young marrieds doing their shopping in pedal pushers at a delicatessen in the middle of the night, the Puerto Rican girls in voluminous cotton skirts, all these women who wanted to, lived for, schemed at, and perhaps actually succeeded in making men happy. New York was full of women. Even at this hour the overflow hit the streets. There were soft tides rising over the island. Peter was full of longing. All he had had to do for the coffee house waitress was to crinkle his eyes and decide to listen to her talk about—what? meem? injustice? art? the Gaza Strip? He also knew where there was a continuous poker game. He felt himself yearning to swim in it, though it was a sucker game. The subway shook the pavement at his feet and he thought, in a shudder of self-pity: In ten years I'll be over forty.

He grinned at this idea, close relative to the child's dream of his parents weeping at the dark mound of his grave. He grinned under his burden of self-pity and nostalgia on the streets of New York, where every Jane seemed to have found her Jack, or at least to expect him soon. *In forty years I'll be over seventy*. He smiled, judged himself hard, was not content with the joke. But as the unearthly Manhattan moon dimmed out into dawn on Riverside Drive, and there was a brief brooding quiet within the city's ceaseless hype and beat, Peter's little joke helped him home and up the open redwood stairway and into bed. Alone. At last he slept.

To distract himself, he plunged and re-plunged into the study of love. He behaved as if he were studying those others, the girls of Manhattan, but in fact he knew that he was studying himself, and this did not displease him. He began to develop his private theories. How can you tell if a girl has a good heart for lovemaking? Well, you make love, but by that time it may be too late for comfort. How do you know in advance? Show her a menu, and if she does not worry over it, but chooses decisively and then eats with good appetite, sweating slightly, she is okay. *Note:* Air conditioning throws off the calculations. *Note:* Fat girls don't count. And in fact it turns out, after all, that a fellow only really discovers the truth about a particular girl when he lives through those precarious getting-to-know-you moments, up the stairway and into the room and beyond. And perhaps there are non-mechanical differences for her, too, depending on whether it is only Peter by her side or, instead, the man she has always been waiting for.

Also look for nervous laughter, sullen moods, the dropped-r finishing-school accent. (All these meanings must be sorted out.) Watch out for the girl who says "fun-and-games" and circles her i's at age over twenty-two. Beware of the bitten nail. Avoid devout atheists, but cultivate ladies who like pious ceremonies. Disregard protestations of cynicism about men, but obey the warning of tension on the dance floor and insistence that a girdle is not a girdle—"just to hold up the stockings." Value a smile that yields. Value a trusting eye. Return it as much as possible.

Peter realized that his experience was limiting his freedom. He was living too much alone with women. He was fleeing toward the comfort of theories and proving things. Well, but knowing the laws of gravity, his weakness for gambling, and the limits of his body did not diminish the pleasure of juggling oranges. On the contrary. Navigation Electro-Computer was up to 13 bid, 15 asked. He had predicted it. He was pleased anyway.

After Elsie, you might have thought that the vision of Sarah—discreet, grateful, and brooding, with her impulses to make him a home-cooked meal—would have tempted him. No. Or rather, yes, but not for long, not while fully awake. For despite his dissatisfaction with Elsie, she had given him something—freedom of action. He discovered an important underground doctrine about love: *You don't have to care.* Love was not like a love song, a lingering, haunting melody, *adieu m' amour;* love was merely third or fourth on the Top Ten of Things To Do. Raised in a very moral American world, he had believed that strong desire must be necessary to success; on the contrary, Elsie was easy on the heart and easy on the body. And why not? He did not need Sarah; he did not need love. He could perpetually begin afresh, and merely begin. He could settle for fun; that is, boredom followed by release—fun-and-games.

Still, those long afternoons with Sarah and her pears and Berlioz in his high studio had unsettled him, unnerved him for other girls. Because of Sarah, he judged Elsie from the heights and depths of other possibilities. He had cared, or wanted to care, or imagined caring. He had forgotten about selling short, he had neglected poker. The newspaper society pages were full of glossy Elsies getting brightly married to well-brushed men like himself, but these were men who had had their college weekends, had passed relieved through a few paltry adventures, and had never known Sarah dreamily playing her fingers along the edges of the dime-sized bald spot in his silky thatch of pale hair. Gingerly those men in the papers had tested their points; they would never discover that a man can be plunged up to the hilt in flesh. Poor Elsies. Poor lads.

Following Elsie and a time of meditation, during which electronics stocks continued to do well as a group, there was an Austrian divorcée named Inga. Inga did marvelous imitations of the Gabor sisters, seven or eleven of whom were her best friends. It seems that one of them met a great movie producer and said, "I hear you are the most *im*-portant man in Hollywood." But by accenting the first syllable and leaving out the "r" in "important," the merry Gabor obtained the word "impotent." Peter listened to Inga tell this charming anecdote seven or eleven times, one for each sister, and after each time she always made sure that attention continued to be focused on her with a change-of-pace remark like, "Dahling, please get me my wrap, I'm *cold*."

With Inga Peter discovered that it was possible to think of a woman as a foam-rubber doll and to throw himself upon her with destructive fury and yet be unable to mark her at all. "I adore the green look you get—green-eyed little boy. You're my green-eyed long green boy, hah?" Afterwards, restoring her face, she would comment, "You were especially good tonight I thought, dahling. It's those oysters, I'm sure. Whatever will we do when the months without *r* come around?"

"I'll figure something out," he said. He did not wait until May to stop calling Inga. And the funny thing was that she never once asked him to explain; she seemed to understand without apologies, and that was more sensitivity than he expected in her. He did see her once in a steak restaurant where he often took dinner alone. She was in a crowd at a large table, and her voice rose above the clatter, in pseudo-Hungarian, " 'Oh dahling,' " she was singing, " 'you are in Hollywood the most impotent man.' "

He sneaked out of the restaurant without finishing his meal. He thought that perhaps his shame arose from being discovered at a dinner by himself, but as he hit the street, cool air and damp, a tangle of taxis, he realized that he was ashamed for Inga—she was still telling that same old story. Her companion at dinner was a well-known minor actor with the thickest hair in the east sixties, a sulky pretty face, and a talent for projecting phlegm, the gripes, and pique. If he had been a few inches taller, he might have been a Hollywood star. For him some brilliant director might invent a thing he would call "Adler Elevator Shoes," and then give him a stool to stand on. He had a great future, if only a genius hurried into his life. In the meantime, Inga kept him down to size.

The next day Peter sold Texas Instruments short. But only a hundred shares. He could cut any loss without serious damage. He also called Dan Shaper in Cleveland and listened to his friend try to be wry about his woe. Poor Dan. Well, he had to make up his own mind and stop mucking around in misery.

Perhaps partly in order not to be caught eating dinner alone, Peter then took up in rapid succession with a secretary in a rival brokerage firm (recently divorced, wouldn't say anything against her husband, but stated firmly that she now wanted a man with the quality of "maturity, y'know?"), a Hawaiian pottery-maker whom he met in a Greenwich Village Mexican restaurant (shyly they later confided that too much spice gave them both uneasy stomachs), and a graduate student in physical education at Columbia. "If I don't go to bed with a man the first time," said the latter, "I never do. That's because I'm fighting a tendency to promiscuity. He's got to catch me from behind—as it were. Peter, don't look nasty. Don't look at me like that. I said 'as it were.' That's just a Freudian slip, it doesn't mean anything." Since a lot of men failed the first time to catch her from behind, so to speak, this maiden from Morningside Heights remained nearly pristinely, albeit nymphomaniacally pure. She was writing her master's essay on "Pushups Since 1900" and believed that physical fitness has never been so important in our nation's life.

Each of these affairs ended with, in order of appearance, a demand of marriage simultaneous with the onslaught of boredom, a rapid surfeit of sweet noodles, pork, and boredom, a slipped disc during badminton and boredom. The graduate student massaged his back, in a purely chiropractic, spinal, amicable way, and assured him that it was a Freudian slip of the disc. He didn't really care for her was the truth of the matter, she promised him. She read his spine like an open book. "Let's face facts. You're what I call a loner. That's an expression I made up. A *loner*," she said briskly and with satisfaction, slapping his buttocks. "So am I. And I'm way behind on my thesis, thanks to you. It's been great. Goodbye."

Other girls had left perfume, beauty soaps, brushes, and various pharmaceuticals in Peter's bathroom. This was the first to leave a bottle of home-brewed liniment including eucalyptus oil. Within a week he was able to juggle again. It was a deep satisfaction to him that he still mended so rapidly. In the paratroops, with a sprained ankle, he had carried a full pack under novacaine and healed before the drug wore off. It had broken the pain cycle, the doctor later explained.

Look at me! thought Peter, again between women, and decided that perhaps his disease of the lapse of love was deeply significant of our age. Personal failures equal public failures —why not? But a man accustomed to hardheaded examination of annual reports was not satisfied by such easy justifications. There should be more to life on earth. The bookkeeper's tables tell more of the story: mismanagement and diversion of effort and failure to use resources. Peter therefore suspended his meditations on the philosophy of love, and discovered that he could eat alone without much risk of being caught at it by going a little out of his way. He took to the movies again. He started with foreign art films, but gradually worked his way up to Alan Ladd Westerns on 42nd Street. He visited museums, and noted that he was perhaps the only person in Manhattan who went alone to museums without looking to pick up somebody of the opposite (or same) sex. He also went to concerts. As his feelings atrophied, he developed a taste for the artistic expression of feelings. But he was not dead yet. He abstained from that sucker poker game in a hotel near Broadway and 96th Street.

He had a thrilling itch in his ears when IBM jumped nineteen points in one day; it lost half the gain the following day—quake in the pit of stomach.

It may be significant of our age, he decided, but it is more importantly significant of me. He folded his newspaper and thrust it over the side of his chair. He thought: I need to do or die somehow, to live and love somehow, or else be content to become a waxy middle-aged man with irritable moods and a cultivated eye. What do I want? Wildness. What do I get? A dream of tired blood. I wait for Dan to arrive in Manhattan. I wait for IBM to announce a stock split. The grape gives its best when it is squeezed, trampled, fermented; I seem to be turning not into wine but a raisin on the floor, dry, hard stale, and pushed to and fro by the ants.

With this over-deep and rather literary thought, Peter fell to his knees and began looking for the raisins that had dropped as he ate from an open box. Crawling about nearsightedly, he had an abrupt fear of assault from the rear. He left the raisins for the maid. He dusted his hands together. It was time to do something about his isolated jitters. It was time to do the same old thing.

Going to the bathroom on this spring evening of verdant self-doubt, reproach, and resolution, he examined his face in the mirror while the birds were busy receiving the season on Riverside Drive outside his window. Back in Saratoga, the dogwood was in bloom and the martins had returned; on Riverside Drive, there were kids a year older, there were mothers with eyes made up a new way, there were girls strolling and boys stalking. From the profile, he decided, he was a but slightly sagging Ivy League tennis player and could qualify to take most recent coeds to the Village Vanguard. From the front, at full face, he looked like a possible handsome young President of the United States, ever so delicately frayed by care, and wishing to care even more than he already by nature did (curlied locks, proud and firm mouth). He was ready. Up arms again, up the flow of life, up girls and girlishness and girldom! Spring has come, Peter my lad, and it is time once more!

But *who?* To whom? This nagging question required a major, statesmanlike answer: *she whom he loved.* Ah, well done. Let the pennants fly.

But what would be her blessed name? Alice, Betty, Carrie, Doris? Mary, Nora, Olive, Peggy? A personal identification, with individual characteristics, a way of opening her umbrella and a way of smiling, a lilt of voice and a glint of eye, these things are important and make the difference between a genuine girl and a foam-rubber doll. Cheep-cheep, said a robin redbreast at his windowsill. He must remember to put out crumbs.

For almost ten days now, Navigation Electro-Computer had been making him some funny money. The stock moved up so fast that he had no sense of a relation between effort and dollars. He had not moved it up. He put through a call to the president of the company to ask just what they were making. He sounded efficient, but he needed to be reminded. It made him a little dizzy. The president cried out gaily to him over the telephone, "Call me any time, Mr. Hatten! Call me collect! You had faith when people said we were just one of those small electronics companies! You like my home number? I don't ordinarily give it out, but for you, sir—." Peter preferred not to think about his paper profits, and then maybe they would go away. He would have liked to try something hard, something outside himself and difficult. For every ten dollars he had put in Nav El-Com, he now had more than thirty. They had researched up a new aircraft stabilizer. Space applications and over-the-counter enthusiasm.

Peter's customers wanted to know why he hadn't pushed old Nav El-Com harder. He had pushed it to the limit of his interest.

He entertained the bird at his window by juggling three oranges, but when he turned for his reward in birdsong, there was only a soft white spot where the robin had been.

4

Resolutely, then, Peter fell in with girls again, and with a particular girl named Irma, whom he met while she was out walking her dog and he was out walking her, although she did not know it at first. The dog seemed to understand at once. Upon seeing Peter, or rather, sniffing him, since dogs have limited vision but trust greatly in smells, the dog, whose name was Peter ("What a coincidence! We are fated for each other!" —"Now isn't that rather pretentious of you? I just *happened* to name him Peter, in honor of my visit to Rome"), began to bark and jump in little circles, which caused a bright flow of admonition, and the dog then suffered a crisis, which was treated with alternate doses of icy calm and furious advice, and Peter being nearby, the cause of all this canine hysteria. . . . He rescued her; he calmed the dog; he smiled; she smiled. And there they were, Irma and Peter, standing in the dusk near the Hudson River, making philosophy together. "Did you know," Peter remarked, the dog safely diverted by a fire hydrant, "that dogs do not bark in a state of nature? They only learn to bark out of futile imitation of human speech."

"*My* dog," she replied; "I have never believed," she also remarked primly (she was not the sort of girl who); "but do dogs exist in a state of nature, Mr. Patten? *My* dog was bred in a kennel in Philadelphia."

"Ah, you know Philly, Miss?" Peter asked daringly.

"Umm," she said, and he knew that in the golden future which lay before them, he should always remember to pronounce it "Philadelphia." Also the dog set up a crisp fresh yipping in protest against his dog-disparaging insinuations.

"It's Hatten," he said, "Peter Hatten. I've been to Philadelphia many times. Victor's. Eugene Ormandy. The Philadelphia Athletics."

"You're putting me on," she said. "All right, we'll try two at that game, Peter."

Irma was a light and metal person who had gone to a fine finishing school, had been finely finished, and now was in town, like Elsie and ten thousand others, for a spell of Show Biz. Having been analyzed at the ages of fifteen to seventeen, she had picked these slightly later years for her Stage of Parental Rebellion, as she named it; she had a little word for it, her own little expression; and she danced in a little off-Broadway musical. This did not mean that she was less pretty or attractive or anything than the girls in the on-Broadway musicals, however. It only meant that she was slightly less skilled. She had just as much heart, and heart is what matters when you come right down to it (if you happen to be coming right down to heart), and she put all her talent and heart and hopes and dreams into her dancing and her walking of Peter, "I mean the dog, silly." She had a strong doubled bud of rump and that balletic stem above. And cute. Slender, but cute. When you can't think about breasts, you can think about doubled bud of springtime rump. Irma knew her own virtues: she had learned a trick of turning her back as she strolled, "conversed," played little teasing games at the stoop of a brownstone on Riverside Drive. She kept herself going with the aid of chicken salads (light on the mayonnaise), filter cigarettes ("I think they're cool, if you remember which end, don't you?"), the love of a dog ("Well, he's almost like human"), and an occasional audition ("But there are some things I won't do even to get on Broadway"). As she confided to Peter, she had already suffered from an important, soul-thickening romance, with a gentleman named Mr. Marvin Magleberg, one of our foremost composers of Country and Western. He was a highly moral person who disapproved of rock and roll because it was a degenerate commercial manifestation of a native American art form, rhythm and blues by name, which should be left to our fine negro people, who are just as good as we are, only they have a better sense of rhythm in such activities as singing and dancing and clapping their hands; she thought an instant, then added: and so on; and this gentleman Mr. Magleberg, this Marvin, he owned part of a Country and Western recording company in Nashville, Tenn., where, it turned out, he also had a wife. A wife! A former band chick! A wife!

Irma left him almost immediately upon discovering his guilty secret. She only waited until she had removed her belongings from his apartment and they had gone to see a musical for which he had written away for tickets in advance. She left him at once, after a month. "Why the delay?" asked Peter.

From her blush, he understood that the delay only *seemed* like a delay. In spirit she had withdrawn her allegiance to Mr. Magleberg of New York and Nashville weeks before. As a matter of fact, she had given Marvin no joy from that day forward (the day on which she had gone through his pockets and discovered the letter, onward), except perhaps the pleasure of being seen with her in orchestra seats. And afterwards, while he watched her white and angry little face on his pillow in the ghostly dark, her stemlike firm-rumped body huddled away from his, the bud closed to him, he must have regretted his duplicity, don't you think?

Peter did indeed so think.

He could feel her slender warmth so near and yet so far, don't you sincerely believe? Wasn't that a dread punishment for the sin of infidelity with a wife in Nashville, a cheap ex-band chick, don't you dig?

Yes. Dig.

Mr. Magleberg's wife, Marvin had tried to tell her, pleading, getting literally down on his knees, figuratively, that is, was terribly cold and indifferent to him and sometimes it made him despondent. Sometimes he didn't know what he was doing half the time. Irma had saved him from the darkness back home, home on the range in Nashville. She had brought life back into his pore lonely country and western heart.

Sure, she understood his problem. Irma lacked not for sympathy and humane feelings. But she held firm to her principles. Cold shoulder and hot tongue was all he got from her. No loin chops.

In answer to her look of flashing morality, Peter dug once again.

But enough of Irma's past. It was her innocence and hope which captivated Peter, not her stupidity; for he too had suffered for love of a married person, and felt as if he had been used as the respondent in one of those Personals advertisements in weird weekend newspapers: SEEK LONELY MAN FREE SATURDAY MORNINGS AND WEDNESDAY AFTERNOONS. Oh Sarah, oh the dream of Sarah. She had used him badly. Mr. Marvin Magleberg had done no worse. In fact, perhaps Sarah's honesty about her husband was even more cruel. Ah, forget it. Nonsense. Foolishness. Now Irma was free and with him always. They would do the *Times* crossword puzzle on Sunday afternoons because they had already done everything else they wanted to do. And Irma thought words are so educational, don't you think? Peter did think. And they would grow fat and amiable together, and then go on a diet together, slimming amiably. Health foods are so good for one, don't you think? Peter did so think. Who knows? They might even marry. Peter considered this semi-seriously, without even being asked if he thought. They *would* marry, later. At his age, with a bald spot the size of a quarter on his scalp, it would soon be time. Soon, or perhaps later. And maybe a sturdy grain of stupidity is healthy in a wife.

They went to museums, and ate in museum cafeterias; and while they recuperated from works of art, Peter explained the workings of the stock market to Irma. He cut his loss in Texas Instruments; he had been right to sell short, it was overpriced and the sheep were rushing to slaughter, but he had made the right decision too soon. He had felt the knife at his throat while some of the sheep were getting rich. Well, he did not worry about a little bleeding. He cut his loss and stepped free. He stored up the experience for future use in another panicky fad market. "Any education costs money," he explained, "also time and expense of spirit. My timing was a little off."

Irma was fascinated. "How much can you make per annum?" she asked.

More hesitantly, like a shy swain, he tried to explain something of the joy he took in juggling oranges in the secrecy of his room. It was private and perfect, he wanted to say, it was a matter of timing. Sometimes it seemed to save his life.

"Per annum," she said, "you get a salary plus commissions, I suppose?"

They went to theaters, mostly musicals, because Irma was not working now and she wanted to make sure that any employed dancers had been hired by mistake or by erotic influence, either negative (homosexual) or positive (lecherous). Peter occasionally had trouble following her logic, but her intentions were usually clear to him. He would buy her long, but he would not sell her short. Sometimes her purity stood in the way of her steady advancement in the life of art. She had tendencies to paranoia—she believed that dancers sometimes used their bodies offstage in order to influence casting directors. "Hmm, a tendency to stark realism," Peter informed her.

"That's not the same as paranoia, except in New York," she observed, switching her rump, and Peter decided that maybe contact with him was making her witty.

"I must be a difficult person," he said.

"No," she replied, "that's contact with Life, not you, makes me humorous, a sense of humor. But you're interrupting, Peter. I was saying. Ever since I finished my analysis and entered like Real Life, I've always known that realism and paranoia aren't the same, but they're similar, don't you think?"

"Let me tell you something. I wish you wouldn't always say don't-you-think," he said.

"I think that's an effort to reassure myself that you're emotionally in tune with me, don't you, Peter?"

He did.

Changing the subject, maybe, Irma informed him that a man of his abilities should be good for thirty-forty thousand by the time he was forty or more. She tilted her head to observe how he took it. It was not a great shock. He had already faced this possibility. Thirty-forty thousand would find him braced, ready, under control, and mostly indifferent. She added thoughtfully: "Per annum." It was one of her favorite learned phrases. Like Shakespeare, she was gifted in little latinities. She ducked her head, twisted, showed him her back in her little gesture. She had milky skin, silken muscles.

They went to tea rooms and coffee houses. They went to espresso shops where the floorshow consisted of poetry read to jazz, and to smaller places with bigger cups, where the floorshow consisted of inter-racial chess-playing, and to capucino specialty places with full-sized cups where the floorshow was just each other, themselves, Peter and Irma, cinnamon and hot milk, exploring the lovers' world of mute satisfaction, don't you think? And then, of course, less mutely, they went to bed. She had a small head and large, muscular hips. She was silent and intent during the act, trying to remember everything, she didn't want to leave anything out; afterwards Irma liked to talk about it. She felt that mature discussion domesticated a confusing violation of her body. It's more a spiritual than a physical action, or should be, don't you know? She liked to wonder about how many times they would perform this action per annum, and figuring on the average of their first month together, she toted up an impressive figure, one heck of a lot of spiritual actions. "Considering your age," she prodded hopefully. "After all, according to Kinsey, a man's best age is around—"

"I know," he interrupted, "but that's before a man is a man. And it's quality that counts."

It was a fine spiritual distinction. Quality, not quantity. That was a gas in addition to a fine spiritual distinction. Irma brooded prettily over it. She also watched his diet and urged him to learn to love spices, as she did. She was noticing that the spiritual average of their first month had dropped slightly by their fourth month. They knew each other well, but she wondered if perhaps Peter would never plunge into her deepest depths of feeling and know her really well. "It take an effort," she told him. "I come from a repressed background during my first, or formative, years, and it's hard to break through to me. I tell you Daddy was a stick! Please try, Petey."

He tried.

"Please try again, Petey. Petey!"

He tried again.

"Petey!"

Afterwards she did an exercise at the window, stretching her arms and tensing her buttocks, belly in, flexing below, her back to him—good for the muscles. "Ooh, the air is nice," she said to the open window. She gazed amiably at the Spry sign blinking across the Hudson. The Spry sign is not fattening. She returned to Peter with one hip lifted, one hand covering her navel, and said roguishly, "Sleepy-boy?"

He tried and tried again.

Placidly Irma accepted his bid to uncover her repressions and placidly she rehearsed all the required responses, did all the exercises; but placidly she discovered that she still felt herself a stranger to the swirling maelstrom of passion. "Ooh, you're like a beast," she said, "and I do like it."

But. But she didn't like it as much as, she understood on good authority, she was supposed to. She pouted and hoped that this sort of thing (you know) didn't make a girl, like, *spread*. Peter pointed out that no, she shouldn't worry, in a way it was a kind of exercise. She worried. A dancer can't just exercise like any old muscles. She has got to be creative all the time.

"Now take you, for instance, Peter. You're not truly muscular—I hope you face facts—but you do have good definition." She studied him hard. "There's a possibility. Would you want to try being creative with me sometime?"

Finally a new outlet for creative expression of feeling occurred to Irma: another man and Peter's jealousy. "Tomorrow," she informed him, running her finger back and forth over his bald spot, "like tomorrow night, that is, I'll be busy. Teddy. He asked me like ages ago. He's like a dance director—a good friend of one anyway. You don't really mind, do you?"

To tell the truth, he didn't. At least not until he thought about it, and then no more than duty required. It must be Teddy who was teaching her to say "like." Alas, poor Irma, he like knew her well. He wanted a space of peace, recuperation, and reading, and he liked to stroll alone on the West Side streets through the dusky, decelerating evening. And so he didn't mind until the third or fourth time, and a certain special abstraction which he found in the center of Irma's customary talkative abstraction—a hard kernel of genuine hooky.

"What is it?" he asked her after a few weeks of this (sick headaches, cousins from out of town, unexpected yawning).

In a wee voice she answered, "Somebody else." She let this sink in. They were at her apartment, the top floor of a brownstone on West 79th Street, just off West End Avenue. It had no elevator. Walking the stairs was good for the legs. "But I can't decide between you. Either a girl's got principles or she hasn't. I've got principles. I had a religious upbringing and went to the church of my choice. Now you talk."

"What about? You've got the pulpit."

"See, you're making me nervous again. I'm nervous. You talk. The problem is—oh, gee, Peter. He isn't as—I don't know, you have so many good qualities, Petey. You're so nice."

"Who is it?" (Ice.)

"Teddy. You talk. Gosh, I feel terrible about the whole lousy mess, Petey. It lacks dignity like."

Peter knew what was expected of him. Rage, tears, sweaty protests, mussing, desperate lovemaking. Forgiveness, violation of her body in order to possess it, more tears, promises, oaths. Sickness, fury, and despair. Instead he declared, "Let me help you decide." He summed up the arguments on both sides, he made some judicious calculations, and then he counseled her: "Pick him."

"Ooh, Peter, *why*?"

"Take my advice."

She pouted, stuck out her lip, stuck out her chest, examined her wrist as if there were an invisible watch on it, tick-tick-ticking away her eternal girlhood, and said, "I feel like I'm japping on my best friend—"

"Japping?" Peter asked.

"Yes, japping, you know, sneak attack, going for another fella."

Peter threw back his head and roared with laughter.

She was furious. "You think I don't know?" she demanded. "I don't realize? Well, I read all about Pearl Harbor in history, honest I did. And besides, you're my *best friend,* we've been together since time began. I really mean it. Gosh, I shouldn't have hit the sack with him, Petey, I'm a traitor to you."

"Did you swear a vow in blood never to betray me? Poor me," said Peter. "Well, I'm not a perfect knight, I'm only a customer's man. Let me tell you something: It doesn't count."

She looked bright and happy and the light came out over her green-decorated green eyes with their green shadow and mascara. "Why are you always putting yourself down, Peter? You may have started life as a customer's man, but now you're like a full-fledged junior partner-broker in the house, aren't you? At least that's what you said, I heard you myself, *didn't I?*"

"Yes, honey."

"Well then. So don't go putting yourself down. You just let me feel ashamed, madly ashamed, it's probably good for my bad, bad, *bad* little soul."

He gathered up his hat, Mrs. Warden's friend's umbrella, and a pair of pajamas he had left on a hook in her bathroom. He wrung out a wash cloth he had left in the sink. Irma watched him with half a fist in her mouth. He started to the door. She was wearing her most fetching bedtime shortie, one of his Ivy shirts, the buttons at the collar of which sometimes caught against the lace edging of her pillow when he turned her over. Ah, turning Irma over to make an Irma Turnover. Her eyes were round as nickels. Below her long graceful dancer's neck, the costume was held out by petite but genuine Irma, and then dipped in a free fall to just above her dimpled knees. Yes, there were real dimples, and when she crooked her knees, they dimpled at him. What is cute? Irma is cute. Her eyes were sad. Her intention was sad. Sadly she followed him to the door, leaned against the wall in the hallway, took her fist all the way out of her mouth, and said reproachfully, in a low voice: "Peter."

He was human. The soft sound of soft her caused him to turn back, half-willing.

"You know what?" she asked.

"What?"

"Just now you look so handsome, like the *Post* Influential, only you have such nice green eyes."

"Okay."

"Oh that isn't what I wanted to say. I always say those things that make you change like that. Why do I do it, Petey?"

He did not answer.

"Peter, I care for you a *lot*," she said. "But a girl needs security, don't you think?"

A gentleman does not close the door on a pair of dimpled knees while the mouth three and a half feet above is moving. Perhaps she could say something important. She might express the wisdom of her dimples and her analysis, her firm embrace and her slow, switching amble. And of the sadness which lay deaf and mute deep within her.

"You never made me feel secure, Peter," she was saying. "I met this nice fellow I was telling you about, I really mean it, he *is* nice, one of the nicest I've met this annum, and he knew all about you—*you* know, I mean he could like guess—but he just cares for me so much, Peter, I mean don't you think that matters? He forgives me all."

The door closed as if someone else had slammed it. He was standing, looking at the door, and then he was rapidly walking. If she had run to his arms, letting the eloquent flesh speak, and not said the word *annum,* his whole life might have been different. But that would not be Irma. Irma followed her destiny and did not disturb his fate. He reeled a little as he walked, chuckling to himself, laughing and gathering laughter. Japping! He leaned a moment against a New York Sanitation Department litter basket, feeling dizzy with laughter, laughter was going to his head, laughter was making his eyes run; he folded his arms into his chest and bent his shoulders to take the laughter simmering up through his throat. When it subsided a little, he pulled down the corners of his eyes and thought: Japping! Or no: pull *up* the corners. It began again. A late shopper glanced sideways at him and hurried on with her bag of delicatessen meats. Peter gathered himself, still laughing, suffering from little high-pitched hiccups, and walked slowly down Broadway, stopping occasionally to shake his head.

Finally the laughter was used up. The hiccups disappeared.

Walking and walking, slowing down, strolling, peering

into the darkened windows of a discount store, he felt that his education in the vessels of love was now complete. He could see nothing more to learn. His ignorance was total. He was disappearing into the final parody of dating. He bought the early edition of the *Times,* had a dish of prunes in a cafeteria, and went to bed. An hour later he got up, dressed, and headed for the poker game. He won six hundred dollars, and this frightened him badly. If they let him win, they must have major plans for him. He put a slip of paper in his breast pocket: *no poker, chappie*! and moved it from shirt to shirt as the days went by. When he wore his Brooks Brothers shirts (no pockets), he tried remembering the message by pure will, and succeeded.

Exhausted, replete, he was tempted next into a long period of continence, during which time he discovered that the warrants of a small electronics company in Cleveland had hidden value in a scanning device about to be brought out of the laboratory stage. He called his suffering friend Dan about it, he wrote letters to him. He sought to distract him from his marital miseries and asked him to look in at the main office of Invariable Cal-Com Equipment. He put a few thousand dollars in it and made a paper profit of twenty thousand in less than six months, without ever growing conceited. He decided to hold the stock for six months for the capital gains benefit; it slumped badly when IBM came up with a radical new method of performing the same operation; he ended the roller-coaster ride where he had begun. He felt neither shame nor regret: his company's fortunes obeyed scientific events over which he had no control. But the gambler's excitement kept his evenings busy with vaguely sensuous reveries, dreams of luxury and power, a persistent fantasy of a Eurasian mistress (he had never known a Eurasian woman). The Captain of Finance slept alone on Riverside Drive, but talked United Artists Hindustani in his sleep. ("Me stunning girl in sari. You mighty Captain of Finance. Us make amour in stereo together.") He did not regret Elsie, Inga, and Irma. His Eurasian charmer evaporated in the electric morning buzz of the alarm clock. He had now cut both his losses and his gains. He told Dan Shaper to come on in.

All this could make him smile while reading his *Herald-Tribune* at breakfast, and the days were full of gestures and amusements, but sometimes Peter awoke at dawn with a vacant nightmare anxiety, and he was holding his breath, gasping, coughing, fighting his way out of sleep, with the hot sheet entangled about his body: *They are pushing me around!* But then, as he heard the comforting hum of the clock and spied the rich gleam of his shoes parked by the bed in the little light off the street, he climbed up from the frights of sleep and realized that he had chosen his women. He had gone from one to the next in search of the perfection he defined for himself —gaiety, wit, grace, and the desire to please. He was making his own choices. And so tomorrow—Marijane or Rita or Julia. Be still, stubborn heart.

But tomorrow he knew that he had learned a lesson. He did not try. He would make do with his patience, with his cinematic dream. He juggled oranges in his room. He seemed to store his excesses of sleep in his chin, in little chinlets; his insomnias made puffiness in other regions of his head. He felt himself swelling with the fluids of discontentment, but the skull was tight, keeping a grip. He wrote to Dan Shaper: "New York is jumping! Don't drag behind!" He thought of his friend as an adrenalin addict, jumping like the island of Manhattan with fun, fear, anger, and lots of sex in the head. But it's vasoconstricted, Peter decided. He'll never slow down. Arteriosclerosis will be the disease of his choice. Himself? Tumor. Insufficient thyroid. *If* he didn't take good care; but he did.

To keep from dragging behind, he obeyed a schedule of exercises. He wore his body down to accepting sleep by spending the late afternoons at pulleys and barbells in the Luxor Health Club, on West 46th Street, opposite the High School of Performing Arts, where delicious, milky young girls, with deep smudges of eye shadow and brilliantly capped teeth, loitered in cashmere sweaters with textbooks on American History and the Stanislavski Method under their arms. Their arms were slender but their bodies were full; they laughed richly together, exchanging the complex wisdom of their experience with men who are casting directors and men who are agents; and then they went in to read about Senator McCarthy in Civics 3. Peter liked to pause and watch them a few moments from across the street, and then he joined the company of men in the Luxor; showering, grunting, steaming, working out and receiving massage, trying to do something about rump and belly, flab and tension. The girls across the street and the club itself reminded Peter of his time in the Army, when Dan's eager yearning gave him all the advantages at the U.S.O. clubs; Peter, withdrawn and calculating, had lived in his friend's light. Training at Fort Bragg, Dan found the gay, mouth-abandoned Southern girls on his passes and furloughs, the ones usually reserved to flying officers; Peter had to take the toothy and desperate ones. Now, of course, time had smoothed and disguised him with money and manners, clothes and maneuvers. And the fact of withdrawn intelligence and suffering. Yes, young as he still was, the girls saw what they called suffering in his eyes, and adored the hard green glint.

Dan and Peter had quarreled bitterly once during the war. A girl. Dan won. He made it clear that he would not play Alphonse and Gaston about Laura. He had won her and married her. But then, itching to be a hero, he had gone for paratroop and, as if to make amends, had dragged Peter with him. Now where did all his going get him? Two kids, a bitchy wife, a struggle to make a buck, a frazzled, fuzzled look in the eye. Good old Dan.

Peter pushed himself through a long program at the gym of the Luxor. Pulleys, barbells, weights; then rope-skipping; then the heavy punching bag; then tapering off on the light one. Agility and control and a dancing manipulation of the bag. It made a dry pattering noise as he guided it, ratata, taratarata, against the board. His arms ached and the sweat ran on his cheeks. He did not stop although he usually avoided overtiring himself. The leather bag bobbed against his fists and he liked destroying it, destroying it, as it flapped back for more. His entire body was opened to sweat in his track suit. When he gave up control-hitting the bag like this, he was usually hitting someone. Who now? Whom was he pasting?

Dan. Funny. It was Dan he was slapping around. This only true friend—why him? He had been much in Peter's mind these past few months. He was going through the last rage of destruction with a girl that Peter had once wanted, and Peter was filled with pity for him, and yet it was Dan's head he slapped back and forth as it hung defenselessly by a metal clasp.

Well, come on in, old pal, I'll do what I can for you. Just don't stand in the way any more.

The girls from the High School of Performing Arts were gone when he emerged at the Luxor's closing time, exercised, steamed clean, exhausted. They had disappeared into their evening rounds of dates, rehearsals, telephoning, explaining. They carried forged identification cards for use in bars; they sat in the bars and told men twice their age that they had so much to give it sometimes frightened them and were told in return, yeah, you'll make it, baby. Or they had gone nicely home to lie on their stomachs under the sun lamp, doing homework. Peter would tell Dan all about the girls from the High School of Performing Arts. They were too young unless you wanted to freak out awhile; they were still fun to contemplate. But now he was very tired. Head down, he lunged into the street and claimed a taxi.

Sometimes, during this time, Peter liked to imagine himself the pet of a giantess, skating across her belly, gamboling in the forest of hair, sucked down by her innards and disappearing into warm caves of love—but that's to be merely a pet. Or sometimes he wanted to be a giant with a doll girl to fondle. Oh those were clever tricks of his mind as he strolled or took a seafood salad at the Senator Cafeteria at Broadway and 96th Street, telephoned or checked a margin account at his office downtown on the Street. He amused himself with these importunating fantasies—first a giant, then a pet; first a pet, then a giant. With a pink, long-lashed, cuddly doll from the High School of Performing Arts. With a broad, hairy, sloping monster beauty from his fearful dreams.

That, he decided, is Mental Health—keeping all the sizes balanced. He wished his friend Dan were in town. He would enjoy the Senator Cafeteria, afire with food, bulbs, and neon, clatter of silver and trays, greetings and business being negotiated, gossip radiating out over butts of cigars, pickles, relish, pot roasts, salads, sandwiches. A deep gong resounded from a machine at the door as each entering eater took his check. Dan was a Jew and liked chopped liver with a sunny dab of chicken fat sliding down it for no reason at all, just for fun, like the lettuce. It was niggling of fate to keep Dan so nervous he couldn't enjoy the foods he was born to. Sometimes Peter liked to pray and say grace over his own careful chow, but there were better and more effective ways to cajole destiny. He was conniving a charge under Dan's fate. Fate needed to be twisted and twirled in the air until it thought itself lucky to be even a historical possibility—no fate out of Peter's hands! Ergo: Dan must eat chopped liver in the Senator Cafeteria.

Peter did his best to hurry Dan on in, and in the meantime, devoted himself to keeping everything calm and easy, ready, under control, his desires hissing out in ferocious half-remembered dreams only when he slept.

But sometimes Mental Health is not its own reward. One night, sleepless, walking, finished with the salad at the Senator Cafeteria, he found himself heading like a somnambulist for the telephone. He was shaking with anger. This time he could not exercise or train it away. The proper form at such a moment is to ride with it. Let the madness ride—*go.* He called Irma. His voice was cool and sweet-talking as he awakened her, slowly took possession. He said: "Peter. Yes, *Pete*. I just happened to be thinking of you, honey. I do that lots."

"Oh Peter."

"It looks as if I interrupted you—were you sleeping?—but sometimes you just have to follow these impulses. I took a chance. Is it okay?"

"Oh Petey, I'm so glad you called, I don't know, gee whiz, things haven't been going so good since, since. . . ."

"We could make it dinner someday this weekend if you prefer—"

"Oh Peter, I won't put my face on. Just come on up, okay? Right now? You really thought about me lots? Are you coming?"

He was alert and going. He was triumphant and in a cab. And yet he was still shaking with anger. She might have said no! She might have been with Teddy or Marvin or some other make-out artist! What Irma did had nothing to do with his fury.

At her door, he was again in proper gear, friendly, easy, and smiling. She had touched herself up a bit at the eyes and there was a clean smell of toothpaste as he kissed her delicately on the cheek. She had changed into a fresh shortie for him. He had always praised her knees. Dimples. She remembered. They chatted for a moment and then, without touching her, he began undoing his clothes. "Ooh, are you some kinda nudist or something?" she asked.

"I like skin."

"Ooh, don't hurt me, Petey. You won't believe this, but it's been a real long time since—I've been nervous, Petey—I've been really *happy,* I mean, but a little jumpy. Don't hurt me, okay?"

He hurt her.

She was making gasping, choking sounds beneath him. Straining toward him, she said, "Don't hurt me anymore, that's enough."

He hurt her.

A few moments later, as he lay buried at her side, his head in a pillow, he felt her starting it again. She was reaching for him with her hand. When she found him, she held him softly, saying, "He's going to be a man again soon. Be a man, I don't care. Be a man, okay, Petey? I don't care how much you hurt me because you care for me. Hey, look." She had made a resolution and carried it out. She turned and lay on her belly. "Yes, that's all right," she said. "I want you to. Hurt me there too."

Peter felt his lips peeling back over his teeth. Well, smart Irma. She had read his mind. She had read part of his mind, but she would not be silent. She had not read enough of his mind to be silent. Where had she learned that command? *Be a man. Is he gonna be a man again?* Was that Marvin's word? Teddy's? Weepy Irma. Squeaky Irma, squeak like a mouse. Muffled slightly, she spoke as her head lay along the pillow, her eyes shut, her face relaxed and peaceful in the little light of a lamp, her breathing slightly hoarse. "Oh, under me," she said. "There's blood. Can you feel it? That's from before. You hurt me, Pete, it was because you love me."

She waited and held her breath and moved in an attempt to help him, humping and adjusting. "Oh!" she said. "You really loved me."

"It wasn't for that reason," he said.

"Careful, careful. Oh, Petey, watch out. Oh, Petey, please be careful. *Oh Petey you're hurting me!*" She began to scream and he held her face in the pillow to keep her quiet. In just a moment it was over. She stopped screaming. He released her. She lay gasping in the pillow. The pillow was wet. He could smell wet cotton and feathers. He slid out and away from her, but she did not move. She lay unnaturally still. Even in his own sudden deep rush of fatigue—now he could sleep, now he could ease down—he felt sorry for her. And then she began talking again. It seemed that nothing could stop her talking even as the tears flowed from her eyes. "Something new . . . I thought . . . because I've been thinking about you. . . . You didn't love me, it didn't mean you loved me. . . ."

He was dressing. He talked very cheerfully to her, glancing at the body on the bed, wishing he could make her look less broken. He felt sympathy in his heart, but his voice was carrying out the other intention. "Some little girls cheat," he said. "Some lie. Some do foolish things. *Teddy*. Some are boring, they talk too much. I wish you'd stop showing me those precious buttocks now, honey, it's the end of the cancan."

She sat up and began to sob. He put his finger to his mouth. *Sh*. It was odd how you could lodge two opposing tenants at once, pity and ridicule: in the heart, pity: in the head, ridicule. He was smiling. *Now* she knew she had been hurt. He grinned at the stubbornness of women. With blood and pain, she could still think love. And she needed words for everything. It was her only way to know the meaning of things. Reality was what passed through her orifices. He could cripple her for life, but if he said the right words, she would smile with gratitude and sleep bleeding and grateful in his arms. Any voice, any orifice, any reality. She was sobbing, trying to stop, hiccuping. He said *Shh* again. He went to the bathroom and found her bottle of Seconol. He took out two pills and flushed the rest of them down the toilet. He brought her the two pills and a glass of water.

"Petey, are you going?" she asked.

He stood by the bed like a worried doctor.

"I'm sorry," she said. "I've been bad."

"Swallow these and go to sleep."

"Do you forgive me now?" she asked. "Say you forgive me or I won't go to sleep."

He said nothing, but she took them. Then she lay down. She made little subsiding hiccups. He stood looking at her. What can a man do to escape love? he thought. I've finally made it with this girl. I came here to break her, and look, now I've made it. I'm the great black knight for Irma. I've made it. Almighty God, save us from the interpretations of others.

She was smiling at him and pulled the covers up to her chin. At the doorway, before he passed through, he glanced back at her smiling eyes. Well, at last she was silent. He put a warning finger to his mouth anyway and pulled the door shut.

5

A few months later came the great disaster of Peter's life: her name was Barbara. Those others had confirmed him in a sour self-concern because they were sourly self-concerned and could not touch him. But Barbara, she was fresh, bright, tender, and, incredibly, she cared about him. It was as simple as that. She quieted his sarcasms; she stilled his angry nighttime heart. She had a naturally affectionate nature as some girls have a naturally graceful sway to their walk. She had responded to the sadness within him with a fierce determination to bring joy (perhaps this missionary intention is a flaw, too); she believed that her reality could penetrate his abstract, starry dream of love (she was brave, she was foolhardy); she liked teaching him to ice-skate again, and to kiss in doorways, and to have private jokes; and yet she was not a wreck of candybox femininity —she was a beautiful exception to all the rules. She had long ungainly bones (if you like a girl like that, you call her coltish), a round-cheeked, anxiously-smiling face, and eyes as eager and contemplative as a sad but undiscouraged child. Frightened or amused, her eyes could suddenly take on a hard black spiked look, but this internal mascara only proved that she protected herself in time of danger. Fine. Excellent. She was looking for her line in life, and in the meantime she decorated store windows and listened for the truth on all sides. She discovered Peter as the object of her mission. Perhaps this was her great flaw—to love him became a nursing mission for her—but how else could anyone who saw Peter learn to love him?

And yet, she had fallen in love with a heroic Peter before he ever knew her. She was not a foredoomed nurse; she loved athletes and flagrant poets and melancholic war heroes, too. She remembered Peter from her first college days at Skidmore in Saratoga. After two years at Skidmore, she had transferred to a school in Virginia in order to be near her father. The old-age daughter of a retired farmer who was dimming out over a book with which he was obsessed, a memorial history of the Lafayette Escadrille, she tried to give some air to his last years. She understood from age six that only her imperturbable gaiety plus the news of Spads and Fokkers kept her father alive. Sometimes she had just stood for hours, doing and redoing her braids by the kitchen table as he wrote. Probably that hard black look had been invented at age six. This shy child, grave and gay, prematurely burdened, brave with death-defying hope and explanations of senility—and yet nothing but a silken, dreamy child—had thought Peter grand, from afar, during his weekend visits to his family in Saratoga. She had still remembered him at Hollins College in Virginia. It was a matter of an eight-foot scarf worn in the snow over a tweed jacket and thick blond hair like a green-eyed Norse god's and the snow crackling when he walked.

"Ha!" Peter commented on her revelation, "I was more Princeton than godly. What a freshman won't think of."

But he had returned alive from the war—no more being squeezed off the stick, into the flak and down through a rapid, hostile air—and perhaps triumph and control did make the snow crackle underfoot. Back at college, he had told Dan that he would make his own rules from then on. No more fear, no pressure from others. Probably that had done things to the snow and the length of his scarf.

She had remembered him with breathless hope, and then he picked her out by fairytale luck, nearly ten years afterward, on a winter weekend in the town where she had gone to school and he had grown up. Did their love ripen quickly? It sprang ripe from their wills. It shipped without spoiling from upstate New York on vacation to workaday Manhattan; they discovered the city together. They took it on the freeway from Saratoga back through the Holland Tunnel. With her small, delicate, old-fashioned face—oval, and oval cheeks, and long straight hair—she toured the city with him, and they explored each other; they hurried home in taxicabs, her face buried in his shoulder, breathless with waiting. The first time they made love, she sobbed with fear and desire, but said, "No, no, no, it's all right, no, no, no, oh I won't say it—"

"Say it!"

"Oh I love you!"

And he found his own throat broken by dry sobs. And she took this for an answer. Perhaps it was, at that moment, even for him.

But sex is not love, though it could seem to be for a time, and could seem to be for an evening or many evenings; there are also long days and weekends and evenings when sex is only the map to love, not love itself, and a bemused couple must look up from the map to find the land and the sky above. The pointing finger is not the star, and even that bright point of light a million miles away is not the star—for its own reality, the star needs a cushion of blackness and its location in the galaxy. Pleasure in isolation was a familiar condition to Peter—pleasure, theories, and control.

And tenderness, respect, gratitude, hope, and desire are not love, either, though they often can seem to be. There were nights when Peter wanted to know why he was a salesman of stocks, bonds, warrants, and put-and-call options. And why there was not something better to do with his clever head and nostalgic heart. And why love cannot replace all the things which a man imagines wanting to do when he puts his chair near the window, his feet on the sill, and looks out over that little stretch of green, interrupted by humming roadway, which runs down to the Hudson River.

Before falling in love, Peter had imagined that love could fill the barren February trees with leaves, twigs, and ripe fruit. He leaned out the window to cool his hot hand on the icicle which hung melting from the sill, shrinking in the sun and leaving its few mournful tears on the sidewalk below. He stroked the gleaming thorn of ice; he cracked it like a tooth; he thought about love and shut the window and put the icicle in the sink. There was no sudden miracle of spring in February. The desire to play poker returned. He had an idea that selling short, if he picked carefully, could make the green dollars come rolling in from the south like the spring. He wanted more than love. Love was merely love, and mere love slipped gravely away, like desire, like youth, like the hope of a future of effort and achievement. This, he decided, at the age when his friends were going through their first divorces, is how marriage becomes a trap. The conjugal ones begin with both love and the desire to make up for all the lacks of their lives; marriage does not make up, and love withers; and thus the agonies of the happy hearth, upon which they revenge themselves for all their disappointments in work, in the world, in hope of grace. He told Barbara about his friends and clients like that, the Stillman Trust—Caroline Stillman was now Mrs. Bobb Anthony; and he handled Bobb's money, too, and he was also cultivating them because Bobb might be able to do something for Dan Shaper when he got to town, but he would have cultivated them anyway; and Bobb and Caroline were perishing in hectic boredom a few years after a love affair which had sizzled in all the columns and in *Town and Country* besides. Committed to love. Oh they had been the brilliant Romeo and Juliet of a season at El Morocco and the Southampton Beach Club. They had gathered a court of columnists and troubadour private detectives, previous spouses and neglected children. True love had triumphed; they collected their divorces, put their children on the custody ride, and married. And now, and now.

Peter understood what Barbara was thinking as he tried to tell what he knew about life in his time: *What do Mr. and Mrs. Anthony prove about anything?*

Well, no sense in answering that one. Life in the world always ebbs away from the secret hopes of soul and flesh. He squinted and waited and admired Barbara's tact. She said nothing. "I don't usually talk so much," he said.

"I like it," she said. "Your voice is so alive when you're disturbed about something. You're like other people—in a nice way, Peter. You care about them—don't you?"

"No," he said.

He dropped the subject. He took it up by another end. He had it all figured out, and abstained. He told Barbara one of his recurrent dreams: he stood stiffly among sheep in a flaming barn; he wore a wet woolen coat; the sheep were crackling and blazing and softly murmuring as the fire took over; they spread their hoofs out, but stood still; smoke of lanolin and sheepswool . . . terrible, terrible. "I'm going to get out of that barn, I'm out of it," he promised her.

"I don't know what dreams mean," she said with the beginnings of her black, closing-down look.

"I take them seriously," he said mildly, "though nothing is more boring than another man's dream. I thought I ought to tell you some way, keed—I'm a barn-deserter. I get out of the barn. Still and because—my coat is *wool,* see?"

"No. You just sound pretentious and ominous, not like you."

"It's like me, B.G."

But in the meantime, there were pleasures with Barbara: kitchen pleasures of good appetite and drink, pleasures of coasting through the city together, easy with half-understood agreements, steady contemplation of the renewable pleasures of bed. Naked and playful, they would go to the window together and watch the Spry sign flashing on the Palisades across the river. Her body smelled as sweet as May wine, as mild and pungent as May wine. She believed that she loved him. Because he needed her, because he would not admit he needed her. Because he made her care for him. With love of Peter her body grew very slender, as if she fed him with it; her long slender bones were gracefully denuded of plumpness; her eyes were hollowed, with a crease of the lower lid and a glowing blue cast of fatigue about them, as if she were an ardent, driven boy; she was a girl, but she too was nervous about love. Peter tried to forget, squeezing shut his eyes and embracing her, that she could invade but not come to rest in his heart.

He suggested that they go to a party. She did not want to go. He suggested it again.

Flushed, yearning, and giving in the act of love, her face became a powdered mask—she was ready to go out. She stood in girdle, slip, elastic and zippered appurtenances before the mirror; she corrected her face. The wan, glowing eyes took makeup. Her face which he had roughened with his beard accepted powder. As trivial as that—disillusion. He knew it was his own weakness. He had never developed sufficient addiction to reality. She seemed to overhear his secret broodings over her preparations for the street. "I would rather stay here," she said mildly. "The party is your idea. Let's stay, let's stay, Peter!"

"Let's go."

The season for May wine was a brief one. Peter felt very cruel and drew obscure satisfaction from this judgment of himself.

The black spikes of doubt, suspicion, and defense in Barbara's eyes made him feel that she too could be cruel in her way. He did not know how. Never mind that.

Out of an unusual kindness toward Barbara, out of an

unusual refusal to despair in himself, he tried to re-invent what Manhattan couples do together in the disconnected city. He planned their evenings. He planned their weekends. He took her walking to see the Japanese temple on Riverside Drive, with the squat, delicate, firmly-smiling face of the Buddha looking out from the court. Then he called for a taxi and said, "Next stop."

"Where?"

"The Luck of the Roaring Camp Authentic Japanese Home-Style Restaurant, Kosher Barbecue, and Espresso Parlor. . . ." He paused for breath while she laughed softly and put her mouth against his collar. "Flamenco Dancing on Weekends."

"A little undiscovered spot in the Village, no doubt," she murmured.

But he took her to P. J. Clarke's on the East Side or Jim Downey's on the West Side because it still pleased the girl from Virginia to have actors and columnists pointed out to her. He made an effort to entertain her. "That's Ben Fugazi," he said. "Can't act in a play with words. Anti-semantic." It was a pleasure to please her and therefore he could manage okay. If there was a sense of strain and effort, well, it was that element of calculation for which no one judged him more harshly than he himself.

Several times he took her for weekends at the house of Caroline and Bobb Anthony in Southampton. He explained that the Anthonys ran a rest camp for the capital gains waifs of Manhattan and their consorts. He squinted through his hard eyes at Barbara and admitted straight on the calculation in this friendship: he handled Caroline's funds, he needed to hold her strongly on his side against a rival from the National City trust department. He had other ideas for Bobb and his new magazine. And the Anthonys distracted him, anyway; it was not merely a career. "You ought to see the displaced persons, part of your education," he told Barbara.

"All Manhattan is like that."

"Mostly midtown," he said, gently correcting her. "Ah, Bee Gee, Bee Gee—*sheltered?* Sheltered. Try Harlem. Washington Heights. The Lower East Side. People live there all year round, honest. But of course I'm a walker, and I guess a girl can't walk so much. Those high heels. Those gangs and muggers. But the Anthonys and their pack—the wander the face of the earth like gypsies. And when they're here, they commute. They have an apartment in town, but four-five months of the year, poor Bobb has to chase Caroline all the way out to Southampton. High life in the jet set. End of elocution."

"I don't mind," said Barbara. "You're nice when you talk like that."

He took her hand and held it a moment.

It rained and fogged the whole first weekend that Barbara spent at the Anthonys. Peter smiled and loafed on the long old-fashioned porch with a large, plump pheasant-hunter and athlete named Steve Schmitt, who was a professional White Russian. Caroline and Bobb had a spat, a tactical skirmish within the extended siege, and Caroline bundled the two small children off to town for a matinee. She explained that she always meant to do things with the children, and now with the bad weather and her headache, she could take them to see the Walt Disney, take a Dramamine and a codeine for herself, and sleep in her seat while giving the children a little love and attention. Bobb flopped about the house with the despairing ennui of a man both dreading and impatient to continue the struggle. He barely spoke to Barbara. A big, sweetish-breathed man, he tried to be polite; he brought her some of Caroline's art books to leaf through; he sat by her side on a couch, sighing and flipping gumdrops into his mouth. He explained that Caroline was interested in house decoration and French impressionism, isn't it? that they had had a little discussion this weekend but it wasn't important and it didn't happen often, and that he had discovered gumdrops as a means of helping him stop smoking. "Have one?" he said anxiously, extending the stubby remains of a roll.

"Thank you, I still smoke."

"Well, it's more important for men. You can't inhale gumdrops. But let's face it, I'm getting fat—well, heavy—and that puts a strain on the system, too." He sighed. "I got my choice. Cancer. Heart." He sighed again. "I'm interrupting you."

"No, not at all."

"The thing is, *you* know, you're a pretty girl, and when a fellow has a discussion like that with his wife. . . ." His voice trailed off. She went on leafing through the book, a collection of Fra Angelico reproductions. Bobb spread his ample flanks on the couch by her side and said, "One thing I wish—wish the rain'd stop."

Out on the porch, playing his hand in the stray droplets on the railing, Peter discussed the market in Czarist bonds with Steve Schmitt. Steve's former wife was a princess and, through this connection, he got to be the promoter of various benefits for free, imperial Russia. Also he was a prime investor in bonds which were still traded over the counter at a few cents on the hundred. Peter creaked back on a wicker chair and agreed with Steve that it was a reasonable risk. He explained to Barbara, after she left Fra Angelico with Bobb fretfully dozing on the couch—once he fell over onto her shoulder—that no one had expected redemption of the imperial Japanese bonds after the war, and they sold for practically nothing, and then thanks to the sound business sense of General MacArthur, fortunes were made. "Fortunes, large fortunes," intoned freedom-loving Steve, gazing down the road to see if Caroline were coming back yet in the station wagon. No, it was the Volkswagen from the drugstore with the candy for Bobb.

"Who knows," Peter explained, "if the Allied Powers might not force the Soviet Government to honor these obligations that go back, some of them, to 1905?"

"The Etat Russe Libre won't have to be forced!" Steve announced proudly. "We'll do it of our own free will. With accumulated interest."

"They'll reintroduce God and free will and the credit structure," said Peter.

"Fortunes," Steve dreamed in the steady Southampton drizzle.

Later, alone with her, Peter explained to Barbara that Steve was not a fool or a madman, not by contemporary standards. There was a steady market in Czarist bonds. There were solid precedents—Japan, Germany. It might be part of some ultimate settlement. And for a few cents on the hundred . . . "Utrillo wasn't nutty, you people are," Barbara said.

"Yeah. Investment is an art."

"Do you really take it seriously, Peter?"

He tried to explain that it was all a game, making and losing and organizing, playing the odds and the rules, and that was exactly why he took it seriously. But of course he did not expect Barbara to understand. And so, because he was a kind man, he tried to explain other matters which she might understand. He held her hand and they borrowed slickers from a closet and walked in the rain. While waiting for the Bolshevik revolution to collapse, Steve stalked Caroline. That amused Peter. Caroline was an important investor. He handled her accounts. That was business. "I have no private income myself," he said. This was a little tease about Barbara's small acreage in Virginia. And he was freshening up the acquaintance with Bobb because he wanted his friend Dan Shaper to come in at a good level with Bobb's publishing company, which had recently sunk a lot of money in a liberal picture-and-text magazine. "A new concept," Peter explained. "Intellectual photographs for college-educated people who don't want to read. The arts, entertainment, and politics without pain, but with a liberal slant—*more* liberal, anyway—and painless."

"I know the magazine," Barbara said dryly.

"Well, it isn't your type. But Shaper needs a decent job."

"You like this friend."

"Yes."

They walked on awhile, sloshing in puddles. Barbara caught a trickle off a leaf on the back of her neck. She giggled.

Five minutes later, Peter thought to add, astounded, "I like you, too."

They went back to the house. Caroline had returned. The children were fidgety in the movie and so she had yanked them out before boy-dog got girl-dog and they were still bawling with disappointment. The servants took charge. Caroline hurtled upstairs and locked herself in her room with her headache. Bobb was practicing croquet shots downstairs in the recreation room. Steve was studying Russian by translating an article from Forbes Magazine with the help of a dictionary. Peter and Barbara went to their separate rooms.

The rain kept up all weekend until Sunday afternoon, just as Peter and Barbara were climbing into his car to drive back to Manhattan, when the sun peeked through and Caroline hurried upstairs to change into a lighter blouse and Bobb and Caroline begged them to come out for another weekend, *next* weekend, the weather was sure to improve, please, *pretty* please, and they promised they would, and to the surprise of Peter and Barbara—but not to Caroline, Bobb, and Steve—they did. A weekend in the country was something to do.

6

Long before Peter decided for sure—he would wait, he was cautious—Barbara understood that he was sliding out of her arms. But since she had decided that she loved him, she could not allow him to slip quietly away. He had said that he liked her, and he really did; and the word had been brought gasping dryly out of his mouth when he shuddered over her body—the word *love*—the word had happened. This slender young girl from Virginia and Saratoga, who had watched him in his red scarf, home from the great city for a weekend in the snow, now discovered sex; she invented and re-invented sex, imagining from her paltry experience that sex was what a man wanted. She remembered earnest girlish discussions, hints, and rumors. She tried to be clever and fanciful, and for love, for the dream of pleasing him, she discovered fanciful, clever, desperate elaborations of whatever sex they had experienced together. She had long, sinuous arms which crept about him and down his body; she had a yearning, devouring mouth; she kissed and kissed, pampered and kissed him. True, this bemused Peter for a while. Who doesn't like experience? Who doesn't take pleasure when the new experience is offered with such grace and hope? Even a dream-ridden soul can be shocked awake. This slender child did *that*? She looked sideways and calculated so greedily? Her eyes studying him—her eyes shut off. First plans and determination, then avid hunger. *Love,* her lips moved silently, *love, love,* opening and shutting on the word along his chest, his belly, his thighs.

He hated her making love to him with that indrawn black look. He pushed her away and took violent charge of her. He drove a runaway machine. She expired like a small animal caught under him on the highway. Then the machine crashed and he dissolved into oblivion.

Later that night she sat straight up in the dark, tears glowing in her eyes, and said in a worn rage, "I hurt down here! You made me hurt! You think it's your good strength, but feel the sheets, there's blood down here!"

He sat up beside her like her twin, sleepy and concerned, caught out of the dark: "Darling, oh I'm sorry."

But she would not let him remain in this sleepy soft consoling state. She was in a fury. "You use your so-called health like a weapon! Good sharp cutting switchblade so-called health!"

It turned him cold. They had made love to exhaustion, she had greedily demanded him, tucked him in with a sigh, heaved and erupted beneath him. And now. And now she was shrilling away about so-called health. "It can be taken away like that," he said mildly, still propped against pillows like her twin. He made a throat-slitting gesture in the dark.

"Yes."

"Like that. That's why I treasure it now. Later maybe it'll be gone."

She put his hand on the sticky place on the sheet. "Peter? Do you love me? Will you *say you love me?"*

Finally it wore him out. He could juggle tirelessly, and quit refreshed; not so this game. He had an ache in his loins and he took to saying, "No, honey, I'm sleepy." And he dozed with distant pity in his heart as he remembered the night before—her laboring body, slippery with sweat, running sleekness, her beautiful slender girlish body, and her eyes full of tears—her prayerful lips at his cheek: "You don't mind? You like this? You love me? Like *this?"*

He guessed that he did. He pitied her, cherished her, admired her, and was bored by her. He did not want to be bothered.

Peter wanted to be immortal, not merely subtly tickled, not merely to twist against thighs and suckle against breasts and be eased and lightened into dreamless sleep. He wanted to be nourished into dreams and reality—to make his mark. But love seemed to create invisible, markless pleasure and nothing else. The body turned heavy and violent and flushed, and then slept, and then was the same body once more. There was Barbara, sweet as a child after her exertions. There was Peter, drifting off. He looked at her and thought: No, she can't do it.

And thought: No, I've got to get out.

And thought, I'll do it myself. If he couldn't have everything, perfect everything he wanted in life, then he could at least have nothing, perfect nothing, the spacious vacancy of his heart. Again he created his dream of quiet in his room with its floating deck on Riverside Drive; the office and quiet, home and quiet, a view of the river and the days going quietly by. He would juggle and keep fit. He would entertain his friend Dan. He was tired. But instead of obeying his fatigue as the stony summons it was, he tried to be kind. They went for a walk in Central Park and then took a cab to the Brasserie. Barbara was fond of this blatant decorator's New York—the faded chartreuse lighting, the pegged leather, the plaster seals on the walls and the Muzak versions of "Feuilles Mortes" and the Moulin Rouge melody. They sat in captain's chairs beneath recessed lights, served by French girls and unmasculine men. *"Le Supreme de Volaille aux points d'Asperges,"* he ordered for her, explaining, "Asparagus is good for the—I forget what, but it's dirty. There are folk songs about it."

For himself he ordered the cheese board and fruit. He was not hungry. He peeled an apple and took a slice of Gruyère with it.

"Why aren't you eating?" she asked.

"I guess I'm a merry jackanapes," he said gloomily, as if this were the answer to her question. "I took dog vitamins once when I knew a girl whose poodle died, but I never learned how to bark. B.G., I like you so much. I'm sorry."

"No no no no no."

Sharply he estimated the possibility of a scene in this restaurant. That would be something new for B.G. No, she was a mannerly girl. But he had better not provoke her. Thinking that, he could not control himself. Funny how the will works. "If you want to dislike me," he said.

"Be quiet."

It was she who would prevent the scene. His own will was frayed like an old rope. She would help hold him tight. He looked at her across his cheese board, her plate of asparagus and chicken. Neither of them ate more than a few bites. A bus boy idly stared at Barbara's Capezio shoes—maroon pumps. Peter felt dismayed by the heavy silence. When he could chatter or look bug-eyed and indignant, he could seem like others. But in silence his mind always fled toward privacy, his several pleasures, his yearning for the control of privacy. Nevertheless, he had decided to receive this gift from her in her due time. He would be exactly as kind as that. She would have to speak first. He would not go till sent. She would have to speak first. Or so he decided.

When at last she understood that there could be no other issue, she did not make a scene. It was as if her tears had been spent in effort and she had none to waste in regret. She did not curse him or berate him or reproach him, as some women do, but she did not wish him well, either.

It happened on an early evening a few days later. When she saw him ready at the door, she only looked into his eyes and said, "There are some things I would like to forget."

"I have good memories of you, Barbara-Girl," he said, with the relieved immediate tenderness of farewell. Together they had admired a crumpled-paper pink flower abandoned by a Puerto Rican flirt in Central Park. Afterwards he had bought her a real flower; she had kissed him openly, in the daylight, on Fifth Avenue, unabashed.

"Some things," she said softly, "I wish I didn't have to think of your remembering. I tried too much. I'm ashamed."

He patted her on the shoulder. Perhaps she could remember his jovial platitude, not her intimate striving. "Don't worry," he said, "I respect you."

She smiled, and her eyes became very bright and hard. "Do you?" she asked. "*Do* you? And you also respect yourself? Just waiting like that?"

She turned her face away and told him to *get out* and he was gone. She had applied her little female pinprick after all.

But he did not blame her. "Get out!" So he got out. He strolled past the houses like little painted gravestones to Village domesticity on Perry Street, through the idle whirl of Sheridan Square; he enjoyed the air, he found his own stride, and then he went home to bed.

7

He ate, he slept, he worked, he juggled, and the identical days filed by. Often now he ached in unhealthy sleep and dreamt through the alarm. Repeated, repeated, remembering dreams vexed him; he spent the nights escaping over coral reefs, sliding, scraping, slipping, escaping only because he was especially quick, like a fish, over chimneys and turrets and towers of coral, over the monumental excrescences of tiny shellfish, but slow, dangerously slow, swimming with torn fins through the long treacherous stretches of loose rock; and the tireless enemy pursued him. "Oh no! Oh no!" he groaned, finding an abutment to scramble over just before he was touched, before the pursuing beasts touched him. Plunge, hurtle, fall. And sat up shocked awake. Peter Hatten was going some place, and sped through the seas with blood leaking from his gills. The salt bled him and dried him. He got up and went to the mirror and fingered his unshaven jaw. He was not yet a fish, though salt was his element. He practiced his juggling in the silent middle of the night and stilled his fingers that way. He kept one, two, three balls in the air. He tried with oranges. When he made a mistake, the smell of orange juice filled his bedroom. His pajamas were stained with droplets of orange juice. The oranges fell and split and spurted into the close air of his bedroom. Then at last he slept again.

He welcomed the morning and thought: *I can still run!* He ran to money and he ran to the Luxor Health Club and he ran to his pure station in space. Despite his dream, he was making himself, and re-making; and not through the illusion of love, but the reality of abstention. He sat stern and smiling at his office during the short day. Then the flesh of a thirty-three-year-old college tennis player, now on its way with an altered metabolism, reluctant to rush the net, was licked into shape by exercise, diet, and steam. He jumped rope. He was rigorous with distractions. He came home exhausted and fell into bed and thought he would not have the dream that night. When Dan arrived in Manhattan, he would have a friend instead.

It was time now to make another trip to Cleveland. A cautious salesman, fair to an old customer, he tried to sell Manhattan to Dan.

"Be a bachelor in New York," he told him, "it's the newest form of slavery. You're a drudge to freedom. With bowed back, you trudge to cocktail parties and openings, dinners and country weekends, toting that burden of liberty. Man, you're a pussycat, you think you love it. But man O man, you squeak like a mouse."

"You're a kidder."

"I'm a mouse."

"You're a juggler."

"I'm a juggler."

"Then tell more."

Peter told Dan more, and then said, "Notice I'm not asking about Laura. I file that problem under—"

"It's still my whole life, Pete."

"Never mind—stop chewing yourself out. Statute of limitations. Like old tax forms. Be done with it."

"Okay, orders."

"Orders. Now I've got to run for my flight." They were sitting in the corner bar of the Hollenden Hotel in Cleveland.

He stood up. He stood silently looking at his friend. He put on the pressure silently, with stern look and bugged-out eyes. Then he grinned and broke the contest. He winked.

Dan had quick, worn, undefeated eyes which snapped up the things of the world about him, furniture, sky, earth, paraphernalia; they got him in trouble, but he was a survivor; his eyes were those of a tough young crocodile, with only the slightest fraying of age to qualify them. There was still Dan's glint in them. To Peter he was still a skinny and immortal sergeant of paratroops. Even slumped with family news in the corner bar of the Hollenden, he had a tough coil inside. The spring was still there. Peter knew how different he was from Dan, and not just in the impenetrable, inward-turning eyes, busy with internal business. The difference was immense, in style, in intention. That these two could be friends gave him a hope that juggling was not his last chance at balance on earth. Dan and Peter could partake of each other's life.

"Pete. Thanks for flying this mission again. I'm pretty dismal company."

"Never mind."

"I'm stuck."

"Cut the comedy, pal." He told him to come on in, come aboard, stop stalling and fly east. He would show his friend the town. All he had to do was cut the comedy.

In the meantime, Peter made out alone. All dealing was suspended in Navigation Electro-Computer; the SEC had found some peculiar trading in the stock by the sister-in-law of the president of the company. Peter was in the clear; he and his people would come out okay. The Air Force was still buying the product for planes that were obsolete but still rolling off the lines. They were manufactured in the district of a congressman who had considerable seniority in budget matters and a consuming interest in national defense. Peter had thought ahead, making a few mistakes, not planning on the sister-in-law, for example, though he should have deduced her from the eager cordiality of the president's voice over the telephone; but enough of the variables remained in strong basic shape. The sister-in-law would cost. But the product and the Air Force and the congressman and the continuous little hints of holocaust in the morning paper were all just as Peter had figured them out. He was in business. He took walks at midnight up Riverside Drive to Grant's Tomb and stared at the marks carved in stone above the entrance to a warrior's hived-over, closed-in, deserted monument: PEACE. He strolled back past the occasional loitering kids, waiting for someone to jump him, ready to fight even if the kid had a knife. He was itching to kick the hand that held a switchblade. He was poised, alert, on the balls of his feet, and smiling because he knew he wouldn't stand a chance if they decided to take him. He wore himself as much as he could by keeping in motion against the close and indifferent city.

Inevitably, however, on one late afternoon in his office at 110 Wall Street, he felt the armor of blessed fatigue suddenly lift from his body as he sat at work, and with this lifting of weight, he welcomed back the jitters, the shakes, the horrors, desire—the soul's loneliness and the body's clamoring. An ant-heap city, making its obscure hive noise, was being sifted, fed, built, destroyed, and rebuilt all about him; he had no comfort or extension in it, and felt like an ant separated from his kind by the gift of consciousness, but punished for his isolation by having no meaning or purpose. There is no place in the hive for the ant who abruptly decides that he would like to reconsider everything under the sun. Like a lost ant, he ran to and fro in his office. His secretary came in to ask if he were missing something. "Yes, just a thingamajig." Yes, just something. He bethought himself: "Get me the new file on NaveeKom, please." He smiled at her, because he was no ant; and she smiled back, because he was her boss and had smiled at her. He sent her back to her cubicle.

Now he had no more doubts. Even the simplest perfection

requires compromise. He went home early, shook off his hot clothes, sat down naked at his desk, and wrote:

> Sarah: Please take me back.
> On your terms.
>
> Peter.

That would settle Saturday afternoon for him. The evenings and the long nights he would live through somehow. By this time next annum, the bald spot on his crown would be the size of a waxy silver dollar, and he could predict its rate of progress as he could predict most of his future.

But if Sarah did not remember him well enough to reply to his note? If she had made other arrangements? He predicted no excess of humiliation for himself. He might be relieved. He would not play poker, he would not sell short. There are even simpler arrangements with which he could make do until time relieved him of the only means he had found to share in human life. There were three oranges in a saucer on his desk. With a fourth, they made a pyramid of oranges. As he sat there, the letter folded in its envelope and the air conditioner blowing on his naked body, he thought of Sarah, he thought of Barbara; he felt his sex with one hand and found it engorged with the thought of sacrifice.

PART 2: DAN

Now this ape loved to tell stories, jump on his trapeze, eat salt and pepper and all manner of spices, and then gaze anxiously upon the world, as if to say, "May I be allowed? May I be forgiven?" He wished only to discover the truth, or so he said. But if so, why did he tell stories, jump on his trapeze, eat salt and pepper and all manner of spices? Because he gazed anxiously upon the world, wishing to be forgiven and allowed.

DAN CLIMBED NAKED AND DRIPPING ONTO MANHATTAN ISLAND LIKE AN APE DUMPED IN A STORM. . . .

You chipmunk with crocodile eyes, you silverfish with cockroach shell, you loping monkey and tickle-yourself baboon, you prune-poisoning pitworm, you river rat of Riverside Drive, you spark of bubbling cheese (causing dreaded pizza-mouth), you crab with clappers and grinding jaw, you skinny beast from mama's lair, you itchy babbler with a head for a heart, you bat-winged cruiser among dog-walking fillies, you mongrel, you slug, you logic-chopping ranter, you no-better-than-Peter-Hatten juggler, you Dan Shaper, you—

But I think this little abstract summary covers enough of the expressions of disapproval with which I have been greeted in the mild climate of a Manhattan striving for triumph in the form of love and nuzzling embraces in the arms of cash. Yes, I have sometimes been criticized in New York, N. Y. It is sometimes rather heavy rhetoric (see above), but I am indeed flawed. Energetic, I am; self-pitying, I am; and there are many other apparent and real contradictions in my character. My teeth are ugly, square, yellow, but solid; my life is filled with melancholy forced marches, and perhaps I deserve no better. So be it. I march to the same doom as everyone else, but not exactly the same. I try to answer age and death by both diddling and loving, foolery and mastery, even as you and you out there. So we all do what we can.

Having given full justice to my detractors, I can now proceed to personal dispraise of myself. Why am I so critical? A touch of modesty has been beaten into me by ill fortune, unworthy enterprises, and steady derogation by my dearest friends. I am a depressed fellow, lucky and unhappy in love. I like to dream of felt slippers and hearthsides as I trample down the Manhattan evening.

I wish I could say that I had cruelly deserted the wife of my youth, that sweet thing who stood by my side through spaghetti and house-loan days, in order to gambol free as an ape in the ripe jungle of Manhattan; for this traditional act—the ambitious and gamboling husband, the wronged, fading wife—might seem to justify by coherence if not by sympathy my later cruelties, excesses, and foolishnesses. *Post hoc, ergo propter hoc,* as that tuneful fallacy goes. But instead I must admit, blushing terribly, that I was a dutiful husband until the age of thirty, submissive, uxorious, laborious, and oedipal, who was finally shocked into another style by a wife's desperate act of intolerance—she deserted *me.* Hear my sad keening with whatever sympathy you can spare. See in your imagination my frazzled eyes, my mouth with its irregular square teeth agape, my skinnified bones rattling. I lost weight, friends. I had trouble with my eyes. Twice in three months I suffered from stiff necks. Yes, she left me.

She left me for a wage slave more slavier than I!

Popped into his T-bird (she liked him square) and off they hummed, consoling each other for hurts! Solid! Swell!

Leaving me with my stiff neck, ruing the day! Aw. Aw.

I shook the dust of Cleveland from my heels, as that old story goes. I quit my job. I found a new one. From then on, *post hoc,* the pattern of my time on earth ceased to be a clear pattern. It seems that a man really can change his life. I had always buried under layers of frowning conjugal intention the true salt of my salt; I had perverse mines of frivolity in me, an untutored native genius for being a jerk, a wastrel, and a genuine solitary in all-night triple-feature movies. In other words, a melancholic who didn't juggle, fighting the battle of Shaper against the world, Shaper against himself, Shaper against God and State, without weightlifting, judo, karate, juggling, or political action to quiet my thumping heart.

I tasted the salt of travel on my tongue. Bus stations, airline terminals. I changed jobs. Again. Maps made me feel agile and alert. Dream of evasion, here I come. There I go. I stroked ticket stubs with amorous fingers and went to check on the *Liberté* in its kennel up the Hudson River off the West Side Highway. I saw friends off and waited till I could pay before I went. (Installment buying reminded me of marriage. I never could make all the payments.) I strolled the ship before it sailed, anyway. Thick hair and angry lips of the Danish girl asking why all her baggage could not be put in the cabin (somebody would console her soon). The tall, bent, hairy-eared financier with a pretty girl who might be his daughter (why in tears? did she *have* to go to that clinic in Switzerland when she would rather . . . ah! she is schizophrenic!). Also on board were the sullen divorcées, the show-biz joy-mongers, reading *Variety,* and one American Indian in madras jacket and space shoes, proving that a Pawnee can have foot trouble, too. Negroes can dance badly. Fat cigar-smokers sometimes write poetry. Lovers can find true love. Everything is possible in this most impossible of worlds. Freedom, freedom.

"My dove, my love," I said to the girl I was with, "speak up, please, my darling. You must eat onions to give body to your voice." I changed jobs and girls once more. Ah, freedom.

There are millions of unemployed in America, but you know? There are also millions of employed. I was one of the jobbing millions. Cool Peter my pal gave me instructions as I took the vows and aspired toward hippitude. He grinned and gave me suave, furious advice: "Who says we have to get married? Is there a law for horses? No, they are caught. Okay. So why take the bit in the teeth and the pole up the back? Not for me, pal. Follow old Peter. Calm that overheated heart. When you think you're in love or have an itch to gamble, try to keep three oranges going in the air."

"Let's have a hamburger. New York makes me hungry."

"You got to learn to make a meal for yourself, pal. Not just hamburgers. Let me tell you something: Keep up your strength. *Cheese.*"

We paused in our strolling at a Tenth Avenue diner like the EATS found near ten thousand American bus stations—"Open Up the Dog House Honey" on the jukebox, a shaky Slim or Pops behind the counter, an assault of fry in the nose. Hamburgers for two—make it cheeseburgers, hold the potatoes. Peter folded his hands. "What!" I said. He blinked those green fawn eyes and kept his hands folded. He said grace in that diner before he continued my peripatetic introduction to town. He laid his hands to rest and squeezed shut his eyes, gradually relaxing so that he had a bland Jesuitical lean softness to his face—that face with so much boiling beneath the lid. When he prayed, he relaxed slowly, as if the music took hold. He finished off the cheeseburger in five bites. He leaned back in our booth, touched a paper napkin to his lips, and smiled. Then he said: "I met a tough lady, Sarah," he murmured, "lots of trouble. I met a sweet girl, Barbara—nothing but trouble."

"Why say grace of it?"

"I'm busy thanking myself for good organs and praying for good use of them. It's that new-time religion, buddy. I do the same before I put three oranges into the air. Concentrate all the time. You got to pray to something."

Open up the doghouse honey
Some cats are comin' in

"Okay. Why pray to yourself?"

"If I have neither torn pants nor a broken leg, nothing to prevent my making out, if I am safe in my Manhattan uniform, I got the whole thing beat. I'm in control. Nobody and nothing can tamper with me. I've got it made."

"That's a creepy way to do it, Pete."

He gave me his long, slow, lounging stare through an

arrogant cloud from his cigar. He let me take it in that he had good definition, he was in condition, he could wear narrow pants and stretch comfortably in them, he was making out, he had all the money he wanted, his wind was good and his eyes were clear, cool, and in control. Usually in a moment of challenge he just lay still and watched, grinning. Waited for his adversary to speak. But because I was his friend, he said, "Do I look like a creep, pal?"

"No."

"Well. Don't let me put the screws on you."

"Okay, thanks," I said. "You've got something special, Pete. A talent. But don't turn it into a camp. These games you play—praying!"

"I'm a fellow got to pray to something, pal. You're a Jew, you don't need any religion."

He wasn't listening to me. He had always been a man convinced. A few times in our long friendship I had been able to move him, but never to change his mind. Funny—I had taken him into the paratroops with me—but I could never understand what test he was giving himself except for that one moment when I saw him hanging in terror on the jump rack. And for the sake of that one moment I could remain his friend, forgive him all this hard control, all this chilled making out. Peter pal. I said: "Do you believe in yourself?"

"Got to believe in something, buddy. I'm the best I got."

He scared me. He sometimes scared me. He was the best friend I had.

We paid for the cheeseburgers and the counterman demanded to know why I hadn't eaten mine. There were fatty scrapings from the grill on the bun. I had said hold the potatoes and onions, but there were potatoes and onions. "Too busy talking," I said.

The counterman shook his head. "Business, always business," he said. "Why can't people learn to enjoy?"

"In the first place," Peter said, "you didn't give him what

he asked for. In the second place—" He saw the look of consternation on my face and laughed. "Naw, I'm just kidding," he said. "My friend's from out of town."

We hit the street and he was still laughing. He explained that I had to learn to give people hell if I wanted to survive in Manhattan. "But I'll lead you easy," he said. "Now another walk."

We headed uptown to the Actor's Studio in its derelict school on 44th Street, west of Times Square. Lounging in front of it was a trio of shaggy boys in jeans so tight that their genitals must have been driven up past their tee-shirts toward their Adam's apples. A dreamy, creamy girl out of a Broadway musical zoomed up on her Vespa to get the Word from Lee Strasberg. She had the face of an angel, delicate bones, a pink flush on her cheeks, large pale eyes, and long, naturally-blond hair held in a clip at the nape of her neck. She alighted like an angel from heaven in her blue Vespa. She got no word from the trio on the stoop. They were discussing their careers and a casting call from the Play-of-the-Week. She had to push by them before they noticed her. "Hey, Melinda!" one dark boy then yelled at her. "Can I run your cycle uptown a sec?"

She floated past.

"Hey! Melinda! I just got to see a fella, he borrowed my transistor, I'll be right back, huh? Melinda?"

"Go fuck yourself," she said.

We walked on in silence. I knew that eventually my broken heart would knit back together. Nearly ten blocks later Peter finally remarked, as we looked at the headlines circling the *Times* building, "Well, that girl has learned to survive in Manhattan."

FRENCH DELEGATION . . . REFUSES . . . ATTEND. . . .

HAVANA REPORTS . . . CONTINUED FIGHTING. . . .

YANKEES COMPLETE SPRING . . . TRAINING. . . .

Peter, my juggler friend in his orbit of balls, instructed

me in the ladies of Manhattan—that paradoxical prey which tracks down the hunter. The hunter has only a popgun, anyway. Then they couple. Let us leave the metaphor. They couple, alone, inviting sorrow, acquainted with grief. They are as fidgety as city dogs. This is another metaphor, but not even metaphors can stop the truth! Peter explained very kindly to me at the end of that long day of hiking and visiting, "You think you're going to go romancing the Melindas? Well, maybe. But you don't know the way yet."

On his smooth, sleek, dour face I read the hint that he knew the way. Probably he did. Yet it was not enough and he did not take great joy of it. It is not enough.

I took nature walks in New York City, along with the dogs of New York, trotting deadpan and nosy beside their several sorts of male masters—the lovelorn, the pederastical, or the merely aging; and the ones who, bored and married, needed the job of walking the dog to get something to do outside the house. I was obliged to pause by fire hydrants in order to scrape the *caca de chien* off my foot (*porte bonheur*!). All over Manhattan I noted these dogs, scraped these feet.

The cats are still another story.

And the parakeets! Ah the parakeets in the windows! The cages, the boxes, the pets! The hobbies!

I, of course, had no woolly, furry, or feathered friend to keep me company. I had Peter, to start with, and he was often busy juggling or chasing or making his pile. Often I stood alone on the fire escape and sniffed the salt air of the Atlantic on a Manhattan evening and thought maybe I should have stayed in Cleveland. With a nose like mine, it may have been the Pacific I sniffed. From eating too much alone in restaurants on upper Broadway my table manners degenerated rapidly, which leads me to believe that table manners are not innate. I took up boiled meat and snatched helter-skelter bites at it without using my knife. Perhaps boiled meat is not innate, either. Apple drying on the sink at home. Bread, butter, and marmalade in the window box. A training manual to translate into English from the Engineering on my desk at the office. Extra credit, extra cash. I owed Peter five hundred dollars. My stepwife making trouble about the kids. Help me, Lord, I am alone and unloved. Unlovable for sure.

I love no one, no one but my kids. And what can I do for them?

And with these thoughts, baffled, I put myself to bed. I was in a state of grief.

And yet I was lucky. I found a new job. I settled into this great new job, writing come-on letters for a mass magazine. Other advantages came my way. I had good health, an accurate ear at music, not much belly, a strong forehand drive, and a nosy look which set me apart from the crowd although it did not make me handsome. Also I have always seen clearly that the free life, utterly free, leads to boredom and slavery, moods and melancholia. Without decisions to take a man grows sad. Therefore I not long ago set myself a duty: to discover true love amid the American ruins of political greatness, triumphant work, and the togethered family. Full of hope, with a good will, I chased the will of the wisp. What did I do? I sat on the parapets of risk and waged my moral equivalent of war. But how? I made jokes. I squirmed, agitated, climbed aboard, and declared myself. All this rustle of need might be sweet to the hearts of ladies. "I suffer," I would later tell Barbara, hoping this would be enough for someone.

This personal grief and labor is not enough, of course. But she might smile happily, buttering toast. "I always knew you were a poet," she might even say, with a soft light in her doubtful eye. "I always knew I would love a poet. Should I cut off the crusts?"

"But I'm a chronic complainer, not a poet! a melancholic! a wounded veteran with a three-per-cent disability!"

Sweetly she murmured, "I don't hear any complaints tonight, Dan."

I could take a hint. She had already cut off the crusts, so I had to eat them separately (*I do like the crusts*). Later we slouched sleepily out of the kitchen, bound for a Sunday of rest, but I fell to silent nibbling, and of course desire flared up from the ashes. Those crusts give strength, I sometimes think. No rest on Sunday for the man full of hope, an agile broken-field runner through nettles of melancholia. (I had scratched legs.) We sometimes staggered through long Sunday afternoons, stunned and goofy with lovemaking, bumping each other, reading the *Times*, touching, picking up, and then finally, at nightfall, finding the Phoenix rising once more out of the Sunday papers. I shall return to Barbara again in good order. In the meantime, friends, I should like to propose for our consideration the prime matter of every man's life in America.

What to do? How to live? The man who believes he has a purpose in life is indeed fortunate—*he does*; and it doesn't matter too much that his purpose is not what he thinks it is. I believe that my purpose was to be a nostalgic lover who optimistically, even politely asked women to be more than human, S.V.P.: I was standing in line, cruel after some gentle perfection, and searching, of course, that fair vision of innocence and experience, tenderness and strength. Ah her way of pulling on her galoshes! Oh her grace at leaving the crusts on the toast! her wrists! her ability to hum Mozart! her firm thighs! her careful driving! . . . Since women are no better off than men, they were charmed, cajoled, pleased, and wounded by my foolish ambition; I wore narrow suits and learned to dance the cha cha (cha) and to mumble the words; I made girls grieve and felt happily relieved of their grief when, like Peter in this, I said to them: "No more, pal."

Was I some sort of monster? Not exactly. Did I annihilate a crowd of tender lovaroonies, cheeks all damp with tears? No. They wiped their eyes of me and continued with love and longing, hoping but warned, dressing and undressing with care, with pursed lips, kicking off their panties but placing their shoes carefully under the bed. They had decided to be spontaneous—maybe; they drew lessons from their mistakes. In other words, I was finding wives for other men.

Like my friend Peter Hatten, I became this way for unhappy love of a married woman. But while Pete was an operatic adulterer, willing to hide in basements and closets, I was different. I blushed and was desperate, but who was that lady you saw me without last night? My wiry, shrill, hysterical wife, my former wife. I lusted after her with an adulterous passion. Boom, boom—the end of marriage.

So what next in my life after that? Parties, happy freedom; shrieks of laughter; forever New Year's Eve, eh? Love equals life. Suffering equals life. Hatred equals life equals love, so let us live it up, down, sideways, and arsy-versy. Sometimes there is a natural progression in the affairs of men. And sometimes, let me tell you, an unnatural progression. Unnaturally, as an ambiguous lover of women, I came early to the love of one wild woman, one wild woman to cross; and turned off in my love, I had then danced like a doomed fly with gluey feet down the flypaper path of narcissism, sadism, masochism, Shaperism —that is, jealousy, quarrelsomeness, broken promises, howls of pride, aches, pains, an occasional cure of laughter. Also I took part in the reform campaign against the corrupt Democratic machine. We felt that there was a chance to bring good government to Cuyahoga County. Though Good Government (young, eastern college, Irish, Italian, Slovenian) did not differ from Bad Government (old, Ohio or no college, Irish, Italian, Slovenian) about Europe, Asia, Africa, and the atmosphere, it took a firm position on Lake Erie water and the Great Lakes drainage basin. I fought my wife at home and Ray T. Miller abroad. I was bewitched, bothered, bewildered, and civic-minded.

All this had tuckered me out. I left Cleveland.

When I came one fall to live in towered Manhattan, it was a brilliant, dry, sun-laden season of quickening blood and bones; the girls were lovely on Fifth and Madison and in the Village; the bright hope and nerve of that city floated me up again. Of course, I had fully complex attitudes of defiance (unexpressed) toward my first trivial job, writing training manuals, and then toward my second trivial job, writing come-on letters; this produced an occasional ugly temper, as it does in most Americans who don't much care for their jobs, who don't do anything they consider important; and like many American men, I trivialized my work discontents by blaming my psychology—that is, my wife, my mother, my father, my sister, my brother, and the rest of the dream world of family, of childhood; and I carried my large blue drawstring sack of disappointments, irritations, rages, ungratified lusts, and the other general-issue equipment of a wily young chap out on his own. But let's be fair: I enjoyed the season and my lungs were healthy. Madison Avenue was lit up like a Christmas tree, abstract and promising as the idea of a future. The rumble of digestion and transport beneath the streets tickled my toes. Fine English shoes gleamed without feet in fine English shoe-shop windows. The cops whistled and the cabbies howled and the old men wheezed and the girls clacked and the kids jabbered and the screech of commerce tangled everything up at midday, at the end of the day, in the morning, whenever. The busses lay athwart the street, but I threaded my way along Madison Avenue like the letter *gamma* through the eye of a needle. I tripped down the walks of Manhattan with heightened spirits after my long rest in suffering. The shirts that I could not yet buy were strewn tastefully on display from the sidewalk, with plastic oak leaves for a spot of rustic color in the shop windows. But I already had a shirt. I had shoes well broken in although not glove-lined with leather—lined with fabric. Someday I would surely have other shoes, better ones, glove-lined. But would I ever walk better? Could a tailored shirt give me more room for breath and hope? *No!* I attended gratefully to the rhythm of the city and would have tipped my hat if I wore one.

My best friend, Peter Hatten, living deep in his double pursuit of money on Wall Street and ladies-in-training, came out of this privacy long enough to tuck me gently into Manhattan. Bachelor Pete showed me the town. Vaguely he thought me in danger of killing myself, not because I had made any serious gestures of the sort, but because *he* had thought of ending the whole business when in a state of jittery love. His Sarah had refused him finally; she wiped him out; she had opted for her husband and less complication. He thought I was more like him than he was. (Intense Dan, Divided Pete.) A truly sympathetic chap, Peter's sympathies were deepened by the fact that he was able to overcome a pitiful conception of himself. He had never married, though when we were both airborne B.A.R. men—jumping over hedges with those heavily personal weapons, as proud of our paratroop boots as if we had stolen them, eighteen years old—we had both thought we were fighting for the Happy Home with some cute bride. We had had the same cute bride in mind. I won her. He had won almost six thousand dollars in a poker game, and spent it on a single weekend. It took me much longer to pay my debt to that bride.

A man changes with weathering time. Life made me somewhat observant. Peter had chosen to be a little bit of a pirate, and to take charge.

Back to the cold war in Manhattan.

"This is Riverside Drive, where the girls live," Pete remarked as he led me on a series of nature study walks for my health, "and this is Madison Avenue," he added on the crosstown bus, since a slow ride is good for neurasthenia, "where the models all live, and this," as we strolled along the East River for a sea change, "is where you can find some excellently stacked and discreet chicks of guaranteed good family."

"But *where*?" I was hard up and put down.

"You want to know more about them?"

"I just want to meet them."

"Poor pal. He's horny," said Peter.

"Not so's I can't stand it." But I was so hard up I could not stand it; bad dreams, shaky hands, bloodshot eyes. Crawling through a mine field under fire and getting my paratroop boots all dirty had not oppressed me as sorely as did my work-empty, love-empty, consuming life. And repetitive, itemized dreams of work and love disasters. And worse—emptiness echoing after down the corridors of days. Me all alone, with a fire escape stairway hanging onto nowhere in the Manhattan Indian summer: lonely, isolated, cut off, all-by-myselfified with a stiff neck in the early hours of morning just from the sheer nervousness of it all. I was vain and arose early, proud of my isolation, horny, making instant coffee, spilling it out, brewing real coffee as an act of defiance—I could be my own bride and family. Like Peter, I could measure out my pleasures in the soot-filled air. ("I don't think so," he said, "but I doubt it.") I sat on the fire escape with my cup of real coffee and invented lives for the awakening multitudes and tucked the coffee grounds into my cheeks, like a squirrel preparing for winter. Then, still puffed up with pride, I entered the subway, and the heat and grit reduced me to Silly Putty in my dacron-cotton suit. Who was I kidding? It's a lovely city at certain intense moments, both hard and cajoling—but what do you do with the rest of the moments?

Peter cocked his head at me and estimated my ability for erotic abstinence. "You're a weak womanizer," he stated evenly—more insults! I had to take that from him! and also philosophy: "A sad sack," he said, "who needs women to carry him off into self-knowledge."

"Also to be cherished a little."

"Okay, okay. By a woman who won't be hard on you at first."

"You know it."

" 'Cause they're all hard on you in the end," he rumbled sadly like a Russian Orthodox priest remembering the plague, famine, earthquake, and civil strife of yore. He wet his lips.

"Lord save us from gambling and determined wimmen," he said.

"You know it, but cut the chatter and *help me,*" I said, abandoning urbanity with a certain faint whine in my voice. He had made those trips to dig me out of Cleveland. He had lent me money and led me to a job. He had taken charge in my distress and doubt. He had even enrolled me in his health club and given me six pairs of long black socks with elastic at the calves. And now I wanted some help. I was out of axis. I was used to short argyle socks. Manhattan had put all my Midwestern habits under attack. *Help!* I said to Peter as he calmly walked me, calculating how much company, advice, admonition, and encouragement was the proper dose for my worrisome case. We strolled and gazed into the brackish water of the East River and felt the weight of the fuming city filling us with hope and that curious lifting, floating, pleasurable anxiety which is unique to New York. At my back lay a waffled row of luxury apartments—ahead, scrubby islands in the river. Behind, doorways and doormen and sports cars and elegant dogs leaving elegant droppings; afore, hospitals and indigent camps and nurseries for drying out juvenile dope addicts, stashed away on sandbars in the East River. O Manahatta!

Peter was commenting, "Things have changed now. Let me tell you something. All the chicks marry Jews, keed, but the style has changed. It's different now. Have confidence. Be warned. Not to make them miserable! To make them happy!"

"No. Aw, no."

"Yes. As happy as intentions can make a man."

"I know too much already about intentions in marriage."

"That's your hangup, brother. Let me tell you—"

I tuned him out as he went into one of his brags about how juggling gives a man all he needs in order to survive this difficult life which throws so many temptations against clarity in a busy man's path.

Once before, years ago, on my first visit to New York, I

had strolled here with Peter and we had dreamed of conquering the city in a single, vague, irresistable King of the Mountain gesture. Now, at age over-thirty, I was a boy again, only with my ideas sorted: (a) making *out* (girls), and (b) making *it* (money). The building in which I lived had a basement with washing machines and ironing tables under two dusty hundred-watt bulbs which hung from the ceiling by long gnurry black cords. After work we did our laundry in that basement. When someone tried to plug in a radio from a double socket, there was a flash and crank of electricity ripping through circuits —night shrouded our eyes, as Homer says—and we all had to wear yesterday's underwear to the office tomorrow. After that we entertained ourselves.

On a warm evening, the laundry room provided a strong male social life, replacing the café, the beer hall, and the locker room for Americans of our estate. We got our kicks sitting on the jumping Bendix; it hopped like an ungainly filly on its loose mounting, that warm sudsy swirl going on between our legs. We discussed toil, trouble, and the iniquity of the divorce laws of several states. About a dozen of us in that building couldn't afford to send out our laundry, although we sent the kids to camp. I was paying Peter my debt at the rate of fifty dollars a month. He always bugged out his green eyes in disapproval and said, "Forget it." But that was part of the scene I wanted to make: no debts. I washed handkerchiefs and stretched them on the mirror above the sink. I did the cotton-dacron shirts in the bathtub, stirring with the pole of the plunger. Once or twice a week I did linen, socks, underwear, and towels downstairs in the basement.

There was one occasional laundry worker visiting our basement, friend of somebody else in the building, who lived in a sleeping bag folded up in the closet of his office. He managed a loan company, but couldn't afford an apartment (he had been *very* eager to divorce, and his wife had the house in Bronxville). He used to pop out of his sleeping bag and use the electric razor before his secretary arrived, and then be ready to discuss and approve loans up to a quarter of a million. For six months he lived in his office, showered and laundered in our building; then, thanks partly to the initiative made manifest by his early hours, he was called in to the main office for a serious talk, a lunch, a pat on the back, and a raise, and could move into an apartment of his own. At eighteen thousand a year he could finally afford a room and a half. Also he received the privilege of personally approving loans up to $300,000.

Like ramblers in the old West, we had nicknames for each other. I put my foot on the hot water drain and said, "Okay, your turn, Remedy." There was no Slim or Tex, but there was a Remedy. This was because he kept saying, "Remedy!" dipping his fine wool socks in warm but not hot soapy water. "Remedy! Remedy!" He used to drink himself up to the task of the weekly laundry. He was a microbiologist doing cancer research in civilian or non-marriage life. He came from the state of Michigan, or was it Minnesota, in which the law stipulated that a wife must provide "a remedy for concupiscence." "Remedy, like it's a goddam disease!" he bawled, stretching the socks on a towel so they wouldn't shrink. "Hey Dan, you think I rinsed enough? I can't stand that detergent itch, you know what I mean?"

I sniffed and felt. "Okay to me."

"It kills the skin, you know what I mean?"

"I also hate an itchy sock."

"Remedy!" he bawled. "Listen, but how do you prove a thing like that? She gave me my medicine in teaspoons! It didn't cure the disease!"

Manhattan groaned in its slow turmoil at our backs. I had done my laundry and now strolled with Pete. Sometimes I had to miss a month or give him only twenty-five. "Forget it!" I had to slip him cash or he'd tear up the check. He sulked and bugged out his eyes at me every time. He didn't mind his own obsessions so much—only mine. But money we could settle. There remained the real question—*what to do with a man's life on earth?* Peter used his solemn word about me: "You have the look of idle sorrow—hair sticking up from your scalp in two little tufts. Angry sleeping."

"Dreaming about missile warfare. End of the world."

"Not every night. Also your wife."

"*Former* wife."

"Atta boy." He smiled approvingly at his pupil. "Do the best you can. That's a point for you. Use the time you have."

"I'll buy me a scissors and a brush."

"Spruce up, fella."

As a matter of fact, I was not absolutely idle in my search for true love. The need to work can lie down quietly with a job in a bureaucracy and be slaked, at least apparently; but love requires a certain initiative, even in our filed-away world. There had been a New York lady in my life just before my New York transplantation; there had been an encounter west of the Holland Tunnel. She came after my conjugal disaster but before the beginning of my New Life. An actress appearing in summer stock in Hiram, Ohio, she loved to play Shakespeare and Shaw. Much of the time she also played showgirls in Las Vegas, and in fact had the showgirls' long legs, those endless legs all the way up, and a chinless face that looked fine goggled behind a glass of champagne, beyond the bubbles, a few inches away. She was not really pretty, she was tall and leggy with a pouting chinless face, and she drank, and she was totally frozen, a solid iceberg, and she had been the old-fashioned concubine of a wild Texas rancher whom she described as wearing oblong ties and carrying a wad big enough to make her choke with daughterly pride. With him she was an iceberg in spring, embraced by the Gulf Stream—breaking up. But that was in Las Vegas, and in the East she played Shakespeare.

Would she become frigid again east of the Mississippi?

How would she make out with a man who wore slender Ivy ties, carried a slender, child-support wallet? Can that cool cat become a kitten, learn to meow? Read on, dear friends!

2

Her name was—well, call her Goneril. I had to strain all on tippy-toe to try to kiss her high chinless face, and when I got up there, just trying, it was likely to clamp shut with firm disgust, thus driving me back down to lower altitudes. I tried to convince myself, with minute success, that she was snapping at the vain and empty air. That lady was snapping at me.

Nevertheless, she seemed to be the only wheel in town (I knew her from the Hiram Drama Festival), and I kept on trying, like Tenzing, trying, trying and hoping stubbornly to scale the peaks. I might have done better to skip her face altogether, but the possibilities for humanity of looking into her eyes and kissing her lips kept me out in the weather. I both stormed and cajoled her. I was a party of one where entire caravans have lost their wagons and perished.

Perhaps idleness would have become me better, for Goneril had several flaws, and one of them was that she was an isolating drinker. It's hard to make love to a stone, a cloud, or a drinker. Though many try. Though many of us make nuisances of ourselves and try. Let us do Goneril justice: Before becoming a showgirl, a Shakespearean player, a Las Vegas concubine, and an occasional actress in pornographic films, she had received a B.A. with a major in Dramatic Arts from the University of Oklahoma at Norman. She was prepared for life as drama. If the struggle for existence involved living-in-the-round, she was ready. She was educated. She had a Phi Beta Kappa key, and, if a boy, she might have become a Rhodes Scholar and a young diplomat with a security record of spotlessly heterosexual anti-communism instead of—instead of a—instead of all that she was. Nevertheless, she drank. I was her escort, wheedling. With foolish Midwestern vanity and morality, seeking to change the world through the miracle of lovemaking, I struggled through many a midtown Manhattan evening in the effort to keep her from getting tanked up. I thought I wanted her to yield soberly, just soberly, because I was nice, tweed-bearing, male, irresistible. She resisted soberly; it was hot within my tweeds. But soberly she liked me for trying, and later kept inviting me to parties in the busy little neighborhood around Sixth Avenue and Carnegie Hall where all her friends seemed to camp like gypsies in studios and lofts. Once she took me home to show me her Phi Beta key. She was also a Senior Lifesaver and a Young Republican (on her Texas rancher's side). She also had a picture of herself waving from a helicopter to a passel of cowboys.

"You look swell," I said. "It's a nice album, too. Aw, please?"

"I like you, honest I do," she assured me. "It's just that I am only attracted to rich men. They represent security, y'know? A woman's lust is stimulated in two ways, by security and by tenderness—" She hit me back onto the couch as I jumped her; I was quick and light on my feet, but she was strong; I tasted mohair, she continued her lecture. "Listen, the motherly kind of girl is stimulated by tenderness, but I'm not it. I'm a girl loves security—a ranch, for example, with over two thousand head of Hereford cattle. And mines. And shipping companies. Honest, Dan, I wouldn't bug you if it weren't true." Now I tried subtlety, my fingers creeping silkily along her silken thigh; she dealt me a karate blow with the side of her hand. "Keep that up and you'll never play the violin again," she said.

"Aw," I said. I never knew there were so many bones in the fingers. About a hundred of them hurt.

She smiled without tenderness, showing large shapely teeth and healthy pink gums; but amused and friendly. "Lust is one of our finer emotions, I always say," she said, "it's so sincere—*look* at you." Peals of merry laughter. "I suppose if I were really nice. . . ." she observed. "But I'm not." Jolly giggles as I got up and paced the room, trying to walk off my sincerity. Then abruptly she became very serious. "I'm sorry I'm not that kind of a girl, Dan. It's upbringing. Nurture, not nature. The way I am. You can take the girl out of the farm, but you can't take the farm out of the girl. I can only do it for *lots* of money, not just money for *me,* y'know, cash on the line, that would be vulgar, but money *behind* the man—there—sitting and multiplying—I like to feel the weight of it." She sighed. "Will I ever find true love, Dan?"

How I found out that she acted in pornographic films was that she invited me to a party to raise money for the defense of her pal Alabam, who had been busted for heroin. The party was held at an isolated outpost in that desperate frontier not far from the Russian Tea Room and Carnegie Hall. It is a land of mystery and many poodles. Alabam, free on bail, or perhaps just played out on invisible strings because the police wanted the joy of following him, was a photographer, a camera man, a pale drawling moviemaker artist with a face like a potato and a voice like a drum majorette from a high school on the Georgia border. The men of this little world of Goneril's were all busy in business, and the girls too, making location trips to Huntington, Long Island, where they gathered about a swimming pool or in a rented house and enacted "Tillie and Superman," "Tillie and the Hairdresser," "Tillie and the Traveling Salesman," "Tillie, Her Husband, and the Boss," and other classic tales of the American Legion repertory. Their contribution to the *Nouvelle Vague* was "Tillie and the Hipster," in which Superzen, the hero, wore both a false nose and a false beard and peddled a book of friendly home poetry from door to Tillie's door.

Goneril was Tillie—a star at last!

"What are you doing with all these crooks and con men?" I had whispered, crowding her into a corner, nuzzling her hopefully in an effort to wear her down. I still thought one could wear a lady down by nuzzling. How wrong I was. Actually, of course, I like nuzzling for itself. "This your idea of security? Bah! Insecure types!"

"These are not crooks and con men," she whispered back indignantly, "these are prosperous makers of pornographic art. They are very well off—some of them contribute to the college alumni fund of their choice. They mostly own sports cars and subscribe to several of our better magazines. Only a few of them have ever even *dabbled* in being crooks and con men."

"Now?" I demanded. "You want to go to bed with me *now?"*

"I thought," she said, drifting away, "you wanted to discuss the sociology of lowlife, but it turns out all you want is that same old thing. What care you for a girl's mind and sociology?"

"I *care*!" I said plaintively.

"If only I were a better person," she said. "You do care. You truly do. Poor sweet Dan. Nice horny Dan. Alas, I'm a bitch—that is, a borderline hysteric with a distorted sense of values and a tendency to prey on men. Ah, well."

And she left me lonely in my corner, studying my shoes, ramifying the laces and scuff, flunking the course in Stoicism 101, with wisps of garrulous marijuana gaiety sifting through my square Cleveland ruminations. I really cared for her mind and sociology! If only she knew! ("Tillie and the Sociologist.") Alabam, seeing I was lonely, tried to engage me in amicable conversation: "So glad y'all could make it to contribute to mah defense fund, suh. Ah hope the people will all turn out foh *yoh* defense, too—*Ah* will. 'Deed Ah will. What they gonna git you fo'?"

"Huh?"

"Nevah mind. Ah *know* it's the code of ouah class—the criminal class, y'know?—nevah to ask questions, Slim. But Ah cain't he'p myself. Ah'm friendly like, y'know? What is yo' form of delinquency, buddy? Due to insufficient or peculiar attentions on the part of yo' mammy—no disrespeck intended—how do you git yo' kicks, rambler?"

Later I chatted with a 52nd Street stripper, a garment center model, and even a few of the industry's prosperous commercial distributors and producers, but my aching overloaded heart was not in it. I was undefended against loneliness, nostalgia, pride, ambition, lust, and other internal felonies. These were my racket, Alabam. I had hopes, like a dog in heat. Superzen winked at me across the room, indicating a willingness to be soulmates. Nope. Nope to that. He was the male star, equipped with a simple heart, a greedy soul, and a large, limber, lazy metabolism. Physically, he was a handsome lad with a crewcut and a boil on his neck, probably due to anxiety. I left him alone with his copy of *Zen Archery in Pictures, An Illustrated Introduction to Eastern Mysticism for Younger Readers* (Quiz Questions at Rear). Boy or man, one should never try to do one's homework at a party—is my motto, based on experience. Never had any luck with homework at a party. Seldom. I sought out Goneril.

"Later," she said. "Maybe."

It was then, dear colleagues, that I took notice how, as it grew drunk outside, her chinless face inclined more kindly toward me from its six-foot-plus-heels altitude. Whiskey in the air joined with whiskey in the veins to create a spiritual influence on my behalf. They spoke kind words of me. She said: "Per-haps."

"When?" I asked. The supersonic boom of hope, springing eternal, popped my ears.

"Perhaps," she said.

"A little later, after the benefit?"

"Perhaps is not a date," she said, "it's only maybe."

Poor Tillie the Toiler, poor Goneril, I think I thought: she is a potential alcoholic and an actual drunk, she leans toward a self-destructive style of life. (At least I so translate my prudery, snobbery, pedantry, and misery.)

I know that many of you readers out there beyond the flowerpot in my window might perhaps appreciate hearing more about the craft of pornographic film art, its promoters and businessmen, its artists at the camera and in the canvas director's chair labelled "DIRECTOR," its lovely starlets filled with hope and its fantastic leading men, such as stalwart Superzen over there, still reading his educational comic book; but basically this is not one of those tales of young American business adjusting to a changing world. Naturally, the implications for business and politics are constantly with us in an age defined by striving—by the abandonment of striving—by striving in other ways. "Love is soul-killing work," Goneril often said, "unless you really care." And she inhaled mightily, inflating herself to full height. "And I so seldom care. There are so few men with ranches a hundred per cent in the clear."

But we are committed to discuss mainly pure love and its annexes at this time. At this point, therefore, I shall merely add the one essential detail in the technique of Goneril's chosen profession. The secret of the amazing false-to-life performances of the leading men in the stag-art cinema industry—this to allay your anxiety—can be ascribed to Stop Action Photography. Feel better now? Yes? Look, they stop the camera, then start it again, they go on once more. Listen, they splice. Pay attention: *they continue after interruptions*. Got it?

Later we'll have to know more about Goneril and her business. She was not simple. It's hard to boil a life down to the bone.

Okay, back to the party.

Superzen was reading and peeking over his book at me and reading again like the boys on benches along Central Park West who are not *really* reading. They desire true understanding and a sample of love to justify the self-love. He wanted to talk. At last he sighed, took courage, tucked the book under his arm, and headed across the room to say, "I understand you're deep, too, according to Goneril. Listen, isn't it the nuts? Being a whole person? Well, at least in this country we got the freedom of the individual."

"It's a darlin' freedom," I said.

"Naw," he said, "y'all and Alabam, you're always putting me on, repeat, puttin' me on. I don't mean in America—you can smoke pot or make movies in America? You *can*? Naw you can't—I mean in our li'l old studio out on Long Island. *That's* where we got the freedom of the individual."

"One of our top freedoms," I said.

"Repeat, smoke pot or make movies in the U. S. of A.? Not on your jollyberries, buster."

"One of our top ten freedoms and coming up fast," I said.

"Repeat, comin' up fast," he said.

The reason for this efflorescence of rhetoric, repeat, efflorescence, I discovered a moment later, is that Superzen had the real actor's zeal and lived his parts, like Paul Muni. He was currently playing an inspector general from Omaha in "Tillie and the Strategic Air Command." He made this obvious when he moved off with his briefcase filled with comic books, singing, "I've got six pence, jolly jolly six pence, six pence to spend and six pence to lend and six pence to send home to my wife. Poor wife."

The party tinkled back over me. Alabam brought me a refill. There was a sharp row of lines biting into his upper lip when he eased up on the smiling; he was older than he looked.

Goneril came up with a frown on her smart, high, broody face. "Listen, Superzen wants to have a conversation, but he says you keep putting him on, putting him down. Why is that, Dan?"

"I don't know, I just can't take him seriously. It's that work he does."

Patiently she showed me my lack of logic. "But you take me seriously, Dan?" She was a little hurt, too.

"Well, two things. First, you're a girl—"

"A woman's work is never done." She sighed. "For a man an M.A. might be enough. He could teach Theater Arts."

"Second, I'm *involved* with you."

She patted my arm with her long paw.

"Number three, I just care about you, Goneril."

"Aw," she said. "Jeez, gosharooney."

However, I was trying not to let moments of feeling distract me. Too often they had led me into the corral when where I needed to be led was astray. "That lingo he's taken up," I said.

"He lives his parts," she said. "Look, he always wanted to make flyboy, but the brass, you know? rejected him for psychological overability, I think it was. Jealous, pure jealous. Now he has his chance to make good. *Talk* to him, Dan. What'll it cost you?"

Well, what would it cost me? This upstairs benefit for Alabam was no occasion for finicky feelings. A gentleman was noisily licking a girl's ear. "Hooo!" she cried. She was wearing orange lipstick and an orange knit jumper, stretching out as she squirmed to show patches of silk, and she had orange hair. He took her entire ear in his mouth. She kicked off her orange pumps with indignant pleasure. When her skirt hiked up, this brought to mind the teethmarks on her thigh and she said to the gentleman licking her ear, "Hey, hooo, hey, wait a sec! Hey, look what this frantic john did to me. He said he was a photographer and just got his jollies from, you know, art pictures, but looks like he was more a—I don't know—kind of thought I was a hero sandwich?"

The man licking her ear and two others nearby abruptly stopped what they were doing to bend down and gaze at her thigh. One ran his fingers like an awed Braille reader over the teethmarks. He whistled. "Take care of that," he said. Another said, "You remember Sonny Tufts? No, before your time—you're just a kid. That was a real star quality for you." The gentleman formerly sucking her ear said, "He must be some kind of nut or something, do a thing like that to a nice clean model." Later Goneril told me that two of the men sold movies for lodges, smokers, fraternities, and policemen's clubs in the New England and mid-Atlantic territories. The ear-sucker was in television on the agency side—square.

The girl looked out like a conqueror over the three bent heads. She took a handkerchief from her friend's breast pocket and dried the inside of her ear. When she handed it back, one of the film salesmen examined it and said, "Say, isn't that the Perry Como fold?"

His colleague replied, "Doodah, doodah."

Across the room, Superzen spied at us over his comic book as Goneril reproached me on his behalf. She wheedled, jiggled, and brought forth, along with her strong female smells, the entire Christian tradition of charity toward our fellow supermen. I wanted to please her. Tanned Superzen—inside he was pale—cast down his eyes. Hidden by the comic book cover, he was reading a volume in the matched set of Dr. Mortimer J. Adler's index and compilation of all the better ideas, the Ideas that have really made it in free competition in the open market—the top ideas of Western Man. He made a binocular of one fist and fixed me in the lens, playfully turning it from me to Goneril and back to me. He flirted and opened his fist to show a wink. He ducked his head boyishly when the mariner's pantomime was done. Finally Goneril nodded at him to indicate that I had been softened up and removed herself toward a tray with a little heap of smoking wienies baked into brown dough. Hot dough. Superzen returned across the room, mouth slightly open to indicate that he really liked me. "I got this library," he continued, "I got started with Aristotle. Next came Aurelius, but I heard his real name is Marcus, so maybe he should come under M. What do you think, Danny? It's Aurelius-Marcus, like Neiman-Marcus? Harh. You think I got thrown off the radar screen in my pursuit of philosophy and it's a red alert, go go *go*?"

"Unh?" I managed to make a sound which indicated neither assent nor disagreement, but rather, a profound willingness to be enlightened.

"Aw, take a little kidding from me, Danny. I run at the mouf a little. It's a factor in my makeup. I was only kidding because I like you. Like me a little back, Danny."

At that upstairs benefit for Alabam, with the curtains muffling the sounds of Sixth Avenue, with the air conditioner fighting its losing battle behind red velvet hangings, with the moviemakers thronging and the wet-eared orange girl saying she once got bit by a chimp, too, Superzen now paused to shift the burden to me. I could make the effort to find him human and he would help. Or I could not. I had a chance. I waited for him to say, *You with me, fella? Like to hear my story?*

He just nodded his head encouragingly at me without speaking.

Goneril passed by and touched my arm, touched Superzen's arm. She wanted everybody to feel just fine. She thought we were making out and passed on.

Superzen shook his head and grinned, clacking a little tongue-and-palate sound toward Goneril. He squeezed up his eyes at her.

I thought he would try his story on me now. He waited.

Alabam floated up in Goneril's wake. "Y'all," he implored, "y'all jes' do whut y'all *wan*-na do, 'kay? Ah mean, have fun. That zenny-boy," he explained to me, "he jes' *love* to level with you, Danny. Y'all hear me now?"

Superzen watched him by, too. He shook his head. Then he rested his mild blue gaze on my eyes, down my nose, through my mouth. I broke on the dotted line. "I'm with you," I said. "I'd like to hear your story."

Well, so Superzen hooked me in. He smiled gratefully. He really wanted to know. He wanted to stop running at the mouth. Like me, he aspired to manliness. But unlike me, he had this little talent; he was a professional stud. In other areas of experience he felt lacking, and he didn't get all the manly power he required out of being a stud, either. For most men, lust and pride are all intertwined. We think of successful lust as a success in life, a vagrant success perhaps, but still a success. For Superzen lust was not lust; it was a mere function, like breathing, which he had learned to control, thanks to Zen and thinking of sandlot baseball, and from which he had succeeded in removing the joy. There was no pride and no mastery in it. It was business. When Zen failed, there was always film cutting and splicing. When baseball failed, there could always be retakes. Something was missing in him as a man and he wished for philosophy to stand in its place, if his brain could only bear the burden. Society is weak. He depended precariously on organ strength, like the rest of us. Precariously. He also wished for friendship and success in swimming under water (more later). He smiled and fought back the flood of words. He saw the look of engagement on my face and spoke at last: "Goneril's a funky chick."

Because this affable comment worked on my imagination—it made me think of Goneril and Superzen, Goneril and myself—my face received a dose of visible grief. The society of artists in the pornography field was no more supportive to me than the society of Bobb Anthony and the magazine promotion business or my family in Cleveland. True, Peter was a friend—a cruel friend, true—but a friend. True, I lay awake at night aching with loneliness for my sons in Cleveland—true. But does society, so attenuated and fractured, do enough of the work in keeping us connected? Plugged in?

No, not enough.

"Aw," said Superzen, letting go, "I only mean Goneril's a pal, I got to say that 'cause it's so true. I read everything the Great Ideas wrote under Friendship, and man, they really got

Goneril put down to a Tee. She's wiggy, but Doctor Adler never said a friend has to cool it all the time. Sure, she buys Seagram's by the six-pack, but—"

Due to his innate sensitivity, Superzen realized that this was not the line to follow either. He wanted to let me know that he also liked her. He would not gossip about her. But we could both, like proud parents, say nice things if I wanted to. I didn't want to. He took a new line. "Sometimes," he said, "I feel like a motherless child, you know? I may be a general in the U. S. Air Force and all, charged with protection of our personnel against instant, inescapable attack by the Roosians —the Australians can take care of the Chinkaroonies; they got good heads on their shoulders and lots of laughs from the kangaroos and all, too—I may live deep in a bunker in Omaha with all my SAC buddies and Goneril and an outdoor pool and all, but I tell you, buddy, at heart I'm just a motherless child. Acting kills the spirit in a man. The soul must not flee its own poor self, buddy, you hear me? It's hard enough to be yourself without being other people, y'hear me talking? Roger and over."

"I hear you," I said, certifying only my ears, not my understanding.

To my left, the girl in orange was patting emergency, consoling Wildroot Cream Oil over the fresh teethmarks on her thigh. Three pairs of hairy-backed hands tried to help. The smooth-handed man from the television agency abstained. He did not think that Wildroot Cream Oil was the proper client to use. He thought they should use Brook Brothers' Antibiotic Ointment, jam-packed with quiet dignity in its tall, slimline tube. In fact, he thought his emergency, consoling hands should use it, but the girl already held three crouching animals at approximate bay. He lifted his muzzle and played hard to get. He ogled her out of a lifted muzzle. He was not got. Once, in the dear dead bye-and-bye, he had held her ear in his mouth. Gone, gone, it was now all gone.

Superzen moved me into a corner. I was susceptible to distraction. I stood surrounded by walls and Superzen, who was still keening, "Hard enough to be yourself."

"Deed it is. I've noticed."

"Are you with me?"

"All the way."

He sighed. "All right, so listen." He leaned closer and gave me a whiff of mouthwash. He was a nice clean boy. He sprayed his oral cavity frequently out of consideration for friends and co-stars. "Listen," he said, "it's not an easy life. The pornographic trade is not for conformists, Danny. You know how your miners get silicosis, I think it is? You know how your X-ray technicians and those charged with our national defense in this time of crisis and the atomic, you know? Radiation? You know about flat feet and the fuzz—oldtime fuzz? Well, listen, I got my occupational diseases, too—maladies—anyway, my little gimmicks. I got troubles, Danny. I do what I can." He paused before the coming confidence and swept a disdainful glance behind him at the petty graces and stylized gestures of partying. There were people. There were merely people, chattering, drinking, fending, arranging. "You know those Madison Avenue chicks?" he asked. "The ones I mean? Blondeness, everywhere blondeness? Aw, you know. Well, let me explain, it's like an occupational disease of my occupation: you got to get your jiving some other way than jiving, you know? That's partway how I come to study philosophy so seriously. Here, let me quote you something: *What means all this? You have embarked, you have made the voyage, you come to shore; now get out*. Ah bleev that, Dannyboy. A man has got to accept his fate. Cool it! says the philosopher. Ah do bleev. So what Ah do think in mah head sometimes—to get mah jiving, Ah mean—is, Take that chick over there, that blonde one. Wal sir, she takes it in the mouth, too. Yes sir, she do. And take that swell skinny one over there, too. Wal, she—"

"Enough," I said.

He looked at me with a quizzical smile and asked in his own voice, "You don't believe me?"

Ah bleev, I thought, but I'm disgusted. "Ah bleev," I said, "but some things are private."

He shook a waggish finger at me. "Y'all should jist ramble on out to the studio, Danny-boy. Ah'm *shore* y'all'd find it more than inneresting. Ah kin tell."

He stopped to measure me again. He wanted my trust, he appealed like a child. He wanted to control me, he played as cool as Peter. He showed both faces like an alternating fan, fading from one into the other: cruel and helpless, cool and winsome.

"You think I'm too show biz for you, lover? Come on, pussycat, I'm just folks, dig. I'm just a plain gal from Southern Cal. I'm just li'l Sue from ole Purdue. For Christ's sake, Dan!"

"Okay, okay."

"Dig me a little, will you? Pretty please? With sugar on it, Danny? With sugar and honey and raisins?"

Sigh. "Okay, I like you, Superzen. Come off it."

Return sigh. Mixed sighs. "We can talk about the great books, that's the ticket. We'll take 'em in our stride."

"Fine."

"And we'll apply 'em to life as we live it—okay? Like the philosopher says: This is our life. I kid thee not."

He blushed at the quotation. He felt guilty. He suffered. He stepped aside in case I wanted to join the orange girl, Goneril, Alabam. The agency man was playing a record of Carol Channing and the orange girl was jerking her limbs and pretending to sing. She shot out her arms, legs, pelvis, head, breasts. Her teethbites and garters kept appearing, no matter how quiet she tried to keep herself. She felt glorious. She felt hilarious. Three and a half men were engaged to her.

Superzen gave me my release, but now I was hooked. I wanted to know what he knew. I wanted to give him some warranty of feeling. Making out was not enough for him, either.

He had a right of feeling, too. I stayed. He smiled gratefully and began again: "Ah bleev lak the Stoic says. . . . I believe, as Marcus wrote in the Great Books, Danny. . . ." He doodled through his roles: misunderstood lad, philosopher, Alabam, stud; he tried to tell me he was a master actor, making out as best he could, not just a tool; he asked my help and he appealed for mercy. I tried compassion; it didn't apply. He was a murderous orphan. I tried to laugh, I tried to bend, I tried to comply; I still got the itch to get moving. There was a melody someplace of undaunted hope, but the music was flatted. What people do is the main thing, not what they dream for themselves. According to Peter, the stag-movie business was big business, written up in the Wall Street Journal, grossing hundreds of millions of tax-free dollars. Superzen could talk and talk, and yet he was still the man who played the Man. And yet Goneril still caused a stir of feeling in me.

Superzen paused once more to discover his mistake. He realized that he had come on too strong. He identified. In his heart he discovered that, like himself, I did not truly care for Alabam over there, eating wienies and telling lies. It was wrong of him to imitate Alabam, even for the sake of demonstrating a talent. I seemed to be, he figured, a judging man. And I was. So he began anew and told me how his life in crime had finally led him to both stardom and philosophy. As a youth he had gone out knick-knacking—ashtrays, costume jewelry, books —"you know, *knick*-knacking. But you don't make good money that way." He took to reading the books he booknapped in order to console himself for poverty. That caused the beginnings of philosophy in him. It was all he could afford. Then he discovered the consolations of good music and got caught with a raincoat over a flute concerto just outside a record shop. This caused the cessation of his career as knickknacker. The Lexington Avenue Merchants Protective Association had its eye on him all the way westward to Madison, Fifth, and probably beyond. Only the kleptomaniac ignores a serious warning. Superzen wanted to escape from unfreedom. He would not be driven by his convictions against society into convictions for petty larceny. That was for pregnant women and other far-out neurotics. He thought it through, step by step. He psyched himself thoroughly with the aid of the books and thought-provoking music that remained in his collection. Music improves the hour of meditation. The ticket was: a new career. But what? How? Picking pockets, selling uranium stock, rolling drunks? Each possible vocation had its disadvantages. As a moral man, he had only knick-knacked in department stores and luxury shops. They figured a certain amount for spoilage and stealage anyway; he was a part of the bookkeeping and faithfully had taken his small role in the business economy. But drinkers did not figure to spend a percentage of their income on being rolled; they preferred to keep the money for drinking. You might sell uranium stock to a widow by mistake. You could get caught picking a pocket. "I was stymied," he said. "I was technologically unemployed, due to inventory control and the early beginnings of my principles. That was over a year ago. Now the principles are firm, Danny, they're rigid. I'll never go back to crime again."

His pale eyes appealed at me. I kept my back to the party. The girl in orange could heal or bruise unaided. I could cease my fret over Goneril. He sighed. The way to my heart lay clear. Tell the truth.

"What happened?" I asked.

He relaxed and shrugged. He sought words, and words came.

He had searched for a new and fulfilling career in this—economy of abundance. He had found Alabam. Alabam was scouting. Alabam had found him. The previous male ingénu in Argosy Legion Productions, Tom Dimples, had met and married a sixty-four-year-old heiress with blue hair and retired to the coupon-clipping business in Red Hook, New York. So Alabam needed to discover Superzen. He did a double-take and, not mincing words, all business, asked him to remove his clothes—"not my shoes and socks, however, that wasn't necessary"—and Superzen had wondered why. It was a strange thing to ask a total stranger in the Astor Drug on Times Square. But as an incipient philosopher and out-of-work knick-knacker, Superzen made it a principle to avoid saying no to anything that might increase his knowledge or firm up his economic foundations. Alabam took him by the hand and led him out of the Astor Drug. They both forgot to pay their checks, slipping dreamily past the cashier.

Kindly Alabam walked all around him in the room they rented for this purpose—being walked around—in the Dixie Hotel on Forty-Second Street. He sniffed and suddenly dropped to his knees for imaginary angle shots and once stuck his finger in Superzen's thigh. Superzen's muscles resisted. That was good. Alabam stated that he liked flesh that stayed firm when prodded; conversely, he disliked flesh that just took in the finger with a wet noise and kind of nibbled it away. That was bad. When he touched a person like that, he feared that he would pull his finger out with the nail missing and a sort of a soggy stump remaining. Firm Superzen was good. Flabby others were bad. "Y'all reckon Ah got good taste, rambler?" Alabam had inquired.

"I dig."

Alabam had said: "Hum. Y'all git dressed now."

Alabam had watched him dress. Superzen tried to put on his clothes with good taste. Then Alabam talked starting pay, bonus, fringe benefits, and legal aid, just in case. This opportunity had opened up—stardom. It wasn't Hollywood, but it was an entry into show business. Lots of people start from the beginning, he had pointed out. With firm muscles a fellow could rise.

"It happened like that, it's my sad story," said Superzen, putting the lamplight behind his head.

I had no reply. I listen to stories, I get involved. Perhaps

I could do something about Goneril. But what could I do about Superzen?

"Just my good luck," he said.

No answer from me.

"I just met this somebody—Alabam. He helped me find myself, doodah, doodah. Ha."

Silence. Silence. Was this a higher form of knick-knacking? I could give neither congratulations nor advice. He did not ask a question I could answer. And yet he was burning for me to speak to him. He wanted me to let go; he wanted to bring me in; I gave him nothing. I felt weakened by another's desire. So often I don't know how to give people what they want. And I want to give something. With Superzen, the moment for friendship was rapidly passing. There was still a glow in his hair from the lamplight. He yearned for a halo and a friend. He had tried and tried. I had failed.

Goneril was crowded onto an electric massage sofa by one of the orange girl's hairy-handed film salesmen. He was in search of his appetite with both hands. Should I rescue her? Go communicate with her? I caught her eye. She waved and winked to indicate: situation under control.

Superzen felt withdrawal. He had made his effort. I had let him down. Suddenly he cried in Alabam's voice, "Aw, come on out! Ah mean, Ah'd shore lak to show you our place, it's a real show-biz setup. Trees, patio, and the pool is shore nice. It's got to be secluded, y'all know? for when Alabam says, 'Cameras, roll!' But it's awful nice anyway."

I could not cross the gulf. There was a look of despair on his peaked, muscular face with its even coat of Mantan. He tooled backwards away from me, grinding an imaginary camera and singing, "Cameras, roooollll."

Apparently Superzen really meant it about enticing me out to the studio, however, because Goneril brought it up, too, after shaking off the salesman and leaving him to do his exercises by himself. "I'd be kind of shy, having you on the set while I was working, you know?" she said. "We're doing 'Tillie and the Astronaut' next. He comes down by mistake in the pool in this space ship, you know? He turns out to be Russian. You know? But I wouldn't mind you watch the other girl, you like to?"

Was this something they went through with all their friends?

"No," I said.

"Aw, come on," she said.

"No."

And she smiled gratefully and squeezed my arm. For almost the first time in the while I had known her, I had the sense of pleasing her. Her eyes looked pleased. I had hope. Then she shrugged and strolled off and left me as lonely as Superzen with my hope.

I was alone and Superzen was alone and society did not fill the spaces which needed filling. I watched what turned out to be another male hero, Superzen's rival, a gray young man named Gray with a handlebar mustache and a long wet hanging nose which had so much inertia built into it that it held, vibrating, *zooingg!* for a moment when he turned, before it decided to follow the rest of his face. "Mahvelous, gaww-joss," this young man was saying to Superzen. Mr. Gray wanted to chat. He wanted to discuss. But Superzen wanted to read, he went back to his book, he loved literature and tales of uninterrupted greatness. I had excluded Superzen from companionship. Now he was excluding Mr. Gray. His own suffering did not cause generosity in him. He felt no brotherhood with his colleague.

Mr. Gray took away his long wet nose. He had poorer resources in the imagination than Superzen, but equal resources with Superzen and D. Shaper for the passing on of unkindness and a coolness in the heart. He too would do his best. In a false false nose over his real false nose, he would bump and pump along in a tale of the Fuller Brush Man from Outer

Space, rehearsing the scene of love because he did not know the play, or take the chance, or run the risk: expelling himself and then splicing the film again with an abashed smile before the silent, bored crew and the drenched ingénue. (Afterwards, coffee.) In most of these films they wear shoes and socks. They are embarrassed and they are of a furtive class. False noses and real socks and controlled-if-possible perturbations.

> "Hi, ho, the wind and the rain
> The rain it raineth every day
> The wind it windeth every way
> Ev! ver! ry! Way-hey-wayyy!
> Hoooo — shee — it!"

Goneril began to impinge upon my sight. In fact, she began to sing and stagger, and finally all six feet of her, yammering an Elizabethan bawdy ballad in her own arrangement, fell limp as a carpet, wall-to-wall down. "Hey-ho, and a hey nonny no," she remarked. Then from below she protested against Lessing's influential essay, "Laocoon," which she claimed to have been the subject of her thesis, and her life in Oklahoma, and her father who died too soon, and her mother who was still alive and nagging; "Nagging? Putting stickles in my ear, honey"; and she had toppled without spilling her glass —the cunning of the career drinker; and she reached for her glass; and I wrestled with her, not for the pleasure of it, which was minimal, which was subliminal but minimal, but merely to get the glass away. But it was hopeless. "Lessing was so theoretical, honey—so all-fired abstract—no feeling, darling —whatcha pulling at me for?" She bounced on her bum; she held the glass steady and drank; she declared that where the bee sucked there sucked she. "And if you wanna pull at me, I suppose you're just gonna pull at me."

When she passed out, I looped her over my arm and lugged her ponderously through the room. I got her coat. I found her purse. I pondered, too, like Lessing at his theories, on why the values of a world guaranteed made of pure form so much depended on sweet matter, transient but transifying. I wished to awaken her, and felt desolate. Abstraction gives us grief, but so does commitment. Goneril had me snowed. I set out homewards.

"Need some help?" asked Superzen, nose still buried in his book.

"Yes."

He put his finger on his place. "Hmm?"

"Never mind, pal."

She wound about me three times, like a cobra, as I tried to prevent her head from going bounce-bounce down the long flight of stairs. I was full of grief and in danger of hernia.

"You can make it okay?" asked Mr. Gray.

"Uh."

"'Cause where there's a will, there's always a way."

"Thank you, friend," I gasped, feeling for the railing.

Superzen and Mr. Gray, now holding hands, mildly watched me manage. I had a focused will. The way was hard. Others waved languidly. There were understanding looks, tolerant smiles. Goneril was their little girl and she was so sl-leepy. "Nice fella," someone said of me in the tone of an approving aunt, "she'll never know what hit her."—"Oh, she's met him before. He's an old friend."—"What's his business, American Legion bookings?"—Whoops. Hair tangled in my legs. She shifted her weight suddenly to let me know she was alive. So much life, so secretly convulsed. And why so topsy-turvy, Goneril pal? Whoops, don't tip me, I'll just go spill if you do.

The stairwell led down into the weary world. Out there lay the universe. Chill out there.

"Ba-ba, yo-all," said Alabam from the top of the stairs. "Real nice a yo-all to fall uppa ma pad."

I staggered out of Alabam's benefit ball into the perpetual noon of Sixth Avenue in the Fifties—delicatessens, charwomen, streetwalkers, and cops. I examined the world through festoons of burden. Goneril kept surprising me. Once she heaved around and hit my panting mouth with her neck. About half the men on the street looked like dognappers trailing a dog with rich parents. There was a poodle with a black ribbon in its tail, mourning its loved ones. It stopped by a hydrant to shed a quiet tear. It whimpered. Perhaps it was just retreating from a formal dinner. The walker at the other end of the leash was wearing white tennis shoes and a shawl sweater and glanced in a superior way at my burden of Goneril. I think I can use the word hoity-toity for the first time in my life. He felt smug about things when he compared himself and poodle with Goneril and me. Simplify, simplify! was his advice to me. My lip began to swell where she had swiped me. It was perhaps 1:00 A.M. I could try to make it the few blocks with Goneril digesting me like a cobra; better not. "Taxi!"

Goneril shook twice and awoke into brief lucidity in the cab. She explained that Alabam said yo-all because he meant both of us. The singular form of the pronoun in Southern is "yo." "I got an *A*-minus in dialects, honey," she said. Then she lapsed into her coma again. I would give her a *B*-plus for comas.

Sixth Avenue was a gray, wind-swept desert, populated by Bedouin ghosts pretending to be swift shieks on the night shift. The wanderers of the evening smiled falsely at each other, or scowled falsely—same thing. They pretended to be on top of the world in this middle-of-the-night midtown of the most powerful city in the world. They ate hot dogs and walked off their sour digestion. They swallowed rebuff all day and tried to walk off their sour dispositions. Sm-mile! Be dapper, be reat, by Ivy or Continental! Smmmm-ile! They coveted the bodies they saw in the magazines, pasted together by airbrush and falsie, and wondered why the streets and offices were so empty of truth. They wanted to be rich and powerful, they wanted to be less bored at their work, they wanted the world not to come to an end. They wanted excitement. They wanted rest. They wanted to be jazzed. They peered into the face of the lady approaching with a mink stole. She twitched away, saying no, and besides, was menopausal. Smmmm-mile! There was an autumn chill in the air. Peter and Goneril knew how to simplify, each in his fashion. So did the lad with the nice comfortable tennis shoes and the sentimental poodle. Why couldn't I?

I would have given up four open-all-night delicatessens for one Ohio oak tree or three maples in a little clump on a hillside. Sadness assaulted me through the windows of the cab. Loneliness. Regret. My babies were asleep in their bedroom of the house in Cleveland. The branches of the oak brushed against the drainpipe outside their window in Cleveland and they stirred at the sound, as if someone were climbing in. They were sore at me, they loved me, they thought I should come back to live with mommy. I saw, I heard, I could smell the restless sleep of a child. At the same time, here in New York, the driver had not thrown the meter; he was high-flagging Goneril home. Screw the company, he was thinking with one eye on Goneril in the mirror. Everybody gets theirs, but he had to drive drunks around town all night.

Where, oh where, was I going in this taxi?

Whither?

I gave him a coin. I said: "Wait, there's more."

I fumbled at the door, I dropped Goneril in the street, I picked her up, I dusted her off, I dropped my wallet. I picked it up, I tried to pluck money from my wallet while Goneril wallowed in my arms; the cabbie sat heavily behind the wheel with one hand out. Goneril toppled again. I hooked her belt onto the doorhandle. It slipped. I caught her before she went. She lay across the fender like a deer brought out of the mountains of Central Park while the brave hunter tried to find a dollar bill. I gave the driver some change and asked him to wait while I tucked wallet in pocket and Goneril over shoulder. One of her shoes had slipped under the cab. When I picked it up, I also found my house-keys. Goneril shifted her weight abruptly and I flopped back against the hood. When I stood up I was goosed by the aggressive Chevrolet radiator insignia. I tried to look on the bright side. It might have been a speeding Buick and I'd have been disqualified for future service. There is always a brighter side. My pants were slightly ripped. They might have been badly ripped. They might have been ripped off. The rip was mostly hidden by my jacket and Goneril's long, undone hair. My luck held. She might have had short hair. I might have lost my jacket. I straightened up and smiled man-to-man at the cabbie. "So long," I said.

"Dent that hood and I'll bust you in the nose!" he yelled at me in farewell. I was still lucky and had not dented his car. He roared away, crunching my glasses. Well, I shouldn't have left them in the street.

I felt my nose with my free hand. Everything was fine.

Still, I had not yet found true love.

Bitter at being thus left alone, psychologically if not sociologically, I toted Goneril upstairs of the Avenue of the Americas and tucked her six feet of feminine dishabille onto the couch. Morally limited by a sense of obligation, I believed it my duty to care for her, although there were girls I have not mentioned back at the benefit and I might merely have left Goneril and my conscience dormant in a corner. Now I did not have the strength to undress her inert body and drag it, together with her absent soul, into bed. She breathed hard about a bee from Shakespeare every time I tried, so finally I buzzed at her, "Psst! Goodbye, I'm going!"

No answer.

"You blasted sauced-up souse, farewell!"

No answer.

"Goodbye! Sleep well! I leave you now!"

She was passed out cold—kaput. As companion, she made the road long. I departed on tiptoe. Why on tiptoe? I was disoriented. I was nearsighted. I was astigmatic. In doubt, I fell back on melodramatic habits of caution. Psst! Tippy-toes and discommoded.

And aimed toward my studio room on the upper West

Side, by long crosstown walk and by subway, brooding over the *New York Times,* and thinking of what a hard hard life it is to be a thirty-three-year-old boy in New York City. The doormen were yawning along Central Park South, the pederasts were prancing, the *poules* were laughing, and the suicidal were thinking happily about how their loved ones would regret all those injustices customarily perpetrated by loved ones. I had no reason to kill myself, since I was the cause of my own trouble (sort out the logic, it's logical, I assure you). If I were to jump off a bridge, I couldn't see where I would go. Beyond ten feet, fog. I was sad. My feet hurt. Oh my lip. My skin itched where Goneril had scraped me with her heel. There were two pieces of comb in my pocket—broken. I wondered if life had any meaning and if, after having new glasses made, I should reread the "Laocoon," by Gotthold Ephraim Lessing (1729-1781), important figure of the Enlightenment in Germany. The cabbie had not punched me in the nose, however.

You know those mild melancholics, intense depressives, awkward exhibitionists, erotic celibates, healthy hallucinators —you know us artist types? Kookie, lend me your comb. If only I were an artist.

Now into the West Side IRT with me. Down, down.

If only the night weren't so black and the subway so hot and my pants so sticky. If only all were beautiful, a few inches less of alcohol in Goneril, a few less cares on my shoulder and ideas in my head. Myopia and fuzzy outlines. Squint: abandon pride. The subway car was hot as hell. I looked for an angel to give me a sign. There he was. Dead? A dead angel, taken by stroke?

A bluefaced man lay throbbing with the vibration from the rails on a seat of the subway car; I thought he was dead; perhaps he was; then the dead man sat up and went on with his crossword puzzle. When I had seen him dead, he was only sharpening his pencil by friction against the underside of the seat. There's that rough metal, you know? He had a face like the Dristan man, sinuses, care, but he had a system. He looked as false, gloomy, and pouchy in the puss as former Vice-President Nixon, but he had a system. He had crossword puzzles and a quick answer to pencil troubles. Peter had a system, his juggling. Goneril had a system, her drinking. Everyone but me had a system.

Systems for making it and making out led me straight back to conscience. There was Goneril, stretched out fully clothed on her couch. Poor Goneril. On her back. She might snore. She might stop breathing. Triste Goneril. Back there, all alone, dress hiked up, thighs spread. Terrible things can happen. She might light a cigarette and burn to death. Slip showing. Garters. That lace is inflammable. Black lace the worst of all. Those airy filligrees, snagging the fingers, feeding the flames. Unhappy Goneril, with many good years still in her. That juicy peach all shriveled by vicious Fahrenheits. That traitor lace, prickly to the fingers. I had not even done her the courtesy of undressing her. She might wrinkle her frock. She might awaken and feel so lonely, feel so blue. *Poor Goneril,* said conscience; *poor me,* said I.

In those athletic Oklahoma limbs there was no tension; in that sappy Phi Beta Kappa head the machinery for accurate appraisal had conked out, due to drink and the devil; innocent Tillie the Toiler lay astraddle a couch which would not lift a leg to protect her against horrible interventions. Assault. Burglars. Sneaky voyeurs. Acts of God.

I struck my forehead and said, “God.”

I changed at 96th Street.

It was my duty to go back and look after her—all those snaps and straps and juts of feminine responsibility, all that weakness and hope. It was enough to make a man's heart diminish in sorrow. A tear formed like a stalactite in my right eye and there was a renewed straining of desire above my knees. The fog, hanging low over the city, wore garish violet city reflected in it. Oh to be in Cleveland again, where the heart is pure and it's Republic Steel you see reflected in the smog. Also I had an outgrown pair of glasses in a closet in Cleveland, where the heart is pure.

You'd think an angel such as I, wanting to do so much good, would just sprout wings and fly through the thickened air over to Sixth Avenue near 57th Street, wouldn't you? Or at least take a cab? Well, I made a quick survey of my portfolio. I reviewed my holdings. A pair of deuces. I was short on cash. My money was all tied up in my investments, such as alimony and child support. Also needed new glasses. A bit of camphor to soothe my lip. I had to take the subway back again; then walk. It was the middle of the night by now: more washwomen, naphtha fumes from the lobbies of buildings, autumnal chill in the early September air. I had a slight jag on; second-winded, I bounced on my toes; I ran up the stairs; I was very tired, too. Without malice or forethought, I had tastefully left Goneril's door ajar for some possible charitable visitation. She lived over a shoe repair. I climbed the stairs, my head filled with sad fantasies of Goneril strangled, Goneril burned to death, Goneril in dire peril. Poor Goneril, lost Goneril, alas, I knew her slightly. I threw open the door.

Just as I predicted, there she sat, smoking a cigarette, already much less drunk. "Oh hello," she said. "Where'd you go?"

I explained how worried I was.

She was touched. I had traveled so far for her, uptown and crosstown, by bus and subway. My second thoughts often thrill my friends. "Gee," she said, "I suppose a girl *could* set herself ablaze for fair. Had an uncle died that way—perished he did by smoke poisoning, mostly from the upholstery. Better if you have Danish modern furniture. Burns clean." Prudently she ground out her cigarette, performing this maneuver with that unnecessary elaboration which indicates serious thought, failure on the drunkmeter test, and leaves the butt spread powdering in the saucer. She then peeked up, peeked around at me, touched the curl at her forehead, shook her head abruptly to let some air in, smiled gratefully, and observed my swelled lip. "Gettin' a sore, honey?"

"No, got one."

"Aw, poor Danny." She kissed me hard and pulled away. She said in a mild sweet voice, "Dan? Want me to do some nastiness for you? You name it."

"Never mind," I said.

"I bet you never tried that."

"No," I admitted, "all I really want is. . . ."

"I know how, honest. I'm good at it. I'm not perfect, but I've practiced."

". . . is true love for my personal qualities," I finished, blushing. (According to Freud, the blush is upward displacement of lowerdown excitement. I upward displaced, head swelling.)

"Dan?" she said. "I think you're nice, you know? You know what I mean?"

I knew. And with true love we sought the origins and secrets of niceness and downward displacement of blushing in each other's arms. She was so tall that I was mostly in her arms rather than the customary Western European reverse, but there was much benefit anyway and we forgot our griefs. We played on the furniture as on a jungle gym. Danish Modern doesn't work for that, though it burns clean. We took this delayed occasion for good fellowship with a lot of kissing and patting and friendly touches like that. You know.

The next morning she awoke sober and made orange juice and English muffins and tea, which she brought to our bed, smiling and not so tall, barefoot, shaking her hair out. After we finished smoking the tea and had a cup of coffee, I bobbed off into the mid-Manhattan noon in full contentment, cartwheeling inwardly while keeping a careful grip on a newspaper. "You know what really sent me about you?" she said. "Really touchin' romantic experience, honey? You know?"

"What?"

"You were so hot to get back here—Dan—worried about me—honey—you even forgot to wear your glasses."

I was convinced that sex had finally begun for me on that wild grave island of Manhattan. Never mind the illusions. Lust of the goat, here I come. Bounty of God, there I went.

But no such luck. I was jumping to conclusions. I could never reach Goneril unless she was drunk, and so finally had to give her up. Those breakfasts were fine, but who can eat pumpernickel bread while encased in the steel helmet of a hangover? Bad scene, man, bad scene. Pete advised me to give her up, but I couldn't go and act on his advice this time because I already had. Farewell, sweet lady. *Dos svidanye.* Adieu. Too bad you like consoling things of the spirits better than consoling spiritual things. Liver trouble isn't contagious, but it's catching on fast. I can't keep up with you. I owed Peter a fortune, or so it looked from where I owed it. My new glasses cost nearly twice what they cost in Cleveland. You're a bit neurotic, Miss G. I think you're a psychopathic personality with delusions of neurosis. You're too greedy though lovely. You're not engaged though you use Pond's. You have soft hands and an abrasive heart. You're in conflict, Goneril. It's only alcohol and money and exhibitionism and power and sex and the place of women and Lessing's "Laocoon" that you're a trifle confused about. You've got yourself a syndrome there, nothing serious. But it wasn't your fault about the glasses. But goodbye.

More spiritual doings in a moment.

3

The Tiger of Third Class Mail at Work?
No.
The Come-On Letter, How It Grew?
No.
I Was a Teen-Age Circulation Hot-Shot? The Song of the Four-Colored Sell Which Looks Like It Was Typed? The Duplicated Personal Signature? The Junk-Mail King? I Threw Up Into My Typewriter and Found Child Support?

Maybe I don't need a title for this part of my confessions. I just did this job. Come Goneril, come night-long worry with Peter, I nevertheless came tramping through the office at 54th and Madison first thing in the morning, dazed and creative, saluting the aluminum stripping (the building had been modernized) and the automatic elevators (the human factor sometimes got drunk) and humming right back at the air conditioning as it hummed at me. The office was already filled with human factors. On an average Monday morning, hung over by Goneril, say, but still shaven, shriven, shorn, and Ivy, I smilingly still could not stand the sight of my secretary. Her name was Rita Rooney. Her breath smelled of raisin-and-nut bread from the Chock Full O' Nuts (with cream cheese) for the first two hours after lunch. When I dictated to her, it always seemed as if she were dictating the menu, chopped nuts, homogenized Kool Aid, three cigarets, and a Dexedrine spansule (for luck and weight control) right back at me. I'm doing the talking; why is she breathing so much, with eyes dreamily crossed? Well, I preferred to compose directly onto the typewriter anyway. But even over the intercom when she announced that Mr. Anthony desired to see me, I conjured up a vision of

Rita's waxed paper with a few crumbs of raisin-nuts sprinkled carelessly over it as she dreamed away the few hours of lunch in a vision of slimness. If fantasy slenderized, we'd be a nation of poets.

"Hiya," I said, striding in to greet her personally. That already is a great accomplishment. You try striding in those pipestem pants; you try saying Hiya first thing in the morning to Rita Rooney. This lady, my secretary, whom I shared with Tom Davenport from the Advertising department (I was in Promotion), gave me a brilliant smile out of a mouth painted like a perfect satiny ribbon, the lips wriggling along each other. " 'Sa beautiful day, isn't it?" I asked Miss Rooney. "Going to be hot as hell."

"Fabb," she wriggled and wriggled, "simply fabb." I decided that I preferred the Village beatniks at Jim Atkin's on Sheridan Square, or the Israeli-style Zioniks in the coffee houses of the upper West Side, with their white or non-lipsticked mouths. Rita did that to me. She was taking noonsies with Tom Davenport. He couldn't afford a hotel room, paid a Karen Horney analyst for his wife, was too shy to borrow an apartment, sweated out renting a hotel room anyway. This meant that she gave me an extra *b* for crispness on the word *fab*, since she was not sure of my intentions about her. She was nervous about this weight problem (the Dex) and guessed that maybe I didn't even lust after her. Cool I remained, and imagined a future of Fabb . . . fabbb . . . fabbbb, Mr. Shaper. It used to be that this accent and speech mannerism indicated leisure and certain girls' schools, but now, given time to read the society pages, Rita could pick up the latest word in the early-afternoon edition over her lunch, a mere twelve hours after Cholly Knickerbocker had got it straight. "He's clyde," she once confided to me, lips writhing with disdain, "you know, *square*. I prefer Leonard Lyons 'cause he has substance, not just gossip, don't you?"

"Fabbola," I said.

She glanced at me with one wild crossed eye as if she feared catching me in the act of one-upping her. She didn't mind sexual perversions (experimentation, she would call it, it's thinking makes it dirty), but one-upping is fattening to a girl; it makes unsightly bulges; it also gave her the anxiety which the idea of three-in-one sex would give my mother in Cleveland. From too much reading in the social service area of the New York *Post* which surrounded Leonard Lyons, Rita had obscurely decided that liberal and experimental sex somehow helped to stop reaction here and abroad; she had not *decided* exactly, she just lived liberally and sincerely, planning to go to bed with a Negro someday. This year the three-in-one tablet, next year the Negro. But the Puerto Ricans would have to wait for another Great Stride Forward. You can't hurry human nature. Tom Davenport had morosely reported, with no visible joy on his henpecked countenance, that he had been the inner layer in a three-in-one tablet composed with Rita and Frederika, the German receptionist. He got sore when I referred to him as Spansule for the next week or so. Frederika was dumb and pretty, the ideal receptionist, though at thirty-five beginning to lose her first enthusiasm for the job; Rita took lousy shorthand, breathing too much, but typed carefully and had a cunning little crossed eye. Since I like to compose my own copy without intermediary, saying "Bllaah" to the typewriter when it turns my stomach, her shortage of shorthand was no pain to me. She copied neatly, on the electric typewriter, changing colors when I so indicated. "Make the YOUR NEIGHBORS WILL TURN GREEN in green, Miss Rooney. WELL-READ ABOUT THE REDS in red, please."

"Fabb," she said. "Capitalized like that? Italicized? How about paragraphing? Every sentence? Special words? What happened to your lip? *Please* caw me Rita, Mr. Shaper. Dan."

"It's all indicated in the margin." As she well knew. But she needed to rub my nose in her efficiency. *Bllach,* I thought into my cream-colored office Olivetti, filling the pit which hid the keys with my last night's supper. Caw me Dan. Bawh. Davenport had been looking liverish lately, too. Maybe new trouble with his wife. Or maybe the three-in-one pill was ceasing to take effect. What next? What next? No wonder he took offense at the spansule notion. I meant someday to tell him that Rita's metabolism was all *geshmasht* by the Dexedrine she took for weight control. Those stimulants seem to constrict the blood vessels in the brain and other organs of pleasure, giving all sorts of fantastic ideas but making it difficult to live up to them. No blood, no joy. But lots of weight control and squeezed ideas. *Bllach.* Laughing is the quickest way I know to dry off the disgust behind my ears, to shake me into good or bad behavior, to jiggle me up and out of troubles. Of course, it doesn't help the Africans or the Asians or the Europeans much—if they know how to laugh, they just *laugh*—but it isn't aimed at solving their problems. And maybe not Goneril's either. Or Castro's. Or Rita's. Or Peter's. Question: Or mine? It usually settles my stomach, anyway. The way camphor helps a cut lip.

An office boy strolled past with the Napoleon-in-Egypt look that goes with this absolutely arrogant profession, provided the boy is white, Anglo-Saxon, and Protestant; he wore a Brooks Brothers shirt, a bow tie, and khaki pants so tight that everybody could read his mind; he flung a black folder on my desk. Stringtied, Top Secret. It contained the latest report on advertising and circulation gains and losses for our chief competitors, *The New Yorker, The Reporter, Harper's, The Atlantic,* and some lesser outlets and intakes of dollars. Oh-oh. Our rate of gain was still the steepest in town, but it was slowing down in proportion to the others, and according to a memo from our consultant statistician, using the present evidence, he projected a topping-out in 17-to-20 months. "When you top out, you cop out," Tom Davenport had once announced to me at coffee-wagon time, and Rita had sighed adoringly—wisdom from the mouth of a grownup. I stared at the graph. There was a crawly jagged line up to a December future, then squash—we ceased to be the phenomenon of the publishing business. Naturally, there would be changes projected at that point, or sooner, if they took the statistician seriously. They might. He was paid like a downtown lawyer. I moped at my desk. I wished once more for a desk in a cubicle, a big old wooden desk in a nice friendly claustrophobic little closet, instead of this aluminum kidney on legs, without drawers, in a "work area," surrounded by office boy, stenographers, secretary, mailers, machinery for producing agoraphobia. It's easy to grumble in an area, but hard to mope. At the grade in the organization where losses could easily be blamed on me, I was like a Greek messenger—off with my job security! *Put your head in the Outgoing basket, please.*

Last item in the folder was a note from my pal Bobb Anthony, the boss: "Lunch today? Talk this over." Bobb sat at his control point in a private office like a humane, sluggish general, sucking gumdrops, with nothing to do but occasionally to destroy entire civilizations. At a nod he might order the deluge of junk mail to be brought down upon an unsuspecting civilian population. He might order me out in the field to sell subscriptions door-to-door. What was on his mind, that fine executive instrument that knew little, saw nothing, but controlled all? Soon I would know. Soon I would have to face the pitiless scrutiny of manifest capitalism. Well, that's our way of life—Gen. Bobb Anthony at the chartreuse push button.

My mouth was dry. Fear for my future. Also Goneril was a dehydrating factor in the economy of my saliva balance. By mistake I had licked my lip and opened the cut.

I carried the black folder with me to the water cooler and stood sipping from a triangular folded cup. A trickle ran out the isoceles. Goddam statistics, graphs, graph paper, and leaky cups. When you're ahead, you're not ahead; and when you're behind, you are collecting unemployment. What would I do for the child support? Well, I'd find another job.

Rita approached too closely, raisins and nuts, as I stood sipping cool water, and said, "Mr. Anthony called. Right now. If you're not too busy." I was still at the gurgle-bottle of spring water. There were droplets on my tie. I had not worn old-school today. Knit, the raveled tie of care, which had flapped in Goneril's face as I lugged her home. Last night had left me slightly verbose, weak in the head and needing the moral support of the classics. "He'd like you to step in to see him," Rita said. I wondered if Tom D. got those if-you're-not-too-busies from her satiny lips. Please hurry up if you're not too busy, Frederika's waiting. Poor tuckered-out Davenport.

I blew at the tip of her nose and she winced. "Thunkyo," I said crisply, Englishing it up a bit. She knew this wasn't love and her mouth wriggled accordingly.

On my way to the boss I stopped to chat with Tom Davenport in his corner of the work area. A few symbolic words to establish my goal for the day: Absence of Panic. Davenport was my colleague in Advertising, slightly my senior in rank and seriousness; Promotion is a more airy occupation. It's the difference between a staff captain and a captain of infantry. He had a morning headache, he reported. Like a lady, he had morning headaches, not hangovers; cramps, not gastritis; his regular physician was a gynecologist, I do believe. "Oh I tell you," he said. That year he was also saying, "Let's face it" and "The thing is, I got this headache." Davenport was loyal to everything. He was a dog and loyal. He was loyal to everything but his own desires. These he constantly betrayed. What he really wanted, let's face it, was to be conjugal, uxorious, with a wife he bedded once a week except during the rutting season, then once extra on the weekend, all honor to trees budding in Scarsdale. Instead he felt it his duty as a modern man, loyal as a dog to the concept of Modern Man, to chase secretaries, receptionists, and others whom his low energy put in easy reach. Because he didn't really want them, he desired only his wife, he had to invent newer and newer stunts, like the three-in-one pill. (*Actually,* it seems more likely that Rita and Frederika had invented it.) Poor loyal fellow used to take the train out to Scarsdale, totally pooped, but feeling awfully loyal as he napped, swaying with the train-motion. He felt himself in the Big League for sex. He was a loyal little-leaguer, anyway, lugging his bat home to mama. Mrs. Davenport (Peg) was a thin and pretty girl who made hungry love to him occasionally. She looked like the assistant buyer at a notions counter. She took his exhaustion for work exhaustion, a devotion to her which kept him driving, driving, driving at his job. Which in a way it was. I imagine him in bed explaining affectionately to Peg, "Let's face it. The thing is, I'm tired." The thing sure was. Together, like the Chinese Communists and Rita Rooney, they had taken the Great Leap Forward into a dazed effort and fatigue. Seeking an identity as Davenport the Stud, he became meeker and meeker, week after week.

"It's not nice to go about seducing all these nervous girls," I once told him as we stood in the men's room, "some of them with this weight problem they have to take Dexedrine for."

He grinned nervously at the compliment. He zipped up, tucking himself ostentatiously out of the way. "How's the boy?" he said. I had made his day. On the other hand, he also had his doubts.

Later he came up to my desk and wanted to talk to me seriously about things. He thought I shouldn't try kidding the folks too much in my letters. The thing is, that was just his opinion. I should just lie straight and friendly on the page and tell the American people we were giving them something the other magazines *wished* they could give, but they just didn't have the know-how. Well, not say it, imply it. But not kid about vital issues and personalities. "You know?" he asked. "Think it up in your own words, Dan. Let's face it, you're the sharp one with words."

"But you with the—" And I made an Italian gesture.

"Aw," he said, "I got troubles, you know?" That was just his opinion, too.

"You make out swell, gee," I said, "considering you got all those troubles."

"How often you see your kids?" he asked me. A little dig. "It cost you a lot, I know, but is it worth it?" Another little dig. Still, he really was wondering if he should maybe marry Rita and Frederika. Well, that triangle stands up as well as many of the parallelograms I know. Also he was giving me the needle. "You're a kidder," he said, "but I have to tell somebody. Only I'd consider that thing, you know, about the P.O.V. Emphasize how we protect American values, the home and country bit, plus the long view, that's the ticket. Consider it, anyway. We're going ahead on the woman package again this spring—special issue on problems, featuring the liberal view on divorce. We're going to say sometimes it's justified. Twenty-three per cent Catholics in our latest figures! Wow!" He moved his head from left to right and then back straight on its socket again. "Risky."

"Bobb wants to see me."

"Risky," he repeated, glad to be part of a team that wasn't afraid to take chances on minority groups. We had faith in the open-mindedness of Americans. Fred was pastor of the Little Old Church-of-Our-Choice in the Dell. "Hey, that's a funny lip you got there!" he called as his parting shot.

On my way to see the boss I wondered why that statistic about our Catholic readership stuck in my mind. Had there been a significant 23 per cent of something in Kinsey, too? Well, despite Pythagoras and Davenport, there is no magic in unalloyed numbers. A secondary quality—no essence.

The boss, big-hearted Bobb Anthony, sat at an antique desk which Caroline, his wife, had personally installed in his office (no work area for him). The desk uncooled the color scheme; it didn't go with the space dividers; it stayed. Oh you interior decorator, but I love my wife. On this stretch of wormy

French wood with green hoofs instead of legs, Bobb placed his executive elbows, he placed the saucer of gumdrops out of reach, he placed his head in his cupped hands, he placed all his attention on me and said dolefully, "Dan, you got like a talent for sweet copy, smartness. But productwise we got to figure out how to use it bestest. Not just adequate, but authentic. I want you to be fulfilled, too."

Translation: If my letters didn't pull trade, I should look for other work. And *smartness*—that's not a nice word.

Line of Meaning: Keep an eye on the circulation charts. And don't say Lung Guyland about Southhampton, even wisecrack-wise.

"How's the family?" he asked. "I suppose you miss them" (sigh) "it's tough."

Translation: Three years ago the company's Operations Research analyst finished his presentation of findings on the pilot project—statistics, market study, analysis of typing pools, depth questionnaire on editorial matter, the works—with a comment to Bobb over lunch: "Oh yes. Take an interest in the help. The team. Infects them with oedipal identification—all siblings together. Break down the barriers. Implement the work concept. The image is—*you're the daddy, Bobb.*"

Line of Meaning: Got to limit time off for trips to Cleveland. The children of divorced employees don't sell magazines.

I told big-hearted Bobb, big-hearted, spongy-jowled, snack-loving Bobb, about how my children in Cleveland had wanted to see what I did when I went to work. One day my stepwife, then still my anti-wife, brought them to the office where I then wrote training manuals. It happened that it was somebody's birthday and we were eating cake and drinking coffee and there were funny paper hats on heads and crumbs in the typewriters. "Oh," said the boys, "work is where Daddy goes to eat cake and coffee." "*And* ice cream."

Big-hearted Bobb was frowning, thinking, Shouldn't get crumbs in the rollers, jam 'em up. But then he came awake:

"Cute!" he said. "I bet they're cute kids! I love kids like that!" The troubled, humanoid frown faded back on. He took off on Monday, Wednesday, and Friday to see his analyst—a three-credit course. "Kids, they're great the greatest in the cathexis department," he said, "mine like that, too—Caroline wants to have you out to the place real soon. You must miss a real home with kids."

Should I thank him?

"The stable family structure," he remarked, "is one of our foundations in life as in the magazine business." He was making an effort. I wanted to return him to his effortless self. A little bit of that higher-priced spread would bring the boss back to normal—not that normal was a happy state for him. On the contrary. But normal at least.

I knitted my brows. "This job is a step forward for me," I said to Bobb. "You know, New York is a bigger town than Cleveland."

"I know," he said resonantly.

Inspired by comprehension, real intercommunicating between Bobb and me, I pursued my discovery to its outer reaches. "New York is more demanding than Cleveland. Intense. It's like the business center of America. Skyscrapers. Why, we work in one ourselves! Commercial and trade."

"More theater too," he murmured delicately. "The arts. Their galleries. The United Nations."

He was drumming with three fingers. There was a sound like hoofbeats at Caroline Anthony's antique desk. I was carried away. "And those double-decker busses on Fifth Avenue."

Silence. Communion. A breach in the wall of responsibility, salary, and stock options which lay between us.

"I suppose you're kidding again," he said at last, with a sigh, "since those double-decker busses went out after the war."

"Yeah. They sold 'em to Mexico. I was kidding, Bobb."

"I miss 'em, too. I used to ride 'em with a girl all the way up to the Cloisters, you know, Rockefeller's house? Blonde hair.

Small firm breasts. That's what makes you the right guy for your job—"

"Wha?" I said.

"Your ability kiddingwise. On the T.A. test you scored exceptionally high in Creative Kidding." He thrummed lightly with three fingers on the antique desk. Heavy drumming would have wiped it out—vibration, splinters. So he thrummed but I took in the signal.

"Bye, Bobb."

He reached for a gumdrop from the ceramic saucer his daughter had made in Creative Crafts at nursery school. You could always see when a paper had been given Mr. Anthony's personal attention by the creative sticky fingerprints. Surreptitiously he put the gumdrop in the wastebasket and went looking for a cherry one. They were his favorite, but he often got grape instead.

On the way out I thrummed with three fingers on my forehead, practicing, and Bobb's secretary thought, Always thinking. Or so I think she thought. But my antique green brain hardly quivered; in its shrunken autumnal state, it lay curled and waiting, suffering from its desires. Cunning. Patience. Self-knowledge and *knowledge*. The problem, Bobb and everyone seemed to say, is Communication. But oh no it wasn't. We communicated too goddamn much already. It's *what* we communicated that bothered me. The President and Khrushchev understood each other all right—they spoke clearly enough—it's *what they say and do* that may wipe us out.

I felt that Bobb and I communicated just fine—communicated incomprehension, confusion, suspicion, doubt, and friendly personal regards. Like Goneril, he meant well. I was being warned as only a gentle bureaucracy knows how to warn that the guillotine is being returned from its vacation in the attic.

"Hey!" Bobb came lumbering after me, ignoring the buttons on his intercom. "How's about lunch later? I can clear my calendar." He seemed to have forgotten that he had already asked me to lunch with him. Or maybe this was a subtle way of being nice after the business about the graph and my children—letting the whole office know that he appreciated me, ran after me, even fed me. There was a caesura in the din of typewriters as he trampled into the work area, peeling dried sugar from his fingertips. "And we can check the zoo!" he said.

After his own feeding on martinis and chops, Bobb liked to stroll into Central Park and make sure the animals had dined adequately. And that they were still there. I also liked to check the park, though I was more interested in the people on benches. The losers sit in Central Park on a nice Indian summer day, confronting nature with silent reproach; some have animals, some don't; some nurse incurable diseases, such as post-nasal drip and Weltschmerz, watching like parents over their metabolic fetishes.

For lunch we ate martinis, lamb chops with paper booties, and fruit salad. Bobb had like this weight problem. Sure, his gumdrops might contain calories, he argued, but they kill the appetite. If overweight didn't exist, America would have invented it. Midtown Manhattan sometimes seems to use work as a rest between Metrecal binges. Slimming is serious; a job is only a job, but clothes are not made for fat boys and girls.

"Well, it's not so bad as all that," Bobb told me. Weight? No, the circulation projection. "First place, not your fault. Second place, every book has its period of consolidation. This is consolidationvale for us. *Ne* worry *pas*." He got that from Caroline, I was sure. "Third place—hell, you want to spend a weekend with us on the Island? How things in Ole Cleveland? You know, I met a girl, Barbara Jones, your buddy Pete Hatten been seeing. You'd like her. My wife knows her from—Caroline knew Pete from. . . ." He was puzzled about how Caroline knew Barbara Jones and Peter. "Smallworldsville," he said anyway. And he topped his hand briefly, non-pederastically, over mine in order to indicate brotherly feeling, friendship, trust, confidence, and that at this stage in his analysis he could hold hands with a man in a restaurant without feeling queer. I squeezed back; he squeezed; we squeezed in unison; the final squeeze clinched it that I probably wouldn't be fired, maybe just not promoted, in case my campaigns failed, and that at the very least I would someday have a weekend in Southampton to remember him by. Pensively we untangled our hands from what might have been.

"It's through Peter Hatten I think Caroline knows her," he concluded. With the hand that had gripped mine he restlessly took up a load of peanuts from the bowl left, by error, on our table. "Ask him to turn you on."

"Well, I suppose I'll meet her someday."

"S.W., huh?"

Small World. Before the boss married this wife and found himself in the magazine business and on a diet, he had been a Jehovah's Witness briefly, then gave up doing the Lord's work to do the Fourteenth Air Force's work (bomber pilot, sitting up there in the sky over Germany, eating Oh Henrys), and now he was back to doing the Lord's work on one of His chosen magazines. Providing the graph didn't ground him. Bobb would never be fired; he had the business equivalent of Calvinist grace—stock representation, a directorship—but he disliked feeling squirmy, anyway. He wanted to build something more than his buttocks. As a youth he had rebelled against his family by finding a seriously out religion; also he had made friends with Lew Ayres. Sometimes he grew nostalgic, overeating at lunch, overtaken by thirst, getting thrown for a weekend nag by his wife, for the days when he did the Lord's work in more direct ways. The three fingers of his right hand were continually busy, brushing peanuts, picking gumdrops, tapping his forehead. His wife Caroline was so elegant that she left out both the consonants *and* the vowels when she talked, trailing only a neurotic sexy breeze in the air behind her; she had her charities (Russian relief) and her men (Anon.), and she lay around a lot on committees. The Russians she wanted to relieve were not Red Russians. They were foxy-faced children of heroes of the Denikin horse cavalries which fought to keep Formosa free in 1917-1919, all over Europe and Siberia. They scraped their ancestral saddlesores raw again in time for the Easter ball. "Hiya, Serge." "Hiya, Prince, howsa boy?" They were caterers or major-domos, and a few worked for the CIA, advising on choice of hors d'oeuvres or Latin countries to be subverted, as the case might be. Their stubborn cousins still needed subsidies from the boss's wife's efforts. They alone upheld the banner of the screaming eagle of the Tsar. What if the rightful government of La Sainte Russie were not reinstated in time to save the Tsar's loyal children from infection by godless Western European ways? What if the Bolsheviki actually succeeded in making collective farmers out of the happy, wood-gathering peasants? It was Caroline's most favorite cause.

Bobb finished the nuts in the bowl. "Let's," he said. He presented his Diner's card. He wrote in the tip, making that odd stifled satisfied grunt which men make when writing in a generous expense-account tip. We threaded our way through the little tables designed for drinking, not eating, on which we had eaten. We would now check the zoo. Bobb walked over to Fifth Avenue and uptown with great purpose. He knew where he was going. His wife liked lions, he liked seals. First, for me, we went through the monkeyhouse. "Blah, smells," he said.

"It's the kids and their peanuts," I said.

"It's the monkeyshit," he said. He was right. The red- and blue-tailed primates crouched, capered, loped, moped in their cages and work areas. "Aw. Aw," I heard myself saying. "Goshalmighty, Dan, you got a strong maternal instinct," Bobb commented.

Outside—*"Blah!"* cried Bobb to underline his point—we paused near the hippopotamus in its deep mud. A child in bloomers, a boy-child with a mama who liked bloomers, a kid whose mother had the notion that bloomers are Edwardian, like Tiffany glass, this desperate child was teasing the hippo; the hippo lay stoned in mud, unresponsive, autistic, catatonic, asleep with its warts and subsidiary worms and weevils; the child climbed onto the fence and fell into the slurpy, turdy, fertile ditch. He was hauled up by his shrieking, bloomer-loving mother. "Aiee!" She screamed like the victim of a Japanese art film. The child wore a subtle smile beneath its pout. It might lose the war, but it would win campaigns. Its mama, Lady Macbeth, was in a momentary breakdown, plucking madly as she howled. The hippo blinked and heaved itself delicately over. Opening its mouth—those shapeless drapes of tumbling pink membrane—the hippo let go with a volcanic convex yawn. Mama screamed at this further insult and the child, dripping hippo reject as it dangled from its mother's hands, gave the animal a grateful wink. The child had paid a small price, *merde* on the face, for a great reversal of fortunes. Its mother broke her heel stamping. "Hire that man!" I said to Bobb. "Enterprising."

"Do you believe in permissive children?" he asked. "I haven't made up our mind yet."

The seals were Bobb's goal, but he had been courteous with my digressions. Now his stride quickened. There were marvelous waxy yellow leaves strewn on the path along with the Good Humor wrappings and peanut bags. It was like Indian summer in Cleveland—banks of leaves and an acrid burning in the air. High clouds. A brilliant sun. Now here we were at last. The seals poked up onto rocks, aw, and pointed their snouts heavenwards, gee. Bobb gazed at me with silent reproach. Sometimes he wished he didn't have to be my father-figure. Because of my dawdling over the monkeys, hippo, and people, we had missed the exhibition of catching lunchtime fish in the air. A seal staggered on its flippers and made a wet awking noise. Moved, Bobb responded. "Kitchykoo!" he shouted. "Kitchy, kitchy, kitchy, *koo*!" They slickly digested their meals in the cool gray sun and failed to answer his entreaties. Maybe, like me, they did not know what he really wanted of them. Any more than did the losers on their benches, playing possum. The child at the hippo moat knew, though. Or knew enough, since his own purposes were clear to him. He wanted to embarrass his mother by getting hippopotamus shit on his face and bloomers. We can use more men like that in this country.

Bobb licked his lips, hungry for seal meat. Admiration made him hungry. Both eating and dieting made him hungry. The thought of his wife made him hungry. He had pangs when he thought of the world's troubles. Doing the Lord's work, he had been slim; as a fighter pilot, lean; now—fighting the belt. Calves heavy in his narrow pants. The pants hiked up on him. There were broad horizontal wrinkles in the lap when he sat down. His garters itched. He wanted to fly again; like the seal, he had evolved too far and his flippers were overspecialized. He was clumsy. Regretfully he said goodbye to the seals for another day. No tears. He would be back.

Excitement had loosened his tongue. He began to tell me his innermost secrets. I didn't want to hear. He would regret it later. Men have been fired from better jobs than mine for less cause than that.

"Bobb, listen," I was saying. He had been telling me about his body. "There's a health food for every lack—" Vitality, energy, or will; take your pick.

"Your friend Peter's a health bug," he said thoughtfully. "He's in good shape. Course, he's not married."

"Some of those foods taste *good*," I said.

"Umm, I like carrotsticks, with a little salt, you know? For a snack? Instead of crackers?"

We strolled out of the park toward the office. We hit the crowd on Fifth Avenue, going every which way. Bobb stood confused, his head higher than most, looking for his bearings. I could see him selling *The Watchtower* and predicting the end of the world soonest. He looked hungry for a meaning in life.

He looked hungry in general. Then abruptly he was reminded of the basic point. He stood amid the crowd and called down to me: "Now hear this. With your help, boy, we're going to climb into the stee-ratosphere, stee-rat-rat-*rat*osphere. We'll not only sell more, paid-up subscriptions, no giveaway gimmacks, I mean gimmicks, than any other class magazine, but also than any other *quality* rag. Now hear that."

I heard. I was at his side throughout this outburst. The seals were over. The hippo-boy was over. I tended to consider the speech a little sanity-inducing joke on his part, but he repeated it on an average of twice a week, usually on Monday at the morning meeting and on Thursday at random. There at the southeast corner of Central Park where the Plaza Hotel gracefully looms, I decided that it must be a complicated put-down, but of whom? Of me and my job? Of himself? Of his wife for marrying him? Of things in general? Later in the day I came around to the simple solution: He meant it. He was like Goneril. He was sincere, and that was the gimmack. "You're right, Bobb," I replied, "and I'll do the best I can." He might have looked foolish to me, smelling his salty, spitty fingertips near the fountain of the Plaza, but he knew how to substitute other pleasures for his slim bygone waistline.

The lights were against us, so I took the time to admire the Plaza, the fountains, the hacks, and their horses. It may all have been a plot—the clop of horses' hooves, the high hats on the hackies, the water leaping in the Plaza fountains—but it succeeded in generating a nostalgic yearning for grace.

"This is a beautiful corner," I said, "beloved by writers since the 'Twenties."

"Hell," he said, "I'm going on forty-five and I *still* love it."

Want to bet he was closer to fifty?

After lunch I wrote my child-support check for the month. Sigh. A moment of gloom. I took the pictures out of my wallet and set them up on the desk in front of me. Must get new ones;

children grow. Then rubbed my hands together. I went back to work on a special letter for the subscribers of *The Realist,* a funny little hip magazine whose subscription list we had bought from a part-time secretary who had managed to steal it out of the shoe box in which the editor kept it. Just how, I don't know. This is business, not crime. We paid her twenty-five cents per name, and with the proceeds, she took a weekend in Fire Island. Ate steamed clams for the first time—then the crook went back to Hunter College, with a major in Lit. I read (researched-up) some back issues of the magazine, which was slanted toward the secular branch of the Lenny Bruce cult. Prophet, not Saint, thank God. Steeping myself into the slant, a toe at a time, I tapped out some sick humor, ritually said "Bllach" into the typewriter, and let's go. "Hiya, Dads. Sick we're not, but disgusted we sometimes are—" *No.* "Hey buddy. Look, you're probably not a magazine subscriber. Take a walk in the evening, pick up on the headlines, browse in an open-late bookstore—" *Bllach.* No and double-no. That blasted secretary, that small-time goon, what trouble she made for me. How could I both conform to company policy and pick up the trail after this narrow band of nonconformists? I mean, if you have to sell an in-group on being an out-group, you might as well teach Lit. at Hunter College.

I was thinking again. Across the work area Rita frowned with her company-spy, three-in-one eyes. I was staring at the freckles. A blouse covered them, but she knew each freckle had been mapped for me by Tom Davenport. She sat at a metal desk with pipestem legs and her skirt hiked up as she typed. Thigh, thigh, then metathigh—why? The Napoleonic office boy ambled past with a fresh cargo of gumdrops for Mr. Anthony. An afternoon yawn hit me and I remembered Goneril. I concentrated. I folded my hands on my chest. Inspired, I unfolded. "I may disagree with what you say," I wrote, "but I'll kill you for saying it." I laughed—but would they subscribe?

Is this the way to woo the Realist? Focus—it is important in selling.

Delicacy is also essential, but my task was not easy. These small-small promotions were sometimes worse than the big ones. Even if it came to the subscribers to some California literary quarterly with 126 paid-up admissions, we would bend all our (my) effort to drag in a few of them with a special letter. Frederika and Rita whispered together in the girl's room, but I slaved away over my cream-colored Olivetti. It isn't that 126 subscriptions made any real difference. But we thought of them as peer-group-leaders, we thought like that, and they firmed up the advertising base. . . . That was it! Try that old story again! I rolled in another sheet. It made a zipping sound. *Bllach.* I sometimes wrote the self-critical words onto the top of the sheet; my fabb secretary knew enough not to type it into the final copy. "As a peer-group leader—jargon is shorthand, pals—you are especially valuable to a magazine like ours. We admit that we attempt to influence the decision-making mass of Americans; a magazine like ours cannot be edited from Big Sur; but still there is an advantage for you too in keeping touch. . . ." I considered this a mildly novel way to sell the product. I tried to imply: Look, buddies, we're giving you something to sneer at in case you're tired of *Time-Life*. Be advanced. Be far out. (I scribbled in the margin: *hp, swng,* meaning: Don't forget to use the words hip and swinging someplace in the copy.) Sneer at us, I was begging them, at a bargain introductory rate to peer-group leaders, stamped envelope enclosed.

In months and years to come I might have to deal with the subscription lists of *The National Review* (right), *The National Guardian* (left), a journal of members of the union of AFL-CIO business agents, a Jewish anti-Zionist newsletter (we are Americans of the Mosaic persuasion, we have swell table manners dating back to before the Civil War, in which we fought bravely and impartially on both sides), not to speak of such major sources of names as *The New Yorker* and the Chevy Chase telephone directory.

The buzzer sounded. Rita said, "Mister Hatten on the telephone." I could see her satiny lips wriggling from across my work area.

"Put him on, please. Hello, pal. Yeah. Sticky and hot inside—the air is coolified. Sure, you say so, I'd like to meet her. No. No. I'd *like* to meet the lady. Trust in the Lord."

He called me the Mahalia Jackson of the magazine promotion trade and signed off. All I meant was that I trusted him to fill my evenings with pleasure and occupation, amen. Back to *The Realist*.

At three-thirty I looked up to notice that the coffee-wagon had passed me by. I would do without. It tasted like boiled back issues, anyway. The wastebasket was half full of wadded-up paper. But there were three sheets in a new manila folder.

At five o'clock I skipped the usual drinks, as usual, but shaved myself with an old Sunbeam Shavemaster I kept in the closet in the men's room, in a gnurry tangle of extension cords wrapped around a drugstore mirror. It was the razor my father gave me when I got out of the Army—single-headed, remorseless, grinding away like the mills of God against my beard. It still worked. The plan for its obsolescence had not been perfected. And it relaxed me to rub the machine against my jaw and think of my sleepy father in Cleveland, still alert to my failings. The grumpy motor massaged my brain. I also brushed my teeth.

At six I would meet Peter at his place, shower in his shower, wear one of his shirts—we shared clothes, we even shared laundry marks, as if the Chinese sensed how close our kinship—and life would begin anew in the gray-yellow dusk of Manhattan. I would tell Peter about Goneril and he would cluck and grin and then he would lead me back into the maze. The girls of Riverside Drive, Village chicks, those lovely East

Side ladies, so patient in their eagerness. . . . But before this, I met the boss one more time that day. He barged in on me just as I was tucking the Shavemaster back in the closet. He said: "You working kind of late?"

And you peeing in the help's john? I wanted to ask. *Lonely, Boss?* But I didn't. While he stood aspraddle and sighing, I apologized. He shivered, took a deep breath, zipped, buttoned. For this relief, much thanks. Also it took him away from fingering his candies. I apologized for working at this hour. I'd rather he didn't know about the shaving, but I also didn't want him to think me panicky because of our lunch and that graph. I winked. "Busy," I said.

Winks he understood. He winked back. Christ, if he wanted to hold my hand again—! But he only said: "Fabb." Making out with the secretaries in the office was okay, while shaving somehow lay in some murky area which lacked definition and clear precedent. Maybe this was because it implied that the beard was growing out of the head on company time. I imagine, given a razor account at an advertising agency, protocol might be reversed; the daily crop of hair could be considered field research, and shaving it a case of market analysis. But we sold deodorized and homogenized sex—sophisticated sex, with deep analysis—along with our politics. If I could talk on the phone with one of the President's speechwriters, also in advt. & promot., as I in fact once did, I could cop a feel behind the files.

Bobb Anthony had a vestigial twitch in his eye. It dated back to the 'Twenties. Winking is *out*; we wink in words nowadays; but the boss was nonverbal despite his garrulity. Like the seal, he stretched, preened, and fished in the air. He trapped an innuendo in the stee-ratosphere.

Bobb winked.

About that conversation with Washington: We had been negotiating with the President for a little text-piece on fallout. We thought it would make a nice Public Service Special. People were getting tired of misunderstood actresses, the problem of integration, and why Johnny couldn't read. They were ready for something major—what to do in case of the destruction of the universe. That was major enough even for us. We could really set our teeth into that. It would make a good theme for the Thanksgiving issue, history and man must endure and the rugged individualism of the pilgrims and stuffed turkey and like that. We put it to the Chief. We went through channels, of course. We're not *Time:* we can't just pick up the phone. We talked with the Chief's man. He said he was waiting for the right crisis to wake up America. The Chief was biding his time. You can lead a man to the shelter, but you can't make him dig.

In the end we decided that major policy decisions should be left to the Luce magazines and Congress; we wanted to preserve our independent critical posture, like *The Reporter*. Only sharper and more homespun. We didn't think it in keeping with our image to add the President to our stable of writers. We preferred sharp-eyed pros. They required less rewriting and were unlikely to cause war with a careless word. In case of war, we would probably enjoy major circulation increases, due to national anxiety, but this advantage would be more than offset by likely hydrogen damage to our plant. The President's man said it was okay by him. No sense in precipitating a moral crisis in the cement industry before we were ready. He said his feelings weren't hurt, but the plug he gave us for the fall circulation drive had a pretty general ring to it.

From the woman's angle, we had thought the President's wife might give us some tips on how to decorate your home away from home, underground, making use of antique folda-way furniture to lick one of the major problems in styling, limited space. We wanted to run it with a red-and-blue color layout—a novel wake-up device to beat certain gloomy implications. Who likes to be cooped up with the family that way, even in a flawlessly decorated living area? Well, we ran it up the flagpole—as Bobb said—but it didn't flutter. I had to throw away a whole promotion series geared to the progressive slant on "Wake Up, America!" Bobb liked the way I had stolen this theme from under the noses of the Radical Right, and yet preserved our magazine's traditional liberal posture (or image).

We stood at the elevator together. Bobb stared at my lip with a worried frown (Boss takes interest in health of Team). "I got a little Chap Stick, you want to try it?" he said. "Last time they ran their ad, they sent me a hundred." He took his head on a slow shake. "Now what am I gonna do with a hundred Chap Sticks? Eat 'em?"

"No," I hastily urged him, thinking, They're probably slimming, though.

"Well, you take care." His head came traveling, he put his face next to mine, his eyes widened delightedly. "Say! Hey! Wow! That's a *bite,* boy!"

I hung my face in pride. "Aw," I said. It wasn't. It was a blow from Goneril's neck. The camphor had irritated it.

"Boy! And I was worrying about you having fun! Man! Come on, Dan, please—aw, come on—please—have a Chap Stick, will you?"

Others came up, saw us in close discussion, pressed the button for themselves. Bobb made a small conspiratorial gesture of one finger to mouth. He considered himself sworn to secrecy. I could trust him with my secrets (Boss like a father to Team). Implicitly. Fellow feeling. Creature comforts. We entered the elevator. As I said, Bobb winked. Four of our fellow passengers blushed. What dreams on their work-ended minds? Guilty, guilty. We shot down eighteen floors to our night-time, part-time careers in what seemed like real life. Rita Rooney and Tom Davenport, trapped in the elevator together, did not even glance at each other. Workaday love was over; conjugal duty and dating now began. The troops marched through the lobby, good soldiers all. We were released from the command of ravenous, organizational Bobb Anthony. The building dribbled us forth into the newsreel evening. Farewell till tomorrow, dear colleagues. Byebye.

We broke step and took a breath, and then went forward on our separated campaigns.

Subway. Down again, across, and up the West Side. The subway disseminated a brutal exhaustion on the muzzles of travelers, a brutal hilarity of elbows and feet. Boots worked for a place to stand. Delicate pumps sent steel-spike messages into competing metatarsal arches. Hands gripped wallets, hands crept cunningly over nearby objects. Pulses were taken by self-made physicians, jammed up against flesh that always craves something, though maybe not medical inspection in the subway. There were kicks, growls, and shrieks. It was rush hour. Neighbors kept deadpans. Many shut their eyes. Blot it out! they thought. No one upchucked today. Someone had yesterday. Blended into the meat machine, an orgy of unwilling togetherness, clothes and limbs and membranes and hair, the mingled breath of multitudes, we concentrated on minding our own business. And yet desire did not desert us.

I wanted to do something personal. I wanted to have a private life. I sought human contact while pinned to a half-dozen bodies I could not see. On the IRT we all shared the population explosion. Humankind was pressing us into faintness, but our thoughts grasped only at salvation by humankind. It had been a long day. Please! Something personal! I felt denuded. My right shoulder ached. It had been to the wheel. Each day was like flipping a little. Each evening I sought to do something which would make me human in this inhuman city. And yet the elbows in my ribs in the subway—like the bloomered boy at the hippo pit—made me flush with gratitude. Fight back, fellas! Return junk mail to sender! Loaf, laze, and wallow! Coffee breaks are not enough. Enjoy a surliness break! Goof off! Drink and eat! Kick and yell! Gefuffle—don't ask what it means—do it! *Love.*

My bruised lips were also chapped and dry from the smiles

I had licked away. False smiling. Business smiles. Let me find my own business now! Ah food, strong bread with sweet butter, that would be an introduction to personal life again. I would favor the evening with some good bread. That might be a start at least.

On the way to meet Peter, I stopped to buy him a loaf of pumpernickel in one of those supermarkets on Broadway which they install in converted movie theaters. On the marquee they advertise lard, you know? Or a special on Mazola? Some of them are being shifted back now to non-cholesterol-producing art movies. Well, anyway, in the supermarket there was this girl, this woman—full in style, no hysteria on the face, a beauty in a plaid skirt and white blouse, strong legs, high breasts, a long straight nose, just a touch of dampness at the blouse and hairline; she was wheeling a cart and rested on the steering bar a hand without a wedding ring. That proved that she was meant for me. For ever after, a woman, a woman! Irish maybe. With a touch of Slav. Of Indian. Of English aloofness. Yet earthy. Perfect, her for me and me for her. Our team! Goodbye, Goneril, you had your chance. You muffed it. Not this darling, my true love. She muffed nothing. She said nothing to me, but she rode that grocery cart with the grace of an angel. For my benefit. She stood on one toe to lift off a bag of flour. For me. Not a large bag. Medium. She lived alone. But she liked to cook. English muffins. Apple pies. Oatmeal cookies. Mm, fresh cookies. How to speak with her? If I came up behind her and said all at once, "I love you," wouldn't she maybe think me a masher, even crude? Possible. So I followed her. Grilled bacon. Bacon and tomato sandwiches for two. On a little marble table. Fireplace. The glow on her face. If only she knew how discreetly I followed her, with consideration for her delicate feelings, instead of just boorishly falling to my knees in front of her cart, she would learn to appreciate me. But she did not notice. Brillo. Ivory Snow. I trailed her in a transport. I wheeled my cart, containing nothing but a long loaf of bread, behind her cart, containing a mounting pile of staples. Jello yes. Jello no. She replaced the Jello on the shelf. She put it back in the right spot. She would not lose my place when I wanted her to read something in a book I admired. She would read the paragraph and hand it back. She would comment briefly. Later we would discuss it in detail. She was considerate of Jello. She would be considerate of me. With a delicate pressure on the bar and wheels of her cart she braked it in order to read the backs of boxes. She was literate. She was an intelligent consumer. She compared quantities of riboflavin in breakfast cereals before making her choice. She made distinctions. She was intelligent. She went to the library near Amsterdam Avenue to read *Consumer's Reports*. But she was not a slave to advice. Measuring the crisp pop of Kellogg's Super "K" against the soft thrill of Wheaties, her tongue between her teeth, the tradition of the New against a fine old flake. I wanted to bite that tongue. Not now, later. I wanted to squeeze it gently. Later. Not now. But I wanted to, badly. At some future date. When I knew her better. When it was appropriate. When it flowed naturally from long acquaintance. When she knew I cared about her, the real her, not merely some ideal of Ideal Woman, not merely some psycho-sensual target. She was not just a pick-up. She was Venus and Aphrodite, she was a careful shopper. She put both boxes down and decided on Kretschmer's Wheat Germ in the jar. It goes wonderfully with bananas and nuts. In the fruit-and-nut department. I didn't blame her at all. I was with her there. I was on her side all the way. I was behind her.

She wheeled her cart and I wheeled mine. She had her hair pinned up and the nape of her neck was lovely, unhysteric, calm, womanly, loving. She forgave me my sins. She knew I was a sinner, but knew also that the worst of all sins is not to recognize one's own flaws. I saw error and sin! within! And yet she knew that I did not wallow in self-pity. Yes, I dipped in a toe now and then, but I had so much to give her. Kretschmer's Wheat Germ is toasted, did she know that? Toasting probably changes some of the original vitamins. That's all right. "Alteration will thy pleasure be." We took our joys carelessly. Untoasted wheat germ is for cattle. We sliced bananas, raisins, and sprinkled nuts on our morning cereal. We took coffee in mugs we bought at the outdoor fair on Waverly Place. We went shopping together because that was how we had met, she and I.

But how to speak those first words to her? So far we were merely grocery carts that passed in the Manhattan night. Quality there. Frozen meat. Liver. Ground chuck. She wasn't poor, she didn't buy hamburger; she wasn't extravagant, she didn't buy steak; she bought ground chuck. She bought liver. She wasn't phony, she didn't buy tripe or brains. God she was perfect. No animals. I bet she had no cats. I felt it in my bones—no cats. She liked human beings better than cats. But how to stop her? How? I mooned along, pushing rubber wheels. I had picked a cart for myself with a little elevated wire throne for a baby. It was inadvertent, but fraught. She could be mother on vacations to my two. She would like them. They would like her. She took an old envelope out of her purse and checked off her list. She had every item and more. Me. She also had me. I was on her list if she only knew. She did not know. She would leave soon. She felt fulfilled. I felt unfulfilled. How to fulfill us both? I could strike up a conversation about Pechter's Russian Pumpernickel. That's what I wheeled in my cart. I could tell her all my jokes about it, my bad puns. How it supports life, it's true, it's beautiful. "Beyond the Pechter Principle"—Freud. "Pechter's in Our Time"—Neville Chamberlain. But she was too young for appeasement. But what if she didn't like Pechter's Russian Pumpernickel? What if she ate Pepperidge Farms bread? Wouldn't she think me odd? Eccentric? Pushy? "Beyond the Pepperidge Principle." No, it didn't have that swing. The rhythm was off. She might call for the manager. The police.

Have me thrown out. For protection against her goons I seized a box of frozen strawberries and threw them next to the bread in my empty cart. Unmelted, they make a brutal weapon. And maybe they would give me an idea. We need ideas more than weapons. They gave me no idea, they did not even thaw.

The master maneuverers say that the important thing in politics is to be on the scene, present, *there*. Wildly I skated up behind her. If I knew her name, I could be more fully present. In England they know each other. They meet at Brighton. They know the same vicar. Here we have to be empirical. Love is a kind of politics. But what did I know about her? She was standing at a bin which displayed rubber gloves to protect a lady's hands from detergent itch. This week only, if you bought a pair of rubber gloves, you got an extra glove free, due to this special offer. She took the package. I knew nothing at all about her but what I sensed in my heart. Maybe she had a third hand. I never said a word to her. I listened to her with the third ear, but I never had the chance to say I loved her, third hand and all. I never saw her again. She never had the chance to make me the happiest man in the world. I was disappointed; wouldn't you be?

At the vicarage, watched over by God on his cloud and the vicar's wife, you can ask her name. At the Gristede's, watched through a mirror by the Pinkerton, you have no rights. History won another round against true love. True, I was shadow-boxing. But the sweat was real. I cared. She did not care.

I carried my bread and strawberries down Broadway in a paper bag.

Even Goneril cared more than she did.

Frederika and Rita Rooney cared more about Tom Davenport than she did about me.

Caroline Anthony cared more about Bobb.

"Youth is full of pleasure, age is full of care," Shakespeare said, thinking of love; but every which way you shake it, love no longer works like that. Now youth is full of care —struggle for an ideal beauty, struggle to fit romance to marriage, the acid resolving of divorce—and only in age do most of us learn to take pleasure easily. Age begins to know how, pleasure sinks into the bones at last; but in age a man should settle to his ambitions and get to work and be full of satisfactions. Still, there are nasty men of all ages, groping in the streets; young men in the basements, old men dancing at Roseland. Youth and age both are full of care. Even Rita Rooney, letting her eyes cross all the way, is fabulously sincere. Bobb, Tom, and the man who wheeled the coffee cart worked at it all night, worked by day; Goneril lived in care as she made her films in magnificent pornoscope; Peter and I discussed; there was very much alike about the quest which ran through all our lives.

Could private detectives find me the girl in the supermarket? Track her down? Learn her habits and teach me to infiltrate her days somehow?

Reasoning and fantasy. *Bllach.*

A group of Puerto Rican kids at a pizza stand was making fun of me. I had taken a greedy bite of the heel of the bread and was chewing with my jaw making clicking noises. One of them tossed me a crust of pizza. He judged me harshly. I too. I sometimes think we all now reason too much about things, Why? and why? and why?, eating ourselves up with insights, I insight you and you insight me and we each insight the other; we brood brood *brood;* but then I look at the way I live at work, what I do with my brains all day, and goddammit, maybe I ought to think more. Is writing come-on letters what for we rose out of the slime with the help of the opposable thumb and the Olivetti? Is this why I battered my way out of my mother's cervix, with my head all bloodied and poor old ma filling the delivery room at St. Luke's Hospital with screams? To write let's-do letters? To smell Rita Rooney's breath and see the bottle of Dexedrine in the wastebasket? To hear Tom Davenport's troubles and bluff with Bobb Anthony? Finally getting down to labor at: "In the coming weeks our lineup includes such vital reports on war and peace, Broadway and Hollywood, as. . . ."

Isn't there something more?

Now the strawberries began to melt and there was a soggy stain in my grocery sack. I held the strawberries between two fingers. I drop-kicked them into the street. Applause. More Puerto Rican kids. I had strawberry mush on my right toe. But the strawberries had only *started* to melt. I limped.

I wanted something more! The days were growing short. It was getting dark. Indian summer over soon. Daylight Savings Time over soon. I wanted more time, more days, more light and air. I wanted to like what I did. I wanted to love whom I bedded. I had plans for the universe. I wanted it to stick around for awhile.

Could I rescue foundered love, foundered marriage and family, by finding Miss Right? (Ten million frayed boys were looking for that same girl, strong, laughing, pensive, multilayered, strolling the supermarket without a past.) I would take her for a weekend with Bobb and Caroline Anthony at their place in Southampton. Gradually she would see me for what I am. Then I would launch myself bravely into business, founding a magazine called *Thank You, the Quarterly of Gracious Receiving.*

What else is there to do?

We're not at the Strategic Air Command in Omaha, running switchboards. We're running typewriters, wheeling grocery carts.

So how else to spend all the power we nonetheless gloriously still possess? Not like the trained seal bobbing out of the salt in the zoo, flapping winglessly under the sun.

Up the stairs two steps at a time. In a hurry.

I presented the bread like a carbine at Peter's door. Black bread with a harsh grain in the stock. Good bread, but unkind thoughts about myself. I knocked with it. The door came open. Green eyes and a smile of welcome. A crisp fresh beige shirt and a black knit tie, just being tied.

"Hi, Pete. What's doing tonight?"

"Games, boyo, games."

4

I believe in reform, and yet, like a stoic rooster trying to be hilarious on a gray dawn, I have laid Zen eggs with the Democratic Party, my former wife, several of my jobs, Goneril, and a number of other projects. Okay, so cocks don't lay eggs; Zen eggs never rhyme; the metaphors are confused; here anyway is the lesson I drew from all this:

The swan's neck is high
But shortening will make it sigh

The turtle's neck is brief
Lengthen it and you give grief

The wrestler has no neck at all
Make him one and he will bawl

Leave everybody's goddamn neck alone!

This conflict in me, between reform of the world and myself, acceptance of the world and myself, between desire to do one thing, desire to do another, produces—well—facetiousness, misery, stubbornness, impatience, howls of rage, whimpers of defiance, and occasionally an overwrought prose style. But as DeGaulle said in *L'Appel,* the revolutionary is a man given to crises of melancholia. Without sometimes being overwrought, we cannot work our will on the world. Let imperfection strive for perfection, then. And let's peek into the pot.

Act Two. Still summertime in September. Our hero has been youthified by the lightened air and dacron-cotton suits. The lip is long since healed. Bobb Anthony left a manila envelope filled with Chap Sticks on my desk.

Summer in Manahatta, mother of waters! Cigar-smoking psychologists in transparent, nylon sportshirts worried away the season with group therapy; hollow-eyed slum kids built their orange-crate fires at the curbs, and howled with rage as umbrella-carrying pederasts offered them a quarter for an old orange box and a bit of comfort—howled for more money; the dry winds swept up the sidestreets, carrying dawn wakefulness to the depressed and insomnia to the worried; ductless models stippled the pavements stiffly with their heels aclack and their unblinking eyes held open (personally) by Helena Rubenstein and Revlon; college beatniks flooded their sports cars into Greenwich Village; fights broke out all day, and the sirens of ambulances screamed for the fallen, the stroked and attacked, mugged by anxiety, unable to breathe. Politics and domestic dilemmas and Man's inevitable fate in mortality pressed more closely at our heels during a Manhattan Indian summer. Radiation causes anxiety and anxiety causes cholesterol and arteriosclerosis stalks the streets. Q.E.D. Drink skim milk. Even if you sometimes think you're powerless, you are. Alas, we usually are.

But not always! Despite weakness, despite madness, Manhattan somehow became a savory summery place, and if you stepped on it, it squealed. In the Pam-Pam's on Sixth Avenue near Eighth Street in the Village, the excited fairies gathered, and an ambassador from the *Reine Blanche* bawled into the telephone, *"Comment ca va? Oui, oui, je viens d'arriver à New York, mon vieux. Oui! Oui!* Everything's swinging!" Much love is transacted in the worst city heat. The trouble is—love is a transaction?

I scampered through Manhattan at stately, sauntering Peter Hatten's side. Once I had pushed him out of the sky and into the war. Now he was trying to steer me down after I lost my guidelines in civilian life. "You look a little ill," he said.

"I feel bad."

"You look it," he insisted.

I felt it.

"Hm. Yes. You look a little worse now. I do fear," my friend meditated aloud, "that Goneril has not been the proper lady for a lad of your sensibility."

"You know it, pal."

"Too alcoholic."

"Which means poor contact. I thought there was something there, you know? But too wild for me."

"Past and future, I've traveled that road myself. We must work out something truer, deeper, more *valid*."

"And a little less tall too, huh Pete?"

The last time I saw my love Goneril alone, we had a valedictory boiler-maker on Third Avenue together. We had something going for each other in this sawdust bar with its swinging door; we had tradition going for us. Goneril gave me the big news in her circle. Superzen's rival superman, Mr. Gray, had challenged his competitor to a contest at who could longest hold his head under water while swimming across the pool of the Paris Hotel. You can't splice and cut here, you can't cheat by thinking of other things, such as minor league baseball! All their friends and colleagues gathered for this fierce tourney. They brought pop, pretzels, candy. Not for quick energy! Also gum! For joy! For fun! They all got up at noon so's to be sure not to miss it. They put on their afternoon best. The girls wore frocks and hats and nice white gloves with pearl buttons. The boys wore cable-knit sweaters and fine Rogers Peet shirts and some wore suits. Connie Adams—I didn't know her—wore the highest steel spikes on her silly little pumps that Goneril had ever seen. Silly Connie Adams caught her shoe in a drain. Served her goddamn right.

Well, Superzen and Mr. Gray shook hands. There is no one more gentlemanly than Superzen or Mr. Gray. Take it from Goneril. She knew them as well as a girl can know a man whom she knows very well from his behavior on the job. Those boys were unfortunate working boys, members of the working-boys class, maybe ignorant—you might say that—benighted, worried, ungrammatical at times—you might say that, too—but for patience, kindness, courtesy, and being gentlemen, you couldn't beat them. I didn't argue. Especially about Superzen. He tried. He had a heart, a soul, a history, and intentions.

Anyway, Goneril felt sad to report the news. But you've got to respect the reality principle. So they flexed their muscles and waved to everybody. Neither one broke training. Not a sip of cherry pop before the contest. Mr. Gray rinsed his mouth out. Superzen read a paragraph by Marcus Aurelius. They stood at the shallow end of the pool and let their terrycloth robes fall to the tiles. What muscles! Chest! Expansion! There was applause. Their handlers picked up robes and copy of Marcus Aurelius. Scatter of additional applause. It was shushed. They shivered. The signal! They dived. And there they were swimming under water, wriggling like handsome tadpoles. . . . It was a beautiful sight. . . . Goneril puckered up at the thought. She forced herself to tell it all. Lying and digressing will get a girl nowheres. Well, land's sakes, both boys forgot about how that pool has an end, you know? You got to consider the pool. In the struggle for life you must consider the limits. Mightily they strove, and mightily they swam, and blop! they both cracked their skulls against the tiles at the deep end. Goneril herself pulled Superzen out. It was judged a tie match.

Now the problem. This failure to gain a clear-cut victory seemed to do something to their nerves, or maybe it was the concussion. Anyway, they had bandaged skulls for "Tillie and the Sultan," with natural turbans made of plaster and gauze, but Argosy Legion Productions was looking for a new leading man. Neither Superzen nor Mr. Gray was really up to snuff. In their business, it's head that counts.

I suffered with them in their trouble. I drank more than I usually do in order to deaden the pain.

Goneril remarked, "There's an opening for you, baby."

"Huh?"

She repeated the invitation. I already talked a little like Superzen. Also I was skinny, but had good definition.

Not for me. No sir. No ma'am.

"I thought you might like a part-time job, a little moonlighting, pussycat. What with all your expenses and like that."

"Nope."

"I thought you really liked me. Give you a chance to show your love and affection—"

"No!"

"—in a businesslike manner. Approved by the group, you know? What people think is very important. I come from an agrarian culture. You can't just put down society, baby. You got to *bend* a little. Sometimes you got to *crouch* to get through life sometimes, baby. Honey. I'll coach you, dig? I'll help you along. We got a patient crew; they're really swell. There's good money in the movie business. You were great that one time. Remember? Remember? When I set myself on fire and burned to death and you saved me? Aw, Danny-boy. I like you, I truly do. Aw, honey—"

No, no, and no.

That is too *confusing* to mix monkey business and funny business and just plain business like that. I tried to explain it to Goneril, but she believed that troubling her head with academic distinctions was a sign of the corruption of intellect in our time. I felt as if I had been swimming under water. I was explaining pathological behavior to the lady who had invented it. There was a pounding in my skull. Goneril snapped her purse shut for emphasis. Okay. If I didn't want to be superman, I just didn't want to be superman.

We said goodbye fondly without plans for further social interaction within the context of our contemporary urban culture of today.

Then, having made our farewell already, we sat together in silence at our booth, doing action painting in the wet of the table with our fingers. We felt that we should not part without accomplishing something more. Goneril seemed a little heavy in the lid. "Another?" I asked.

"Don't mind if I do," she said primly, snagging the waiter by his apron as he passed by on business. She had the knack of coming awake at the moment of crisis.

The waiter returned with his cork tray and we both sighed. The whiskey searched through our pipes along with the beer in an amicable collaborative quest after meaning. "The Harp That Once Thro' Tara's Halls" suddenly came to mind as one of the most wondrous works of man. The Wurlitzer juke box had thought of it at the same time as I did. What good fortune, what luck. Goneril and I were filled with philosophic charity for all humanity in general and for each other in particular. The Wurlitzer, all lit up, played its song just for us. Then it rested. It lit down. Pensive silence in the air and chips of glass on the floor due to someone's previous error. To forgive was divine. The boiler-maker had contributed both recuperative silence and splinters of glass to civilization in our time.

Goneril arose at last. She touched my shoulder. "Don't move," she commanded me. She searched into my eyes. "You've found it. Keep it. Don't move, Dan."

Goneril went floating out into the dusk of Third Avenue toward her date of the evening. I remained at table in an attitude that may have looked like dejection to the waiter. It was not that. Goneril knew. She wanted me to have it. She wanted to find her own taxi. She wanted me to keep it. I was sorting myself out again.

Peter listened to my story as he might have listened to a client who had found a bad investment on his own. He knew Goneril better than I thought he did. He did not judge. Everyone must pay the price of his education. Sometimes, for example, those wild little electronics promotions work out. They have a gimmick and it fires. Or it misfires. Never mind. Now back to normal duty. He turned his calm green gaze upon me and made some suggestions.

During the next few days, Pete and I visited various friends of his skirt-pursuing interregnum, before he had got himself committed to his present girl. There was a gracious Indian lady with a Brahmin spot on her forehead; sinuous, sensuous, and soothing, she had much delighted him; also she was a water-colorist; she had painted him into a delicate mythological study in which he appeared as a tiger and she as a languishing and submissive maiden. "It's gouache, they call it in Hindustani," he said. Some months ago he had bid goodbye to Miss India with a dozen long-stemmed American Beauty roses, thinking of possible future kindness, and now here I was, hoping for present kindness.

"Foresight," Pete said about himself, hitching up his pants. "Besides she's great. Expert. They got like a little tradition in India. I keep an account at the florist. Give you the number. You lift the phone—roses, carnations, orchids, daisies—insurance, buddy. No extra trouble. And turns out she is *great*."

"What a woman has, every woman," I glumly philosophized, "is what we want, the real diamond, the flower opening—if we can open it. But we demand prettiness, wit, expertness instead."

He looked at me as if I were a drag. I often was. Well, both Bobb Anthony and Goneril had pulled me down in the recent past. Love and money were problems. In the less recent past, there were other problems—money and love. And the meaning of life in a society without a public, shared sense of hope. Oh, a drag.

"That's the setting, man, and you can't tell the diamond without the setting. Now this Amanda-baby, listen, she got—"

Amanda-baby had loved to undress him, bathe him, suavely raise him to joy, and who cared if her romantic Hindu sari gave off a faint odor of mothballs? The prospect of a full airing of Indian-Pakistan border troubles delighted me. "But do mothballs make you sneeze?" Peter asked. There was a spoilsport concealed within that juggler pal of mine. Her apartment had a view of the East River and the borders of the Bronx, so why fear an occasional sniff of dichloricide? What's so great about flowers to smell?

"Do, do come in, please."

The oiled top of her head as she bowed in welcome. Her hair was plaited in long braids, then done together in a sleek crossknot. First rich hair, then face appearing upwards with ample smile and strong teeth. She had a wide-moving, bowing, sweeping way of walking across her tile floors. There was tea in little cups and a stack of recent quality paperbacks. After she performed the preliminary rites of hospitality, I discovered marks of aging and hardening on her fine Eastern countenance. Well, that wasn't so bad. Why not? Wisdom of the ages and thirty-eight years—so? But Pete soon established a nostalgic rapport with her that made any interference from my personal wave length a case of international jamming. No. I left them, claiming a stomach ache, with a certain resentment for my pal Pete, the Indian Giver. She said to me. "Do, do return someday, please," and blocked Peter's exit with a thigh that had the strength and resolution of Krishna Menon through her sari.

The next day I was still unsettled. "Christ! You give and you take away!"

"Easy, boy. Let me do it my way."

"Make up your mind!"

"Follow me and you're okay." And his green eyes were fixed anxiously upon me. Pete liked to imagine himself more controlled than any human being can be. He knew that I saw the failure within which made the effort necessary. He was anxious about my judgment. Well, I had no right to expect him to save me into fun, even though he said he would. And he was my friend despite failures and troubles. But I also suspected the possibility of serious displeasure if I didn't follow exactly as he chose me to follow. He was my friend, but there was something hard in him. If I did not accept the terms on which he gave friendship, he could become my enemy. He could be as controlled and relentless in hatred as he now was in friendship.

He lit up a cigarillo. "You're going to get mashed in the dating machine," he said speculatively, "less'n you learn how to ride on top. We got to get you some experience, boy."

I did not answer.

"Sorry about Amanda, kid. Just happened is all. Sorry."

He understood that I needed to be let out on my own awhile. I shook off the leash. So on my own there was also a girl of twenty-eight, Debbie, who lived with her mother. You know those girls of twenty-eight who have cute virginal ways? She was always being shocked; she wrote coy notes signed with a little picture of a toy animal instead of her name; men bothered her though she wanted to be a lot of fun. "Like I mean I want him to really like me, the real me, first. Do you really feel you know me, Dan?" Her mother was desperate to get the real her married; the daughter tried to care. She just wanted to be a lot of undergrad fun at twenty-eight.

Cute, ten thousand times cute: bangs, round cheeks, toreador pants, cute gestures, winks, dodgings, opinions. "Oh dear, oh dear," she jigged at the telephone, winking, "but I have a visitee, Ronald. I don't think it would be polite to have two visitees, do you? After all, I have enough trouble entertaining one visitee, don't you think?"

Round juicy hips belied the cuteness; nubile, ready, with dark insomniac buried eyes ("I read a lot"). Pendulous lips and white teeth for biting: a mug, a chipmunk mug with biting equipment. A thin layer of pompous flesh covered her. A mop of the thickest hair I could remember, baby-shampooed and sweet-smelling, tumbling, doll-like, cute. Bristling below, a full large sex; and the grinning moppet facelet above. She squirted her kisses like ripe plum juice into my mouth. A muzzle of face she offered me; jokes, giggles, transports of somersaults on the broadloom.

She was learning sex by relearning being a child—pushing, fighting, biting, giggling, pulling at my hair until I atrociously tickled her. "Oooh, you're strong," she cried, "your hair is strong, you're not wearing a wig!" I growled and said something that played the game of the big bad boy. She gave a chipper cry in the agony of pleasure, chirping in the night like a bird, astonishing herself at this womanly impulse but trying to make it girlish; "Kum! Kum! Ooh I like it when you kum!"; and when the juice ran and her eyes seemed to explode, she then sobbed like a child.

Afterwards, she was cute again. "Ooh, you're strong. You're smart too—don't you think? I bet you think so. You're *sharp*."

This sharp girl, I thought, cuts others; cuts herself, too.

Though she and her mother had a nice view of Manhattan from the top of a midtown hotel-apartment, I again said *nyet*, since her soul rejected me without her knowledge. "Byesies!" she cried. "That's the plural of Bye, Dan—Bye Many Times." Finally a man her mother's age first visiteed and then married Debbie, and I wonder if she has stopped circling her *i*'s. (That's a fun penmanship, friends.)

And then there came out of my life, shortly after she came into it, a compact little blonde actress who disliked me on first sight though I also found her cute, and found her cute again, and finally she liked me a little. Virginia admired Henry James (the later novels), had graduated from Bennington, and possessed unusually shapely bones in her knees. But feeling *for* me is very important *to* me. I just wore her down to liking me. Love at first sight is usually a judicial error, reversed in lower courts; but attrition is not very romantic. I had to let myself out in my own custody. She later married a rock-and-roll singer whom she had met backstage at the Apollo Theater, whither she had wandered in order to congratulate him upon successfully fecundating a hand microphone. These pure little dimpled things do dearly love the smell of guitars and exertion. She plucked out the slivers he picked up from sliding around the stage in silk pants. I should have been warned of her finicky nature by the way she went sniffing about me, tucking her nose here and there, complaining in her finishing-school accent because. . . . I blush to say it. I can't say it. Let me let her say it.

"Dan, you have no smell."

"No?"

"No nice Bee Oh."

"No?"

"Do you *have* to shower every night? Is it *necessary* to your obsessive compulsion? Do you have to be so square? Are you running away from true earthiness, darling?"

"I'm a boor you mean?"

"Bore I mean," she said, pouting. That word usually signals an end to serious enterprise in love. End of Ginny. Nearly the end of emulation of my investment-counsellor pal.

One evening—and it shows by what small signs good friends know the end of their road together—Pete drew me out of my brooding into a nightclub with some directors of an electronics firm whose stock had gone from three to one hundred and seventeen, account taken of splits and year-end dividends, in a little under four years. Pete had climbed aboard early. These men were not scientists, they were the accountants and money-men, they were made of beef and had meaty, striated jowls, as if they had gained a pound for a point, a hanging thigh and a pendulous belly for each split, a tangle of broken capillaries in their eyes for each year-end report. We sat among red brocade and spooned up our Béarnaise sauce and drank. They were joyful and made me sad. Then they were sad and made me sad. At the tax-deductible board over which we leaned, waiters hovered, the maitre d'hotel smiled; Courvoisier and bourbon stood among our company, and the Mills Brothers, in person, were singing for us their oldtimey favorites:

I want a paper dollie
Justa call my own
A re-all paper dollie
Like I left at home

Which are not the precise words, of course. One of the vice-presidents, Charles McGannon, who had earlier showed me a picture of his daughter, Sharon, the one who was killed in the Jag accident, cried out while they sang: "Aw! Isn't that beautiful? Isn't that about the most beautiful you ever heard? Isn't it? Beautiful?"

"I'll tell you something," said Pete.

"Isn't that just the most *beautiful*? song you ever *heard*?"

"You got hold of a thought there," Peter said, living dangerously.

"Aw, I mean. Aw! Aw!" This awed man was growing richer while he tax-deducted himself one step nearer to arteriosclerosis, stoking up with cholesterol pie and anxiety pudding and guilt because he gave his daughter a car to drive the mere three blocks to campus; he was living it up and dreaming, courtesy the Mills Brothers, of the swing on the front porch of the McGannon little frame house in Albion, Michigan, where he had once been Andy Hardy, or at least Mickey Rooney. He took his thyroid tablet in a sip of bourbon, spare the rocks, and lay back to dream of the boy that was.

Uppa lazy river
Goes a friendly bum
Uppa lazy liver
With a Tum-Tum-Tum

Oh you expense-account riches of Manhattan, without which a hundred square miles would return to swamp. The souvenir alligators would take over the deserted pleasure dome at last, with their pals the Miami Beach turtles and the Atlantic City goldfish. Acres and acres of those tall buildings and intimate retreats are built into the granite stilts of tax laws, with intermeshing loopholes for ventilation during the immensely hot days around April 15. Imagine the expense account gone! The restaurants of Lexington become the abode of wild animals instead of tame beasties with lacquered hair and powdered plump arms; snakes and small critters of the field play on 52nd Street; chirp of bird replaces tinkle of cocktail piano; the cry of the heron and the gull is heard over the land. Dogwood and crab grass break through the asphalt, doing their softening and crumbling work; and vultures circle in the sky over the blackening bones of doormen. In a bartender's skull, a small bird finds perch, eating a pickled onion.

"You're not taking in the Mills Brothers," said Mr. McGannon with delicate reproach. "Your mind is wandering. Probably you're in a hurry to get home to the little lady—you married, Danny?"

"Divorced, Mr. McGannon."

"Caw me Charlie."

Peter remarked, when he saw how I had diminished during that swollen evening on the town, that maybe he should not be my Leader any more. Not for steaks on the tab of flourishing small companies with Defense Department contracts. Nor for their whiskey. Not if I was going to show up so sullen. "You again," he said, "don't you know it's Out to be socially conscious?"

"Don't you know it's Out to be In or Out?"

Touché, he made with his Ballantine-commanding fingers. Non-U. Dragsville. He agreed, but defended himself slyly. "I even supply a girl for these chaps, that's how bad I am—girl name of Freddie." He grinned. "Hm. Like I did for you." Renewed flash of grin. "Trouble with you, pal, is you don't appreciate whores. I s'pose Goneril is something else."

I shook my head stubbornly.

"I want you should meet our gal Freddie someday. You will."

It was a gloomifying evening. One of the executives wore gloves, it gave a touch of elegance to his search for pleasure; he seemed to break them off his hands, like a fop of a snake peeling for the spring season. Beneath, there was mottled, hairless skin. "Let's go someplace else—let's go to the Copa," he kept saying. "Peter, take us some place else. How about the Copa? Don't they have a good show this week, what's-her-name's husband?"

Peter studied him with his mild, focused gaze. Later that night he would juggle away the furies; he might visit Amanda or Freddie; he was educated in the ways of avoiding tension without drugs. He inspired the confidence which is eagerly given any controlled man.

Nevertheless, despite money and juggling, despite chicks and control, Peter was following a map into unmapped jungles. There, amid the screaming beasts, control would do him little good. It would do him good, but not enough. When it stopped doing good, it would leave him at the mercy of the uncontrolled and the excluded in his own heart, that wildness which could then claim no right of satisfaction. His nature was discontented, metaphysical; he could not pretend the flower of feeling was just a paper flower, kept in an envelope, put in a glass of water for fun and then dried out, shrunken, hidden. You can't trick with love and work as Peter was doing. (*As I was doing, O Lord. As I was doing.*) I worried about old Pete. Back to me.

Then came some turns for the better on the Christmas projection at the magazine. Tom Davenport was happy. He got big new Columbia Records, United Artists, Renault Dauphine, and Book-of-the-Month accounts. He kept a pair of helium-filled balloons with a picture of the Dauphine floating above him, anchored by a string to his drawers. His desk had drawers. Also one of my random mailings drew the highest percentage of year-or-over subscriptions of any junk-mail appeal in six years. Bobb Anthony smiled upon me and took me to the zoo. This time we made the seals at fish-time and lunch afterwards. Also the monkey-house. Also the people on benches. Over the second martini I started kidding him on the square, which is one of my usual defenses against the strangulation of boredom. I suggested an article for the magazine on "Dieting as the Last Frontier." It's the big problem still available to most Americans. We can do little about politics and the future, can do too much about love and marriage. He perked up. I began to listen to myself. Dieting could provide an inspiring account of struggle and failure, strength of character and social responsibility. It's bedrock Americanism, with a suspenseful triumph which makes the wearing of sports clothes esthetic, or a tragic fall into an orgy of malted milks. Technique, chemistry, physics, and Metrecal can help, but in the last analysis, it is the lonely individual that counts, fighting his desperate battle with the box of crackers in the dark hours of the night. Here lies a modern saga of determination, cunning, skill, and planning. Losing weight is that moral equivalent of war, I argued, which so many have sought in vain, in war and elsewhere.

There was a long silence.

"Too controversial," Bobb decided, with eyes hooded.

For dessert we consulted the waiter. He shrugged. We had to make our own decision. They were both equally good. Bobb had the chocolate mousse. I had the *zabaglione.*

As we walked back to the office Bobb told me that he had put in for my raise and was sure it would come through. But I had the feeling that he saw a limit to how high I could rise on his team. I was a good hitter, but kind of hell in the dugout. Just a little bit, you know, snotty? Not that it made any difference to him. I had a kind heart when you got to know me. But much as he liked me, he truly did, I was really swell, I was sort of—you know—*Jewish?* He did not offer me one of his mints and hurried into his office to be alone with them.

I gave Peter postdated checks for the money I owed him

and extracted a promise to cash them, one on the first of each month. He promised. Peter kept promises. He saw me coming up from the brine, gasping for air, my lungs bursting; but now on the beach and ready to go. "Hmm," he said. "Now let me tell you something."

"Cash them!"

"I *said*. But now I've got another idea. Take that one away. Sit down and let's talk her over."

I obeyed.

As the Bible says, "They drank and were full of drink." I made love and was full of love. But the situations are not parallel. The drunkards satisfy themselves. I hoped to be satisfied by another. "An important distinction!" Dan the Pedant said to Peter, index finger raised into the air to defy contradictory testimony. Gently Peter moved my finger out of his light, like Diogenes being patient with Alexander.

"Have a smoke," he said. "And the drunkard doesn't satisfy himself, either."

"No. No."

"Only juggling *really* satisfies, pal. But have a cigar."

I shook my head at the snapped-open leather case. "Peter, you used to listen. I was kidding Bobb Anthony, but I'm straight with you. It's not dieting. Not yet. Not for many. If politics and work have lost their meaning in our lives, we make love bear too much of the burden."

"I'm listening, Dan." His curious long lashes fluttered against the eyesocket shadows on his cheeks. His eyes lay in deep shadow, though his face looked plump and his body fit. The eyes were those of an emaciated man, withdrawn, brutalized, and watchful. I became aware again that Peter was deeply depressed and that all his comfortable pleasuring of himself, his ease and sardonic control, were merely the way he kept the lid on. He would blow it off someday. He would explode. And yet, with Peter cool and me frantic about work and love, it was he the happy one now. Happy though depressed. Haha. What a world in which keeping the lid on the major troubles means a man has control! We were sitting in Peter's high-ceilinged studio, surrounded by space and glass, within sight of his bar bells and his tumblers in a corner and the little plate of oranges by his chair. Peter sat in the one heavy chair, his knees up, his head shrouded in shadow. As it grew dark, the Spry sign across the Hudson came closer. There looked to be slick puddles of oil on the slow river. Peter stood up and gestured me toward the comfortable chair. I refused it. He sank back. He chose carefully from his cigar case, just as if there were differences among the slender cigars he fetched out; he picked one from among its identical brothers, ran it under his nose, sniffed, back and forth, ducking the rough texture and delicate aroma, delectating; and at last began to smoke. All this ironical silent activity saved his having to make ironical judgments on my state. I could get angry and say, "You're wrong, take back those words," but how could I say, "Take back that twirling sniff of your Upmann Maduro Maduro No. 4?" Smoking a cigar is easier than making up one's mind, and often does no greater harm. Peter's being a stock salesman did no special harm; his widows liked to discuss IBM and their deceased husbands with him. Even his being a salesman of flattery and candlelight dining did no real harm—it merely confirmed his place as an easer in life, an enjoyer, a backward relisher, bemused and entertained and wearing the narrowest Continental styles.

It was also a pleasure to be Peter's friend. His juggling kept him fit. His smoking of cigars was easy on the lungs. We sat in his bare, white, luxuriously large and white studio on Riverside Drive; we had a view of the Palisades and the Spry sign and the spectors patrolling Riverside Drive at night with their smaller, four-footed spectors or their skirted or pedal-pusher spectors; we talked together, like old friends, with long slow silences while we made up our minds.

"You can't live like a joke!" I nevertheless said. "Who do you think you're illustrating?"

"Whom," he said.

"Take that thing out of your mouth and answer me."

In a corner, growing like a plant, was the one disorderly element in his sparse and controlled life—the tumblers, the juggler's equipment, the weight bar for lifting and a little pile of extra weights, like fruit on the tree. Metal proliferated in a corner of his room. Peter occasionally glanced at it as a man glances at a loved woman—for assurance that he and she are still there, in connection.

"Answer!" I said.

He sucked thoughtfully, bugged out his eyes by a delicious act of inhaling, held the cigar between thumb and forefinger, the eyes retreated; he commented evenly: "All right. You want some politics? Go start a movement. You want some frontiers to conquer? Go open up the Great West. You wanna be inner-directed, pal? Go learn to juggle. I'll lend you a book. It's *absorbing*. Or inner-direct your sweet masculine self into a hot job of work and grow up to be a tycoon, why not?"

I shrugged.

"Otherwise," he said, putting the cigar back in its thumb-and-forefinger notch, "don't bug me with the impractical. Adam chose Eve because there was none other. Let's not sweet talk. Here's your problem: *now lots of others!"*

I bowed my head before this implied sacrifice of womanhood. So many of them, sacrifices and women! So much responsibility!

"I'm somewhat like you," he said. "I am sometimes thrown for a loss by my unusually clear memory."

"Melancholic."

His face twitched in a fake smile. "My only hope? Not caring very much."

"I haven't reached that stage of development yet," I said. I tried to tell him that reviving makes sense. There is dying and there is reviving. Dying happens only one more time than reviving, than at least a partial revival. That's considered a fighting chance in any gamble. I tried to say that there are joys, there are others, there were my sons and hope, there was work still to be found and done, there was always this reviving. "It would be ignorant to forget what's happened already and what is coming. I agree about that, Pete. But there are a lot of chances before it happens."

He looked at me from his shadow and smoked and gave me the chance to say more if I could. I could not say it to him. The grounds of hope are not very precise. But at least I remained silent, did not stumble, did not convince him, but remained stubborn. For very different reasons from his, I was learning to equal him in patience. Suddenly he smiled broadly and sat forward.

"All right!" he announced, conducting the firing squad with his cigar. "I don't ask you to give up your ideals. Far be it from me and on the contrary. This is the time of mucho ideals —*maybe*. That's a consumer product, too. Ideals. Are You Making Love More But Enjoying It Less? Okay, try true love, it's truer. So there's this chick—maybe!—she has like a little amble to her walk, I like her myself but there's this little problem, she. . . ."

Always thinking, Peter would always first consider the problem in this Barbara he was considering for me. Peter had no hope of anything but making out. He knew how to make it, how to make out, but no trust elsewhere. Ready or not, he was never ready. But rover, red rover, Dan could come over. Barbara had a problem? Come on over.

On that long evening of balked conflict with Peter, watching the reflected river lights blinking in his window and listening to the soft rush of traffic down the highway, watching Peter and listening to him, trying to answer him with answers I had not earned, not yet, perhaps not ever, I bit my lips and clenched my fists with intention to solve Barbara's problem, whatever it was.

And mine. And mine.

Why so hasty? I was in a hurry.

Why so opposed? I did not want to go Peter's way, though it seemed easy for him and my own road lay confused under salt floods. I wished to go out building sea walls against grief and I wished to laugh in Peter's face.

5

My friend Pete, as you can see, was unwearied by his semi-productive exertions on his friend Dan's behalf. His form was good, and in this game of girl-watching and girl-finding, it must be the form that counts. I say "semi-productive exertions" because my failure to make a true, tender, chipper, joyful connection was mitigated by the incidental brute socializing which may often accompany basic rejection. Is that too formally stated? Okay: I made out often if not well. Parties, receptions, openings, and other social duties came to fill the idle hours in my harassed thirty-five-hour workweek.

Let us now imagine together how I might halt this round. There came to be a real Barbara—let us imagine an imaginary Barbara. For example, standing in the IRT subway on a velvet early evening at the West 96th Street-Broadway stop, we would meet another friend of Pete's, that very Barbara girl, let's say, and she would put out her gloved hand to me in dramatic formality, with a thousand and eleven violins playing beneath the trains and the lights blotting away the shadows beneath her eyes, and we would make soul contact at once, right there, with the scenery watching, no? "I'm a window decorator in a department store," she would hoarsely murmur, because you got to have dialogue.

"A kind of advertising writer. Shake." Because one good line of dialogue deserves another.

She could have described herself as an astrophysicist and I would not have listened very closely at that moment. I was absorbing her presence through my pores and trying to keep from laughing for joy. I was being tickled all over, head, heart, and higher regions. I don't believe in love at first sight, as I've already patiently explained, but this was sheer perception. You know—Keen Analytic Intuition meets Joy in Life. That's not love at first sight, friends. That's just plain good sense. What worked itself out of her glintings, her glancings, her shy turnings of her ankle as she chattered on, her challenging smile and her fluttering lashes, was this: she was a genuine girl, a womanly girl, a girlish woman, one of the rare surviving examples of that beautiful species: just the Barbara for me. She had a frail fringe of hair fallen from the coif over her neck (careless) and a fringe like the shadow of bangs combed across her forehead (deliberate). And she was old enough for laughlines about the mouth, but no frownlines; laughlines up from the corners of her eyes, but no frownlines; just a delicate tracery of thoughtlines, consider-lines, feeling-lines. The top button of her blouse was undone. Joy-lines and maybe-yes lines. I could see one freckle floating on high proud flesh. She was tanned from weekends at the Hamptons, and as she laughed, I could see where the tan ended just below the freckle, and then lace cut off my prying. *Barbara.* Richly brushed hair and creamy skin and full laughing cheeks. And a high curve of rump under her skirt. And witty? Very smart. Smart-lines around the eyes.

The workmen rebuilding the station were packing it up for the day. They took down their caged electric bulbs and disconnected their drills and let the dust settle. They heaved by us like infantrymen being led to the rear for a rest.

Peter observed the debris of excavation going on in my heart and murmured, "Dig We Must for a Growing New York." And whispered, "Boy."

Barbara was wearing a double-breasted and belted trench

coat, as if trying out for a British spy movie. She had a small, flushed, round, lascivious face and stood with heft, it seemed to me, secure on Barbara's green earth, which in this case happened to be the cemented subway station. Two people meet, they like their way of standing, they make quick decisions: *connection:* we all three knew it. Somehow, in straightening out the introductions as we waited for the Seventh Avenue Express, it came clear that she had never been married, but that she knew people who had been married; in fact, her best friend had children, one each by two unsuccessful marriages. "Lucky Eunice! I'd like to have a child," Barbara said in a rush of heavy feeling.

"Well," I said, "then let's take the Local."

In the ensuing laughter at my small joke (Dan is suave! Dan makes joke!), my friend Peter ducked out and Barbara and I did take the local train down to the Battery, talking all the while over the roar of the subway, deciding, bantering and bumping, deciding, tricking with our bodies, deciding, strolling in that little park at the jag-tooth end of Manhattan, deciding; and later, at dusk, we had a snack of roast beef sandwich followed by Jello. This was all our stomachs could manage in their agonies of anticipation. "Hell, let's take a cab," she said.

We had decided. We returned to her apartment by cab, rolled about on the carpet, and fell into various postures that you are supposed to fall into only under the stress of strong emotion, and sometimes not even then. Well, I did like her. I felt grateful that I could still invent these games anew after my season of salt in the wounds instead of on the ripe tomatoes.

Wouldn't it be nice and romantic like that? A true Manhattan romance? With rumble of subway, sudden conviction, and clever luxury in the body? I sometimes remember it that way, and there really was a soar of wings in the air about us.

But it wasn't quite like that, in earthly fact. The wings started out as pinfeathers. Pete old pal simply unloaded her on me by taking me around to her place. Sad way to meet a girl. One of Pete's discards. But that's how all his girls finished, in the discard pile, and so the fact is not a severe judgment of her. Even the oranges he juggled eventually hit the floor and split when they didn't turn electric blue and fuzzy in the heat of the vacant days.

Anyway, I did really meet her, it doesn't matter how. Love at first sight is immature, but instantaneous perception is, well, love at first sight. What comes after the beginning is what matters.

Barbara betrayed, at odd moments—we come now to quibbles—a cautious calculation in her large, lidded eyes: *What would he like now?* She sought to please, overeducated in love, but she was sincere. This is a popular commodity in Manhattan. "I sincere you loverly," the boy says. And the girl replies: "I sincere you very much, too." There we were, Prince Dan and Princess Barbara, gallantly writhing, breathing hotly with all the rush of nature in our ears, lord of perfumed, heaving breasts and queen of flushing, tense, gambolling body—next thing you know, we could be Mr. and Mrs. D. Shaper, third house down the block in Forest Hills. "I sincere you four children. . . . I sincere you a barbecue pit. . . . I sincere you duodenal ulcers, a Corvair, and long blue evenings before the teevee. . . ."

Barbara carried the divine essence of wife like a perfume on her breath, just as I exhaled the essence of husband—that longing for completion in the accepted mode. No experience can teach us, nor age do anything but kill us. Such as we have no faith in statistics. We listen to our hopes anew each time. We like kids.

"You do? I do too," she said.

But we were both also running scared. One black marriage was twisted like a burnt-out cell into my heart, a cold romance with Peter and who knows what else was a part of her burden—we had our doubts built into us, too. I even dared to guess that love might not be the final station on my way. We were not quite alike. She was longing for love, that girl Barbara —a husky healthy long-legged Village orphan with a father high and dry in Virginia. Despite her large bones and flushed cheeks, she had obtained a delicate education. She had prepared herself for the perfume on her breath. Love, O Love; Hope, O Hope. Miss Whosit's, Skidmore College, Hollins College, graduate year in Paris, and she buttered toast nicely.

And she *enjoyed* hand-squeezed orange juice, hand-squeezing it.

When with improving fortunes I looked for a new apartment, something with more dignity than my furnished room, which was known as Alimony Studio, it seemed convenient to pitch my camp near Barbara's digs off Sheridan Square in the Village. The upper West Side was my port of entry into the second adolescence of divorce. Time to cross over this way-station. The past was folding into the past; the future seemed friendly, filled with Sunday afternoons on which I would neither kill myself from the George Washington Bridge nor iron my shirts. Like my loan company friend, like Remedy, who had found a new wife—a nurse at St. John's—I could now send out my laundry and forget my housekeeping skills. That was a phase of evolution, up from the struggle in detergent toward a white-collar humanity, which I was pleased to pass. My raise came through. Bobb clapped me on the shoulder, exhaling congratulations; Rita Rooney breathed hot Dexedrine at me; I could imagine the end of my debts.

Just before moving down to Christopher Street, I attended Remedy's wedding. His bride was an orthopedic nurse with strong wrists and back; she used to work in a sauna bath, Remedy told me, but met a lot of intellectuals; apparently the remedy for concupiscence had been steamed into her. All the frazzled cotton-dacron lads from the Alimony Studios were there. Some of them I had only seen in the basement, doing linen and undies. We crowded into the meeting room of a semi-kosher restaurant on Broadway at 102nd Street. (It also served tacos and tequila. Changing times.) A Tammany judge performed the ceremony and insisted on making a little speech: "Concrete experience is the mother of invention. Plaster walls and sublet floors do not a domicile make. Permanence, a ninety-nine-year lease, a land contract, including air and mineral rights—these are the very foundations of our American family of today. You who have suffered unhappiness in the prefab-home environment are all the better qualified to cement a lasting—" I decided the judge was in the building business on the side. Turned out he was especially interested in a crosstown freeway, and left a lot of leaflets on the table next to the punch bowl. Paving. Urban Redevelopment. Concrete and cement.

"Who's that? Who's that?" Barbara kept asking as we drank pink champagne. I wanted her to know my fellows in this world of inequitable taxation. I whispered in her ear, loving the flutter of lobe against lip; I muttered deadpan, but each man's trouble was mine. They were my buddies.

"Loan company manager, two kids in Scarsdale, Mental Cruelty. Television camera crew chief, five children in White Plains under age eight, Catholic—legal separation. Art Director, no kids, two analysts. She got him by the—"

"Who's that?"

"Fred Lazslo, I told you about him. Wives north and south. Marries for pregnancy, divorces for adultery. He doesn't hurt much."

"Doesn't he hurt other people? What about the children?"

"Yes. I meant he doesn't feel it much."

"Who's that one?"

"Don't know him. Does sheets, shirts, and underwear and scrams back upstairs. I think he's a weeper. He goes back to his wife within six months from today."

"Maybe she won't have him," Barbara said.

Remedy traveled about the room, filling our glasses and slowly turning red and urging us all to kiss his darling orthopedist. She wore a woodsy scent. Her gown must have been left in a cedar closet since her last wedding. Remedy pulled me off into a corner with him. "Oh if that wife o' mine could only see me now!" he whispered, wild-eyed.

"Ex," I said.

"Hunh?" He meant his former wife in Michigan. "She'd *plotz.* She thought I couldn't do anything without her, and she wouldn't do anything with me. Not anything that counted. Nothing I mean *real,* man. Had to have my teeth fixed from grinding 'em. She thought I was finished. Well, it almost did. Finish me. So now look at Stella over there—man, I tell you, she's Insatiable City."

The judge had to go to a meeting of the Transportation Committee, Washington Heights Tamaya Lodge. He told us all to be sure to have automobiles, only way to get around Manhattan, gonna cut a fast road through town pretty soon, clean out those Spick gangs lurk in Central Park, so long now, fellas. It had been nice getting to know a fine bunch of non-Spanish Caucasian-type voters like us. The party began to break up. A couple of the boys said they planned to do their laundry tonight. A Bendix, hunched and stately with its churning belly, should have stood up there with Remedy and his bride as the matron of honor.

Me, I was moving on. The magazine was treating me like a member of its happy family. I had had a nice clap on the back from Bobb Anthony for discovering a new way to dun elapsed subscribers. Shame. You got to get at the guilt. Guilt is always there, lurking in the nasal passages. You have to nurse it along. You approach it from unexpected angles. Icicles in the heart. Fluff on the mind. Whispers. Insinuations. You can't afford ignorance. You can't leave yourself in the lurch. If you didn't have high standards, you wouldn't have subscribed in the first place. (Of course, some of them may have subscribed in order to receive the free Art Linkletter record.) There is so much you need to know in these troubled times. Our readers will be the first to hear if China, when Elizabeth Taylor, about outboard motors. It's a weekly Conversation Piece. Over coffee. With klatch. When you drink your Martini ("tini") and you ask for a refill ("sweeten it"), what else you going to say, chaps? Art movies? Bertrand Russell? The revolution in house design?

Plenty to say if you are prepared! (Art movies are invading. Lord Russell is important and so is yogurt. The ranch-type with picture window is changing with the changing times; now it comes underground, with lead walls, and no window at all.) Plenty more! Discussion points! Insights! You can't afford to bore your friends, it's not friendly. More and more distinguished people study our pages carefully for clues. We wanted to share it all with you, you, but you let your subscription lapse and hurt our feelings. . . .

"Dan," said Bobb Anthony, "how many days is it till Christmas?"

The bonus! I thought. It came to me in a flash.

He put his hand on my shoulder. Well, not on my shoulder, but on my desk. A warm breath of gumdrops. The thought was there. That last letter—the one about our hurtie feelings, signed by the Reader Service Editor (Subscriptions)—had nearly made him cry. We had discussed what to name the R.S.E. Uncle Bill? I was kidding. Jack Taylor? Too folksy. Timothy Parkinson, Jr.? Effete. We kicked it around. The next morning Bobb came running into my work area, shouting, "Dan Shaper! Dan Shaper! Dan Shaper!"

"Yes, Bobb Anthony," I replied, rising slowly from behind my kidney.

"That's it! That's it!"

The name we finally made up for the Reader Service Editor was mine. Bobb's creative idea of the month. It took away a little of the reality I was striving for, but in my rising phase I could afford it. With the help of true love, laughter, and my immortal soul, I might still keep things sorted out.

I survived my first winter in Manhattan. There was spring with Barbara. Summer would find me a survivor—feeling friendly toward the world—and so it did, and so I did.

Barbara did not exactly convince me about living in the Village, but when she found me the apartment, I fell into it without further elaborate thought. She decorated for me—slightly-used Danish and Amsterdam Avenue American. Hell, a place to live in is merely a home. And my raise wasn't *that* good. I merely increased the percentage of delinquent readers who came to know shame for leaving our magazine in the lurch just when we wanted to increase the advertising base. ("Aw, come on, subscribers—you can't afford to be without accurate poop on the momentous steps that lie ahead—and Cary Grant discovered a new cure for mental illness—and will Cuba, won't Egypt, can't Africa . . . ?") Barbara and I took to lounging and scrounging and loafing together (try it on good-as-new Danish furniture, friends! cricks in the back!), going to parties and movies, doing nothing and making love, tickling each other and trying out different things off the furniture, on the broadloom, in the crickless bed. It was pleasant and easy, and when it seemed too marital for me, wounded as I was in my recent conjugal Iwo Jima, I simply stayed away from her for a day or two. She understood. Understood? All right, bided her time.

Okay. Unlike a wife, she was even warmer when I returned. She cared, her heart throbbed for me, just me. Like a wife, she knew how to bide her time. In sex she made no pedantic demands for performance, unlike my former wife, who often had an expression on her face as she turned off and said goodnight: "Okay, you got a B-plus this evening." But Barbara did not grade me; she *cared*. Consequently I had the sneaky, Oedipal satisfaction of imagining my former failure like a space shot orbitting about us, swinging rhythmically through the universe and squeaking back by radio: "A-plus! A-plus!"

"You're still reacting," said Pete. "Watch out, you'll be caught."

"I'll be careful," I insisted.

"Caught," he said. "You notice that black look she gets?"

"No."

"Like spikes. Black as can be."

"No."

"You'll be caught, buddy."

"Careful," I said, though those A-pluses did bemuse me. Once or twice, of course, I had my doubts ('To doubt is human'—Dan Shaper, *circa* 1960). For example, I discovered Barbara's eye watching me across the pillow, figuring out how to do good to me. A cold eye, it seemed at the moment, encased within this glistening triumphant female body, sleek for action: a coldly doubting eye. Well, who doesn't take an occasional B-minus? And what woman doesn't wonder and worry?

It's true that the weeds of pride and ambition and revenge often sprout in love's garden. It's true that the past grows wild. (I'm an organic farmer.) But if the plant is strong enough, the weeds will disappear.

Such weedy moments, such wondering and worrying aside, I drifted contentedly. We ate jam sandwiches and I smeared clover honey on her breasts and licked it off, thereby achieving an effect of honest old-fashioned humor; also it led to noisy tickling, happy struggle, giggling, shouts and silence. We took showers together. We rode the great ride. We refreshed the dream of pleasure, and ran dripping through spacious rooms. She kept flowers everywhere. And all this—pleasant thought—was temporary! I could stop when I liked! When we wearied of closed rooms, we strolled without aftergrouch on 8th Street, stopping to buy me a shirt or her a book, sitting still for a beer, aged thirty-little and twenty-much. Barbara's flesh occupied her bones more intimately, courtesy of the nourishing distractions of love. Her breasts grew larger, as if she were about to give birth to me. I even, discreetly, stammering, found myself saying, "You haven't—we haven't—a *mistake*?" No, it was merely the sweet ease of flesh that changed her. Her slender crest of ilium, that bone at the hip, was covered by a silken pad. Looking upon her, a friend of ours said, "She's happy! That's what it looks like!"

I felt proud enough to do nothing about it, just to be delighted and proud. I now believed in more than rescue of the capsized. I began to suspect the possibility that, for whatever reason we were put on earth, we could also create joy for others and for ourselves. I had my life organized. It was easier to go out to see my kids. I was even making a little more money —doing my job well.

In my new grace, Bobb Anthony was taking good notice of me, and Barbara and I spent a long summer weekend at his house at Southampton on Long Island, out there where the Brooklyn accent thins out, nearly disappears, and the bleeding madras shorts on the men come from bloody India. Bobb's most recent wife, Caroline, had handsome heavy shoulders, a slim body, a perpetually parted, astonished mouth, and an accent that economically used *w*'s for *r*'s, *l*'s, and *w*'s. "Hew-wo theh," she murmured, holding out a soft paw, "I've hehd so much about woo." She also sometimes used *w*'s for *y*'s. She carried a parasol into the sun when she greeted us. No freckles allowed on her shoulders, bare though they be.

Authentic bleeding madras impressed me; so did finishing-school girls, ladies who once were finishing-school girls, and the habit their husbands cultivated of floating martinis on swimming pools. An Air Force Reserve major named Steve, recently married to an aging heiress, spent the daylight hours in the pool, paddling about with glass in hand, swaddled by a rubber raft and thinking about Caroline Anthony; in the evening he floated into the house, supported by boredom and anxiety, and wore a girdle because his wife had loved him for his figure when he had been a Regular Air Force man. He was pooped and impatient to be a widower. *Money money money*, as the poet says, *water water water*. And each martini with an olive olive olive. New York society, as everyone knows, is a small town, and my pal Barbara, in the days when she had been Peter's Barbara-Girl, had also known Steve Schmitt. They had all known Bobb and Caroline Anthony. Like many unhappy people, they kept busy knowing people. Caroline and Bobb were both impatient to serve him—Bobb because of Caroline, Caroline because of Steve. There were complications.

"He has this drinking problem Steve does," Barbara said, "but he's charming. He doesn't work and he abuses her in public"—she was speaking of his wife—"only words, doesn't hit her, not in public, but I've seen her with black and blue marks. But I think he only hits her when they're alone. At least I never saw him swing."

"Savoir-faire," I said.

"He's part Russian, I think. Holy Russian. They're on her shoulder mostly."

"What?"

"The marks. It's not tooth or nail. You know, *love*—he hits sometimes, I think."

"A true White Russian gentleman would consider the cut of the dresses and hit her in the belly, where it wouldn't show."

"Don't be sarcastic, Dan."

I heaved a great sigh.

"And don't give me those sarcastic yawns, either."

It was discouraging to see how Barbara took on the manner of this world. She was adaptable, she was willing, I grew indignant at her generosity in such moments. She was in conflict with the world without being in the least rebellious. That's a paradox, but not really. Well, stubborn Dan, I heaved my great pretentious objectionable sighs. There is always that miracle of privacy and intimacy—flowers and eyes and the slow turmoil of pleasure—and then the loved one politely looking through you. Discourages me sometimes. But the privacy is real and so is the society. I say to myself: Clunk, get that through your head. Nevertheless, I felt encrusted and heavy with salt, like a discouraged sea beast trying to climb the evolutionary ladder. I was impatient.

While Caroline led Barbara off to show her the room where she would stay, Bobb put his arm around my shoulders and said, continuing something he had in mind about me: "The stee-ratosphere, rat-rat-ratosphere." Christ, he was drunk before lunch. What was bothering him? Steve? "Not just class, but quality." He was talking about the magazine, just as if it were Monday morning. He lowered his voice to conspire with me: "We'll hit the top, Dan, you help. It's prostitution buddy like we're doing to a class or quality product. *Cheapening*. That's what I was called onto the Board of Directors for. We're making it cheap." Happily he clapped me on the shoulder. "We'll hit the top! Can't miss with this quality product we got!"

"Nice place you got here in Lung Guyland," I said.

His elation departed. "Caroline found it. Long commute, all summer. Stay in that apartment all by myself."

"Wanna play?" asked a hoarse littleboy's voice. It was Steve. He was a White Russian patriot on his first wife's side. A Cossack by marriage, he had kept up his interest in freeing Holy Russia. He was a thick athlete, like Bobb a former pilot, but I believe now mostly a friend to Caroline. Three years ago he co-hosted the Russian Easter Ball, but he hadn't worked much since. "Hey, you guys want to play croquet? Barbie? Dan? Where's Barbie, getting smashed already? Where's Caroline?" Steve used his on-the-job training as an honorary Russian refugee to co-host the official croquet match.

Barbara and I did not play, but we enjoyed the late afternoon coolness on the green behind the house. There were motes of dust in the air, floating. There was sun and salt, sky just above, sea just away. Here on this island lay an arrangement of acreage with outsize houses, reduced servant quarters, summers of leisure in which the circular driveways were filled with Alfa Romeos, Mercedes, and sporty little cars—few chauffeurs; changing times, but still that summer lassitude, luxury, routine of pleasure. Not too far away—potato farms for Manhattan.

I wanted to take Barbara for a walk down the road, but she felt that this would be impolite. Since she had met these people with Peter, it was a heavy time for her. She had stayed here with Peter and was now with me. She wondered what they said. She tried not to think about it, but she knew how they talked and she thought about it. She needed to have her own way now and I gave it to her. Despite everything, despite every strain the click of croquet balls and the beeping cries of the players somehow pleased me: summer leisure on the playing fields of Southampton. There were prizes and bets and traditional jokes. No wars would be won. But time could be passed. When Steve bent at his home wicket, showing a wide twin acreage in pale pink flannel, Caroline stood behind him as he waved his matching pink mallet back and forth between his legs. He was measuring for distance and velocity. "You're a big man, Steve," she drawled, like the girl in calico in the first reel of a Western, "you're a big man and y'move like a big man."

Steve straightened up to smile at her, bent over again, eased his great haunches on either side of the mallet, and, wiggling, sighted along the peen to ball, wickets, and pole. Caroline watched; Caroline held her breath; Caroline made a little airy pout of admiration, eyes fixed on the troubled expanse of pink flannel.

I felt sad. Show me a contented man and I'll show you a blind one. But why should Bobb Anthony's agonies infect me? He was singing to himself: *Scoobie-doobie-doo.* He liked jazz, but he was contemplative.

Steve bent lower, the flannel was stretched into tight horizontal wrinkles, he swung the mallet in its practiced arc.

Scoobie. Doobie. Doo. Bobb was praying for disaster.

Clunk!

Steve's ball shot through the pair of wickets and hit the

pole. There was a little clatter of applause. He glanced up with his boyish, free-Russia face and smiled with gratitude at Caroline. She had inspired him. She was his inspiration. Without Caroline he might not have made that daring flight through the dusk over an uncharted twenty-two inches of grass.

Bobb, still watching his wife and Steve with shy concentration, whispered for my ears alone, "I'm a big man, too. And I move like a big man." But he missed a try at zonking Steve's wife's ball. He glanced back at me with bitterness in his heart from the middle of the court. It was lumps in the grass. It was Caroline's not noticing his bigness any more. It was her heart's going pittypat for a man whose hobby was the Grand Duke Nicholas. It was fate, a statistical projection, like the graph of the magazine's growth. But of course, my letters had started to draw and the statistician was wrong.

While Bobb played out the match with the others, Caroline and Steve stood humorously fencing with their croquet mallets near the home pole. Caroline looked lovely in nubby blue silk pants and a blouse which revealed her shoulders for all, plus Steve, to see. Steve was a fine fencer, like any honest Russian, though a bit heavy on his feet, like some Russians. Caroline managed to change her clothes six times a day, for each of the six seasons of the day—lounging pajamas at breakfast, sport or riding clothes for after, bikini for swimming (a deep, dimpled navel), lunch frock, afternoon sport corduroys, cocktail dress, and evening display to please Bobb, Steve, and the rest of us. That makes seven, but she sometimes missed a stage. She looked lovely as she bent to the children when the servants brought them in for an afternoon kiss, full of grace. Then Steve and she went on fencing, giggling furiously. "Don't chip the mallets," Bobb pleaded. "If they once get out of balance—"

"There are extra mallets, dear," said Caroline. *"En garde!"* With one knee bent in nubby blue silk, she challenged Steve. Bobb kept missing shots, straightening up and sucking a fresh gumdrop, and missing his shot again. He finished last. Everyone congratulated him on a hostly self-sacrifice. He brightened up at the bright side of things.

On the way back to the house, Steve walked with Caroline and Bobb tried to talk office with me. Boss relaxes. Boss has good time and friendly chat with favored minion. Boss suffers bravely, provides inspiring example. He laughed over-loud when he mentioned Tom Davenport and Rita. "Classic case, huh?" he demanded of me.

I avoided answering because he did not know about Frederika, and that made it an exceptional case.

"But Tom does a good job, and hell, I'm not narrow-minded. Doesn't interfere with his job, nor hers either, by God. Good men, both of them."

This grammatical confusion showed a flash of insight, but he did not follow it up. A pause of death. The loose eye wandered toward witty Steve, transmitting electricity into supercharged Caroline. More courage on the way from Bobb.

"Glad to see you're getting along better now too," he said with a significant wink which took in all the Western Hemisphere, possibly except for Cuba, plus Barbara. "Man isn't happy, doesn't do a good job. Happy man—good job. I hope you won't take that amiss. Now you're happy—well, you saw the revised 18-month projection. No coincidence, believe you me."

He kidded me not. Let's face it. Between you & I, the thing was, a happy man does a better job.

"And hell," he said, rolling both eyes piteously toward his wife and Steve, "what Tom and Rita proves—'cause Tom is not your make-out-type fellow, he's quiet—is a married man . . . is a married man . . ." He swallowed hard. ". . . is a married man can still get in his lumps." Bobb was growing a bit distracted and needed a drink. In the golden light of the sunset Steve and Caroline were comparing sun tans on their forearms and then on their collarbones. "So don't delay," Bobb finished, leaving me to figure out his thought at the highest executive level, and trotted past Caroline and Steve into the house. "Got to make sure they brought the ice, the ice!"

Barbara came up and held my hand. We watched him up the steps, flopping like a seal. He was a fat man and he moved like a fat man.

Barbara and I spent a chaste weekend because there were so many house guests, there were so many events, and the party had a "theme"—Roman Festival; we were deafened by foolishness, blinded by idiocy; we could hear the lion groaning in the cellar; we both got a little drunk and, like a good suburban married couple, barely knew each other. One of the servants had to be stationed near the lion's cage to keep the drunks from getting mauled as they stumbled down to play kitchy-koo with the nice cat. Bobb would rather have had a nice floppy seal, but Caroline made the animal decisions in this house. I have no idea how long it took to get lion smell out of the house. The king of the jungle had considerable distinction in the world of scent. It stank in all directions. Like little green headless imps, the long-necked air wicks stood on futile guard duty about his cage. Our host's small chow, which had a sensitive nose, like mine, whimpered miserably all the three days we were there. I know it was not envy of the larger animal, for involuntary sounds of anguish came to my lips, also. Barbara confined herself to saying "shush" when I sought to discuss the subject. I feel duty-bound to issue an adverse report on the humor of the weekend: "Better run over to the city to find a Jew for the lion." "*Ars gratia artis*—we should be in pictures." "Yes, lionized, harh, harh!" In fact, they didn't even get the gentlemanly *C* for wit. Well, that's high life for you. A more thoughtful lady took the theme of the party as History Made Real—an effort, like charades, at improvement and adult education. Now she knew more about the glory that was Roma than she ever could learn from magazines, books, movies, and other such impersonal sources of learning. "Of course, travel is different," she said. "It's really. . . ." But then she couldn't think of a synonym for *broadening*. "I mean it," she said. "I love history, it's so inneresting, I mean, you learn so much, I mean it's a fun activity?" she asked me.

I assured her she was on the right track.

The great beast prowled his cage belowstairs while a little combo played "Jeepers Creepers" on Saturday night.

> Jeepers! Creepers!
> Wheredja get those eyes?

He roared piteously and stank mercilessly. He got those eyes in captivity, in his Work Area. He got that smell in the same place.

On the last night of the weekend, some of the accumulated carrot sticks, pickled artichoke hearts, and raw cauliflower we had all ingested began to take aphrodisiac effect. There was boredom and fidgets, empty rattling through the halls and mere busywork in the bedrooms. There were deep currents of trivial feeling which crossed official boundaries: we were well-acquainted, over-acquainted, without necessarily being friends, as if bound together by a lion-hunting expedition; so much mustard gaminess all around seemed to move the guests in ways that croquet matches, drink, and lion-teasing no longer satisfied. Steve read the weekend edition of the *World-Telegram* and brooded over a new victory of the Soviet or Interloper Russians, which implied a defeat for the genuine Russians of New York, Hoboken, and Paris. It wasn't Bobb's fault, but Bobb grew fidgety under Steve's glare. Our hostess, Caroline, had become as pensive and nervous as Goneril on the way through one of her lonely drunks. Like Goneril, she needed more from life than roles in some of our finest pornographic films and good grades in graduate school; or more, in this case, than a Georgian house in Southampton and a secure place in the social and cash registers. Caroline snapped at her children and the servants took charge; she seemed not to recognize the lion, but the lion, king of the beasts, merely yawned; Caroline took a Dexedrine spansule, stood next to a tall blue vase of fresh flowers, and watched the sunset all alone on the veranda, a morose pout on her lovely snub-nosed face and her pale blond hair all tumbled carelessly about her shoulders. She had a fine pair of shoulders. It's sad to see a lovely hostess with fine shoulders so sad.

Plump Steve, waterlogged after floating on the pool all day, ignored his own wife and mooned after Caroline. Unshipshape, he lurched across rooms with a heavy, stubborn dimness in the eye. He was not so dumb. Caroline needed him and he needed to be needed, as the B-24 had once needed immaculate, eagle-eyed Captain (later Major) Steve at the controls. He slid a cigar into the tall blue vase of fresh flowers and cigar butts. They stood together on the veranda with the cigar receptacle like Tristan's sword between them. Caroline and Steve remained immobile in the sunset, mutually electrified.

Caroline's husband, Bobb, morbidly haunted the two of them. He asked her if she had said goodnight to their kiddies. He asked this in a pushy voice in front of Steve. He failed to consider the needs of Caroline and Steve because he thought a great deal of his own, thinking these needs were for Caroline because he had no steady knowledge of what they were for. I believe he did suffer, however, from a hurt, continual longing for all the children by his three marriages and one paternity suit settled out of court. He referred to the children as his "gumdrops."

Caroline had a tomboy, pug, low-bridged nose drawn in by pouting; Steve a small snout which had stopped growing while the rest of his face thickened in the Russian phase of his career; Bobb, our host, a pretty, straight, but awfully delicate nose for a big man. I notice details like this in times of crisis. Later that evening, after dinner, a crisis occurred. Leaving their noses out of it, here is the story of Caroline, fat Steve, and the slot machine: The . . . Story . . . of the . . . Slot . . . *Machine!*

(And still the story of Barbara and me, looking for our proper place together. Barbara and I were involved.)

I begin. As souvenir of one of his divorces in Reno, our host had carried away a genuine slot machine. Painted in carnival colors, with a malevolent, mushed, cast-iron face, it waited in a closet on spindly legs, like a hypnotized monster from the movies. We stare into the face of the machine; it is trying to tell us something, if we only understood. ("For the sake of science we must awaken it into earth speech by feeding it the food it requires, Doctor Serendipitus. It is our duty." —"Heh, heh, heh, Yas, Hm, yas. Give it a nickel, please, Nurse Wanda.") In a secluded closet off the children's playroom, it stood on its weak, spraddled legs, with a bottle full of nickels on a little shelf beside it. Well, not exactly a bottle; it was a chamber pot, bought at great expense at Serendipity, which is a chic little antique and junque shoppe on the East Side of Manhattan. There was this slot machine, there were these nickels, and there was this sign above the chamber pot full of nickels: "Honor System Prevails." In Bobb and Caroline's house the idea was that you play the machine for the sheer game of it and replace the nickels in the pot for the next hobbyist. Does this bring back memories of that nutty intensity which prevails among genuine no-honor-system players? No, it's a sterile risk. Cutified by Serendipity and no real expense of nickels, you can hide in the closet and pull away to your heart's content.

Well, Caroline, our host's wife, went back through the playroom to jerk the machine after the children were abed. And fat Steven, the former pilot, followed her. And her husband accompanied them in spirit, though his jealous legs would not be moved. Anyway, he was needed at the Duplicate Bridge table. He went on flipping gumdrops into his mouth from the little saucer at his elbow. Steve and Caroline had left the doors open. She was wearing a tangerine Roman robe; her long pale hair was down over her fine shoulders, admixed with the tangerine straps of the gown; she laughed through her little nose. They left the door of the closet part-way open, for air, and you could hear the whirr and clank of the machine, and her small voice saying, "Two cherries and a raspberry. Whoops. A raspberry, two lemons. Ooh, missed again. A lemon, a joker, a raspberry." She pronounced these words *chewy, wazbewy, wemon, jokah*. Occasionally there would be a crisp tumble of nickels and she would squeak for joy, "Three plums! Three sweet plums!" (Thwee pwums!) "Mmm, I just *wove,* to feel the *pwums,* coming *in!*"

Just strolling, I strolled back to see the machine which gave so much delight. Who knows, I might also see the pwums come in. I don't play Bridge. Barbara was downstairs, communing with the lion. I was wearing silent rubber soles, alas. Alas, the closet door was ajar.

Steve stood closely behind her as she played the machine. His pants were down around his ankles. Her skirt was pulled up and looped over the hairy forearms of the Air Force major (ret.), who clasped her with active interest. Honor System Prevails, I thought; the degradation of gambling. This way, with the nickels supplied gratis, there is no risk. The machine was set so that she won with three cherries. And Steve, the former war hero, stood with his pants hobbling his feet and his long black woolen socks held up by garters on his plump calves and his head against her back while she bent over the machine, as if he were a curious doctor listening to her spine. A Cossack by marriage, he rode to the slot machine. He never once let go. Neither did she. She giggled and bounced and pulled the arm of the machine and swayed and tilted and flipped and bounced and flipped some more and tried to help it into a winning score. She fed, fed, fed the machine its nickels; and in, in, in they went; and her small-small voice squeaked with delight when there finally came a little slippery silver stream in the trough.

"Oooh, jackpot!" she cried.

But before this time, of course, dismayed Dan had turned away. My stomach hurt.

I went belowstairs to join Barbara, wistful at the lion cage, watching it sleep. The lion stirred and grumbled like a grandfather. "It dreams," she said, "it's having sweet dreams."

"Shocking," I said, still shocked. "Terrible. No shame. Waw meat, gwistle and all."

"It's the animal nature," she said, alone and dreaming in the stench of the beast, pure, lovely, and entranced. Abruptly she seemed to awaken from her lion-brooding. "But I know you, Dan, you've got something else on your mind. What's the matter?" She shivered and shook her head. She was trying to leave the lion for me. This beautiful effort deserved to be rewarded. Upstairs, at the bridge table, Bobb was popping gumdrops—cherry, lemon, lime—into his mouth. His wife and Steve were being unspeakable.

"That slot machine—" I began.

"It's a pretty cute decorating idea." Out of the corner of her eye she was still admiring the lion.

I stared. Party madness. How hard it is to tell the truth, to hear it! How hard to see truly! We stumble over fact, wandering through the party, but then what do we know? Not very much, even about ourselves, though the great party is intended to reveal the world to us, open us to the world. And yet it's easier to speak the truth loudly and badly—to be a Truth Trumpeter—than to make the truth count for understanding when we care about the consequences. The only truth that matters is the one which takes us down the road a piece. All the rest is mere signifying, mere gossip, mere party bravery. . . . Something like this went through my head. I could drown, I could chortle. Which? All right, chortle—cockcrow on the dungheap! Leave Barbara out of it. Not fair to Barbara otherwise. Wait for unity until unified. Barbara was obedient rather than moral. She accepted the fabric into which she was woven. She took it because it happened. If I were critical of Steve and

Caroline, she would have been gently indulgent of me; if I were indignant, she would have said firmly, though frightened of making me angry, "You have no right to judge, Dan—do you?"

She was frightened by danger, not committed to judgment. She would not see the connections between the dizzy horror of this life and the unclosed distance between us. Certainly it would make trouble. But I had no right to disturb her now by indulging my outrage. And so I avoided disturbing Barbara's distrait party humor; I said no more. It's not necessary to be true to oneself at a weekend in the country. It's not even necessary to be true to others. Barbara should enjoy her lion without gossip from me. I could bear the burden alone. The slot machine was no leaping monster of the apocalypse, corrupter of the middle-aged. Caroline and Steve were the necessitous who are the mother and father of invention; it was a case of low-level weapons testing; they tried to bring reality into their lives with the help of nickels rudely borrowed, as best they could they twied. Oh poor chaps. What silence, what silence.

When at last I told Peter about it, he made a face and said it was a filthy thing—"Ah, you're right. Offensive at the very least. Poor taste, I agree. But you know? They're trying. Let me tell you something—" But then he put his face near mine and began to laugh. "You feel *shame*? For *them*? Okay, I'll share it with you, pal, share and share alike." He shook his head delightedly. "Well, you're right, that's one way. Shame. Hm. I knew a girl like that, she had a funny down-homey name, Irma she was, she learned something from the animals." He grinned. "I mean the animals midtown, the delicatessen animals, y'know? Say, how's BeeGee?"

I did not answer.

"They are *trying,* pal. Irma was like that, too. Pick up on it, will you? *Trying*."

Like Peter, Caroline and Steve juggled in their awful privacy. It did them not enough good.

And so the seasons passed. There was no war, there was a succession of world crises, and Barbara and I were patient. She got used to my facetiousness and my mean, blue isolations. I learned to ride with her occasional chattering edginess, her dread that she was anybody, a speck in the Manhattan air, nobody. We could put up with a bad weekend now and then. Peter no longer frightened her. The idea of Peter only frightened her a little. She could laugh a little and let go with the people who had known her with Peter. My sons, when I went to Cleveland, felt that I was climbing out onto firm ground and wanted to stand on it with me. Barbara and I had time and health on our side. We were in a condition to wait for developments.

6

At Thanksgiving time, Barbara made a little banquet for me, not for friends, just for Barbara and me: a cool house to blow on desire, hot food to satisfy the stomach, and not too much of it. But her smile, her voice of ease and control, its burr of Virginia. But crispy celeries, sweet butter, hot rolls, and delicate Rock Cornish hens, with bones so sweet that I wanted to take them in my teeth and crunch them into twiggy morsels. Ah she knew the ways of the body. And we talked. We floated in fine conjugal ease. Outside there were fragments of Manhattan flying every which way, toward Sheridan Square and toward nothing; in our warm nest there was nesting warmth. Barbary, is there a snag in all this velvet? Aye.

Look: everyone has to watch out for what he needs. We need, we love, we even sacrifice for another; but we are always watching out.

Let us aspire to love. Let us remember the way of the world. When we soar into those loved and loving eyes, we see the soul looking out. And need stares cunningly through the soul which looks out. Which does not make the loving and tender soul less tender and loving.

But when we seek perfect communion, we sometimes find unconscious cunning.

Well, why not? She'll find it in me, too.

One day after Thanksgiving she remarked that I must owe a lot of invitations to friends who had had me to dinner or drinks, filling the idle hours of Manhattan. Sure, quite a lot. Well, wouldn't I like to ask them up to her place. Sure, why not? And thus repay all those debts? Yes? Get them off the old conscience? (See the half-aware cunning which looks out of her innocence and generosity.)

"But I'm not really so worried by debts, Barbary. They like having me." I thought of Goneril and Debbie and so many tense ladies with the elastic line of girdle showing through skirt and the double-track of fret between the eyes. No, I didn't need Barbara to pay these debts for me. And Peter looking over everything, my devious pal. No.

"Yes, but still it would be nice."

"Yes, okay Barbary, okay, nice."

"Okay, a week from Friday?"

"Okay."

"Okay. Leave it to me."

At the time I was interested in other matters, two French films I think it was. I'm a focused fellow. I did not listen well enough. Those okays battering back and forth should have warned me. "Let's make the double feature," I said.

"Let me have your address book. I'll send out the invitations, okay?"

I handed it over. There was a small qualm about letting her see for herself how few irresistible, fascinating, and delicious girls lay interred in my book—just names. But Barbara and her stately pride—she would be neither jealous nor smug. As it turned out, she was glad to invite them. She invited them all. She invited everybody, couples, singles, male, female, the long and the short and the tall. And her friends. And her friends' friends. She wanted to return our obligations in a formal way. But she wanted more than I saw; the party gave more than I was willing to give, it offered too much.

It was a large party, with lots of ice, liquor, and food, and a heap of umbrellas outside the door. The heavy sky above the Battery was not moved to rain, it merely lay across the blue like a log, but that's how big the party was—enough to provide a heap of timid umbrellas. Peter came without Freddie, thank God. He had been seeing too much of that far-out old pro. It occurred to me that maybe he was interested in Goneril, which would be a big step up from Freddie. Finding all my acquaintances from Alimony Studios, from the magazine, gathered like this—from Peter, out of the dating machine, from the network of family and Army and college days, all tied together in Manhattan—made me a little drunk. There were too many connections. There were too many short circuits. Plucked from their places on Madison Avenue or in the towers of Central Park West or Upper Broadway or the Village or Midtown, these worn, subtle, experienced faces came to remind me of how fast history rolls over onto history, tide upon tide, in this port and issue of hope, our Manhattan, this heaven of pleasure and impertinence, where every man abides amid abstraction, craves significance, is showered with the dust of glory and the threat of immediate ruin. Men met women and started anew for the thousandth time. Women met men and tirelessly asked the same old question, *Will you bring it all together?* And showed by the glint of cruelty in their eyes that they knew he would not.

Goneril, for example, arrived on Alabam's arm, gracious

and elegant, and from that possessive and finicky way she took Alabam's arm, I learned something about him: he was homosexual. Goneril's high face was dimpled with pleasure. "Such a surprise," she kept saying, "such a surprise." She was talking about me, not about Alabam.

"She asked iffen Ah'd come along," Alabam explained. "Ah got off, you know, boy? Ah got me another appeal."

"Glad to have you!" I uttered like a host.

"Mah new counselor—he sho do know how to appeal. Appeal, 'peal, 'peal, evah since last Christmas."

"Great!"

Goneril touched my chest, dithering. "Listen, I've got so much to tell you, honest!" she said. The rib cage gave a hollow, thumping clang where she attracted my attention by means of her mailed fist.

"Oof," I said.

"Why y'all doubled ovah lak that?" Alabam asked. "If'n y'all been injured, Ah got jest the counselor-at-law."

"It's *yo*," Goneril said, "in the singular. How many times do I have to tell you?"

Contritely Alabam hung his head. I straightened up and put in my elbows for better defense. "Go on," I said.

"Well, I hardly know where to begin. I'm being analyzed!" I made a cautious symbolic grunt, also signifying, *Great*. "My doctor," she added coyly, "he, my doctor, a tall very handsome Pee Aitch Dee in psychology, he's not really a *doctor* doctor, he says I should give up the game—"

"What game?"

"My—uh—*star*dom."

"Our flicks," Alabam explained cheerfully. "Ah say she ought to 'peal for a stay a exe*cu*tion."

"But how would I pay for my analysis?" she asked.

She was asking a rhetorical question and paused. I had no solution. I made a rhetorical shrug.

"If'n he's a real imitation doctah, let him give y'all an

answer a that one," said Alabam. Being out on bond seemed to act as a stimulus to conversation for Alabam.

"Willikers," I said.

"I don't know. I'd have to go to Hollywood and work in that trashy television. I just—don't—know."

"Gosh."

"Do you know any other way how a girl can live, Dan?" She meant other than performing in stag movies. There must be something. But the mind boggles. Alternative positions in commerce or industry involve a descent from the glamor of the silver screen.

"Well, at the moment—" I stated simply.

With her face mooning above me on high, I could imagine no worthy post for her as a secretary, salesgirl, or receptionist. How could she make the leap from psychopathic success to neurotic anonymity? Where lay respectability when the laurels of both art and commerce had already crowned her bared forehead? It would take a doctor with at least a Pee Aitch Dee or better to open up these questions, and even he might require years of close study at the portals of perception. Fortunately he was interested in her case and gave her a special rate, the same price *his* training analyst charged his wife. It was the professional discount, he explained to Goneril, and she in turn explained to me. "It's like buying chairs through an interior decorator."

"Lak gettin' yo film from Mexico through the Mafia," said Alabam. "Yo got to deal with the politicians."

Every man finds his own portion of truth in the flux of his own experience. Bless yo, Alabam. Amen. There were new guests arriving, shouting happily at their station in our space. I had duties.

"Already," Goneril said, "Dan, you hear me? Already I'm learning how to be more spontaneous."

"Swell."

"I have honest impulses all the time, Dan, you hear me?

Ooh, there's Peter over there. Dan—it's so fine to see you again like this. I really like it. I do. I regret I made you jump so many hoops. Today I like it, Dan! You just let me drop, and now just when I'm making such progress in my analysis, it's the quick kind, you know—?" She paused expectantly. I recalled the drape of her body over my shoulder, my broken glasses, the pieces of my comb in my pocket. A new assault from behind, someone slipping a small damp hand into mine—Debbie. The weeks fly like years in Manhattan, rapid, full, irremediably gone. "I really like it now. I do. I *do*. Seeing you," Goneril said, one eye casing Debbie, who was moving her hand in and out of my abstracted grip.

"Excuse me, I have to be nice to company. Say, how's Superzen?" A distracted host, presenting the guests to each other, I did not stay for the reply. "Say, here's my friend Debbie—"

Debbie was pouting by this time; she had also paid us a visit. By coincidence she too happened to be in analysis, but with a genuine doctor. There is this distinction among the girls of Manhattan. Some have M.D. doctors. Debbie, being Debbie, had deeper considerations than health on her mind. "It's so important to be mature, don't you think?" she asked me. "No, I mean seriously. Really. I mean really mature, not just staid."

"It's vital."

"What do you think, Mister—?"

"Alabam," I said, introducing them.

"Mister Alabam. Do you follow the psychology of politics?"

"Yes, all the time. Listen, chile, yo like to be maybe a starlet? Ah'm a big-time maker of special films."

"Yes. Yes. Say, have you heard how the Russians got that way from how they were treated as children? They haven't grown up? They're aggressive? Hostile? Immature?"

"Swaddled," I said.

"Yes, that's right! Now I remember! They've been

swaddled too much! I've always had this secret yen for self-expression as an actress, Mr. Alabam."

"Ah think we jes' might show y'all how, Miss Debbie."

"Yo," said Goneril.

"You mean educational? documentaries? television? or true feature-length-type stories?"

"Wal, yeah. They sho am. Innerested, honey?"

"I'll tell you frankly, Mr. Alabam. I'll just come right out and say it. I don't suppose you're used to my kind of girl, but that's the kind of girl I am, truly. I've been raised that way. I've heard all about you film producers who prey on young girls you meet at parties, and so I'll tell you the truth. I'm interested."

As I slipped away, I heard Alabam, deeply concerned, declaring to Debbie, "We've got to stop swaddling them Roosians *at once*. But first, Ah think maybe y'all should see the type film we make."

Ah, New York! Friendship, love, power, contacts! People from all over! The United Nations! Negroes, Jews, Christians, Mohammedans! Musicians! Gerontologists! Italian counts with tufts of gray hair brushed back over the ears! Actresses and models! Painters! Action painters! Zen Buddhists! Action Zen Buddhists! Policemen with graduate degrees in Sociology! Patrons of the arts! Pederasts, some of them queer! Others just killing time while they waited for Garbo or Marlene. Alley-way thugs on principle and pornographers from Hartford! Pals, buddies, chicks, chicklets. Babies, honeys, loves, dads, pops, and distinguished tourists. Many others! Oh life begins at Manhattan soirées. So I lounged about, enjoying things, while capable, nervy Barbara managed her evening. I crowed with laughter at my friends' jokes. I wished Frank Sinatra records didn't always have to be played at parties, but my motto is, Live and let live, even people who say "swinging" for anything besides barroom doors and porch furniture. There was a peculiar elation in the air, and if I put my little finger on it, I felt that it would rise like an invisible nipple to my touch.

But where? It was like mood music in fi so hi that only a dog's ear could make it out. I twitched, I growled, I prowled amid the elegances of Barbara's six years in the same apartment. And yet there was something else—a soupçon of a soupçon. Someone or something was a joker. Peter kept to himself, sprawled in a chair, his long legs arrogantly stuck out in everyone's way. We barely spoke. Goneril waved, but stayed away from him. Something wrong. I felt a little like poor Bobb in Southampton. But no painted slot machine on spindly legs. And Barbara cared for me. Something, something. I went from Sheldon Kurtz to Debbie to Ronnie van Holst to a musty, irrelevant Mr. Carrington from Columbia University (General Studies). He was building his character around a pipe and smoked rum-scented tobacco. The answer lay some place else. The question was unasked.

Barbara disappeared with Goneril into the bathroom. Was that the question? Alabam had left Debbie and gone with them—*why*? I tried the door. It was locked. Why? I didn't know the rules for such a case, being just an immigrant from Cleveland, so I took my hand from the doorknob. But I worried. The sense of Barbara with Goneril and Alabam behind the locked bathroom door fretted me just below the reverie line. I couldn't quite see why. I looked to see if Peter was with them, but Peter was alone in his chair, dawdling through a book. He didn't usually look at art books at parties. He didn't usually hide like that. I am a careless driver when I have a few drinks in me, so I don't drive, then. I took my hand from the doorknob and thought I'd think about it later. I was fuddled and went grinning like a party fool to the Mr. Carrington of City College: "I hear you're interested in James Joyce—"

"Yes, my field is Anglo-Irish. Joyce, James Stephens, Yeats, the Irish renascence, the whole *megillah*. I'm at NYU nights. I was just explaining to, ah, Debbie here"—tamp, tamp

—"how I don't think a doctorate should be required for tenure if you're making genuine contributions in your field—"

"How?" Debbie asked.

"At least I personally don't care a darn about it, ah, ah—Debbie?"

Peter was grinning in his chair, with his eyes glinting and his hand relaxed and spent, two fingers holding a cigar. He had let the book fall. I had neither the answer nor the question and the bathroom door was locked on Barbara, Goneril, and Alabam. Was there some sort of protocol for such cases? Why was Peter smiling?

Fret and fuddlement. Dull static below the reverie line. But then the bathroom door suddenly opened and three trim characters came filing out, one by one, first Barbara, then Goneril, then Alabam with his fatty sly mug. They had had their talk and why worry? Anxious is enough without adding worrying into the bargain. I took a drink to raise the sugar content of my blood. There they were. All okay. Barbara okay. Goneril and Alabam. Alcohol affects the blood sugar positively. It absolutely did with me. No questions, no trespassing, no fooling. I had delusions of non-persecution. Laugh when you feel anxious is an adequate working rule.

I poked about, chuckling for hospitality's sake. "Yummy," Debbie was saying to Mr. Carrington, tilting toward him and inhaling, "a man who smokes good tobacco goes straight to my heart." She was showing him heart. He could make out the shadow between small, squeezed-up breasts. That was probably heart, but he looked away. "Blow some smoke here," she said. "I love it."

"It's aged in rum," said Mr. Carrington of Pace Business College. "I got a car, I got my own apartment." Now he dared to look back at her and the shadow that was surely heart. "I'm sure I'll get tenure next year."

Debbie thought she had him now. And she did. She cast upon him the blazing, adoring look of the girl who wants to make out with men by taking them over. She sought to be feminine. Like a missile-launching crew she sought it. Debbie was working on Mr. Carrington, it was all systems go, and her X-ray eyes generated a peculiar hot sterility as they burned toward Mr. Carrington. Modestly I held my hands over my genitals as I crossed the field of her operations.

Barbara's scotch arose like an invisible extra brain in my brain. I stopped thinking about the three of them in the bathroom a few minutes ago and Peter's odd smiling watchfulness, and thought about Debbie and Mr. Carrington, and stopped thinking about them and just thought about sweet floating nothing. Ah how rich and soft to have no dreams. What vague dreams when you have no dreams. I was the child magician again, nourished by suckling, heavy with milk from Heller's Instant Booze on Greenwich Avenue. My mouth was surely a little slack. I felt like Superzen with his concussion that interfered with reading, but in compensation gave him double vision—what every true-blue philosopher wants. I was a little stately and sleepy and awake. My little finger was happy about things. It and I allowed as how (generous small finger!) we might wait until everybody had left and then give Barbara a hand in cleaning up. After all, it was partly for me, else why invite all the folks in my address book?

They started away. Obscurely compelled into an idiot grin and ducking bows, I found myself at the door, saying goodbye with a drink in my hand. Goodbye, goodbye, goodbye. Somehow anxious again. Still worrying.

"Bye, Dan. Congratulations. I hope you're very happy."

"So long, Dan. She's a lovely girl."

Goodbye, Peter. Goodbye, Alabam. Goodbye, you former Air Force major. Goodbye, lion keepers and lion hunters. Goodbye, Goneril, say hello to Superzen; goodbye Karen and Ella and Rosalie. Who now, soft friends? Mr. Carrington and Debbie. Sheldon Kurtz and his split self. He had planted his jokes like Johnny Appleseed, but no one watched them grow. They did not grow. Bye-bye, all.

"*Ciau,* man." (Sheldon's head waggily working.) "You go pretty fast, keed. What's the date?"

I thought to answer, "Today's the twenty-first," but then all at once it came to me. I realized why this evening had a familiar sheen on it. I was as beamy and balmy as my plump friend Remedy in the back room of the formerly kosher restaurant. I understood the obvious. I caught up with everyone else in the world: *This was my engagement party.* Without my knowing it, I was supposed to be married next! Oh, ow, ouch. My brain jiggled up and down my ears and shook out a message to prudence: *Look what's happening!* And prudence sent back a rush telegram: *Use your head! Rush hour this time!*

Without my knowing it, Barbara had staged an engagement party for us?

For us?

For *me*?

There was a sick lurch in my belly. Control. There was a rackety pounding in my skull. I forgot to ask what she had been doing, locked so long in the bathroom with Goneril and Alabam. This other scheming was an important matter. First things only. Control. I would wait it out. Sour ebbtide of drinking. My heart was ready to jump, but I waited.

After the guests had all left I glared at Barbara across the debris of food, drink, and ash; surrounded we were by ruined cheese, wisps of expired cigarettes, half-finished glasses, emptied bottles. Someone had forgotten his umbrella. Someone had left his wristwatch in the bathroom. Control. Barbara lowered her eyes beneath my silent accusation. She was upset about something, but I let myself take precedence. She submitted. Her face was flushed and miserable. So she admitted. She was wrong! Scheming! Wrong!

Then I put the accusation into words. How outraged I was. How I thundered. Her lip quivered. It is said to be the lower lip which quivers, but in her case I believe it to have been the upper. And her nose twitched. Tears on the verge. Guilt! She had no right to maneuver me that way. She felt guilty for having misled and misinformed poor Dan Shaper—me, just a small child of divorce from Ohio. As Barbara yielded to shame, I grew mighty in wrath. I scowled, I was filled with indignation, I was cold as ice. I arose, majestic and blind. I may even have lifted a finger in the air, the index finger, indicting her for callous manipulation of a tender new bachelor orphan.

You know? She did not answer at all.

I helped her pile the dishes in the sink for the cleaning woman the next day. Then I bid her adew.

7

Days passed. Weeks. I sulked in my tents for a while, alone amid that skinny Danish furniture. I forgot to water the plant. Its leaves turned red, turned brown; it perished. Barbara continued to be present in my head. What we used to say to each other returned to pass the time in our absence from each other. Clear: I missed her. I wished that I could learn to juggle, like Peter, and thus put the universe to rest in perfect circular motion, perfect balance, perfect stillness. Instead I tried to forget Barbara by remembering her badly; how, for example, she seemed uninterested in my past or present, my children, job, or family. What I was to her was what I was. Isn't that egotism? Isn't that just needing me? Isn't that something bad? Finally one day a few months ago she had asked a question: "Do people's noses get bigger with age?"

"Mine will. Cartilege, hey?"

"What does your father's nose look like?"

"His ears are bigger'n mine, too. And there's hair. He's seventy, he thinks. He has no birth certificate. When I'm seventy

I'll have a big nose, hairy ears, but maybe a birth certificate'll keep down some of the cartilege."

"Oh. This is one of your facetious times."

"I'm sorry, Barbara. You caught me by surprise. Interested? He was born in a town called Kamenetz-Podolsk, but not exactly in the town. In the Jewish section. The ghetto," I finished smugly. "Those who stayed are all dead now. No relatives." To answer the look of horror on her face, I said, "My nose will probably thicken considerably, beginning soon."

"Oh, Dan, you don't have to make fun of everything."

"I'm nervous about your questions."

"Do you care for me, Dan?"

On the radio, I heard the music to:

Now Uncle Sam wants yew
Says put away that git-tar

and here beside me Barbara was asking, "Tell me you care." The earth hurtles out toward the infinite, civilization is in fugue, the lands and peoples have lost the reins, the end is surely coming; only we don't know if it's for one at a time or all together, and that's essential; still we want to be loved quickly, loved absolutely, truly, now; we must be loved now, right now. Will our noses have time to thicken? That depends. There's a statistical possibility. On the salt flats of Manhattan, with its airports seeping into the bay, an inch or two a year, its tunnels of pipes and wires, its piled-up, shored-up ruins of skyscrapers, its radar stations and fuzzy towers, Barbara was trying to make love do all the work, so put away that git-tar. But I cared.

"You know what?" I asked her on that day when she had finally asked me a question about something other than Barbara. "We have to learn to get excited about something else besides love in this country."

She smiled. "There's always money."

"Naw."

"I mean success."

"Well, I suppose. But it's all mixed up with love."

She put her finger in her mouth and, looking cute, said, "The race problem. Unemployment. The hydrogen contest," conceding them to me for the sake of harmony. She smiled humbly. "Do I recall correctly?" Then she looked at me as if to say, You must have it your way, and that's pride. And it was. And therefore I took her to bed. And then all the pride, questions, doubts, and dreads were stripped off—her exquisite shivers when slowly I awakened her from behind, her white smile, turning over to look at me with the points of teeth showing.

"Wait. Wait. Wait."

"I'm with you, Dan."

"I'm with you, Barbary."

Swaying over her, looking into those two narrowed eyes, shivering myself with the miserly pleasure being cautiously portioned out—Barbara was difficult, she had a high edge of frigidity—swaying and swaying, looking, looking. . . . She was not frigid. She was frightened and unsure. Pride. No pride. Forgetting pride. The smile widened, the eyes became wide and fixed; and I possessed this beautiful creature with her eyes gradually opening, then squeezing shut until she cried out, and we were aware of nothing together, not even oblivion, until once more I was awake to the beautiful edges and joinings of her body, the silver edge of eyelid, the quicksilver precision of lip to skin, of ear to head, as if she were fashioned for an accuracy in the flesh because accuracy of spirit is only known in saints who love no single man or imperfect creature, but all men and imperfect creatures. She loved me, I loved her. That was enough. It may not be the whole truth, but while it was strong in me, I had no other, and felt no need. For pride, no pride; for fright, certainty. Now it was I who wanted to give all the questions merely one answer. The single answer is persuasive though it dooms us to nothing but love, sharing of the act of sharing, and the final dismay of our hopes in love.

Why not give up to ecstasy? Why not give up later, if need be, to the passion of failure? Why not just ride my anger with Barbara now, try Debbie again, try Goneril?

The hydrogen contest and fallout, the race problem and integration, unemployment of millions and the mis-employment of nearly everybody else did not hurt me in the bone, though they might dissolve the marrow. They made me scowl and fret, they made me shrug and try to be funny, glib, persuasive, deciding. When I was not thinking, I could dismiss them. But Barbara hung me up without an answer. The pain in my pride and gut, my own step-by-step hopes for the present and future were what caused me to flag. Surely it would be better to do battle for humanity elsewhere, but we do not choose our battlefields. We do not head for the frontier to seek proof of manliness; we find ourselves at the frontier for good reasons, not psychological ones, and because we are there. History and fate, hunger and the need for a home have put us where we are. Within the pressure of our common humanity, we choose the options the times give us. Even seeking to make our own decisions, we must follow the needs of our bodies if these decisions are to be true ones.

Alas, my caution and pride. I was suddenly doing silent battle with Barbara. Better battles might be fought elsewhere, wars more worthy. I felt restricted.

Still, she had no right to make plans for me and give parties announcing what I did not announce to her. She had no such right. Ultimately we listen to our secret histories. For my pride, the plant was dying in its pot. The top leaves were brown, but the thick underleaves still had some dusty green juice in them. I peeked at the leaves as a lonely man peeks at himself in the mirror; I went to the sink for water and forgot why I was there; I drank water I didn't need and the plant was perishing. With pride, too, we try to do too much work.

Sometimes, like any man who lives alone, I fell into a stuporous wild depression of an afternoon, late, after work, when the sugar goes down in the blood and before I took my first evening gin and tonic, and I wanted to cry out to some girl passing in a cab: "I love you, love you! Love *me*!" At such times Christmas carols made me weep and I flew with a nutty smile up and down the slopes of Riverside Drive. I wanted to wire to this unknown beauty of my life: "Join me! Come quick! Hurry! Marry me!"

But which? Who? Goneril in her own pornographic madness? Amanda? Debbie? Ella? Karen with her impossible floating isolation? Barbara? They too had their late afternoon blues, but we could do nothing for each other. Thank God for the grassy slopes to climb, the gin to drink. Not that I drank or climbed all that much. Just enough to open my pores to sweat, to put the sugar back in my blood. But sometimes, released, sweating lightly in a bulky knit sweater, with a drop o' sugar circulating in my veins, I wondered if maybe Barbara . . . Barbara . . . if I hadn't been too hard on a human being. Didn't I also try to work things my personal way? Force things to go my own way? Yes, I do and did.

I saw little of my friend Peter during this time. We were too much alike, but he made out much better at it, juggling, joking, and getting rich. Once, to kid, he rented a liveried Bentley to take a girl to the New Yorker on upper Broadway for a revival of *Sunset Boulevard*. "Open the gates," he intoned like Eric von Stroheim, "without Peter Hatten there would *be* no Coprophil Electronics Corporation." It was a new issue he managed. The girl in the car didn't matter. He was making out, doing okay. "How's my Barbara-Girl?" he asked me. "You still on the outs, fella?"

Like a shy swain, I sent her flowers. We went through a stiff and careful evening. We began again, but I made it clear that I would not be pushed. We started again, slowly this time, from our full stop of misunderstanding. Have I mentioned that she had a father in Virginia? I had already asked to meet him. I know what you're thinking. All right, I *asked,* I asked again,

I wanted to make the trip. We would go to see her father together. That everlasting trip by the young couple to meet the parents. The rock didn't get tired, but surely Sisyphus did. We would eat home-cooked meals, though Barbara had no mother to home-cook them. The trouble with looking for either adventure or security is that you are likely to find them. Here we went again—*love.*

Barbara and I floated in the conviction of being important to the world because we cared. We were on our road to Virginia to present me to Wolbrook Jones, "the father." On the way to the West Side Terminal, the cabbie told us that both Franklin Delano Roosevelt and Jimmy Dean still lived, the one chained in the basement of the White House, the other in the basement of MGM Well, we get to be important any way we can. The cabbie had found inside dope. But what if the White House doesn't have a basement, only a utility room with washer, dryer, and gas-o-matic furnace? What if MGM is built ranch-style, with no private cells?

On the plane I fell asleep, sleep crept like a fluid up my legs. I went into idle gear. I remembered a snowfall over the Cuyahoga Valley of Cleveland fifteen years before, and my first important girl, her name was Winkie—she played the piano and had fat solid flesh, like good mild cheese—now she had daughters who hogged the telephone. Here I was still courting. Time takes its good time passing for me. I was still getting ready to be polite to a parent.

How can I tell the truth about what happened next? I think it is my fault, but I am no martyr. I think it is Barbara's fault, too. Is it that I could not be all things to one girl? Or that she could not take enough from me of what I could give? Or that—?

I would like to tell the truth about myself: quick, decisive, slow to learn from experience, filled with afterthoughts, obsessed with truth, self-centered—whew! I overvalue friendship and love; I am also sometimes indifferent and not interested.

Hell. The only way is by letting the story tell it. The story of Peter, too, since we are halves of the same apple. (Which one has the stem?) Let me trace the way back to Peter, to Laura and my sons, to Barbara. And then go forward if I can.

Peter to Dan: "You think writing copy makes more sense than selling stock?"

"Naw!"

"Well then—it makes no sense!"

"All right! Everyone knows that!"

We were shouting at each other through the forest primeval. But it was Peter's whitewashed room. Cigars, a bottle of Courvoisier, Scarlatti on the hi-fi, our ancient companionship together. We were shouting together, as we had for fifteen years, through the war, school, and marriage. About the Meaning of Life.

I yelled on: "Superzen, Goneril's friend, is just trying to improve himself, too!"

"All right! You agree!"

Peter made a little flipping, juggling gesture with his hands. Fingers flopped upwards. Tip of tongue showed. Eyeballs white. "Then if we spend most of our waking hours in foolishness, why not finish off the rest? The part you assign to love? Why not? Why not!" he screamed.

I thought of the boil on the neck of Mr. Gray, Superzen's rival, God knows why. He too was anxious. Peter had his boils inside—the outside bland and easy and working out with the tumblers. He was sore at me about something—about Barbara. Now I begin, only *begin* to understand someone I thought I knew like a brother. (Question: Who knows his brother? That's an expression, I guess.)

After studying judo and Sarah, whom I never met, Peter had taken up juggling very seriously and passed his hours with oranges, two, three, four, five. A faint smell of orange juice in his apartment. It reminded me of new babies. Split oranges—a bachelor's babies. But he persisted; he had a talent for balance and neat circling. He always wanted to juggle one more, one more: that one more was always the important one. Unlike judo, juggling requires no other person, just another orange. He said to me: "I want to learn to be, ah! patient. To keep the ball, ah! rolling. To balance and wait! You understand, pal? I like too much to hurry, but I don't like it. The important thing is to lose desire."

"Does it help?"

"Age helps. There's a girl name of Freddie helps me. Let me tell you something: I'm learning. Funny thing, though, not desiring doesn't help. It only means the reason is different—in a hurry to get it over, in and out of life. Not the same as losing desire."

Smell of orange on his hands. Superzen too had vocational smells on his hands.

And Barbara. What more can she do than love? Like the juggler, the lover has limits beyond which he cannot pass. Despite love, there is more.

Beyond the window where Peter and I sat in abrupt silence lay the black solid pack of river. It was invisibly moving toward the sea. There were droplets of spray and rushings of water beyond what we could know from our perch in darkness in Peter's studio; there was a salt harbor breeze up the waterway. Peter and I averted our eyes from each other. We looked at the Hudson; we smoked cigars; we each saw a different river and breathed a different smoke. There was a long way yet to go. That long way of truth and revelation, ending our friendship, could not much longer be avoided.

For the moment, even in stiff silence, I was still grateful. Scrupulously he had been my friend. I had been his friend.

When I lost my wife and job, I lived for weeks with no strength in my upper arms and shoulders. I could barely lift them. I felt the muscles invisibly atrophying with an accelerated age, although in fact I could do with them whatever I needed to do. When I lost the woman I loved to another man, the pain filled my belly and below, a heavy shifting drawing in the sick innards.

I thought about rousing myself, but to think about it made the weakness stir again in my belly, made my shoulders hang in shreds. I could not decide to be alive once more.

I had constant trouble cleaning my glasses, the film forming and re-forming each time I wiped them. I drank a great deal of milk, like a homesick child, but my digestion remained poor. I suffered through the long night and then slept feverishly until noon.

I thought of all that in Cleveland, visiting my sons. The scene of my death—the scene of failure. And the boys growing up with suspicion and love compounded. Family matters. Back to Barbara.

How hard it is to tell the truth; even when lost in grief we construct, the eyes roll, we try to build a mathematics that takes account of anarchy. It was as if I anticipated the disaster with Barbara, but did not recognize it. I thought I wept for my sons, but perhaps I was merely preparing myself for sorrow. I went to Cleveland to see my children and saw what was happening to them in a house without me. On the airplane back to Manhattan, tears began to form as I sat stiffly with the lunch tray in my lap; they rolled and rolled down my cheeks; I was sitting propped up, tied in, politely bawling with an attack of public melancholia. The stewardess, biting her lip, stood jiggling in the aisle and asked if she could do anything. They must get lots of emergency flights for funerals, I thought, the honest tears still flowing. "Yes, someone died," I said, weeping, weeping, lying and weeping.

She got me an aspirin and a Benzedrex inhaler in case my ears hurt on landing.

You see, I make a joke of it. A poor joke, but mine. And it wasn't really like that. Wrecked by Barbara and Peter. And yet it was not all jealousy. This girl Barbara made me feel tenderness. I understood what it was—at last!—to want the best for someone else besides my children and my own self. The last night I was with her before that trip to Cleveland, I awoke to see her peacefully smiling face on the pillow. I felt my own head clear into ease. When she lay on her back like that, her naked breasts spread, flat, and loose, I felt pity for her weakness—the inevitability of age within all that twenty-eight-year-old girlishness. She would open herself for me, taking and grasping for life; but now she was merely drowsy. Someday the veins on her hands would be sharply bluish against the delicate skin. She would try to lose weight too many times. Time would bruise the back of her hands, those breasts, that eager smiling gaze.

I drifted toward sleep, buried against her, my mouth seeking hers. She was willing to love me as I was.

Later, dimly half awake, cramped, I kissed her arm and turned on the other side.

Then I dreamt I was again in bed with my wife, but not as it had always been, anxious and driving, a competition with her hips. No. I cared enough. I cared intelligently. Peacefully smiling above her, I had gently insisted, "Not like that, honey," and she had obeyed me. I distracted her with caring. And we made love like kindness. And in that dream she said *Yes, like that, thank you.*

I awoke with my buttocks back to back with Barbara's. Touching in this comical, tender way, I had to accept the fact that asleep, dreaming and wishing, with the sheets still mussed by the slime of love, I had returned to my wife. Unreality can banish reality. The nightmare triumphs by an impossible transformation.

Barbara awakened a few seconds later and asked why my face was wet. "I'm crying for happiness," I said.

Love wants to be deceived. Therefore she did not tell me she knew I was lying. There was a black look like spikes in her eyes. Where had I seen that look before? Silently we clung to each other, first for comfort, then wriggling like fish, intermingled, interpenetrated, convulsed, drenched, seeking to create light by exchanging fire. When at last we fell away, we could hardly see.

8

Now, at a certain midpoint, I need to gather up what I have learned thus far. Having no power corrupts; having absolutely no power at all corrupts absolutely. In the crisis of meaning which afflicts us, in a time which avoids the prime questions of life on earth (we amuse ourselves, we wait), I like others sought to find the meaning of life in love. Religions, wars, and brave jousting seem impossible. Therefore we put too heavy a burden on love. I counted too much on it, I still do. So did Barbara. So did Peter, in his way. So they still do. We all thought to free ourselves into the air, wafted on wings of love, but found ourselves mere earth-bound jugglers again. We toy with freedom like do-it-yourself hobbyists. Comes trouble! Comes joy! We seek to give it up. Why? The heart in this world becomes a machine, a crank, bare works burning against itself, love and feeling, smoke and hurt, nothing. It cannot run on its own volition. Therefore we seek the fuel in oceans and mines, winds and mountains, below ground and in abstract space; therefore we find salt flats and wind-swept deserts. We stumble and rub salt into our open flesh.

PART 3: BARBARA

"Friend," said the lady, "that for which you have suffered I grant you without delay. You shall be refused no longer. You will be refused nothing. I give you my love and my body."

The troubadour thanked her warmly and accepted her gifts.

"However," said the lady, "you may yet suffer and take joy from me. I wish you well of both."

AT FIRST, BARBARA WAS A TARGET. *She would have preferred to be an archer or even an arrow. . . .*

Barbara-Girl Jones, who disliked the name Barbara-Girl, believed that to be called by her right name would be a great good, but it seemed to be a good which would follow only from circumstances and a state of being. Therefore she frequently put up with the name Barbara-Girl, biding her time until she could enforce her real name upon the turbulent making, unmaking, and remaking universe of Manhattan. She studied, watched, waited, and bided her time. She had learned to smile and she had learned to listen attentively and she was gracious by nature, and so she had merits to compensate for her secret judgments of herself. For she gave herself only a passing grade in Conduct of Life.

Visited late on one of those smoky afternoons of autumn in Greenwich Village, Barbara-Girl might be found curled up on the hooked rug in front of her fireplace on Perry Street, noodling gracefully through a seed catalogue. There was a shelf of books about "Method" and other methods to study acting; there were several rows of art books; there was half a shelf devoted to dancing, both ballet and modern, and a history of Mime, pronounced "Meem"; there were many shelves of novels and poems and outsize gift books of all species and tastes, geological layers representing the jellyfish boys and crustacean men with whom Barbara had bided her time. Amid all this hullaballoo of Manhattan cultivation, books, records, wire sculpture, ink sketches, arts and crafts and courses for adults, Barbara was trying to choose among varieties of parsnips, turnips, and hybrid tomatoes for the sharecroppers of her farm in the highlands of Virginia. Cute Barbara. There was also an appointment book and a telephone with a black coiled slither of cord and a neat pile of hairpins in an ashtray as she leaned upon the tufts of rug before a small, expertly kindled fire. Self-sufficient Barbara, sweet Barbara. Her grandmother (now dead) had hooked the rug; herself (not yet fully committed) had built the fire. Outside, in the courtyard off Perry Street, there was an ailanthus, the tree of heaven, surviving expertly on earth. Inside, as she governed over her life, biding her time, Barbara wore white duck pants, stained with ink (she drew), and a silk blouse (she was careless but elegant). Excellent Barbara had a gay, pouting, bright, little-girl face, a big girl's trained and generous body, exceptionally long-waisted, and a shrewd disappointed head. Her mouth wore little notched turn-downs at the corners. She was deprived though there had been plenty of men to discover her by telephone, by talk, by importunate request and shy courtship; they had made their way into her life through the courtyard of white-painted brick, peeping through the windows at the neighbor's Dufy prints and plastic mobiles; and chief among these men was Peter Hatten, her deep clever odd wry stockbroker pal.

She knew that he had something important to say to her, she even suspected what it was, but she felt in no hurry to hear it this time. She tried to think only of parsnips growing upside down with their heads snugly in the earth; she concentrated on resistance against weevils and worms. "Why ever," Peter was asking as he strolled smiling into her room, sniffing woodsmoke like a cautious animal downwind of the fire, "why ever do you spend your Saturday afternoon with a seed catalogue, hey Bee Gee?"

"Because." And she blushed. She took a small income from the hillside in Virginia which was being sharecropped in garden vegetables for her; tomatoes, parsnips, crisp dusky green beans, abrupt radishes; not mere corn, tobacco, or cotton; cab fare it meant, and silk blouses, and ladylike indulgences; she had also given Peter a set of hand-carved French juggler's toys for his birthday, beautifully tooled, balanced, hand-rubbed, polished, ready for flight; and when she visited back home, she strolled in the fields, commented on the changing weather, and bit happily, like a proprietor, into a sun-hot spurting tomato. She carried a pocketful of salt, she loved the taste. When, crossing Sheridan Square, she found grains of salt in her coat pocket, she licked her fingers and smiled. This was an advantage getting through the traffic of Sheridan Square. Somehow it seemed tactless to discuss her income while living among artists and esthetic stockbrokers, and so she said to Peter's question, "Because."

"I know," said Peter, who also knew what her income came to. Not enough to make any important difference if you are looking for money, just a small grace note for a girl's survival in Manhattan. "Say, that chimney doesn't draw so good, does it? Let me tell you something: smoke, hey girl? Maybe you ought to move into Washington Square Village."

"The kindling was damp, Peter. Sit down."

But he had already sat, stretching toward the fire his long legs in their fine narrow Italian corduroy. "I know I'm early. Let me read—hm—look at the pictures while you take care of business." And he removed her Senior Class yearbook from between a volume of Gurdjieff and a paperback edition of Edmund Wilson's critical essays. Bad news; Peter brought bad news tonight; his green eyes were half closed as he pretended to read. "Hollins College," he said, "let me tell you something, I never knew a girl graduated from Hollins College before."

"Near Roanoke."

"I knew a girl near Roanoke once, she came from there, but I never knew Hollins College. Funny."

"All right," said Barbara-Girl, mimicking him, "let me tell you something. You tease me while I finish with the seeds."

He emitted a short amused electronic blip, as if he had

some private pun in mind, too weak to share but pleasant enough for his own use. "Then we'll talk," he said, "later. I take a certain pleasure in just enjoying you, girl." And he lit a cigarillo and lay patiently toasting near the fire, easy as he liked to be, watching her touch a pencil to her tongue and make her decisions. No corn at all this year. No more tobacco ever —soil tired. New nitrogen fertilizers, then a diverse crop of eatin' vegetables. Lazily Peter blinked in a flickering ray of sunlight while, outside, late afternoon strollers, dressed for country, marked off another autumn Saturday in Greenwich Village, grateful for crooked streets, sunny stoops, and Village ease. He heard a drunken stumble in the hall and went to look, because he was always curious about instances of the loss of control. It was only a painter managing an enormous limp canvas around a bend of the stairway. Peter watched, making his little hum of judgment, and then returned. "Like unborn foam rubber," he said, "mewls and squirms."

Barbara did not answer, though she was supposed to ask him what he was muttering about. She wet the pencil with her tongue and marked some margins.

Peter sighed upon beautiful Barbara-Girl because he carried some rather sad news to tell her. Rather sad, yes sad, somewhat sad. He was the messenger of difficult tidings and felt as uneasy as a messenger might. But how ever could he speak while she took notes in a seed catalogue? Suppressing true feeling breaks the easy rhythm of an intention. She was making it difficult for him. He tried to drowse, his legs twitching, wanting to be up and galloping through the Village, filled with juice and wishing to be away. His eyes kept opening of their own will.

Peter stretched his legs toward the fire, shifted his weight, and made a little bunch of rug to pillow his head. Mildly he smoked and considered the layers of paper quilting the walls. Beyond, in the next apartment a bottle fell. Butter-fingers. No, Gallo-fingers. It must have been the janitor, who wore war surplus khaki undershirts and had once showed Peter his Purple Heart ribbon. He kept it in a Macy's box along with some photographs of himself in the hospital and a recording he had made at the USO to send his folks, saying that he was feeling pretty good and the doctor looked at him today and Sonja Henie was gonna give a show for the boys, they promised. "Go on, it's real, touch it." Peter had touched the ribbon. "It's real, ain't it? You can't buy that kind." "Oh, it's real." "I could show you, want to?" "Oh I know, I believe you." "When it rains, I tell you, I can hardly stand it sometimes. Of course, you can't remember probably, you was just a kid."

"I was in it too."

"Course, the next one's gonna be easy, just buttons. Buttons and woo-*whoof*." He made a Mae West shape in the air. Peter realized afterwards that he was making a mushroom shape. He was smiling happily around brown studs of teeth. Then his face darkened again. "When it rains, I go nuts. I got to deaden the pain. You know how that is? I get this itch in my side. When it's damp. When it's gonna rain. My wife thinks I'm just loafing when I ask her to clean the hall, but I say, shit, Uncle Sam give me a Purple Heart to prove it. What's the matter with women they don't take nothing for an answer, Mr. Hatten? You're a smart man, now you answer me that."

"You got me there."

"You fuckin' right I got you. I got you by the bloney. You want to see my letter from the doc at the Vets?" He burrowed in the box for a brown manila envelope and waved it at Peter.

Peter, who had been decorated for heroic rashness, had said, "Man! Wow!"

"You kidding me? I got a eighteen-per-cent disability."

"Don't let 'em take it away from you, the bastids," Peter had said. The janitor was unloosening his belt. "Just let me drop my pants a minute, I'll show you. I got the scars."

Peter had held up his hand to stop him. "Friend, I know. I trust you absolutely. I can see from your face that you are a man who has suffered in his lifetime." He had then put his hand down: "Shake." And made his getaway.

He dozed, smiling.

The telephone rang, it softly buzzed, and Barbara was saying, "No, no, I'm busy. No. But thank you, Larry." And then she was back, closing the seed catalogue, fallen quietly beside Peter on the floor, gazing into his face as he opened his eyes from his dream of evasion, juggling himself into perfect liberty out on Washington Square in the brilliant October sun. "Ahoy Peter," she said, her small face calmed, quiescent, ready for fret.

"Something to tell you!" he cried out, as if caught in his thought by her troubled eyes.

She bent to kiss him on the lips, very softly and murmurously, as they settled onto the familiar rug by the fire. "What is it?"

"Later," he said, "let me tell you something later," and sighed, and flipped over to grasp her and pull her down upon him.

"What?"

"Just a sec."

His gestures were short with her, his heart was absent, much as always. What he had to tell her could wait a few minutes. First they would make love, easing this fine autumn afternoon down toward chilly evening, with the warmth of the fire spattering an excitement like rain upon their bodies as they lay together on the rug. She got up abruptly, moved swiftly to the lamp; then the fire was their only light and she was clasping him. There was that chameleon alteration of a woman. On the street, in the routines of a day, Barbara smiled, all easy cleanness, straight and slim, a busy American Girl; then the furry, muffy sex when it was lifted and spread for him, and the odor of lust which gradually, beautifully, supplanted her fine soaps and perfumes. She lay spread below him and clasping about him as he entered with her full permission; her legs crossed over his back, pulled him to her; she smiled, her wetted teeth sent forth a glitter of light and pleasure into the world, her eyes going out of focus hilariously, gravely, then squeezed shut: *welcome, welcome, welcome!* Her smile full of welcome took him into it until the one smile seemed to belong to them both together, all through their tolling bodies.

He almost forgot the message he was bringing her.

But when they uncoiled and lay together stretched out by the fire, he remembered it afresh at once. He sat up. He shook his head clear. He shook his head reproachfully. "Ah, Bee Gee, Bee Gee."

"What is it?" She turned her face toward the fire and lay still. She knew.

"It's all—"

"I feel cold, Peter."

"It's over between us," he said. He apologized for the cliché and for the accident of the afternoon. He had meant only to tell her and to have a cup of tea on their friendship, to try to explain, and of course he couldn't explain his peculiar ways to anyone, his point of view about things, but still. . . . Well, she had done nothing wrong. There was not even another girl, though true, there probably would be. It was just his nature. He had the itch to move on, he was not sure, he was fatigued, he was Peter Hatten and that's the way it was. Probably it was silly to apologize. He didn't usually. But she was something special in his life. He continually asked the question: Why can't I have the most beautiful girl, the most loving one? A very beautiful girl, a very loving one was not enough. He wanted more. He gritted his teeth because he could not juggle five oranges, but he could not juggle four either, and not three very well. He wondered if Barbara could understand how odd that made him feel. He would like to believe that she understood. He wished to find the something more in life that could satisfy him, and pleasure did not satisfy, love did not; there was something more. He would find it, or until he found it, he would remain a young man looking, managing and making out if not best and most tender. That was true, too. He would remain a young man for awhile. What's-his-name, Gallo the janitor, didn't even know Peter was old enough to have made the same war. He tried to explain to her how it was about being young in this way, waiting for everything, keeping his age waiting in the air. There's a gamble in beating the odds in favor of losing grip; there's a skill to it. He sat up, naked, and tried to explain.

Silence from Barbara. Firelight glowed on the stiff mask of her face.

He would like Bee Gee to try to see it his way.

Silence.

He scrubbed his scalp with his dry knuckles. "Why don't you say something?" he asked.

Silence.

Okay, it was probably better her way. While he waited for the answer which he realized he did not really want or need, he quickly dressed. He would fill her silence with a space of talk. Being kind to her, he would be kind to himself. "I'm mobile and evasive—way I am, Bee Gee," he said, trying to grin and get his shoes on fast. "There are three things in a girl that scare me off—possessiveness and I forget the other two." He waited, but she did not speak. He sniffed. A thin rope of woodsmoke was curling out of the fireplace. "I don't mean you were *possessive,* kid, I just mean how I see it. I'm peculiar. Evasive. Wanting to take off, you know? The girl I liked best was married—she left me lots of room. You see?"

She sat up to look at him. He paused. She followed him with her eyes but said nothing.

Speed and garrulousness were the big advantages against a Scene, he reminded himself. "I'll tell you something, Bee Gee. You can't beat nature. I made myself that way. *Nurture,* I guess. But listen: I'm sorry. You're a sweet girl, probably the sweetest. You were awfully sweet to me."

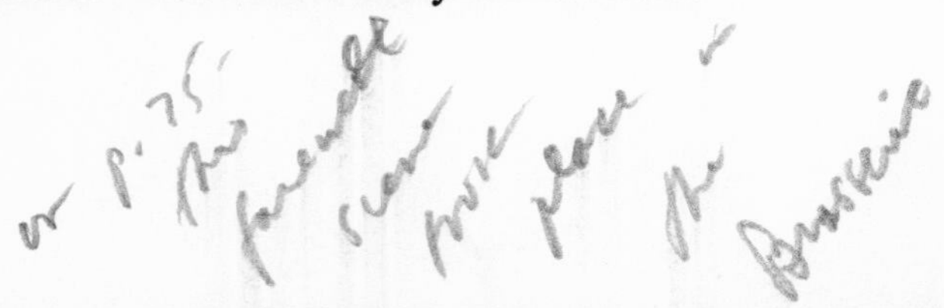

She sat cross-legged in the light of the dying fire, wearing nothing, ripe, naked, and hanging, making no move to hide her nakedness. She watched him dress. She handed him his tie. In their twisting on the floor they had torn the cover and first pages of her seed catalogue. Someone had kicked it, someone who lacked control. Carefully she put it together again.

"I'm sorry, Barbara-Girl. I am. Honest. Please say something. Aren't you cold? Wouldn't you like me to get you a robe?"

Her voice was very calm, very quiet. "Perhaps I knew. I think I knew," she said at last, "but I didn't." She sat unmoving, her shoulders glowing in the firelight, her face in darkness. "I certainly should have known, but *why didn't I?"*

Peter stood by. It was difficult, he wanted to leave, but courtesy demanded that he wait till she dismissed him. He believed in common decency between people. She should say something mean and cutting, she should hurry; and then at last he could go.

"Why don't people understand about you, Peter?"

He knew how to waste the air with that old question; it bemused him too as it flashed overhead every day of his life; he did not know how to answer it. He shrugged.

"I'm cold," she said.

Peter got her flannel robe and tucked it around her. She was squatting by the fire like an Indian mourner in a story. He put his hands very intimately upon her, tucking the robe between her legs and over her breasts, because he didn't want her to catch cold, too, in addition to losing a lover. The thought and the action made him feel kind—operationally concerned. Gently he patted the flannel to her. He liked her body, that was part of it, but he also felt kind. She did not move or resist, but when she turned her face to him, he found it running with tears. Her breathing remained steady—only the tears flowing through some deep breach in her control. There were no sobs, and Peter thought, she should shiver, do her good, psych her up a little; and to bring her out in the open, he grinned, winked, and said, "There's no one like you, Bee Gee. Don't move into a Project—stay in this place. I like your apartment. You have style. Let me tell you something: it suits you."

"Get out of here," she said.

"Um—Bee Gee?"

"Get out."

He was buttoned and ready. He could be gone in an instant. He suddenly felt a constriction in his chest and his voice was hoarse. "I'm trying to tell you I'm sorry. I know I'm not good at it. I'm terrible at it. But I'm sorry, Barbara-Girl."

"Go. Go. *Just go.*"

At last he was dismissed, free as he wanted to be; down the hall and out, unencumbered; out onto the street, walking off the cramp of his legs in the Greenwich Village evening. He hated the weight of brooding and expectation on his back; he disliked a fireplace that didn't draw; he pitied a girl who sat heavy and naked without shame in her sorrow.

2

How easy it came to Barbara to divide into small spinster tributaries. She flowed idly, becalmed and flattened out. She painted a little, she read, she took great care with her job as designer of a department store fashion window. She walked barefoot behind glass on Lexington Avenue, directing the barefoot boys as they draped silk and tweed over cream-colored mannequins. She could be seen through glass from the busy street, silent, finger to lips, thinking; or head upraised, thinking; or hand on shoulder of assistant, resting and considering a sprig of plastic fern, a palm branch, a paper flower. Royal palms, magnolias, cyprus, and Bougainvillea; all in photograph, in water color, in poster, in seriagraph, in papier-maché or in slippery polyethylene synthetic. Silently behind glass she arranged the pretty mannequins in their pretty world. She was given a style for each season, a fashion for each resort, and put a nest of crumpled travel posters at the hobbled feet. She watched the boys doing what she told them to do and thought, even the word *mannequin* originally meant a kind of boy. And took comfort in the company of barefoot boys and plastic dummies.

At the end of the afternoon, she hurried home to the apartment on Perry Street and changed into easier clothes. Her salary paid certain expenses, her income paid certain others, and as to the rest of what she sought for her few years on earth, her needs were not great. How small-small I have reduced myself! she decided, smiling as she passed the Chinese laundry on Bedford Street, doing little chores on her day off, just strolling. She believed that it is a man's duty to lead a girl toward being a woman, to lead a woman toward risking herself in life. Instead, Peter had led her into these small-small requests of the days unfolding around her; he had prepared her to live alone, not by fortifying her with love but by sapping her trust in others. Poor small-small Peter, she thought, smalled straight into the crevices. Trusts only, merely, minutely himself. No matter how he diminishes what he takes and gives, it still comes to be too much for him. She waved to the Chinese laundryman; she bought a box of corn flakes at the grocery and then remembered about the shoes; she had a cup of coffee at the counter of the Howard Johnson's at Sixth Avenue near Eighth Street while she waited for the shoe repair man to finish. She saw someone she knew—a buyer from the store—and they chatted with difficulty, the buyer convinced that she did not remember who he was. She left her coffee and strolled back down Greenwich Avenue past the Women's House of Detention, crossing out of the sun.

She decided that she understood Peter. She satisfied herself even about the violence of his lovemaking, black silences with abrupt frantic appeals, wedges of strain on his face and, worse, glimpses of horror—*he's not simple.* And yet he had been nice, considerate, pleasant through the lounging hours, and had cared to his limit for the limit of his time. When he called her Barbara-Girl, it was because he liked her. He was one of those fanatic voyagers who adopt the dulled tourist, make a trip complete; they know how to smile, listen, stroll and make friends on deck; they grasp for dear life at strangers, and in return, give a furious display of agility and light, leaving a poignant memory of shipside intimacy—but they turn away as if by signal at the sound of the bells on the buoys in the coastal fog. They are the most vivid people in the world, they pour out feeling, they continually make their testament, they leave an ache of vividness after, but the wanderer is made for wandering. He stretches out his long legs and squints his green eyes and makes off. No return voyage. Adieu, she thought, it's never goodbye.

And so she was in no hurry to be found by the next man, who might also be both vivid and a voyager, how to tell? The telephone buzzed, but she did not run to it. Sometimes she watched it buzz, and she barely moved, humming with the music from an FM station which kept her company in her silence, while she waited patiently for the telephone to stop, please, and then went on with her book. She was taking a reading course in French. She liked Gide, Stendhal, and Baudelaire, but Camus seemed too stylishly abstract. She had her own ideas about things. "Small-small ideas," she once said, "but mine." And she was given credit for being an Original, an unanxious twenty-eight-year-old girl who had made a nest for herself in Greenwich Village, without caring about any of the fashions, those that said to be married, to be Beat, to travel, to get rich, to go to an analyst, to take overdoses. She just settled into her nest, enjoyed her health and comfort, did her pretty job, and let time span her. She knew very well the dangers of the love-me look, how it makes men run; and she found fair humor in the fact that the chaps who most ran from the responsibility of a woman's weight had, beneath their sharp chatter and brutal testing of the wind, their own look in the eye, that love-me-anyhow look. Juggling Peter had it. Thousands of the anxious jostlers of anxious Manhattan had it. Sometimes she spied it from her store window as she put tweed over the chill flesh of a doll. It admired her from the street, but gazed with wistful longing at the mannequins in their stiff, submissive, plastic waiting.

The months flowed past in this easy, spinsterish fashion. She asked the janitor to fix the faucet and looked at his Purple Heart when he brought it in. He had something else in mind, but his eyes met hers for a moment and then he went quietly. She spent a weekend in the hospital having a cyst removed. This cyst at the base of her spine would have been her twin sister, twenty-eight years ago, had it developed; when the doctor described it to her, she knew a moment of melancholia—*maybe I'll never have children, only cysts.* But she still had time for everything. She thought of taking guitar lessons. She decided to wait till she needed a change. She met visitors in town, friends of friends, and saw all the plays. She rather liked being the extra girl. She was put on expense accounts and shook hands goodnight and learned to wriggle out of the irate grip of men bursting in their clothes. Secretly, many of these rabid, stuffed, pawing men were unresentful. They ate well and drank well and maybe there was just too much talk about the rest of it. They found it nice to be given credit for vigor by a clever, friendly girl, and have to prove nothing. The physical change in her own life, the absence of a man in her bed, the smell of him and the grain of his body, was less difficult than she had imagined when she imagined herself in love with Peter. Did he arouse her much less than she, in her own pride, had insisted? Perhaps; face that thought another time. Put lust and pride away; try comfort awhile.

She awakened sometimes with a bitter ache in her cramped

thighs. Dreaming at dawn, she broke awake and willed the dream away. Then she watched the first light of the courtyard fall softly over her bed. She noted that there was no recognizable face in the dream, there were no clasping arms, there were no green eyes aslant on the dream's head. The thought was a small victory. She smiled and got up to make herself real coffee in the percolator, not instant. Now that she cared very little about Peter, was not even hurt in her pride, she found that she liked her breakfasts alone, her evenings free, her hours after work to do as she chose. New York was a pleasant blue-and-chocolate, cigarette-and-alcohol town to go floating upon. Her own way. Her own lazy choices. She was in no hurry for anything different.

This news she broke as kindly as possible to the gropers, the hurt lads, the prideful list-keepers, and the big spenders from out of town. She had heard all the false reports about love that she needed for a while. She was in no hurry to repeat the news. She liked falling asleep alone to the music of WNYC-FM, "New York City's Own Radio," and waking up for a high-protein breakfast. Then to the store for a look at some swatches of cloth and fashion cutouts. It was like playing with dolls all over again.

Occasionally, with sadness, wonder, pity, and the sum of it only a slight twinge which engaged her lower heart, her lower angers and appetites, she thought of Peter. Oh, Peter. But he was doing okay, and that was the news of him from the occasional friends who said, "Peter—you're still interested in Peter?"

"Yes, why not? Tell me."

"Nothing much to tell."

"*In*terested."

"Well, making out. They say he got a big new account, some upstate widow, and they say he—oh, you know—"

"Peter has the wash all hung out," Barbara said, interrupting, and then she sighed. Poor Peter, who called her Barbara-

Girl. But that was all. She wanted to hear no more. She could see him now as clearly as if she had invented his posture and costume in honor of the new season. The meaning of his abstracted life on earth was as unclear as if she had made some terrible mistake in putting him together for the window. He was sad on Christmas and Thanksgiving because he had no wife, no steady hearth of affection, but not on Halloween or New Year's Eve, when there was usually a great party, a great chick. He learned to deal with the sadness by sleeping, by strolling, by movies, by his practice and exercises, by crawling into the crowd of Broadway or Times Square; he learned not to try to cope with it by gambling or drinking, which left him sick, depressed, and available to grippe. He learned to control the joys of holiday parties by taking a firm hold on the girl and telling her how to go with him, when, up to what point, and leaving why to her anxious imagination. At about the time when she thought she finally had him managed, it was suddenly the end.

"It's over between us, honey. I'm sorry. I am."

He had made no promises. The girl believed the promises she had made herself because she liked his green eyes and lounging ways. She had mistaken grace for submission. And then Peter once more took his position behind glass, silent and perfect.

Barbara felt that she understood him because in a way she was like him, but of course without the screwy male jumping from girl to girl, onto one girl straight out of another girl. She was a girl and modest, she was a girl and careful of herself. But like Peter, making it, making out, dealing with files, reports, and widows from his office, juggling away the evenings, she wanted to manage her life and make perfect decisions for herself. She too juggled, though without oranges flashing through the air. So that while Peter managed love by hygienic wenching, she managed very simply by giving it up. Perhaps it was not that Peter had been a great love, merely a great lesson to her. But he had touched her, though it was behind glass, like a barefoot boy in her display window. Yes. As a brother perhaps, but deeply. As a perverse brother.

For a long time she could imagine the arms of no one else about her. Peter was jumping like a rooster in his village now, but if he grew weary of this form of chicken pox and decided to come back to her (classic formulation of the spinster's lonely dream), she would not have him. She would not punish him. No mean reversals. He would smile shyly out of those green eyes and push out his legs in the chair and say, "Let me tell you something, Bee Gee," and she would just say No. She knew that Peter, clever Peter, would understand—and also that he would not return blushing, eyes downcast, like the abashed knight in the dream. That was stale fantasy, another insomniac indulgence for when the clock roared its ticking across the room at her in the blackest hour just before dawn. After she let it run its course, taming the clock with fantasy, she was praised a few hours later for a new idea in displaying Caribbean spring fashions, gay prints with purple velvet ribbon and *"le chic francais"* (Irish lace). She said thank you to the vice-president of the store and wondered why mere Peter, mere love, could still crack her sleep with their trouble and distraction. *"Un jour,"* the vice-president was saying, "the *magasin* must send you to Paris for us. I see! in you! a flair!" He breathed intimately: "I see in you, Miss Jones, a flair!"

"Thank you."

"*De rien,* Miss Jones."

Ronnie van Holst, one of the boys who worked her windows, had a shrewd, sympathetic, sisterly insight and said, "Let's exchange telephone privileges, Barbie. Either one of us has the agonies, she can call the other at any hour and talk it over. Sometimes it's nicer on the telephone. I don't mind being awakened unless I took a Seconal. Deal?" Barbara thanked him from the bottom of her heart, but distantly. She did not know how to tell him her story. She did not want the bad news about his sailors at the thinking hour when she was telling herself her story.

He looked hurt. His ladyish mouth turned girlish. Barbara to the rescue, teasing.

"I don't mind sitting up awake," she said. "I solve the world's problems. Last night I got Red China into the United Nations without losing face for America. I designed a costume radiation detector you can wear with almost anything. And last week I wiped out segregation throughout the South over a cup of Sanka, with sugar and cream, that way there's no depression. But you're awfully sweet, Ronnie—you can dial Barbara if it's a bad time for you, honest. I mean it."

Ronnie was hurt but brave. It was Barbara he had been thinking of. She had cut him off when he had honestly wanted to be generous. Later he described her as "a tough broad—*nails*." He liked her despite what he said to his special friend; but how else to talk to his special friend?

Unregretful Barbara had quit the silence of her country childhood, days and nights of it; she temporized; she abandoned the breath of Virginia fields and woods and the slow evolution of her father's perishing will, his long dying into himself. She kept her own counsel in the close fret of Greenwich Village, she kept to herself. She fell in love with a medieval song by Guillaume de Machaut, "Adieu M'Amour"; let it turn again and again on the record player till it was scratched away, a sad little song, a little sad song; "farewell, my love, my sweet princess"; she found herself a little relieved when the song she loved best could no longer be played, and did not replace it. She gave up grief. Proudly she sacrificed melancholy. She believed it to be the recourse of the weak and she put it away. She made a busy life for herself, knowing that this too is a recourse of the weak.

She never called Ronnie in the middle of the night and he never called her.

In response to her letter, her father's doctor wrote to her

that he was a tough old man and she shouldn't worry. He was getting just a little deaf, but he had never much listened; his stubbornness and preoccupation would probably increase with time, but that was nothing new; his heart and lungs were nearly perfect, and the prognosis for his arteries was for no marked changes in any limited span of time. She paid her father a visit. This time he forgot to ask what the devil she was doing up there in New York. He did not ask why she was not married. Maybe it had not occurred to him; it did not occur to her any more, either. *"Adieu m'amour, ma douce princesse."*

3

But just then her life changed once more; Peter did it. When he finally paid a new call on her, it turned out that he had another classic formula in mind: Introduce Lonely Pal to Prize Chick. She felt both courtesy and courage flag. Peter not only gave her up, he wanted to pass her on! Shame made her lean against the door: pretty-pretty flush on her cheek. Smiling and gabbing, he was presenting his old friend, his life-long buddy, fine fellow, let me tell you something, Dan Shaper, just returned from a marital war in Ohio and a wounded veteran of civil strife. A wide and easy smile out of Peter's smooth face.

"How do you do?" Barbara said, but wanted to cry. She bent to take the telephone from the floor to its shelf; she straightened a row of fallen books; she glanced with hectic eyes into the mirror and wet the corners of her mouth with her tongue. *No, meet it, meet it.* For a moment her eyes shamefully met Peter's, and then finally she noticed the nice eyes of Dan Shaper, nice yellow-brown worried eyes, slightly frazzled. He understood that she was in trouble though he did not know why. He was frowning and trying to solve the puzzle by studying her with great concentration. He was sorry if he had interrupted either the trouble or the working-out of it. He was willing to leave at once if she wanted him to. She read all that in the flecks of his eyes and his solemn little bow. The blue vein on the back of one of his hands throbbed, but she did not interpret it.

"Please stay," said Barbara. "I'll make coffee. Look—my new machine! Italian! Or you'd rather have a drink?"

"Where are your seed catalogues?" Peter boomed out with his false social heartiness, his voice even louder than the tick of her clock at the hour of desolation. "I promised Dan the seed catalogues. She has a farm," he said, repeating for his audience of two what he had already said to each one alone. "Barbara-Girl is an exploiter of the peasants, she's an absentee landlord, she's mistress of her own estate. And that's Greenwitch Village, let me tell you, boy."

Outside, there was a dreamy false spring after the long winter cure; or was it spring? She lost track of the seasons, her store's windows were always ahead; and inside here was Peter again, now presenting his friend.

He had already described her to Dan without stint over a dinner briefing at the Old Salt Sea Food the night before. Friendship between pals demanded that everything be sent smoothly flying into the air, Manhattan chicks were all to be hand-rubbed and deployed skywards; they twisted and twirled, they whirled so nicely; but no kidding about the kidding, it's serious business, like those funny little electronics companies on the Coast. He had had to wait for the right moment to issue out Barbara-Girl. Earlier would have been too early. He went on pitching his pal, taking his time about it, easing him in:

"Oh yeah, after possessiveness I do hate a smoky chimney and a lot of moles on the back. And also a Ph.D. in physics who thinks he's a salesman and blabs about the military business in automated data control systems he ain't really got firmed up. But take that Bee Gee, I didn't mean to get strung out on business, she got a nice clean back," he had said to Dan, "firm little rump, dance lessons, you know? Neat. Only a kind of cyst right there at the base of her spine—like a steering knob, fella. You remember the necker's knob on your high school jalopy?"

"What an idea," Dan had said.

"Aw, it's not big, it's sort of funny. Use it with one finger for automated steering. She's really sweet, tops, I mean it, keed."

"Let me find out for myself."

"You're right. You'll see. She's a champion."

Peter was nervous. He was standing near her fireplace and discovering that Barbara was a stranger to him. His eye fell on a book which he had given her, and on a seed catalogue which he had crumpled and ripped with his own bare toes, and he did not know her. She had a champion back and he had told Dan all about it, but he watched her move about the room and she was still as strange as life to Peter.

On edge, he sometimes diluted his thought with jabber. Then later he might turn as dry as paper. Nerves.

While Barbara made busy with the coffee, rattling cups, measuring, touching drawers and cupboards, she understood very well what Peter was trying to do and had done. How free of him? So free: she could ignore him and his projects. "Sit down, you-all, please!" she called from the kitchen. Let him stretch out his legs in his chair, let him squint and fill a space. She could see him pulling at the books on her shelves. Let him feel guilty, let him go scheming and riding his nerves. She would not be passed on. She could make her own decision about Dan Shaper without Peter, without reacting either against or for him because of Peter. Dan was just a young man who had somehow found his way into her closed circle. He was just another edgy Dick Whittington come to make out in Manhattan. She could choose or not choose, as she chose.

She put some dusky grapes in a plate and popped one into her mouth. There was a burst of sweet and then pits. She swallowed the pits.

Thus she returned to the room with her soft Southern smile and her cool, intelligent, gray-green eyes; she had a tray with grapes, coffee, cookies, cream, and sugar—not Pream, not instant coffee, not sugarless sugar; she knew she walked well and both men were admiring her. She didn't mind admiration. In charge, just slightly livened by the presence of Peter, her cheeks scraped red from within by the idea of him, she made them laugh, she made them make her laugh, she even accepted their impromptu invitation to dinner. "The two of you? I'll be impossible," she said.

"You'll be possible," said Peter, "just improbable."

"I declare." But she gazed calmly at him, waiting for him to bow away. He took a sprig of grapes. She knew that he had already received the signal from his friend Dan that, yes, right about this girl: *great*. She had given them her back several times so that they could communicate by the telebachelor nod. Peter scowled, eating grapes. How boyish of him. How truly boyish. He would live up to the bargain, but all at once regretfully. He had grape pits in his mouth which he would save until he was outside. Before he could spit them out the janitor caught him and said, "Where you been keeping yourself, Mr. Hatten? I got the itch a lot since I seen you last."

Barbara and Dan went alone to Chumley's on Bedford Street. They both liked the feel of the place. Its aura of a pub in the Aulde Village, the encrusted door and the creaking little ramp of stairs, a nesting warmth against the evening chill, was more important to them than the work done by the kitchen. Who needed food? You can eat every day. A meeting like this takes place only once, only once. . . . "Only once in a lifetime," Dan Shaper recited stalwartly, blushing. "I can't help it, I mean it." And they studied the ancient bookjackets lining the wall, stained by years of smoking and frying. The waiter was

Chinese. They both ordered English grill and ate only the sausage. The waiter, a chess-player, made no comment.

They took dinner together again the next night, and the next night, and the one after. They obeyed a curious set of rules developed for their special case. First of all, they did not ransack Peter. Also they did not deal with each other in anything but delicate, seemly, innocently foolish fashion; Dan gripped her hand only to shake it goodnight, like a chivalrous and shy Manhattan knight, a fierce suffragette's gentle cavalier. They talked about the day's news. A Hollywood teen-age favorite had been arrested with bloody shoes for kicking to death his toy chow ("I was trying discipline like my analyst said, but I got carried away"); they remarked that it was a difficult era, what with China, Algeria, the Soviet Union, the United States, and insufficiently inhibited movie stars. They compared notes on movies and discovered they liked reality and rhythm, disliked stories without a beat. The compact cars, the new conservatism, the Manhattan real estate boom, the uses of fallout shelters, the decline of baseball, the New York newspapers, action painting, poetry to jazz and FM radio, all were brought under close scrutiny. Barbara sometimes felt as if she were swimming under water, but with a safe mechanical lung; she could do it forever, it was so easy, easy. She was grateful to Dan for being slow with her and rebuilding the strange world about them in stylized shapes and colors, like a record-album cover. If he stayed here, safe and abstract, well, there would be nothing lost, nothing gained; there would be nothing hurt. The actor's dog was a newspaper dog, mere currency. Slowly she was content to let Dan lead her. Maybe he would not stay in this place. His handshake goodnight obscurely moved her to admiration, wonder, and pity. So much courtesy in this shy one.

Then at last one evening they talked about Peter, as if this friend to both of them, friend in very different ways, were a problem to be solved by great patience together. "Let him tell us something," Dan said. They measured each other across linen, dinner once more at Chumley's, and tried to force entry of their friend Peter's life. What did he do with himself besides keep his eye quick and body lean, invade girls, stroll streets, make money in his brokerage firm? They could hear him saying, "Enough, boy. Quite enough, Bee Gee." Yes, enough in a way, but not enough. These pleasures were of the body, but decided by Peter's mind; they had become styles of exploration, a means to random grace, like religion and wearing clothes to those devoted to fashion and a fashionable God. ("That's sociology, boy," Peter would say, "I mean, is there anything worser?")

Barbara was no longer smiling as they talked. But Dan was thinking about her teeth, which were white, even, and small, and they pleased him. He was discovering that there are friendly and unfriendly teeth and Barbara's were friendly. Her teeth were beautiful, were unangry. He didn't care how he had met her; he knew that Peter's way of touching a girl was not his —they might as well have been of different sexes. Peter had taken nothing of what Dan wanted from Barbara. He thought of how Peter had drawn him into New York. Peter had offered him a style. He had shown him his own way and put the best possible face on it. "He was good to me—kind," Dan said.

"He tried to be kind to me."

Yet Barbara and Dan both said, in veiled and discreet ways, that Peter was a dangerous man for the two of them. For Barbara because he called her Barbara-Girl and then hurt her. ("Stop psyching me, Bee Gee.") For Dan because of his handsome, prosperous example of reducing a man's vital decisions toward mere whims about girls (where to kiss and when? how soon to bed and why not now?), about money (wait six months for capital gains, don't churn your account), about pride and the tokens of pride, exploring the nervy city with his nervily merry and predatory eye. He leapt on the town, oh he was a chief of it; both Dan and Barbara were secretly warmed by being his friends, enormously pleased to cluck sadly over the fault they sensed in him. It made them seem provident to themselves.

"Curious how he gambles in the market," said Dan. "Why does he need it? He doesn't really care about money."

"And says boy to everyone."

"Even girls."

"That's just what I was going to say," said Barbara. "I declare."

"Read your mind."

And they crossed little fingers like children and made wishes. Neither told the other his wish, but both knew: *Love, love me quick, care for me.* Dan also wished that he would never again have to use the New York *Post* as a source of conversation. Barbara also wished upon her department store window, her magpie accumulation of observation, her busy response to the chattering world—*simplify, simplify.* They continued to strain their feeling through Peter, who had said, "Out of a hundred vital elements, including what the Chinese do, what the Russians do, what the President does or does not do, I can predict—say—seven with certainty and forty-four approximately, and that puts me on the right side with fifty-one per cent. Do you think this gives me a profitable advantage on the market?"

"Does it?" Dan had asked.

"Enough to make a dollar? Let me tell you something: When you figure in the monstrous and capricious and the trivial improbables—hey man?"

"Well, does it?" Dan asked, knowing how Peter liked to keep his control of things.

Peter smiled blandly, without teeth. (So Dan reported, and said to Barbara: 'You have nice teeth.' And she said: 'On with the story.') "No story," said Dan. "He said yes and no. He gambles under control, as he does everything. No more poker. He juggles and pulls out okay for himself."

"Which is all right in gambling or juggling," said Barbara.

"Which is all right in gambling. Fifty-one per cent might be good enough. In juggling you have to know everything. You have to be perfect, one hundred per cent. You have to forget about everything else."

The waiter retrieved Dan's napkin, which had fallen to the floor. He brought more coffee.

Having discussed Peter, they returned to each other through the circuitous route of Manhattan gossip. Jokes about psychoanalysis (both brushed by it), jokes about home towns (both touched by them), news of family and connections back there; good news of being both familiar and extraordinary on a special turf. Dan explained that he made his living as a writer of come-on letters for a magazine ("Come on and subscribe"), having graduated from whatsamatter letters ("Whatsamatter you didn't renew your subscription, whatsamatter you didn't send your check after you filled out the form?"). His promotion made the matter of child support easier. He put his children between them in a ritual way. "I know you miss them," she said. "I do," he said. "Lands," she said, "you can tell me."

He initiated her into the folklore of the child-support underground. Impoverished divorced fathers call their children long distance, making a nickel do for a quarter in the ears of the long distance operator as they feed the pay telephones. "One dollar and twenty-five cents, please," says the operator, and daddy uses just five nickels, rhythmically pounding the base of the telephone box as each nickel descends to give a deep, melodic, quarter-of-a-dollar tone—another version of the naked oiled J. Arthur Rank slave and his annunciatory gong. Highly larcenous and symbolic, yes? Dan inquired. She smiled dimly. "Well," he said, "it's us or the Bell Telephone Company, it's a revolutionary situation! My group survives by guerilla warfare in the booths of Grand Central Station." With his recent promotion, he could afford to use quarters for quarters. "Getting bourgeois," he said, "a tough-fisted old phone man like me."

Having discussed, Dan and Barbara fell silent; he took

her hand; he looked into her face. Her eyes on that evening seemed to have a velvety glow in the smoky light of Chumley's on Bedford Street in Greenwich Village. The chess-players were playing chess, the thinkers and arguers were thinking and disputing. Barbara's eyes glowed with a deep, velvety patience. And on that night, having discussed Peter and the telephone company, having discussed their home towns and their parents, having made their courting jokes and fallen silent, having put a velvety glow in her eyes and a calm warmth in Dan's heart, they returned to Barbara's apartment; they kissed with great friendliness, they undressed back to back, he admired her, they went to bed together for the first time as if it were the thousandth. In the morning she awakened him with orange juice, and they made love as if it were the first time. "I'm afraid," she said.

"Don't be afraid," he said. "I'm afraid too, but don't let's be."

4

"Would you like me to bath you?"

"*What* me?"

"All right, *bathe* you, darling, with an *e*."

Dan and Barbara sprang into pleasure like creatures born to it, but long deprived. At the start too wounded by their history to be passionate, they relived the course of adult lust, beginning with abrupt embraces and desperate possessions, then finding their way like fortunate jungle explorers into a sunny, confident luxuriance. The first time Barbara suggested bathing Dan, he even thought maybe he was dirty; laughter erupted from her thrown-back head, "I'll tell you, I'll tell you!

I'll tell you that if it occurs to me!" Then he thought she wanted to baby him, and let her, because why not? But it was not maternal babying that she wanted. Exotic flowers lay buried under the cool pine of her Southern Baptist heart; she pulled and stroked and let the suds and steam rise about them; but being American, she gave up this service all at once, impulsive and frantic, and simply flopped into the tub with him. And they embraced in hot perfumed water, her lips biting into his shoulder and slippery desire opening like a Japanese flower within her. They climbed out, they dried each other carefully; they lay down together at a steep angle, pensive, floating on nighttime seas, quiet and ceremonious in soft communication, letting time settle like water about them, until she whispered to him, through him, with a curious formality, "You have all my permission"; and then the seas swept over them with a tidal flow and they breathed as one breath together in the deep.

Later.

Later she told him that for a while she had felt safe, closed and slick against the world, like one of the mannequins in her store windows. Now no longer safe; unsealed.

He said it was better not to be sealed tight, better not to be safe.

She listened to him and lay still.

Later she told him about the dirt paths across her father's farm where she grew up in Virginia, and how she wept when her first mount died—

"You had a pony?"

"A *horse*."

And how her father, a peculiar country scholar, spent most of his energy compiling a history of the combats between Spads and Fokkers in the war of 1914-1918.

"Fairly odd."

"Yes, but what was fairly oddest is he didn't work on the Civil War, let's say the Confederate Navy. You want your back rubbed?"

"Just right here a little. Yes."

Leaning back and forth on him while he stretched, sighed, closed his eyes, she said, "Pa flew one of those Spads. Lucky for him. He's so shy he couldn't pronounce the other plane."

Dan lay beneath her hands, saying, "It's so nice because."

"In twenty-five words or less."

"Yes, or more—"

And she gave it up to roll onto his back, lying there with her heart thumping and just wiggling her rump once or twice for the sake of sweet friendship. They talked; she tried to explain about Manhattan to Dan—all the immigrants from far countries are constantly telling each other why. Life on that island was more personal than the combat of Spads and Fokkers, though sometimes in despair in that ancient other war, a pilot might simply circle above and drop a brick onto his enemy's cockpit. "Oh yes!" said Dan. "I read about it on the back of the Kellogg's box when I was a kid—"

"Listen to me, Dan."

He flipped over and held her head against his shoulder and listened. As they lay like two tucked-together spoons, she tried to tell him about the gasping intensity with which she cooled her overheated, longing heart to the required busy immobility of New York. Her mother had died at her birth, and this is very strange; she had been raised by her father and housekeepers and boarding schools, and these are strange. She had come to New York looking for love and motion; in order to get it on Manhattan's terms, she had to refrigerate, stay still. A hot motor grinds up its heat to make the still cold of the deep freeze. (*Peter,* they both thought.) She had sat in corners at parties, smiling till the bold ones came up to tease and trick with her; she hoped for the shy ones, but they were merely to be captured—she was not a capturing woman; she waited. Oh! oh! maybe that one! she had sometimes thought, but lost him in the crowd; perhaps to be predatory was the way? But the predatory bird damages its prey in its beak, and she did not want a damaged man. What other man is there? she had wondered. There must be another kind than the reforming homosexuals, the Don Juans, the worried stylists of Manhattan whose faces never age, but their gums retract, their teeth go bad, their chins unravel, and their necks get pouchy or scrawny. Pities and disasters and a few smiling favorites.

But Peter takes care of himself, they decided again, without speaking of him.

And while talking, no, after falling into a silence between words, that silence which decides whether a man and a woman mean more than service for each other—that silence which is like the darkness between the stars that gives them their radiance—the telephone rang and it was Peter. "Hey boy," he said, "you find a girl and you leave off with your pal? Let me tell you something: that how it is? What about dinner tonight?"

"I'm with Barbary."

"I don't know that, boy? *Ah declah.* I *mean* you two and me and my lady. Listen, I won't describe, you'll see for yourself." When there was no answer, he added sweetly, "Look, is Bee Gee embarrassed about me? Come on, boy, the past is past, everyone's had lots of baths, we're all nice and clean—" Dan winced while Peter just babbled it over smoothly again: "Talk to me nice, boy."

The word *bath* made it a challenge. All right. And anyway, if Barbara had been touched by Peter, it had been a mere touch to teach her what she wanted. Sweet chatter, smooth clatter. Who hadn't been searched, cut, bled in this world? Busy Manhattan would wash you down the drain unless you held on to what you know for yourself and let the rest swirl by. The sewers lay boiling beneath the city. Barbara and Dan had heard the music in the conduits, but believed they could listen, sniff, peek, and stand free. Peter thought he could go strolling in the depths and come back with clean shoes.

This time it was no very complicated joke. It turned out that he merely wanted them to meet his new girl, Freddie.

They took dinner together in a midtown steak house. Like all Peter's companions, Freddie had beauty, and hers was that monumental beauty composed of a brazen host of flaws. She felt that Mary Magdalene was her psychic sister—she too had been a call girl. She suffered from a head cold, but regally. Being a prostitute and suffering a runny nose were two equal imperfections. Her large, vague eyes stared and rolled myopically. They looked down a slightly hooked nose with a small sharp droop at the end. A glistening head-cold jewel lay at each nostril. The creamy skin under her chin doubled when she laughed, putting a sudden softness to her face; but then she remembered and lifted her head to its patrician heights again. Her rich pelt of blue-black hair was streaked with gray. She had a widow's peak. Her mouth, rather small, hid small but perfect teeth—no imperfection here. However, she frequently opened her mouth to speak, and now there was plenty of imperfection released toward the sky: "Oh my dear, my dear sweet, I mean it was a magnificent book, so—I mean he like understands people, you know, humans—so magnificent, I mean—*groovy*." She refused to stand up, knowing that her great courtesan's head, lolling, lifting, blessing, *requiescat non in pace,* was her finest feature. Despite the delicate skin, her wrists were a trifle thick. She wore no precious stones except a pearl choker above the low-cut velvet dress. The night lily blooms without jewels (who's counting those pearls?). No one could take eyes from her, man or woman. Someday a reformed homosexual might marry her, made huge and proud by her groovy past.

"Why did you leave Paris if you liked it so much?" Dan asked her.

"Darling, I was busted," she said. "I got in trouble with one of their finest families over there, darling. Like they thought I was after their son and heir's fortune, but I mean all I wanted was his *money,* darling." Still searching for the *mot juste,* she held up her little finger. "It was the living end, sweets."

Peter laughed aloud. He was a smiler, but he seldom laughed. He was busy approving publicly of Freddie.

"Now I can get *Peter* money. I don't need *his* money, that mucky old foreigner. I got an American friend in Peter who likes me a lot, don't I, mm?"

She put a hand on his wallet and squeezed, saying, "Mm-*mm*!" and made an ecstatic face. "Plenty Peter money, mm?" Then she lifted her patrician face and looked at them from an imaginary height of elegance. She was playing elegance against the vulgar joke. She had the habit of trying to make herself interesting.

"And now you boys just excuse me a sec, okay? You too, BeeGee."

She studied the tip of her nose in her mirror, sniffing and wriggling to practice it. "Tomorrow I just trip myself out to Lonn Guyland to see Miss G.," she said.

"Who?" Dan asked. He had an idea.

"Do a little turn with her, y'know? It's a change from turning the tricks in my lonesome. Mr. A. wants me to wear snuggies, can you imagine? Cover me up next to myself like that?"

"You're going out where," Dan said.

"But I like to look nice all over anyhoo," she said as if this were an answer. "Lootwise it's best."

Dan stared. "Alabam," Peter stated. "Goneril." He met Dan's eyes hard to put an end to his questions.

"Oh yes, that sweet Mister A. he shows like a creative imagination Goneril calls it, you know? You know Superzen —poor *poor* thing? I always thought he was the grooviest, *reading,* and *thinking,* and such a good *swimmer,* and now that awful head trouble—oh Petey, you're pinching again!"

He shook his head with a mild grin on his face. "No I'm not pal. That's just getting ready to make you black and blue all over. I'm just getting the range, pal."

"Well, like I said—scusi. I'll be only a min-oot." She snapped the mirror back into her purse and arose. With narrowed eyes and pointed finger she slowly revolved until she found her direction. Stately, stretching herself tall, she turned after a few steps to wave. They were watching. She could proceed with confidence.

"Hey, pal, what do you think?" Peter asked Dan while Freddie went away to spend her hour in the powder room.

"You're kidding."

"Great kid, isn't she?" But his face darkened and was abstract, and over it fell an abrupt stiffness, the lines of control running from the flanges of his nose to the corners of his mouth, and both Dan and Barbara grieved for the still person within. They were silent; they gabbed to fill the silence. Freddie left her vacuum behind her. Valiantly they talked. Peter attended, head slightly tilted, to their labor of politeness. "You're lucky, you two," he said. Then he caught sight of Freddie ambling among the tables, bestowing her smile and her hand, and he pushed his chair back to meet her, grinning. "Next time you stay away so long, pal, whyn't you at least send a postcard?" And turned to Barbara and Dan with that wanness again: "You want to cut out, you two? Then cut out."

"Are you dismissing us?" Dan asked.

"The check is taken care of, boy. I made some crazy money this week—toy money, but *green,* chappie."

Freddie nodded happily and said she was so pleased to make their acquaintance at last after Petey had told her so much about them and they would surely have lots, lots more to talk about next time, travels and all, things and all—"Soonest, okay? Say oui. Say oui. Say like adios, chico, that's what all the South American millionaires in Paris say, 'cause they always speak French with an accent—"

Peter kept his hand on the nape of her neck. They were both smiling. She blew Dan a kiss, pursing her mouth till it was very small and made a little wet noise.

The air outside was heavy, filled with a fine grit, an unnatural city heat that caused a slime of discomfort without warmth. It was that different heat left over after a day of exhausts, exhalations, flow of wastes and by-products, labor of machinery and unceasing commotion. They held hands like children home in the cab, and then, with tea at midnight in her kitchen, went on touching hands over an enameled table. Poor Peter, they were both thinking, and thinking how impossible for anyone to be his friend, how impossible to stop hoping for him. He too had to survive in that air and time. After his juggling, he loved best walking down Broadway on the upper West Side, just sauntering, or wandering down Fourth Avenue among the used book shops, interested in the kingdoms of France and England, the lives of the courtiers; he would pick out four or five books and hurry home to settle in his reading chair with them; he was fond, clever, and quiet; and yet he appeared in public with a schizophrenic whore, and played all his brasses.

"Oh, he's a confusion," Barbara said. "Maybe we could just let it go."

"Probably that's better."

The memory of her life with Peter was like a rising spume of smoke, very remote and faraway over the roofs of Perry Street. Outside there were parked cars and tough kids leaning against them and sudden eddies of air to drive away the smoke. *Adieu m'amour*—what nonsense to make a song of smoke and smoke and smoke!

"I thought you wanted to talk about him," Dan said.

"I don't. Let's walk once more around the block and then I'll. . . . Let's have a drink at the White Horse, I feel like seeing. . . . No, let's just do nothing. Let's stay here."

They sat in silence at the kitchen table with kitchen noises settling about them. Dan let her go into herself. She was making an effort to control her excitement.

"He's all-time," she said very slowly, trying to use the right slang. She sighed and gave up. "He's unusual."

Dan smiled because she returned to the subject so quickly, just as if he were not there as witness. She had said to let him go. "Did you know his friend—Jacques What's-his-name—always wears those foulards?"

She sighed again. "I never heard about any other friends. Just you. You date from when he made friends."

"You make me feel like a dodo or something else extinct."

"You're unusual."

He took her hand again. "Am I all-time?" A swaying wind came up from the port just after midnight, bringing a faint salt to the Manhattan air, and the branches of the tree in the courtyard were singing. He shut the window just before the rain began. As the first spatters sounded on the pane, spreading the dust, he turned swiftly upon her and lifted her into his arms. He did not wait for her to nestle herself against him, but pulled her strainingly to his shoulder. Breathing her hair, he could smell her soap and cologne, despite their sheathing in the day's dust and anxiety. *"Am I all-time?"* he demanded. "I need you to make me feel it. I've had a little bad luck."

"It's the thing a man needs," she said as she pried his hands loose, "—the best thing to complete a man. Perfect is no damn good."

They both grinned with astonishment that she should find something so wise to say just because he was hurting her in his embrace. The mood of nervous unease was broken.

"Sit down," she said. "It was easy." She pulled her skirt between her knees like a schoolgirl. "I won the insight title last year."

She poured fresh tea. Like the creak of the kitchen, the long day was settling about them. Dan went to the cupboard and brought back the pot of marmalade and cut them each a slice of black bread. He put the bread on one plate between them. "I'd like to visit your father," he said.

"What? Down there?"

"Let's make a little trip to Virginia. I want to learn how to say you-all to people."

She hid her confusion by entering the joke with him. "Only when talking to two or more—that's your first lesson. And you'll have to bone up on airplanes."

"Prehistoric Spads and Fokkers."

"Y'all remember!"

"How could I forget? Someone else told me, someone I once knew. I'll buy balsa models and study good."

"Dan! Why?"

He went to the trouble of making his most Jewish shrug.

She folded her hands and her eyes filled. She remembered the ache in her eyes of insomnia, but she had not felt this bite since meeting Dan, and now, as tenderness soothed her, it was as if she had simply stretched herself into sweet comfort in her kitchen at midnight. There was a warm rain on the city outside. The unbidden tears washed her eyes. Her body felt both heavy and comfortable to herself. Dan was looking at the shoes under her chair; she had shaken them off her feet. She would have liked to tell him that she loved him.

5

But despite their joy in each other, they were not contented. They had bad habits in love, bad histories and determinations. Though Dan wanted to be cared for—*tell me I'm all-time!*—he feared being moved from his own few inches, his little square of fought-over reality, his jokes, his teasing, his mournful inwardness about his sons in Cleveland, his elegiac sense of what he had lost in life and of time passing, his pride at surviving, his astonished pleasure in the sparks he struck. Like Peter, he took positions, he husbanded his health. Peter was more skilled than Dan. He trained. He lounged and had presence, and the more Manhattan pressed down at him, the more he ambled and stretched in this powerful repose which he had built for himself. Sometimes he would scrub his scalp with his knuckles —that for nerves—that was all the sign he gave. But Barbara had caught Dan sucking in his stomach as he stood in a room, as he lay abed with her. He was as wary as a child. He made jokes about becoming a champion athlete when he grew up. It was not mere vanity. He was still mobilizing to travel light in disaster.

Did he want no responsibility for her? to his feelings for her? Was he just another stricken lad in Manhattan, making out? Barbara thought: Surviving! That's not the way to be all-time!

Without quarreling, they had a quarrel. Barbara understood how she had caused Dan's side of it. Before their trip to Virginia, she arranged a party for his friends, her friends, their mutual friends, and he took flight after it. He thought he was being pushed. He wanted to meet her father, but he did not want to be pushed. He had warned her that he was used to bad luck in love, and though this might have completed him as a man, as she once said, it left him afterwards a nervous loner. Bad luck can also do that to a man. She had been too generous with him. Freedom in love was a snare and a delusion—he had all the theoretical knowledge customarily branded onto the skull these days; but any hint of being instructed or put in an arranged place made him exchange the complication of his feelings for a pure, polite rage. How well did she know him? Not well enough. Her principle about the party had been all wrong: include everybody. Peter was there; Dan's old friend whom he called Goneril; others. It might have been heavy going but fun to remember. It wasn't. A miscalculation. Barbara had miscalculated and Dan was wrong. They brought themselves much trouble.

There was one lucky side about the party. Bobb and

Caroline Anthony, separated for a few weeks, each thought the other would turn up and so both did their sulking elsewhere. But there were the terrible moments with Goneril—Barbara believed that Dan should have protected her—and then there was the separation from him afterwards. He thought she was trying to announce their engagement, to slide it in. Maybe he just could not accept the parade of their lives in Manhattan, Debbie, Peter, the window-dressers, their friends. And yet it had been amusing, some of it, that was the word—amusing; and Goneril and her accompanying Alabam had been both terrible and somehow amusing. Goneril gained immunity from Goneril; if not self-generating, she was at least self-innoculated. The terrible part of the evening might have been borne happily if Dan had not cut himself off from her. He had been kind in his cool way, but then angry and in retreat. Well, she recognized that she had no right to push him like that. She was trying to make him be what she thought she needed. Maybe she really needed something else.

Dan did not know how he had left her with Goneril and so caused Barbara to fear him. He did not see enough into Barbara's universe of dread. But who else could have seen?

It became clear to Barbara why Bobb Anthony did not appear. She also thought she knew why Peter came without Freddie.

Barbara believed that Dan should have protected her from Goneril, though she did not ask protection. He should have watched. He should have stopped it. Perhaps he did not know enough about Goneril, but he should have known.

The guests made their way by subway and cab into the Village; one careful boy, Sheldon Kurtz, carried the address on the little R.S.V.P. card in his hatband. Someone dropped a mauve glove at the doorway. There were downtown, uptown, midtown ladies and gentlemen; they swirled about Barbara, letting her get their drinks and letting Dan get them and later, getting their own. Peter lay slumped in a chair, pulling on a cigar, his long legs sprawled out and his hooded eyes alert. He smiled and waved at Debbie and a little actress and the odd little buddies that he had dug out of coffee shops, offices, and fashion shows. The little girls whom Dan had known in his time of little girls—the little girls Peter had led him to—chirped and posed and pouted and said, "Ooh, you really are," to young men who confessed to their interesting vocations. There was also a knot of violence, initiative, and madness: Goneril, the wild tall chick, with her attendant Alabam. Dan had told Barbara about them, he had warned her, he had asked her to be amused or not to invite them, but he had not prepared her. "Such a surprise!" Goneril purred, leaning forward to examine Barbara as if she were a small commodity on display. "So this is what Dan really likes."

Peter was sighting along his knees to Goneril and Barbara where they stood and talked. He could not hear them across the babble of the room, Alabam shrieking with laughter to acknowledge an introduction to Ronnie van Holst, but his eyes shined with anticipation. He sniffed the future in the air. He did not move. Goneril circled and circled at a distance, figuring Barbara out but doing her own talking. She wanted Barbara to feel her presence; she needed no other answer for now. Then, bearing Alabam in her wake, she swept back across the room. It was as if she had to retreat first in order to will trouble to Barbara. She did not wish it naturally; she had to take time to will it. "Hello, I'm—"

"Of course. I'm your hostess," Barbara said coolly. "We spoke only a moment ago."

"Um. You're a *nice* girl."

"Ooh," said Alabam, defending Barbara, "not jes' nice. She's, you know, honey,"—and he made a circle of thumb and forefinger, indicating perfection—"she's *à la carte.*" And smiled to the judges in the highest gallery with triumph at his compliment. He also tried to catch Peter's eye. Peter was squinting at the wall just behind him.

Goneril took down her drink in a long mannish gulp, put

the glass away, and then stepped into a speech which she began all in a rush: "What I mean, chile, got to talk to you. I have this little crime deal working for me. I went to college, just like you, sister-honey, but the trouble with one of these crime-type deals going for you is then you get unemployed but there's no unemployment, no disability, y'know? And then pretty soon you are old and gray and nobody cares, *no*-badaddy. There's a lack of social security in the crime line, honey." She made a sad brave face. "However, there is kicks." And she sang a little tune: "You can't take that aw-*way* from *me*-ee." But she was not done yet. She was in a mood to confide. "All I wish in this little deal is you could have a friend, y'know? I got associates and colleagues, I get laid, sure, but like a *friend* friend, you know what I mean? Alabam, okay. But there's something, must be something—" and a look of puzzlement crossed her face "—there must be something more. To *count* on. You know I went to college?"

She smiled and turned away, as if to remove the weight of obligation. She was much obliged, but she did not want to obligate Barbara. Her turning away at that moment was an act of kindness. She went for a fresh drink.

Barbara said to Dan, "I can see why you liked her."

"Who?"

"Goneril. She's touching."

"No, not quite."

"I know you better, Dan. I don't mean you wanted to 'take her away from all that.' I mean she's just touching, something about her, that's all."

But Goneril was one of those girls with elephant ears when people were talking about her. Or maybe eagle's eyes. She either saw or heard Barbara being kind about her to Dan, and so she swayed up on her stilts, ready to carry her project forward, exaggerating her drunkenness, and just lay her head on Dan's shoulder, looking up to wink into his eye. Though she winked at Dan, she was wigwagging signals from within toward Barbara: *Don't be sorry for me, you bitch, sister-honey.*

I'm a bitch and don't you dare be kind to me. She timed the signal to Barbara and then slipped her hand inside Dan's shirt: "Ooh, no undies," she said. "I do hate a man who wears tee-shirts, don't you, Barbara-Girl?"

Barbara just smiled at the cruelty. She did not stop to figure out when Goneril had had the chance to discuss her with Peter. He lay sprawled in a chair across the room, leafing through a Skira volume about Fra Angelico which he had given Barbara when he called her Bee Gee. ("B.G. For a rainy weekend in Southampton. P.H.") Barbara said, "We need some fresh glasses," and left Goneril and Dan there with Goneril's long paw gathering a fold of skin on his chest.

As soon as Barbara turned her back, Goneril removed the hand. She said to him: "She's a great chick, Dan. You're smart. I give you credit. Christ maybe you and Barbara have it made, oh Christ."

And went to join Alabam.

Dan stared after her, talked with a friend—party time! —forgot her. Elbows, shoulders, mouths. Party time. A sleek uncomfortable fun was dripped like oil over faces. The room shrank. No one was listening, all timid, brazen, exalted, scared, talking, making out. Peter had kept a little space about him and was turning the pages of the book. A party philosopher, whom Peter had once snubbed, came up to hector him. "Hey man, I've discovered a truth," he said.

Peter made his eyes hard.

The party philosopher pulled at his cuffs and then at his collar to make sure they showed the requisite strips of white. "You know what? It's a thing I thought of. People never forgive anyone they've hurt. See, it's not only the victim gets sore, it's—"

"People never forgive anyone," Peter said with a smile, relaxing. "But I do."

"You think so?" the party philosopher cried eagerly. He squatted by Peter's chair. He had a very thin stalk of a neck, which now bobbled at about the level of Peter's knees. "Look, you remember me, Sheldon Kurtz, we met at Jacques' place, I back shows?" He bobbled his head to encourage assent from Peter. "Well, about human responsibility to other humans, I always operate on the theory—"

"Wrong already," said Peter.

"—theory that—"

"*Wrong*. You're dead."

A couple who had just met was bumping knees, elbows, arms, saying Excuse me, pushed together in a corner behind a tubular lamp. They were frowning with desperate excitement. The young man found the glimpse of a pink strap pulling into a pink tuck of flesh as he said Excuse me to the young lady the most beautiful thing he had even seen. The girl listened to his Excuse me and understood what it meant and thought it the most beautiful phrase she had ever heard. The girl was a model in the store where Barbara worked. The man had come down from Alimony Hall, where Dan had met him in the laundry room. He too was looking for True Love, that love which comes only by surprise and lives happily ever afterward, and now he had found it. The man's hand flew to his pocket to make sure of his pencil so that he could write down her telephone number. When he asked her for it, the girl said, No, no, I'll just whisper and you remember. That's my husband over there. You'll remember if my lips make it, won't you? *Oh please*. Now watch: *Gramercy 5. . . .*

Another inmate of Alimony Hall, an instructor at Barnard, was saying to a girl as he spilled his drink on her foot: "I dreamed I was T. S. Eliot in my Maidenform Bra—"

"Teasa Who?"

"Tee-*ess* Eliot."

She wanted to tune in for him. "Wasn't her picture on the cover of *Time*?"

Peter, making his escape from the party philosopher, leaned over to prompt her as the instructor stood aghast, abruptly sobered and detumesced by ignorance. "No, Debbie, that was another girl—she lives in a world of her own," he hastily added to the doctoral candidate. "Debbie's like that. You ought to try it sometime."

The candidate mourned. "All my jokes are academic. One thing about my first wife, she understood them."

"Debbie understands, too—don't you, Debbie?"

The pursuing party philosopher heard the last few words. He said to Peter in a voice calculated to include Debbie and the young man, too: "Don't you think we outgrow the oedipal situation in the first marriage? and then we go on to mature relationships with the onslaught of . . . uh. . . ." His eyes dilated and then came to a focus on the young instructor. He began again: "People never forgive anyone who's ever hurt them, that's something I realize with a new force now that the progress of integration in the South—"

But Peter was off to the bar and the party philosopher took after him in hot chase. Peter Hatten was the kind of man he had always wanted to be friends with. He had so much to give if only Peter would let him. If people would only listen. If he could only talk with Peter Hatten alone some evening, really exchange ideas. And feelings, oh feelings about things. There was so much to express in every man's life. Sometimes, at a Manhattan party like this, he almost came to despair despite his firmest resolution never to give up. "Peter!" he cried.

Debbie listened to the young instructor's explanations about T. S. Eliot. "I've heard of him, sure," she apologized. "Isn't that Gerry Mulligan they're playing? Brubeck? And I know all about Robert Frost, too, the spry elderly poet. It's all this noise." She waved at him heavily with her mascara-laden lashes. "Like I'd so dearly love to be really up on things. I really and truly do dig the theater and all, you know?"

Peter, heading back again, having shaken his philosopher and put a Vivaldi concerto on the machine, nodded encouragingly as he went by. After his shock the young instructor was making a stern effort to follow orders and dig Debbie. "Girls are really intuitive," he said, working on his own line of reasoning. "That's their forté."

"And how!" said Debbie. "All I know is it's sure mine." She was making a great effort to follow this spook. She knew it wasn't nice to think of him as a spook just because he was this creepy-colored schoolteacher, but she didn't like to hide her true feelings from herself. "Will you ever forgive me I didn't know Mr. Everett's poetry?"

"Surely."

"I really do have some fine qualities."

"Oh I'm sure you do."

"Like I got this natural sense of rhythm, too—I bet you dance like a *dream*. . . ."

Peter looked up from his chair at the tinkle up and down the scale of Debbie's laughter and the answering restrained chuckle ("Ho-ho. Ho-ho.") of the young man. To himself he had already named the young man Uncle Tom Crow. He wondered if it were true, as he had heard, that the bright kids in colored high schools had to go to Laughing Class before they went on to college—a special course in learning to laugh with restraint. Ho, ho. Ho, ho. Well, he had intervened at the proper moment. Otherwise Uncle T. C. would never have gotten over his sense of betrayal by Debbie's ignorance of the classics.

Behind the tubular lamp the man who had found true love was sulking. The lady, who understood, was intimating sadness. They would have to share her with her husband. No other recourse in a difficult life. She identified the Vivaldi correctly.

Then Peter's eyes glinted on Barbara's across the room, pair on pair, with a frankly pleased, calculating smile. He took pleasure in the light managing of things. Barbara smiled back, but they did not approach each other.

"One thing I've learned about politics," the party philosopher was trying to tell Dan, "it's the art of the probable. Sometimes power tends to corrupt, you know? Now you take General Lemnitzer of the Joint Chiefs—" The party philosopher, his moon face leaning close on the long thin neck, his eyes wet with feeling, gleaming with the true dope, became a military expert after the second drink. The first drink was for Freud. The third was for the sadness of it all.

Peter went up to rescue his friend. "Hiya, boy. Say—whatever happened to George Fielding Eliot?"

"Christ! Old 'Fielding' Eliot! Didn't he play for the *Herald Tribune*?" Dan asked.

The philosopher began a strategic retreat. He knew it was a newspaper, not a ball team. Both Dan and Peter took pity. "Let me get you a drink." "Here, try one of my cigarillos."

"Small cigars, aren't they?" said the party philosopher, reaching eagerly. "I've always wondered about that. I hear they make 'em from the pressed stems and scrapings, gather 'em up in a new scientific process, a composition paper wrapper—"

Peter looked at Dan as if they had, together, made a terrible discovery. Like most bores, the party philosopher was not insensitive; he was merely determined; the glance of icy green made him shiver and redouble his efforts.

"According to all the statistics about smoking, the tars and resins in cigars or cigarillos—assuming you don't inhale—"

Goneril was not done with Barbara. She had been waiting. She did not want Dan around when they had their moment together. She saw him talking with Peter and someone else. She had been calculating the moment of maximum crush in the small apartment. Now she weaved through the party, past advertising men, models, decorators, a rich lawyer, the couple divided in half by the tubular lamp—hiding behind a narrow pipe as if it were a mighty oak—past Sheldon Kurtz, the party philosopher, past Debbie and the man she now truly loved, who was an instructor at Barnard, past the boy Ronnie who worked a window in the store, past the husband desperately studying the tubular lamp through his contact lenses, past others, past Peter; she came stalking Barbara through the voices that said "Hey! I'm—" and the smiles that tried to stop her. She found Barbara again, clutched her elbow in her long hand, and continued, drunk or pretending to be, talking to her like an old friend or enemy, with a speech that she had only interrupted for the reasons of patience and convenience: "The picture business, hell. I went to college. The picture business stinks. So I got Peter to find me a friend, y'know? A nice safe john. He found me one okay, wasn't long since. He likes actresses, they all do, y'know? You know the type? A grateful safe john appreciated my college education and I'm an actress, is what he wanted. He wanted me to walk around and me say, *You're a big man and you move like a big man.* That helped him. A kook. Well, who isn't? Tell me that. The kook-type deal soothes the midnight chagrins, y'know, sister-honey? And do you know what else? Goddamn kook. He really was big—big and fat and you know what more? Well, he wasn't such a big man how it counts—no bigger'n a little finger, seems like, honey—but that's big enough to do me the damage he did."

She stopped and watched Barbara for a reply. None yet.

"Wish he'd stuck to the kook-type deal. That damage he did."

There was the energetic wound-up whir of a Vivaldi concerto. Barbara cocked her head as if to listen.

Goneril smiled at Barbara with a certain amount of admiration. The girl knew how to wait. Then Goneril said quietly, "I think you are acquainted with him." Still no answer. Well. Very good. She went on with her speech: "I was stoned out of my head and careless with that little pinkie. You're a lady, but I bet you know what I mean. We both went to college, didn't we? There's something I got to talk to you about. Private. Tell you *pri*vate-lee."

Tall, leaning, drunk, and purposeful, Goneril gripped Barbara's elbow and abruptly pushed her toward the bathroom. Barbara braked her heels against the rug. Goneril had lost her patience for a moment. Silly girl. She made a little chirping noise to herself. She smiled and said, "Look, honey, Alabam is going with us. You got nothing to fear from me. And anyway, you think I'd want to hurt that little Barbara-Girl? Aw."

The party was spinning about them. Ronnie van Holst was explaining to Peter that he should wear only Italian shoes. "Such narrow *feet,* Mr. Hatten. You should have accessories to match." Debbie was discussing poetry and things with an instructor at Barnard, and telling him how young he looked for his age—"Just how old *are* you, Mr. Carrington? Your type complexion I can't tell age very well." —and he was telling Debbie she looked young, too. ("Well," she was saying, "with every passing year. . . .") There were voices and glasses chinking; there were smiles and costumes flashing. The philosopher was bearing down on a late arrival. Vivaldi and Monteverdi were two of his favorite composers. Dan was chatting and being polite. No one particularly noticed the little group of three pressuring into the bathroom. Barbara let herself be moved.

Inside, Alabam locked the door. It was an efficient action. It was as if he had suddenly turned down the volume control on the party. He softly pushed the seat over and sat on it with an eager smile illuminating his face. He was sweating. Goneril was in no particular hurry. She looked into the mirror above the sink as she spoke, pulling the skin back over her cheekbones, nipping it back behind her eyes in order to test the effect on her jaw, all the time talking and talking. Abruptly she came to the point.

"The thing is," she said, "there's this British doctor, he sent me this kit, honey. By mail. He believes in it, it's a principle with him, darling."

"I don't understand you at all," Barbara said.

Alabam's grin widened; the sweat trickled from his cheeks. He said to Goneril just as if she had not done all the talking: "You tell her."

"You see?" Goneril asked.

"If you want to tell me something, please tell me."

Goneril took a deep breath and turned from the mirror

with all the lights on and the tiles blazing and the small clean smells of the bathroom rising in the heat of the three bodies locked there together. "I'm pregnant, but I got this kit. I just need someone to help me with it. I'm gaining weight already. You got a nursy look about you."

Barbara felt that nothing was real in this cell outside her life. It was her apartment, her bathroom, that was her tube of toothpaste, those were her brushes and towels; she had put her face in that washcloth; nothing was real.

"Ah'm too nervous," Alabam said, "that's my trouble."

"He's too nervous," Goneril said.

"Wouldn't mention it otherwise," Alabam said, "but Ah'm too nervous. It's mah way of life, y'know? Good at mah way of life even if Ah'm nervous."

Goneril put a possessive hand on Barbara. "You come to my place or I'll come back here later. I want *you,* honey. This English doc's kit. Just three things is all: tincture of green soap for keeping clean, catheter—that's a long like needle, and clamps-a-majigs for keeping the opening open. Wash well. Insert needle. Find bag of waters. Prick, whoosh, it's done. Ten minutes is all there is to it."

Alabam giggled. "Ah wish Ah wasn't so nervous."

"He tried. Jabbed me all over. Ooh, it hurt. Wrong place is not the recipe, honey."

"Ah'm *nervous,* Ah told you. Ah wasn't cut out to be no doctor."

"Well, you find someone nerves of steel and there you are, honey. Like you. Smart and nerves. Just like Sweden, that's the recipe. It's the *novum organum,* if I remember my college education rightly. But you got to keep clean—those fakers are careless, you go blindfolded to a house in Jersey City and they don't care, they save on the tincture of green soap; that's how you get butcher shops."

Barbara felt sick. Why was Goneril doing this? What weakness in her did Goneril hope to play upon? why?

"If you miss the first time, jab and I bleed a lot—no

nerves of steel—you have a cup of coffee and wait. I won't mind or complain. I'll explain you everything you have to do. No sweat. You have like the aptitude, I can tell those things. You will now, won't you, honey—?"

"I don't have to listen to this."

"But you do!" said Alabam. "Ain't she all-time, Miss Gee?"

Barbara was fumbling with the lock and Goneril was smiling because she had so much trouble unlocking the door to her own bathroom. Neither Alabam nor Goneril moved to stop her. Goneril stood near the shower and stiffened one finger —the pinkie—and pointed it at her as if mildly requesting her gracious attention. When she finally worked the lock and flung open the door, Goneril said softly, "You have to listen, because you did. You're just like me, sister-honey. What if I told you it's Dan's—what then?"

Barbara whirled on her, her face contorted, but still not knowing what to say. She felt that Goneril had spoken something like the truth. Yet she knew it was a lie. She knew that Goneril was in trouble. She knew that, for reasons she did not understand, Goneril was appealing to her, but that if she answered the appeal, Goneril would hurt her badly. The appeal was genuine; the intention to hurt was real. Accused truly or falsely, Barbara felt caught.

"I thought maybe you'd help me," Goneril said, "but you won't."

She remained in the bathroom with Alabam and locked the door as Barbara left.

Barbara went up to Dan to try to tell him what had happened, but he was standing with a puzzled smile at the door, saying goodbye to the first departing guests. She put her hand on his shoulder despite the strange smile he wore, but then she caught sight of Peter, watching her, and she took her hand away.

She thought that perhaps silence and ignorance were better

than understanding in love. But she did not want to be sacrificed to vulgarity or a joke. She wondered if she were becoming someone for Peter to use as fuel in his line of chatter. "There was this funny girl from Virginia, never mind her name, she came to learn the facts of life. . . ."

In the next moment, as if to prove once more that calculations about people only touch the truth, only jab and prick at the bag of truth, she found Goneril jammed into a corner with Peter, who was white-faced, whispering furiously at her, "I thought I told you not to fool with her! Leave that girl alone!"

Barbara's approach rescued Goneril. She wriggled away from Peter to take Barbara's hand. "It's all right, isn't it, sister-honey?" There was a tear like a contact lens on each eye. "You're not going to help me, are you? So it's all right."

When Peter touched their two locked hands, Goneril let go. He led Barbara away. "I'm sorry, Bee Gee," he said. "Don't let yourself even think about it."

"I don't understand. But did you see her? That girl is in hell."

Peter shook his head angrily. "Of course! Of course! But you're not supposed to join her. Haven't you learned yet? People want to involve you, especially you, Bee Gee. You're the kind of girl people want to involve."

"That poor creature."

"No, no, *no!* Please take care of yourself, Bee Gee." The green animal eyes were looking with great concern into her face, and then he was gone. She had an after image of his eyes warning her, but when she blinked and looked around, he had already left the room. Someone had turned off the record player. There was a heavy swell of quiet.

Goodbyes. They had been happening without her. "Bye-bye, honey." Smiling, knowing, bland, and malicious. Barbara stood with Dan and answered the goodbyes.

Ronnie van Holst was the last to leave. "That Miss

Goneril's friend left his umbrella," he said. "Tell me where he lives and I'll return it."

Dan told him. Impatiently he cut off Ronnie's congratulations on a fine party. "So long." Ronnie scampered off.

Then: "I'll help you with the glasses." He was emptying ashtrays into the fireplace.

"No, let's put the ashes in a plastic bag," Barbara said.

Perhaps Dan should have protected her from Goneril, but how? Perhaps he should not have let her be invited. Perhaps she should be angry with him. Peter had been the one to watch over her, not Dan.

A silent hour of cleaning up. Their ears rang with the silence.

At the door as Dan left, the janitor stood waving a bottle of Gallo Thunderbird. "I got the itch again!" he called out happily. "Woo-*whoof*!" He made a Mae West shape in the air. "Next time just buttons!"

For a time after the party Dan and Barbara did not see each other. Dan believed that she had planned to announce an "engagement." Even the word seemed ridiculous. He had helped her with the dishes and then said goodbye. Though she was angry about Goneril, he did not know it and it was his decision not to see her. Barbara believed that he should have watched more carefully. He should have stopped her. But she also believed that comprehension is an illusion. Love—or so Barbara still hoped—can happen although the final misery of isolation is irreducible. She could love Peter and he could be ridiculous. She could love Dan and he could abandon her. It happened.

She heard the janitor howling in the hallway. "Woo-*whoof!* Buttons!"

Just as Dan never mentioned the discovery of Caroline Anthony and Steve Schmitt at the slot machine, so Barbara never told him about how Goneril had put forward her claim and called her sister-honey while Alabam sat watching and grinning on the toilet. She would never tell him that Goneril had crowded her into the bathroom with the news of her kit from the English doctor. She would bear this burden alone. She would never tell him. She never did.

6

They considered driving down to Virginia, making a slow sea change from Manhattan southward, learning the country and each other at the same time. Like many lovers, after their trouble in love they sought to tie themselves more closely together as the proof that they did love. Dan wanted to stop at a beach on the Atlantic shore, perhaps in Delaware, and watch the skinny sandpipers at their continual bug-mining in the sand; he wanted to eat shellfish in a seaside restaurant; he imagined the two of them holding hands on a hillside over the ocean. But instead, they had jobs and obligations; there was a hurry. Barbara picked up the tickets one lunch hour and came with them to Dan's office. The staff looked up from its typewriters as she made her way through the open work area. Barbara checked the tight rules for fashion on the women who work in offices—sex and severity; at her store, she decided, they took more chances on being fun to look at. A secretary with a satiny ribbon of continuous mouth—that must be Rita Rooney—swiveled all the way around in her chair to stare her down. While Barbara stood with Dan at his desk, both of them made shy all at once—work was one thing, real life another—Bobb Anthony came bounding out of his private office. "Glad to see you chaps back together again!" he cried. He licked his lips. He wanted in. He wanted to be a part of their lives.

Caroline and Bobb had patched things up. He was, as usual, hopeful. But Barbara did not want to follow his lead. "You've lost weight," she said instead.

"Aw, this new diet." Bobb blushed. "Safflower oil, you know? Caroline found out about it. I must be allergic. Nauseous all the time," he said happily, "so it works. Instead of drinking lunch I go out and check the zoo."

They could not decide whether or not to congratulate him, and so said nothing, both saying it together.

"So long, you kids. Dan—you show her around the place, okay?"

Barbara thought that he looked worried and ill despite the smile. He was a sick man and he moved like a sick man.

Afterwards Dan told her that her visit to the office seemed as strange to him as his children's coming to his office in Cleveland. There was poor connection between what he did all day and what mattered to him; there were connections, but those of a comic nightmare. Still, there was a gain. Now when he talked about Bobb in his circle of power, and about Rita, Tom Davenport, and Frederika, Barbara had a picture of the dream. She had heard the actual shuffle of the papers that they shuffled. If Dan said *power* about Bobb Anthony, she could interpret the word. It was part of their intention together for her to know what he meant. It was part of their intention for him to know what she meant. But they were not in a hurry to exchange visits in their jobs again; the increment of understanding was not so great as they imagined it would be.

They flew from an aluminum-and-glass airport at Idlewild toward the backwoods town in Virginia with its heavy humid chill in the air, smell of wood fires hanging low over the pine clusters, loiterers in wool shirts and dungarees. The airport took DC-6's in a flat saucer between two rows of hills. They rented a car and drove through town. Barbara was tense; her eyes glittered and she held her purse tightly in both hands, like a child entering a new class. She wanted to justify her father, the town, this corner of the world to the stranger she was bringing to it. She showed Dan the sights. The dirt roads which she remembered from her childhood were black-topped now. Hot-rodders went spinning round and round the courthouse square, souped up, coked up, jazzed up, inspired by television tough-guys, shouting, "Man! *Man*!" They stopped and strolled through the square and drank from the stone fountain in the little park, given the town in 1923 by "The Marks Dept. Store." Dan made a pun on the name. Barbara took his arm and held it tightly. The old men squatting on the steps of the buildings around the square blinked, spat, and watched the teevee in the window of the Auto Supply. Jawing away the day, they discussed the races, taxes, and the nawth. And not whether China should be admitted to the United Nations, but rather, whether the United Nations should be admitted to the United States. "It's already there!" cackled one geezer. "I read it's already there in Noo Yawk!"

"Aw, I meant the *Yew*-nited States," said his friend.

A tandem of two cars went screaming and roaring past, mufflers gone. Dan said to Barbara, "This is practically Sixth Avenue. It's getting to be one long street in this country."

"Shush," she said. "You Yankees come messing down here, y'all go right away *thinking*."

Dan kissed her on the forehead, the nose, the mouth. Barbara let go her anxiety—that confusion of home-town childishness and courting dread in a time and place made strange to her. They strolled back to the car with his hand tight on her arm. She said, before they got in and drove on, "I want to tell you something, Dan." He knew by his joyous pride what it would be—gratitude—but he did not want her to say it. He kissed her again.

In the haze and laze of springtime Virginia they found that they thought the same thoughts, made the same jokes, and didn't need to talk much. Since Dan's anger about the party (he had felt manipulated), since Goneril's assault and appeal (Barbara had felt used), silence between them suited Barbara much more than talk. It was as if she were still depressed by the quarrel although they had passed through it. They had each passed through it alone and rejoined the other on the other side. She wanted him to hold her hand. She was not sure about the rest. Silence and ignorance might be the rest.

Dan had not given up the effort to understand everything he could. Barbara was issue of Wolbrook Jones, and this man was strange to him. He fretted over finding the daughter in the father. Wolbrook Jones had an old parlor in his house, set apart as a library in which he studied and kept files of his correspondence with airplane manufacturers, aviators, libraries, and museums. After he sat in this room awhile each morning, he shuffled into the kitchen and worked with a pencil on a child's yellow ruled pad, inscribing with enormous frowning care his fantasies of heroic gallantry in the air. With spindly shanks and massive forearms, he hunched over the kitchen table like a wheelchair invalid, scribbling through an endless dream of youth and glory. He kept models of the several 1917-1918 Spads and Fokkers hung from the ceiling by string tied to thumbtacks, the struts made of thin wire and no plastic any place: good balsa wood and carved bits of twigs. They hung from the ceiling above the place where he sat and wrote. When a storm blew up, and winds shook the house, the toy planes drifted in abstract air. The flies clung fatly for dear life to the ceiling, the planes floated in a deathly element. Wolbrook Jones stared impatiently at his model airplanes, wishing reality would find him again. Arthritic, both shrinking and gnarling, he looked like a trespasser in his own clothes. Bent over the chipped white enamel kitchen table with his tongue wetting a stub of pencil, he struggled with his memory of graceful ease in the air, frets of hair in his ear and nose, distant, horrified by the world, released from it. He reminded Dan of the ga-ga old men of Bickford's on upper Broadway, clipping the New York *Times* and reading their scraps of paper and huffing into their coffee cups.

Barbara read his mind. "Of course I take after my father," she said, "but I'm *different*. And I was born of a mother, too.

Dad is very old, you know. Almost fifty when they got married. We all get strange someday, Dan."

The milk was thick and rich, though it was town milk, and Dan let his belt out a notch. They walked in pine woods and through sunny pastures. One evening they all three of them went to the movies to see a Western, which Mr. Jones watched glumly because no hoss can replace a monoplane, and afterwards they had chop suey sundaes at his urging (diced fruit over vanilla ice cream). "I got good digestion, I been coming to this parlor all the time," he said. "Only one they never remodeled. Ever try a bourbon sundae? Best thing for the gut—nourishing. Soothing when you get to feeling mean, Mr. Shaper, you ought to try that up there in New York." Dan made a note to try to find a place where he could persuade the bartender to pour a jigger of bourbon over a scoop of vanilla ice cream.

On this evening they went to bed near midnight, but on other nights they discussed awhile (the race problem, politics, wars, airplanes) and then went to bed before nine, in separate rooms. Barbara knew that Dan was thinking when he went up to his room, and thinking about passing the rest of his life with her, but she tried not to worry him. An hour later he would creep barefoot down the hall—away by dawn. Or sometimes he just stayed in his own room, listening to the country night, and the next day they lay together in a damp field under the searching sun, under a sun which was hot on parts of their bodies never exposed to sunlight, swelling and greeting the spring weather. As he held her in his arms like a kitten in the sunlight, and she fell asleep on the loose soft loam, little bursts of energy went off in her body, first in her thighs, then in her arms—a buzz and hop of electricity—and then in the center; but now it was no longer anxious, undischarged electricity, but a subsiding, sighing, sleeping moving toward him, a sweet relenting of the total mobilization of her life. She slept. He lay awake, holding her, his open eyes focused on the sky against which wisps of cloud silently ran. Then suddenly he slept too. When he opened his eyes again, the sun sweet and hot on their intertwined sprawl, his first thought was: I love her. He was tasting the wet salt of her shoulder.

"I love you too," she was saying softly. "Hot. Hot. Hothothothot."

If Wolbrook Jones understood, he said nothing. He seemed not to remember courtship any more. Some days his legs were good and his wind was bad, sometimes he breathed okay and his legs gave out, but he did not worry his time; he came to focus very closely on chivalry over the Rhineland and let the rest of the world go mind itself.

But on their last evening in town, he suddenly asked Dan, "Like to show you my stand of pine tomorrow morning, eh?"

Barbara looked at Dan with frightened huge eyes, pleading with him not to be offended if her father made formal requests for information. She understood that Dan believed himself too old to be questioned by a parent, it was out of an Andy Hardy movie, it was from another age. The next morning Wolbrook apologized; he would be busy with mail all day. They finally went for their walk in the buzzing dusk and Wolbrook said, "Pine grows fast, it does, in this country. But then it ain't good for much either, except for firewood. Which is what we do with it. Burn it." The old man had heavy gray eyebrows which hung in tufts over his eyes, like the fur of some winter animal, and Dan could not see if anything was happening in the eyes. He was saying, "Course, they make paper, too, and send it up north. They chew it up with acid in the vats. But the paper, y'know, ain't no damn good? Rots after a few years, just rots and turns yellow? All that acid?"

"Yes," said Dan, falling into line.

"It does."

They entered the thin stand of pine with its blue dying glow among the branches. There were spiders in the trees. Below, strips of sunlight lay unraveled on the soft earth. "Some kinds of wood, y'know, they can make skeletons out of?"

"What?"

"Skeletons of planes—framework? Used to. Still find them

some places, I bet. Ever see a wooden plane, wooden skeleton, I mean, covered with some kind of stretched skin?"

"No," said Dan, wondering if this were his long way around to a more difficult question.

"Guess not. Museums maybe. Want to turn back? I'd like a pot of coffee now, get chilled easy. Used to fly, y'know? Bones chilled up there in an open cockpit, boy." And he turned anxiously to this young man about whom he knew nothing, who was traveling with his daughter, who had come to stay in his house, and he asked, "You think Barbara has sense enough to put the coffee on before we get back?"

The next day Barbara and Dan were returning to Manhattan, strapped into sanitized seats of a DC-6, served plastic pork chops and paper coffee, humming through the never-no-think land of the air. "Poor Dad," said Barbara, "but don't be too hard on him."

"Am I hard on him?"

"Sometimes I'm a little vague myself, darling."

"Am I hard?"

They held hands and talked about the passing beyond life of those who live overtime. They wondered how you would know if you had finished your span. They wondered if you had the right to ask yourself this question. Dan reported what a doctor had once told him: Almost everyone dies with dignity. At the end, whatever we have decided about ourselves, however we have loved life or failed at it, we are all reconciled. Mortality made them sigh.

A squall came up, lightning flashed, and the airliner bobbed and jerked like a tree being axed to earth. A very fat man whose safety belt barely reached about his sweating middle began to pray in loud wails, and his wife said, "Sha! Everybody's looking!" A young woman spilled coffee on herself and giggled hysterically, "It was just hanging there, coffee without a cup, right in the air!" The stewardess ran up and down the aisle, tugging at seat belts, and then fastened herself in with a fixed gray smile on her face. Dan said to Barbara, "You okay?"

"Okay."

"Let's finish what I was saying. Men used to begin their lives with love and end it with ambition. Now we begin with love and ambition and finish with ambition and love—no good order to things anymore."

"Do you miss good order?"

"Yes, I do. I do."

Barbara watched the fat man's wife crooning and shushing him in his huge hairy ear. She had given up warning him of disgrace. She was now trying to take care of him. She had a hand on his bloated belly and she stroked him as if he were a baby with colic. Barbara sighed and turned to Dan, who was smiling at her. "I suppose it's harder to get on with things now."

"We're supposed to think about bombs and China and the future—we keep busy in smaller ways. Airsickness. Income tax. The dream of perfect love. Dreams of freedom."

The airplane hiccuped brutally.

"Would you like to worry about the population explosion? They say we'll be twice as many in the year 2000. People will be sleeping and standing in shifts. Think of the congestion in the bowling alleys. Your magazine may triple its circulation. A lot of them subscribers! Would you prefer grander worries?"

"You're a tease, Barbara."

"Yes, you would."

As suddenly as it came, the squall disappeared. The pilot droned an unintelligible apology. Because the fat man was outraged by the static on the pilot's microphone, the stewardess repeated the formula speech about occasional inevitable atmosphere disturbances. Also unintelligibly. Another complaint from the fat man. The stewardess offered to write it out for anyone who could not hear it; her face was still blanched, swollen, and airsick, and the trim blue skirt and slender legs seemed to belong to some other girl who had sought adventure and fascinating contacts in a romantic occupation.

Barbara said to Dan that there are people like her father, who bear risk and even seek it out, and others who merely diminish through life. Different ways of being mortal, different ways of confronting the self. Her father did not consider his soul in splendid isolation; he governed his old age by the actions of praise, ferocity, and danger in his history. They were past, past—that was terrible. He still flew over the Rhineland with the shrill scream of wind in his struts, his eyes in goggles and a leather-helmeted head, peering out of a cockpit buffeted by the stream. He knew who the enemy was. He knew what his chances were and how to improve them. Wolbrook might be thick and slow with age, but he remembered speed and agility and could continue to treasure himself. He would die thinking of life.

Barbara and Dan thought of death and looked into each other's eyes and thought of love. They believed that to be alive must come to mean more than flying a monoplane toward a lonely tournament. More than an ascending income graph and a pattern of skill at keeping oranges in the air. More than oil on the waters, more than washing salt from wounds. More. More than dressing pink dummies in a window. More than writing letters that produce seven-per-cent results on Class-A mailing lists. Other matters and more. Barbara and Dan needed to mean enough for each other to give value to their failures and sense to the further intentions of their lives on earth. Their hearts laden with yearning told them that they had not come to an end of joy or sorrow. They were at the border of undiscovered country.

"Thank you for flying Trans Coastal," said the stewardess to each and every descending passenger. "So glad to have had you aboard this flight," she added when a passenger was slow getting off. The fat man was very slow and so she said, "Bye now."

He winked at her. His wife said, "Harry. Move already." Dan said to Barbara, "We can learn from everything." "Let's. Let's."

7

A few weeks after their return from Virginia, Dan made a trip to Cleveland to visit his children. Barbara was blue for him, happy for him, and blue for him. She stayed home evenings, turning the pages of a book, listening to music, waiting, astonished at how peacefully conjugal she felt. After work she might have a quick dinner out, to have her fill of noise; one night a steak and baked potato at The Derby on MacDougal Street, another night spaghetti at the San Remo amid the busily explaining couples of the Village, another night a cold salad and hot chocolate at Cafe Manzini on West Third Street because she liked the melancholy artiness of its décor—wire chairs, foreign newspapers on spindles, Tiffany glass lamps, and taped music of guitars or Kurt Weill songs. Most of the time she just hurried home and made soup and eggs for herself, and honey on oatmeal bread for a bit of sweetening. And waited. Cool jazz over an all-night FM station.

It was very different from her spinster patience, like the difference between the dreamy waiting for the alarm to ring in the morning and that clenched waiting for sleep to relieve a midnight; perspectives of the day rather than the limits of insomnia. Her anxiety that Dan go well with his sons seemed a little fond and foolish to her. A man secure with himself is a man secure with himself. Right. Perfect. Could she make a man good, virtuous, strong? Well, that's no job for a woman. Rescuing souls is no job for a woman; nor reforming them. But she could do other things. She could make a plastic mannequin look almost human, and if she could practice this art, perhaps she could also help to make a place for Dan alongside her and with himself. What she was doing was outside and around him; it was not done to him. He was no longer that perverse creature which a bachelor like Peter became—his own bride. She would fuss over Dan, worry and fret him, delight him, and now he could face down the roadway toward his children without looking at himself. She sat at the window which gave on Perry Street, touched the curtain, and wished it were the grain of his body. Once they took the habit, her hands liked to keep busy. *I should knit,* she thought. Such sure-sure decisions, like the designer of a store display.

But life was not so easy for this down-homey girl. For just at the time when she felt replete, filled with Dan, physically filled and stretched to her full, she would suddenly, on an evening away from him like this, discharge the burden and be filled merely with a vacant grief. Then she remembered how hateful he had found the goodbye-sayers at her disastrous party for him; how he had coldly abandoned her; how she had meant well but he had taken it for something else—a vulgar possessiveness—and yes, he was almost right, it almost was, but she had meant only that she loved him. Those goodbyes, his and Goneril's and the others, still echoed in her fearful hollowness of heart when she was left alone on a Saturday evening. She knew that love to her meant smile, touch, and presence, not mere understanding; it meant Dan's presence and he was gone, and had deserted her before; she knew that solidarity is love, that their fullness together was love—not comprehension, not the possession of one soul by another. She thought and was confused and thought some more and played the new recording of "Adieu M'Amour" which Dan had given her to replace the one eaten away by use, and she feared that she could say it in many ways, what love is, and she did not know what love is. All she knew was that Dan was gone visiting his children and she was alone. What is love? Is it anything at all if it cannot reduce the familiar misery of isolation? She had been content without it and put grief away; and now, despite Dan's love for her, she went stumbling in grief through a Saturday evening. The memory of his care did not give her ease; she had what she wanted and she had nothing; she could remember only that he had abandoned her to Goneril and said goodbye to her in a cold rage, and that now he had left her alone and what else was there?

The walking wounded: those grieving for comprehension, melancholic because they have not found what they want to do in life. They say they want to be "understood."

Making-out and making-do.

She remembered Dan's words and his ceaseless revolving in the grip of discontentment. The air of Perry Street seemed filled with grit, like an invisible seamless paste folding over her lungs, closing her heart in. The time was heavy, the air was heavy, the din of trucks and voices never let up. The triumph of her freedom—a pretty girl making out alone in Manhattan! —had forever departed.

She thought she might take a hot bath and eat something and then perhaps feel better. She turned on and off the lights, brushed her hair, moved ashtrays, let the record stop itself and left the machine on. What right had he to upset her life like this? What right had she to open herself to this man? She felt dizzy and sat down. Desire and illness, a dizziness in the head. She swung her head down between her knees and waited till the blood was pounding in her temples. She sat up, blinking as if awakened.

Ronnie van Holst had invited her to call him at any hour of the day or night. Now this made her smile. When her life had been hopeless, it had at least lain even and uneventful; she had felt no need to call on Ronnie for an hour of telephone talk. But now that Dan had given her hope, had blessed her with love, she was filled with dread and needed help. She looked at the telephone, tempted, but she did not use it. Still, she had thought it through. Now that she admitted needing to receive life from others, she might call upon them. She had learned to conceive it.

The bath eased her a little. The tightness of her breathing was relieved. She patted herself dry with a new soft towel.

When the telephone rang, she jumped as if the catastrophe had been planned. It was Peter, asking to come up for a cup of tea. No, not asking—demanding. No, not that either—pleading. "Barbara. Barbara-Girl. Will you help me, Barbara, will you?" She had two thoughts while she tried to see what to do. When there is so much trouble everywhere in the world, Peter, why does your own trouble stand so close to you? All right, that's familiar enough, but why so close to me?

While she listened to him, she brushed her hair, which was down after her bath, long and silky, as Peter used to like it, saying that she reminded him of a cartoon witch; and while she brushed her hair, she thought: So you're a loner, are you? Loner, you can't stand being alone. And she was saying as she combed this hair, thought these thoughts, "All right, Peter. All right then. I didn't know you were so fond of tea."

"Hahaha!"

His harsh burst of electronic laughter, following so soon after the imperative yearning and desperation of the words, made her hesitate again. Peter worked out his plans for everything, it seemed, even the decision to despair. His laughter was trying to say that he was still on top, deciding to be unhappy. It rushed into her ear out of the black sieve, making her dizzy. No, no tea tonight, she thought; "Peter, I don't want to see you."

Too late. He had hung up and was on his way and she must look as well as possible, put on the mask, defend herself. Peter would make even his trouble flash brilliantly in the air, magnificently his own. She mobilized to meet him, and went to her mirror with a vanity imposed upon her by Peter; she peered anxiously into it as she blackened her eyelashes, not for pleasure or beauty but to keep her eyes private; she put on a mask of make-up to keep Peter at his distance, and then she addressed an envelope. It was to Dan. She would write him all about it after Peter left. She left the envelope leaning against the mirror, the address where he stayed in Cleveland aslant in reverse reflection, alongside the pots, tubes, bottles, brushes, creams, and lotions shining like stars about it. And the gifts of perfume from Peter and Dan and that vague Doug who had tarried awhile at a timid, long-faced distance until she met Peter. And the little soaps and toy animals and all the accreted souvenirs of a pretty girl's floating on dreamy, groovy Manhattan. She sighed and rubbed her knuckles across her teeth. Hard work ahead. Peter was on his way.

Nevertheless, as the buzzer sounded she let him stand and sound on while she went to the window to catch one glimpse of her courtyard out-of-doors before she admitted him. A sparrow, eating crumbs on the window sill, looked up at her with beady reproach. It took its ragged winter feathers away when she lifted her hand to her hair. The sound of busses backfiring did not ruffle it, but the flicker through glass of a woman, watching and thinking, rent it from its small pecking. She wanted only to be friendly; it shot straight up into the sky without a sound. Then she answered the door.

She looked at him and gasped: "Your hair!"

"It's turned white," he said.

Then she began to laugh. "Oh, Peter, it's melting."

The cowl of snow disappeared as he shook his head. "I walked. Fresh snow, this time of the spring—another surprise, Barbara-Girl. Let me tell you something: feels good." His cheeks were pink and his angry, overjoyed step filled the little apartment. This bore no relation to the desperation of his voice on the telephone, but the voice still had its grating edge and the eyes were cold and fixed. If he was in trouble, most of his armored body still kept its hard integrity. But he was in trouble.

"Peter, what's the matter?"

"I've been practicing my juggling," he said, "you know?

That's why I have to rent a high-ceilinged apartment. Surely you remember that ceiling?" And his high harsh laughter filled the room. "Well, I used to be able to do four balls, going on five. Now I can only do three, going on four. Something's happened to me. A change." His mouth broke in a fixed deathly grimace, the teeth showing, and Barbara was astonished at this first sign of age in him. His teeth seemed lengthened, he was having gum trouble, the teeth were marked at the narrowing roots by tobacco stains. Then his mouth was opening and shutting and there was that terrible laughter again. "I've lost the touch," he said. "I'm going downhill, I haven't got it anymore. I'm ready to die."

"Peter!" she said angrily. "Stop that silly laughing!"

Abruptly he sat down and was silent, looking at his shoes. "You're right," he then said. "That's one reason I thought of you. You talk sense. I shouldn't giggle." When he turned his face to her again, he was smiling, sleek, confident, and stilled. "I'm no maniac. I'm sorry I upset you. Jittery."

"What's the *matter,* Peter?"

"Nothing. You have to expect it. Things go all wrong. The center does not hold. I function, but it's all dead. I am no longer among the living."

"You're *what?*"

"It disturbs me, you know, Bee Gee?" He sat very straight and purposeful, still smiling, and said, "I've got no one but myself, but that is nothing at all. Hm. You don't understand. Let me put it your way: I am having a nervous breakdown. No, wait. Listen. No hallucinations, no delusions of persecution, no loss of major control. Orifices, outlets, and valves in A-Number-One condition. Just an old-fashioned something, to wit: *No reality in my life.* No reason for either being here or killing myself. I've studied how to juggle and make love and enjoy my life—no point in it. No nothing. No, no, and no." He smiled demurely. "For purposes of intercommunication, and I want to intercommunicate, and also concision, and I wish to be concise, I shall call it by an old-fashioned word—sometimes the old-fashioned ways are best—nervous breakdown. Can't take it anymore. Take *what,* you might ask, Bee Gee? Don't even know what I'm to take or not take. I walk around the streets with my soul in a balloon tied to my finger, but the string has been cut—no balloon. No reason. No response. No go, it's gone, Barbara-Girl." And he showed his gums triumphantly, running his tongue over his teeth. "But I know your name, I'm in contact. I even know *my* name, I know what I'm doing and this is hardly an appeal for help, since I know Bee Gee cannot help me. Barbara-Girl. But I wanted to tell someone anyway."

He waited to see if she would interrupt. He raised his hand like a pedantic schoolteacher.

"Melodramatic? Perhaps. Nevertheless I tell you the truth, Barbara-Girl: I can no longer juggle four balls." He leaned forward and said, "Go ahead, smile. I give you permission. Please smile, my friend."

Barbara remembered the sound of Peter's voice over water as he sang to her on the dock at Southampton: lap of gentle salt breeze, dusk, moon rising, distant shout of weekend visitors. He had an easy baritone of which he was proud and he had crooned to her. She remembered his gentleness, his distance, his gentleness despite the distance of not caring very much. In the falling dusk at Southampton, he had given names to each of the sandpipers pecking their snacks in the sand; Bobb, Steve, Fritz; each one had a character and he told her why and made her laugh. Poor Peter! poor Peter! she thought.

His cheeks were wet. He was smiling at her and wiping his face with his hand. There was a smudge on his forehead. "Selfish tears. Don't pity me. Only selfish tears, Barbara."

She watched this in awe. A man was weeping. It was like hearing the snowfall, its passage through the air, its slow dissolving on the earth, a sound that must not be heard.

"Don't pity me," he repeated. "Just selfish and selfishness is all I've got."

They're tears all the same, she thought, and darted forward toward him and pressed his head lightly to her. "Oh Peter," she said, "I just can't see how anyone can tell it so clearly and still insist—"

"I'm not well."

"You seem just *quiet,* Peter."

"I get sick in my own way, with excellent clarity. It's part of my sickness."

She touched his cheek and bent to look into his eyes. There was a faint smell of tomato juice on his mouth. "Feel better, please. We need you big and strong."

"Okay, Bee Gee. By executive order."

"You've been drinking tomato juice. Are you on a diet?"

He grinned crookedly, showing stained teeth. "You think I'm getting fat? No, Bloody Marys. But Barbara!" And he put himself to her again, with the cunning of a lonely child. He said softly: "Barbara-Girl, I need to make contact somehow."

"Not that way, your old way," she said, extricating herself.

He let her go and went to the window which gave onto her courtyard. It was snowing, the snow sifted down as if the universe were gently rocking; and it was still clean—that impossible pure Manhattan snow, sweet at the moment of fall. "No," he said, "that's the way I've tried so much, that way. You're right. I've won and captured, but made no space for myself. You're right about that. Another victory, another notch—eventually you weaken the weapon with notching your victories. Just let me sit with you, Barbara?" And fell silent, blushing like a boy at his repeated, repeated appeal. And in a stammering, discontinuous way he began to talk to her for almost—Barbara suddenly understood—the first time in the years she had known him. He had jabbered, joked, teased, flirted, but now he was addressing her. What he said still seemed (this was Peter, wasn't it?) less important than his manner. He formed his thought and explored its style. He discovered where it led, then uttered a desperate little summary, then went to the window and stared at the deepening snowfall in the silent court, then turned upon her with a quick quirk of facetiousness, then went on. He told her as much truth as he could in this way tell. And the hours passed.

He had wanted to marry Freddie, he said, a girl named Freddie, you remember Freddie? Far-out and stupid, but he wanted her. Why? Because she was able to make him feel something. You know what that means, to feel something? To *feel?* Yes, you know, Barbara. But can you understand what it means to a man who has closed the flower of feeling? Closed it tight? Shut it through every season of love and striving—no love and no striving?

And then his pacing and blank gaze out the window again. Spaces of talk and spaces of silence. As much truth as he could find in them.

But Freddie made him feel bad, she was mean, she was a boiling ant hill of conniving and she made him sick with jealousy, that was all Freddie was, that kind of feeling.

More snow, more silent looking. Again he turned back to Barbara with a puzzled, long, humorous, sallow face. He smiled, showing a stained tooth. "A surprise to me," he said.

"What?"

"When I knew she was with some Oklahoma oil man—some Stetson or other—how I felt, Bee Gee. . . ." He stopped, talked, stopped, stared, paced, and talked for hours, but as always with him, there was his trick of focus; he made himself real to her, even in his untouchable dodging; the hours passed and she was happy to be in his company, though the only emotion she could name was pity. Maybe she too was cruising after strong feeling within the sudden quiet of her life with Dan, and pity would do for awhile. "Bee Gee?" he said. "I can't juggle so good anymore. I'm not steady with the balls or myself. I'm losing out."

"Oh Peter, you're thinking foolish thoughts, talking foolish thoughts, talking foolishness."

"I thought I wasn't cut out for this kind of life, that kind of life. I was right, but—question—maybe I wasn't cut out for any kind of life, huh Barbara-Girl?"

With a peculiar canniness on his face, he watched her shake her head, and then he cast his eyes down. Then he went on.

"I want to die."

There was absolute stillness. He meant it, and at the same time he calculated its effect. She was filled with horror, both for his meaning it and for his calculation, and she said, "Nonsense. What you need is—"

"A rest? a vacation? a checkup by a specialist? dinner by candlelight? reconciliation with my aged parents? a cruise of the Caribbean with the over-30 club? an advantageous marriage? a new sports car? a fresh young thing with long blonde hair or an understanding and experienced divorcée with both feet on the ground? protein tablets and a sunlamp? a new set of tumblers? What? *What?* The salt has lost its savor, so you tell me, Bee Gee."

She pressed her lips together and waited, she just waited, resolved not to be angry, but wondering what she could put in the place of anger. He would offer a substitute. She must be cautious. This was not her domain. Peter had capacities for control and he sought control.

"I've been through all those remedies and more. Chicks. New woofer, new tweeter. Grand chicks—you, for instance. Let me tell you something: I've got me my junior partnership. Any car I want I rent, I don't like owning anymore. I can go around the world if it suits me. What next? A psychiatrist?"

"Do you need someone to talk to, Peter?"

"Haw!"

She waded straight in. "I don't mean deep analysis necessarily, but someone who can help you work through. . . ." She turned away. "I know exactly what you're thinking all at once. I lack a sense of humor."

He made his peculiar new forced croaking laugh. He put his face close to hers and said 'Ha!" but the light of appeal and gratitude in his eyes did not recede. As if betrayed by his eyes, he went to hide at the window again. Outside, in the courtyard off Perry Street, the snow was no longer softly piling up upon itself. There was no wind; the snow had stopped. But it was after midnight, and the city had come to a halt in the snow. This man claimed so lightly to be destroyed and explained himself with facetious eloquence; he tricked and played games and made her out a fool; and yet her rhythm of breathing was broken by him. Was it because he had never loved her that she still treasured a hope about him? She knew very well that the nurse is released at the end of the convalescence.

He returned from the window with worried concern on his face. He was always just in time, it seemed. Coolly he tuned in on her. "I'm sorry," he said. "I know how all this sounds."

"Please, Peter, just tell me how I can help you."

He shook his head. "I know you want to be kind. I suppose I'll do something about it myself. . . . a psychiatrist, as you say. Don't you remember what I think of that unhappy breed? their tight little mouths? Or their decisions to be spontaneous, and so they are spontaneous?" He made a tight little face. He made a spontaneous face, but it was an ugly grimace, showing his gums.

"Is this really the time to make so many judgments, Peter?"

"Any port in a storm. . . . Quite a storm outside. Look, a humpback of snow on your window sill. And all this while we were talking."

And all this while they were talking. . . . went the words in Barbara's head as if she were considering the troubles of strangers, the Manhattan troubles of Manhattan strangers, perpetually striving and gabbing on the anxious island. She saw Peter watching her with his hand opened as if to juggle or cup one of the balls he liked to flip into the air, and remembered his Sunday morning trick with the oranges—oranges up! oranges down! oranges all around! And all this while he was talking.

"For you, when love is over, it's over, Barbara? For me

it's never over. I'm still in love with the scrawny little beast with scraped knees I knew in junior high school. I kissed her once—she sucked my lip like a Milky Way. Caramel. Hotness down to my ankles even now when I think about it. She had eyes like a squirrel's. But I admit it's a little dim in recent years —knees and eyes like that. But you, Barbara, I'm still in love with you."

Poor Peter. He looked hard into her eyes to head off the thought, head it off, stop it now, that he could not come to the end of love because he could not carry it through to the end; and so she only thought, *poor Peter,* which meant the same thing.

"I love you forever, Barbara. In my own way. I never stop."

She felt an odd elation as he maneuvered about her; perhaps it was the juggler's joy in herself. No. No. Dan loved her and Peter needed someone. Peter could finish nothing, could love no one; but also needed help. She felt pride in her body very much like lust, it *is* very much like lust, she thought; this must be what men like so much, conquering the frontiers again and again through our bodies. They take such joy in pride. Pride—they suffer so from pride. And then she felt another flood of sorrow for the maneuvering, manipulating, agonized creature before her. "It's so cold," he was saying.

"The heat goes off at eleven. We're supposed to close down."

"No, I mean outside, Barbara-Girl. Nuclear changes in the weather, you know? Radiation or something—the winds. Maybe we're all finished. May I spend the night here? On the couch? *Please*?" It was a snowfall which had broken all the rules for the city in spring. The green of ailanthus in the courtyard was nearly gone under thick white. The snow creaked under its own weight. "Just on the couch, Barbara?" There was mingled in his voice the excitement of the fading storm outside and the imploring jitters of what he called his "breakdown."

Barbara abruptly recalled the childish sense of late-at-night, those forbidden and secret hours when the world sleeps and only the inner circle is awake. She had stared into the teeming mystery of her own soul in the house in Virginia. At dawn she knew nothing more about it, but she *knew*. This time of the night is misplaced in Manhattan, but not lost; disaster returns it.

"Barbara-Girl, are you listening to me? Let me just stay on the couch."

"I suppose so," she said. And this concession was punishment for pride, punishment because she knew she could love someone and he could not, and she had no right to pride herself on this. "Just there, but just there—oh dear, that will never work out. I know you, Peter."

"I promise!"

A sigh, a sweet sigh; and Barbara knew she was sweetly sighing and bit her lip; Peter was busy with all his tricks, making her aware, transmitting his disease of awareness. He caused her to be sweetly yielding and languorous; she was aware of it, she disliked this automatic response. "You promise," she said severely. "Please keep your promise. There's something about you that never keeps promises, I feel."

He lowered his eyes contritely. "I'll keep them to you even if I don't keep them to myself."

"Stop playing Tom Sawyer."

"Penrod. I'm not up to Huck Finn. Too cute."

"I said Tom Sawyer. Listen to me."

Wan smile, lip hiding teeth. "Wasn't I listening, Bee Gee?"

No wonder he can't juggle anymore, Barbara thought, his shoulders are sloping wrong, Lord he's tired. He looked as if he were falling through space all closed in on himself, falling without a sound through dry galaxies.

"I promise," he said.

Like embarrassed grown brother and sister, they undressed, washed, scrubbed teeth, hiding and not hiding, looking and not looking. His body was very familiar to her. He was like a brother now. And all the same, Barbara knew, for whatever his reasons and hers, he had been the man who awakened her from her fretful Village sleep. After the farmer's daughter had come to New York, this salesman had shown her the sights, the Empire State Building and the Statue of Liberty; he had taken her on the boatride around Manhattan and showed her how the skyline could be seen like notes on a clef of yet-to-be-sung melodies. He was not a brother.

She sat at a low tufted bench, removing the girlish mask. She turned off the light at the mirror after she creamed away her make-up. The chill from outdoors was seeping into the room. She scampered into bed and hid there with her nightgown. She put it on under the covers.

In a moment her heart stopped pounding. She smiled to herself, holding her wrist like a hypochondriac measuring excitement by counting the pulse. But who was counting? She was not counting. The lights were out and there was only the bluish phosphorescent glow of the mound of snow against the window. She could hear the catch of Peter's breathing from the couch. Barbara felt oddly comforted by the presence of this old friend in her apartment, this loveless, hopeless, grieving old friend, and despite the oddness and gravity of the occasion, she fell asleep with a start like the reverse of frightened wakening; a click—she flew off from herself. Her habit when she slept alone was for careening lifts into harsh nerves, descents into oblivion, elevator rises and falls into sealed dream compartments, visions, anxieties, corrections, and regrets. Now she merely slept.

She may have been away for half an hour when she felt breathing nearby and awoke calmly, cool and refreshed, knowing exactly where she lay and whose breath it was—Dan's. But it was not Dan's and she felt no less calm. "Barbara. Please," he was saying.

"Please?"

"Please let me hold your hand for a few minutes."

She gave him her hand and, sighing, he rested his cheek against it, his body sprawled ungainly on the floor. The apartment was settling and creaking in the sudden winter cold. Barbara waited, thinking he would make some violent move now, something she could ridicule or fight away. No. He seemed content. He seemed grateful. Her hand, stretched out like that against his cheek, was growing cramped. For a cramped hand, she thought, the lady might be lost. No, no, surely not.

The bristles on his cheek roughed against her skin. There was a grain of beard, there was an anti-grain, back and forth. Her arm, held tight, began to ache, and she longed for the sweet sinking back into sleep. And she pitied him. He had no reality. The sharp drawing ache in her heart translated the practical trivial cramp in her wrist. She said: "All right."

He did not answer.

She paused and said sharply, irritably, with a dizzy stupefaction at her own voice, "Come into bed then, you'll catch cold."

He paused and, sighing as if unwilling, slipped in beside her. She moved away from him. He did not try to follow. He seemed content to lie in the little trough of warmth where she had been. And it seemed to her (she knew she was hiding from herself, she was trying to trick herself, she was disguising the inevitable fact from herself), she fell asleep again as soon as her own part of the sheet was warmed by her own body. She deceived herself into sleep. Dreamily, irritably, she accepted him into her bed, dozing, hardly permitting him to know her—not permitting—giving herself away.

She awoke with a lurch of shipwreck. Convulsively she arched her back and the nightgown was pulled up in a noose about her neck. She awoke on the wrong side of disaster; she was lost and the dark ruin was hanging over her; she was foundering in icy seas. "Peter!" she cried out, "I don't allow it! I don't! I don't! You have no right!"

But there was no strength in her after the cry. She was down in the icy salt of the North Atlantic. She sobbed and turned her head and sought oblivion, but could not even freeze herself to death. As he crouched between her knees, her body foundering in the crevice of the bed under his diminished heft, he swayed, he twisted like a sick child, his eyes tried to find hers; his gaze faltered, his head fell, and he was sobbing; but his body did not retreat. "Barbara, don't play." He swayed and took her, groaning softly and pleading with her, "Ride with me, don't play, Barbara, ride, *ride,* just ride with me one more time!"

In the depth of this alien wave, she looked at him with a pious, puzzled mien. It was as if the black ocean asked mercy of its bobbing, swept prey, saying, Don't be cold, don't freeze, let me consume you alive. She felt a hot tear fall from his face onto hers, and this was a signal that she seemed to have been waiting for. A voice, her voice, her voice despite all her decisions was whispering to him; her hands were stroking his back with hard, long, imperative pressure. "You had my permission all the time, Peter. Don't fret. Don't fret now."

But neither terror nor pity nor love can end the long troubles. He rushed into her, he did not flow, he did not fly and soar, he seized, took, and slipped from her grasp; he was all effortful pride; he lay gasping and sobbing on her breast and she comforted him as best she could.

8

When Barbara awakened late in the morning, with a vacuum cleaner angrily searching in corners upstairs, she felt the queasy seasick lurch of shame located in that same place in the belly reserved to jealousy; but shame has a sweeter, sickish taste. The machine upstairs was sucking up dust and air, squealing, heaving great boastful gusts. Peter stirred at her first movement. She shrank away. He waited an instant and then slipped out of bed. She felt him watching, standing naked by the bed and blinking. She kept her eyes squeezed shut. She knew this was cowardly, but even as she pretended to be asleep and fooled no one, she felt herself dimming out; the act followed swiftly upon the child's imitation of it, her fists opened, she departed from herself for a few moments.

Then Peter was standing by their bed, fully dressed, pink-cheeked, hair combed with water, slicked down, himself sleek and grinning, with an incongruous stubble of beard above the neatly knotted tie. "Hey Barbara-Girl?" he said. "Open the eyes."

She did. There was a taste of cold fever in her mouth. She lay like dead, stiff and twisted as if caught by death in the midst of a flight from crime.

"Hey Barbara-Girl, I really felt bad last night, honest, I'm sorry I came on at you like that."

"Leave me alone now, Peter."

"Bee Gee? Hey? I didn't know what Goneril was up to at your party—you believe me, don't you?"

"Go."

"Okay. Let me tell you something: it was the blues, you know? And about Dan. I just didn't like thinking about it. Having you two in mind like that—"

"Go."

"I didn't mean any harm. Not really *harm* harm, anyway. I suppose no one does. Sort of jealous maybe, but listen, Bee Gee, I only wanted to make things clear and straight out here among us—"

Heedless of her nakedness, of the chill of death in her limbs, she flew out of bed with her arms flailing—"Get out! Get out! Out!"—and it seemed to her as she stood alone, naked and alone and sobbing in that room, that he scampered away like some quick animal, like a rabbit in danger. She could hear his light steps in the hall, as if he were skipping. As she squinted in the ferocious winter sunlight at the window, she could almost see his tracks, woodsy leapings as he made off for cover in the snow. She then lost him entirely. She even seemed to lose the thought of him. She stood naked and frozen in the shadow behind the curtain, awaiting her clothing.

How did Peter pass the remainder of the day? He thought. He most frequently passed his time at the trade of reading financial bulletins and annual reports, and talking with his clients by telephone when he went to his office; today he did not go to his office. Probably he ate snacks (he liked health foods, he ate lightly); probably he drank coffee and made up his mind. He decided all day long, and at the end of the day, he had decided. He telephoned Dan early in the evening, without yet having shaved or washed, feeling Barbara like a validating aura still clinging to his body as he put coins in the pay telephone in a booth in Grand Central Station (how did he get there? wandering, walking), and repeated, "No, I'm not drunk, pal. I thought you should know—can't trust any of them—object lesson, buddy-boy. Couldn't help myself. Really wanted to prove—"

And sighed when Dan hung up on him. Had bet himself that he'd never get that sentence out. Everybody interrupting him lately by making him stop in the middle. As if they already knew the rest.

He sat in the booth, frowning because he believed this very moment would find Dan speaking with Barbara and she would be saying, "Yes, it's true. In a way it's true. I don't suppose I can make you see how it happened. It's true."

Then Peter went to his highceilinged studio to wait for Dan. Interested in finance and credit, Peter understood that he considered his friend a debtor and had been disturbed by Dan's profit in an abandoned investment. But he also knew that his scheme to collect the debt was a non-commercial, non-gain transaction, and as he puzzled, he dropped a tight orange and heard it break, squirt. No marked skill at his chosen craft. You have to go with beautiful unconsciousness with the oranges, you have to ride without command, you have to fly high with all three, leaving pride behind. No marked skill here. Marked skill at brooding, at being densely Peter; but these habits were not good enough for him as he skipped across the middle of his life. Trouble, trouble, when pride and health leave the man who trusts too much in them. Trouble; no more simplicity, no more switch-blade health flashing out when he willed the button be pressed. He felt weakness and complication on their way into his life. Sucking the broken orange, he went to the refrigerator for another. He could only keep three in the air, never more. He had lied to Barbara. But he had told the truth to Dan. He had lied about his juggling. He had told the truth about Barbara to Dan and he had told the truth to Barbara about himself, both in the night when he felt alone and isolated and in the morning when he was angrily sated. Both truths were part of the portfolio. Dan had broken a pledge to the society of formal lovers. It was a secret pledge; he had not known that Peter had enrolled him; but Dan had abandoned his friend. You don't have to make promises to betray them. But now Peter had fixed things. Dan could not go so free as he thought. One more orange. Barbara desirable after Dan desired her. Try that orange. No. No. More trouble. But now he could last it out, and if an orange fell, he would begin again, juggling with a cracked orange. Hup, hup, hup, *hup*. Not too high. In an easy arc. Think with the flight, not with the oranges. Don't think, ride with them.

He retrieved the fallen fruit and it leaked on his hand as he answered the call from Dan, who was now back in Manhattan.

"Meet me at the Howard Johnson's on Sixth Avenue at Eighth Street," Dan said.

"That's a hell of a place to meet, buddy."

"Meet me there."

"Makes you feel like you're on a turnpike, that place. What's the matter with you? Why there?"

"That's where I want to see you."

"You sound like you're looking for a quarrel, buddy." Frowning, he sucked the juice on his palm.

"First meet me at Howard Johnson's and I'll see."

"*We* shall see, boy," Peter said.

"I'll see."

Dan stalked him in the damp and wet doorway of the restaurant. Nearby there was a newsstand, a paperback bookshop just closing, a subway entrance with loose papers chasing down the stairs. Within the Howard Johnson's, late on this evening, marcelled homosexuals chattered and tough ones planned their missions; a few other eaters, loyal to ice cream in this curious delayed winter of March, took up their sundaes avidly; the softly shifting glow of the juke box bathed the faces of the lonely, the hunting, and the discussing couples. There was a bleat of busses as Peter approached, waving a hand in greeting. There was a spatter of wet in the air.

"Is it true?" Dan asked.

"Hiya, buddy."

"Is it true?"

"Yes."

"Did you have any reason?"

Peter was shining with alert pleasure in the beginning of the conversation. At last the conclusion to an experience! feeling something again! He took a deep breath of the fine cold March wind swirling through Eighth Street and across the intersection. It did not occur to him that Dan might hit him or that anything like a vulgar Village street fight could interrupt this odd conjunction of two old friends. He said: "Everything has reasons."

A negro cat in blue jeans, a short cashmere coat, and Italian sandals, with hair blondined so that it looked almost green, was soliciting in the subway entrance. Entranced young men were floating elegantly past, back, past again. The boy began to hum a little tune to himself and to the universe. Peter desired to await a reply from the universe, something he could share with the green-haired cat, but Dan seemed pressed for time and so he continued his little speech: "Let me explain, pal. You came to town and I had a nice deal. You were lonely —sick with yourself—*remember*? Remember how it was? I tried to help you. Now it's you has the nice deal. You lucked out good. And me? Well, you didn't help me, so I had to help myself."

No answer from Dan. There were fresh gusts of wind down Eighth Street, into the subway entrance, across the hurrying and the huddling out late in the evening.

"You see, don't you now, buddy?"

Dan was staring at him like a stranger. "You're crazy off your head, Pete."

"Maybe." Well, give him the stranger look right back. "And you're smart, funny, and pretty for a man. Let me tell you something. You've got it made. But you haven't got the big thing which I have."

Dan stared.

Peter screwed up his face in a grin, pushing it forward, showing his teeth and whispering, "No truth in you any place, boy. Nothing but—listen, whatever I do, I *do* it, I make out. But you—*square*!" He hoped the green-haired crooner was listening. He said, "You hear me? You're ready to lie down like everyone else. You want to slide by the same easy way. You want to make a nice little hole for yourself with canned water and supplies for a lifetime underground. You think you can beat the game with a tight door and a Bee Gee. A little lady by your side. Yummy. That same old scene. Well, wrongo. I wanted to show you! Wrongo! Wrong! You're nothing but square, nothing but lies, nothing! Nothing more—nothing at all!"

Dan made a little grunt which was perhaps intended to continue the discussion. He wanted to see clearly, he wanted to understand the charge against him. No man fails to feel guilt when accused of total fault. Thus the madman has an important advantage on the man who listens; for does not the listener then say, Maybe true? Maybe I fail totally? But Dan thought of Barbara and this gave him a narrow sense of what to do. Jealousy and fury taught him a simple act, and he knew a terrible moment of exultation—jealousy, fury, pride, hatred, and a vivid bone-and-blood joy in the wet March air of a doorway. He then said, "Here's some truth," and drove his fist as hard as he could, with a short flooding lunge, toward Peter's head, all the while thinking: No, the sensible thing would be to hit him in the belly or below. I'm still being a gentleman.

Perhaps that's what Peter meant when he said he had no truth. He neglected striking his enemy where he could destroy him most cruelly. Peter took the blow leaning on his cheekbone, crying out "Ha!", whirling and coming back flailing, head down, uncaring, like a child in a tantrum. He was hurt. He felt great joy. His body flew unencumbered toward Dan through the salt air of the city.

Now imagine a great drawing away from what the world recognized at once to be more than a mere street brawl. There were chattering idlers who fell silent; there were sighs of satisfaction from watchers ("Olé," murmured the boy with green hair); there was a priestly hum on Sixth Avenue; and within this stir, Dan leapt on Peter and bore him to the slushy, littered, laden sidewalk. Someone said, "Oh my, lookit." Someone said, "It's quicker than lung cancer, hey Mike?" And then the awe of disaster fell fully over the watchers. Trained by the isolation of cities, they observed. They studied. All understood that his was no anecdote—blow, cry, man fallen and man running. Dan meant murder, although thus far the crowd knew more about his intention than he did. He struck wild, unfocused blows with his fist, exploratory thrusts, returned in slow motion by Peter; and only as Dan splintered a tooth, as his knuckles were cut and clothes filthied, did the pure lust for murder gradually arise in his throat. It was with a dizziness of triumph that he realized that he wanted to destroy Peter, just that, nothing more, merely to kill him and this was sufficient truth unto the moment. And the communication seemed to pass almost instantaneously to Peter, his old friend, and Peter was up on his feet, gasping, roaring, thrilled in his turn, with cunning slits watching above the cut cheekbones. Peter was no longer thinking of the boy with green hair, he too was focused, he said, "Don't mess with me, buddy."

Dan lunged with arms extended and took a world-darkening blow to the chest; the universe tipped and the lights drifted out, as if the rheostat had shorted; retching, Dan fell, and calmly wondered if he had broken a rib, and thought over his mistake in not watching more carefully (Manage the rage! he thought); and Peter stood over him: "Enough?" Dan breathed wet snow. His fingers clenched over a handful of softly silted sidewalk filth; he waited; he listened to this word *enough*. "Vavoom," said the green-haired boy. "Go go go." Then Dan thrust himself at Peter's ankles with a tackling hook suddenly rendered up from wartime memories, feeling his body light and contracted despite the dark gasping in his chest. They were down on the sidewalk together, rolling in the slush, Dan using fists and elbows to hurt, break, maim, and Peter using fists to hit back and protect himself; Dan was not aware of any effort to stop the blows against himself, he was conscious only of his target. And yet neither of them, covered with sidewalk slime and blood, struck out with feet or knees at the vulnerable private parts. They were still gentlemen obeying the rules though their coats had been torn off in the brief gasping respites.

Dan felt his attention wandering. It was like the war, out swinging under a parachute again, dangling and rushing down, swinging toward death among marionette strings and toy explosions, and thinking not about death but about the label on a box of cold cereal which he had studied over breakfast as a child. Lou Gehrig likes Wheaties with milk and cream and sugar and fresh fruit, don't get dirt in the magazine of the B.A.R., don't break the ankles or knees, the soul is not immortal but has consequences. And swinging down from the sky to life and death over the green world which sent up little puffs of cream; down, down. And now, on Sixth Avenue, rolling in slime, he had a glimpse of a girl in a taxi, slowing down, her elegant courtesan's head lifted, making little astonished pouting motions with her lips, kissing the air. Freddie gazed myopically at them through the window. Abruptly she leaned toward the driver and, at the same moment, the cab sped forward and away. Or was it Freddie? Wasn't it just another girl cruising in a cab? Down, down, he swung, and his ear was scraped raw against the pavement; there was flesh shredded loose; Dan thought: Can I hear the bowels of New York as I crouch here, my ear to the pavement? Beneath him there was the passage and discharge of wastes, the labor of electricity, all the perturbed, buried powers of Manhattan. And there was pain from his ear. The powerlines sang below, tangled through sand and rock; sewers, managed streams, gas, electricity, telephone, and abandoned conduits controlled by no one. Peter was standing over him with eyes abstract and horrified and joined fists coming down like an ax. And then Dan was no longer a gentleman. He decided. He struck swiftly and from below. In this instant it was finally settled.

Peter stumbled. He was coughing and helpless, blood choking up from his mouth. His body went slack; he fell, his knees were wet and his mouth was ragged, gaping; one shoe had been torn off, and through the rip the sock showed a yellowish, shell-like ankle; he was lying in vomit, he had soiled his pants. Dan stood above him, tugging him toward a parking meter, all his life shrunken to a passion to drop his friend on it, sharpened to an ecstasy of hope of hitting him with a parking meter. Peter, through the blood which surged up in airy bubbles, gasped, "Okay, boy, you're okay," and Dan let him fall.

"Mister," the green-haired mother's helper said, "Hey, Mister Big-time! They called the cops. You want to come with me and I'll put sweet stuff on your hurt?"

Dan shook his head. The gesture brought him rushing back to himself. He had dropped his friend onto the sidewalk near the parking meter—it was slick with blood and excrement and the slush of feet; there was an ambulance on the way, there were police on the way. The green-haired boy was smiling and mouthing at him. Dan felt horror for what he had done. Within the horror, he felt triumph. The green-haired boy said, "Man, you are now in the *Bright Lights*. I'd take me off to my place, big-time man, I was you—"

There was the turning red eye of a police car swinging down Sixth Avenue from Fourteenth Street.

Dan sprang into the street. He dodged through the traffic on Sixth Avenue, out and across with brakes and horns screaming about him, then through the parking lot at the corner of Waverly Place, down alleys and across Washington Square, pacing himself in and out of the shadows of the dead buildings just off the east side of the Square, marked for destruction with taped crosses on the windows. He stopped abruptly in the darkness of a ruined stoop. What could he do for Peter? What could he do for himself? Why was he running in a circle? He cupped his hand over the torn ear. In this silence he listened to himself. His horror must not mean that he wander blindly behind enemy lines until he was caught. There was no escape on the streets. The police and punishment would not relieve him of his horror. He must move slowly and cunningly. But he could not. He started back into the light of the street and stumbled against a wet box filled with crumbled masonry. He stopped again. He forced himself to take a long slow breath. He put his hand back over his ear. He would be a clever soldier and find his way home. But he could not be clever. He heard footsteps and broke into a frantic run.

"Hey, Big-time! It's me! Your *friend*!"

He ran and ran with his mouth gasping and his heart hurting.

He made his way up the back stairway to his apartment. He crashed open the door with his shoulder, snapping the lock. Luck: the lock broke, but not the door. He stood in the darkness with a crazy triumph beating about him. No one. Nothing. Emptiness and silence.

He fell into bed, bathed in substances he had never before known, thick blood, fierce shrill wordless tears, a black reek in which he had been dipped; and then finally he lay with his eyes fixed on the sky beyond his ceiling and the one beyond it and the last bricked ceiling of mortality above him; he lay like a stone in age-old, grave, unthinking submission.

9

When Dan called her, she would not see him. When he went to her apartment anyway, she would not admit him. He then stopped like an overwound clock. For a time he heard no ticking within, no feeling, no motion of desire or hope. He was ill, he hurt, he felt the hurt as mere stoppage. This was perhaps a contagion from Peter; to feel nothing, to be absolutely still and silent within was Peter's disease. Dan was ill; he had the flu; the bruises on his body became swollen welts. On his right forearm there were three delicate perforations, toothmarks, which suddenly opened up and exploded like seeds into ripe infection. A rooty stringlet of infection led up under his arm. Many of the oozing scrapes and bruises merely turned sore and black, but this arm ballooned up, huge and ungainly, a stiff rubbery stump with the stretched skin a torture to him. He sat with his arm in hot water, trying to draw out the disease, enervated and dizzy in the steam as he crouched above the bowl. Finally a doctor came to give him penicillin. The doctor shook his head as he filed his steel away in his bag and snapped it shut. "Human teeth—the worst. A shame on us. Worse than dogs or rats. We put such *dreck* in our mouths, that's why. That's the main reason."

He finished a bottle of aspirin; he slept; he drank gin and lay fitfully abed and went through a half-hallucinated week in which the days and nights were all contained within alternating efforts to make Barbara answer him, to lift Peter onto the parking meter, to force Barbara to reply, to bury Peter in the filth of his own body. He wished to destroy, forgive, destroy. He was weeping in the dark for his old friend and praying he had not hurt him. He was wishing him dead and burnt to ash. And dreaming despite all his efforts to treasure reality, not dreams, that Barbara could be a stranger to him, a virgin child with flowing hair he met as she ran down a hillside through a bank of flowers to be discovered. What kind of flowers? Dream flowers for an absolute dream lover.

In his illness he grasped at this dream purity.

The doctor gave him the third penicillin injection and suggested massive vitamin injections—"Just for fun. Why are you smiling?"

"I was thinking about flowers. Don't they make vitamins from flowers?"

"Rose hips is for health nuts. Synthesize them is better—more economical. Are you a health nut? If you are, do me a favor next time. Stay away from human teeth is my professional counsel to you. Listen—a couple shots of B-12, folic acid, B-complex in the bloomers—you need a little pickup, my friend."

"Rose hips," Dan murmured with satisfaction.

He slept himself out and bathed himself carefully, easing his sore body into the hot water, and slept again. That hillside never altered in the seasons, its bank of flowers, Barbara with her flowing hair loosened, running, a sweet breeze as he waited.

Then the penicillin and aspirin brought down the fever. He seemed to have a click in his head, the dream ended, he sprang upward from daymare and nightsweat. The clock began ticking. He sat up, blinking, and threw off the blanket. He held out his hands—steady. One arm was still slightly swollen, but the pain had faded. Awake from his dream, something went out of him that could never be put back. It had seemed essential, like a piece of his gut, and it had become diseased and it was removed. Even if he began to miss it later, it could not be put back. His arm throbbed; there would be residues, deposits, invisible scars; the source was gone. Youth must be gotten rid of eventually, it cannot be retained without disease, it must give way. Peter had tried to live under his infection of purity; for Dan, corrupted innocence would give way to the next place in history. He thought of calm seas and hot sun.

He found news of Peter by reaching his secretary. Out of the hospital. The body can support a great deal. Peter had given an explanation to the police which did not mention him. It was a bizarre concocted story, but now, with an end made to their old friendship, Peter's story did not concern Dan. The reason for his assault on Peter had also been covered over by the fight itself. It had served the purpose of drawing out his jealous rage. Sometimes it happens. This, he knew, is the only excuse for revenge—now anger ended. He had left it dissolved in the slime on the sidewalk near Howard Johnson's on the Avenue of the Americas.

He turned back toward Barbara and she was gone. She had left New York, moved out; in a few days, she had simply withdrawn and the tracks were already brushed over. Did she have any right to be angry with him? His jealousy lay curled and waiting. This happens, too. Could she believe that the blame for the fight lay in him and she had nothing to do with it? He looked impatiently in a mirror and saw only himself, frowning, frazzled, stubborn, with dark stains below the eyes, one of Manhattan's false boys of thirty-three; he gazed out the window at the jagged, musical skyline of Manhattan and prayed for new possibilities for Dan Shaper—tenderness and the hope of giving up anger, pity for Barbara, willingness to sacrifice. The dense air of Manhattan, seeming to free him, seeming to stifle him, had brought him to a hope of generosity, like a basement nurturing a vagrant root carried in with some other package.

When he put through a call to her in Virginia, she would not receive it. Her voice said to the operator very firmly and formally, "That person is not here." He sent her a telegram asking her please to talk with him, waited half a day, and then called again. *"That person is not at this number."*

He sent her a wire: ARRIVING TOMORROW. He did not wait for a reply. It did not occur to him that she would leave her father's house and he did not expect her to meet him at the station, though he had given her the time of his arrival. He hired a Ford and drove through the courthouse square, around which the same hot-rod kids whipped away the long afternoon, and down the black-topped road which he remembered as if it were the map of his own childhood, scraps of Southern town, country garage with tar-paper roof, the ungraded turnoff and the long drive until suddenly a weathered and spreading house appeared on its little knoll.

She had heard the Ford and stood on the porch wearing a loosely fitting flowered cotton housedress that must have been hanging in a closet for years after being checked on the order form of a mail-order catalogue. There were freckles on her forearms and she wore no make-up and there was a pale burst of delicate lines at the corners of her eyes where she had frowned in the sun. She was barefooted. The dress was too long. It was as if to defy him by presenting a rural stranger to his eyes, but he was not deceived. There was Barbara from Perry Street behind the freckles and the Montgomery-Ward frock. There was the girl who had been tried by the edge of broken glass in Manhattan and there was his lady. She stood on the porch. They had it straight out under the sky with no other greeting. Her face turned blood-red in the setting sun and she said, "Was that the way to settle things between us! Was that the way!"

Not a question. He answered it as if it were a question. "It was between Peter and me. What was between you and me—"

"But who was important, Peter or me? Why didn't you

think of me first? Why didn't you leave it just between you and me?"

"I am not. . . . I live in this time," he said slowly. "You're right. What was for you and me is for us to settle. But about Peter and me—"

"Why didn't you just forget him?"

Dan had once found Peter sitting cross-legged on his bed after a shower, his hands folded and his eyes closed, his sex hanging like an uncropped tail, his hands minutely throbbing together in prayer. It was early on a Friday evening. What are you doing! Dan had asked. *Praying*. Why! *For grace. For success in all my enterprises. For mercy.* And then the winning smile. And then marvelously clothed in an elegant, very narrow suit, every gesture floating with the juggler's charm and nothing but money in his pockets.

"Forget him," Barbara said, "why don't you?"

"Yes, I can now. Now I can. You know what he's telling people? He was beaten up by some rough-trade sailor who thought he'd made a pass."

"You were wrong to be so brutal."

"I'm sorry I did it. If I hadn't, maybe I'd be sorrier. But I wish there were another way. I had to lose this friend. That way."

She touched the loose screen on the front door and pressed the rusted mesh against the frame with her fingers. It sprang when she let go. "What about me, Dan?"

"I had to think about him first in order to think about you. Maybe that was wrong. Sometimes you have to be wrong first in order to be right afterwards."

"Well." He was not sure she was listening. Was that person at this number? She did not let him know for sure, but her face began to compose itself behind its strained rural mask; she was Barbara thinking back to New York and Peter's wild, willful lies. *Grace, success, and mercy*. She lowered her head, but kept her eyes on Dan's, waiting for him to make further decisions.

An old Negro on a bicycle lurched toward them in the ruts down the road. He studied the house, studied the package he was carrying, turned his bicycle around and headed out again. Dan watched him down the road, sighed, and then began once more to say that if he had done wrong, then he had done wrong. He saw nothing strange in her curious knack of making them discuss his rage as if her part in it were beyond reckoning. She seemed to ask to be privileged, just because she could not be. "You have to let me be wrong in my own way, Barbara—" Ah! Now he did remind her. "If you want me to accept your being wrong in your way."

Slowly she turned toward the red, raw, plowed field to the right of the house. "Did I ever ask you to forgive me—?"

"*Accept*, I said."

"—forgive me? No, I think not," she said softly. The rich sun turned and turned, bathing them in a golden dying afternoon light.

"I do anyway, Barbary."

She did not answer, so he repeated his words.

"All right," she said at last.

"We've decided? We've settled it between us now? Everything that's important before the beginning? We can start now?"

The small capillaries of her eyes were reddened by fatigue, by staring. She leaned against the weathered pine. She touched his hand but said nothing and looked away from him.

"Yes, I think so," he answered for her, and now she let him see her troubled face again. She stroked his hand with long pulling caresses. "Yes, I think we'll live elsewhere. Not here."

"But not in New York?"

"But not in New York either."

"Does it make so much difference?"

"Not so much," he said. "Some places are less practical —from now on we'll try being practical. Let's try it." Then straightway he took her in his arms.

"Sometimes I'm foolish," she said. "I get depressed. I can be lonely without notice."

"I'm ready for that. Sometimes I'm surly."

"Sometimes I'm the most confused. I get stiff and careful then. You can't talk to me. You just have to wait."

"Frequently I'm intelligent. Recently I gave up the dream of perfection."

"Sometimes I follow someone's lead because he seems to know and I'm not sure. If someone shouts at me I start to cry, I can't help it. Sometimes just whispering is as bad as shouting, too."

But her eyes were dry and shining. He kept his arms around her and said, "We'll have the chance to practice all our faults, don't you worry."

She stood near him in her mail-order cotton dress. There was the smell of lemony soap on her skin. "Come say hello to my father," she said. "He wants to ask if you know a good history of the Curtiss-Wright turbine." But she did not move. She just waited and let him hold her lightly. She put one warning hand on his arm. She meant to tell him to make up his mind from everything he knew, leaving out nothing that might rise up to trouble him later, and she also meant to influence his decision.

"We'll live in a practical way together," he told her, "a job and a place. We'll cherish each other." He had the conviction that his spirit looked around corners, even if it was only the next corner that it looked around. "We'll marry."

"This evening," she answered him, "we'll just ride the easy evening. It's beautiful country, isn't it?"

"But we're started on our way," he said. They had gone completely past the place in her road where she and Peter had met; Dan had decided completely about her. She felt easy and powerful because her hand and her holding attention to his arm had ministered to this decision. But he had decided for himself. He accepted his victory.

"Oh," she said at the door, stopping short as if suddenly remembering something, "do you love me, Dan?"

"I've begun. You're the salt of the earth."

She nodded her head to the compliment. "Even if—?"

"Even if anything."

"Wait. Peter's smart," she said, "he believes love is impossible. He tried his best to teach us. He did his best to convince us."

"It doesn't settle things. That's true. I can't stand writing those come-on letters very much longer. That's true, too. But anyway—"

"I'm going to have a child, Dan."

In the stillness of the Virginia evening, his breath stopped, the wind in the high pine branches stopped; she stood with one arm upraised, holding the door. She would not speak until he did. He knew that they could not expect the gift of reality all at once; they could not claim it as their right; they could seek it. He said that he loved her. She said that the child was his.

He said: "That's the best kind. I like it better that way."

She moved away from him, flushed with anger. He turned her back into his arms to say that she must expect trouble from him. She gave him her black, roused look.

"And maybe from me!" she said. "Even now, I don't know everything I might do sometime."

"That's true, too."

He put his arms closely around her, and after a moment, the chattering hot anger seemed to flow away into the evening. He held her and shook his face against hers and tried to make fun of her. He knew that she was ready to look up and smile at him. The time of doubt was in abeyance. The back of her neck seemed to lose fever at his touch. Coolness. Joy and grief mastered. He felt certain of her. He took hope in his further portion in the world. He teased for her smile. He knew she was about to smile upon him. He knew it. He knew it. She put her head against his chest and began to cry.

SALT is Herbert Gold's sixth novel. Among the others are *The Man Who Was Not With It* and *Therefore Be Bold*. He is also the author of over forty stories, fourteen of which were collected in *Love and Like*. Mr. Gold has edited an anthology of fiction, *Fiction of the Fifties,* and an anthology of non-fiction writings, *First Person Singular: Essays for the Sixties,* soon to be published by The Dial Press. He has received a number of important literary prizes, including Guggenheim and Hudson Review Fellowships, an award from the National Institute of Arts and Letters, an O. Henry Prize and a Ford Foundation Theatre Fellowship to work at the San Francisco Actors' Workshop. Mr. Gold has been a Judge for the National Book Award in fiction, and has taught at Cornell University, the State University of Iowa, and the University of California at Berkeley.